To Captain Avyn Fumio Yata,
USAF Academy Class of 1979,
and Lieutenant Commander Marshall Atkins,
US Naval Academy Class of 1979.

The good die young.

D0311074

PATRICK A. DAVIS

A LONG DAY FOR DYING

POCKET STAR BOOKS
New York London Toronto Sydney Singapore

This book is a work of fiction. Names, characters, places and incidents are products of the author's imagination or are used fictitiously. Any resemblance to actual events or locales or persons, living or dead, is entirely coincidental.

An *Original* Publication of POCKET BOOKS

A Pocket Star Book published by
POCKET BOOKS, a division of Simon & Schuster, Inc.
1230 Avenue of the Americas, New York, NY 10020

Copyright © 2003 by Patrick A. Davis

ISBN: 0-7434-7429-5

First Pocket Books printing July 2003

10 9 8 7 6 5 4 3 2 1

POCKET STAR BOOKS and colophon are registered trademarks of Simon & Schuster, Inc.

For information regarding special discounts for bulk purchases, please contact Simon & Schuster Special Sales at 1-800-456-6798 or business@simonandschuster.com

Cover art by Ben Perini

Printed in the U.S.A.

THE COMMANDER

"A chilling murder mystery. . . . Davis combines convincing police procedure with plenty of head-scratching clues, twists and dead ends. . . . A bona fide thriller."

—*Publishers Weekly*

"A crafty, detail-rich mystery. . . . Deft characterizations keep us engaged."

—*Booklist*

THE COLONEL

"A plausible conspiracy thriller that keeps getting more and more complicated until all the threads are tied together, pretty much at the last possible moment. . . . Fans of Nelson DeMille will find this one entirely satisfying."

—*Booklist*

"Gripping twists and turns and the revelation of a top-level conspiracy will keep readers on edge."

—*Publishers Weekly*

THE GENERAL

"A terse, gung-ho military-thriller debut. . . . Lots of action."

—*Kirkus Reviews*

Acknowledgments

A number of people were crucial to bringing this novel to fruition. First and foremost, I'd like to express my gratitude to my good friends Bob and Katie Sessler, who once again labored through the early drafts and helped me refine the story into something readable. Thanks also to my informal circle of proofreaders for their perceptive comments and their brutally honest critiques: Bobby and Kathy Baker, Dennis and Becky Stefanski, Martha Jones, Andrew Hobbs, Cecil and Barb Fuqua, and Marilyn Page.

In addition, I'd like to express my appreciation to my Air Force Academy classmates Colonel Dennis Hilley and Lieutenant Colonel (Ret) Mike Garber, for keeping me straight on the military aspects of the story, including the dramatic changes in the Pentagon, since the 9-11 attacks. My deepest thanks also to Dr. Bill Burke and Dr. Carey Page, for patiently imparting their medical and forensic knowledge to a layman; to CMSgt Maximus Smith, for shedding light on the nuances of the C-32 aircraft; to Louise Burke and Lauren McKenna at Simon & Schuster/Pocket Books, for believing in my ability to write entertaining stories; to Chris Pepe at Putnam, for helping launch my career; and to my agent and confidante, Karen Solem, whose steadfast faith in our eventual success never wavered.

Finally, I'd like to thank my wife, Helen Davis, and my parents, Bill and Betty David, whose faith, support, and love still inspire me.

Author's Notes

To those military readers who are familiar with the Pentagon, I'd like to say that I was intentionally vague or misleading on some of the locations of key Pentagon offices. In light of what happened on 9-11, I didn't feel comfortable in precisely placing their positions. Could terrorists with mayhem on their minds learn the placements of these offices? Of course. But not from me.

I also followed this same cautious approach when describing the entrance into the private compartment of the C-32 aircraft. While the details are generally accurate, there are a few key differences from the actual way the mechanism works.

Ironically, my concerns over these points reflects how America has changed since 9-11. Even while writing a fictional story, I was constantly aware that I didn't want to put down anything that an Al Qaeda wanna-be could somehow use. Hopefully, I've succeeded.

Thank you for understanding.

PAT DAVIS

A LONG
DAY FOR
DYING

1

MORNING

I heard the faint beating of the rotor blades long before I saw the approaching helicopter.

It was a cool spring morning, a little after sunrise, and I'd just stepped out onto the porch of my rambling farmhouse in rural northern Virginia. I gazed toward the east, past the grass airstrip my crop-duster father had built thirty years earlier and the farm fields he no longer owned. Searching the horizon, I finally saw it. A speck, coming out of the glow of the sun. I checked my watch. Almost seven-twenty. Right on time, and I wondered what I was getting myself into.

My regular job is chief of police for Warrentown, Virginia, a quiet town of four thousand, roughly seventy miles west of D.C. Occasionally I also moonlight as a consultant to the Office of Special Investigations, the air force's primary criminal investigative branch. I'd taken the job as a favor to then-OSI commander Brigadier General Gary Mercer, who'd lost a lot of his experienced personnel to the better-paying jobs in the civilian world.

To stem the bleeding, Mercer hired on a few former investigators like myself—I'd put in twenty years in the OSI, retiring as a light colonel—to consult on the more "sensitive" cases. By sensitive, General Mercer meant things like espionage, major drug rings, murders—anything that might garner the attention of the press or Congress or the four-star constellations at the Pentagon.

Since the military isn't exactly a hotbed of crime, the consultant workload is pretty light, and I average maybe three cases a year. In the past, I've always looked forward to getting called out as a change of pace from the Andy-of-Mayberry routine. But not today.

The reason the helicopter was flying out to pick me up stems from a conversation I'd had earlier with Colonel Charles Hinkle, the current OSI chief. I'd been in the shower when the phone rang. Mrs. Anuncio, my live-in housekeeper, had banged on the bathroom door until I finally yanked it open, a towel cinched around my waist, dripping water all over the place.

Ignoring my scowl, Mrs. Anuncio stuck a portable phone up to my face. "Man say must talk. Important."

"I don't care. Tell him I'll call back when I'm dressed."

Mrs. Anuncio made like she suddenly didn't understand English. She stood there, holding out the phone, her square face locked with a stubborn gaze.

Christ. Sometimes I wondered who really worked for whom. I repeated irritably, "Mrs. Anuncio, tell him I will call after—"

That was as far as I got before a familiar voice chirped out at me. "Marty, pick up the goddamn phone. *Now.*"

Mrs. Anuncio smiled smugly. I sighed, blinked water from my eyes, and took the phone. As she turned her bulky frame for the door, she announced breakfast was ready. When I asked for an omelet, she bluntly replied that she'd made waffles.

I could only smile at her response. Mrs. Anuncio had worked for me for almost a month before I figured out that her gruff exterior was mostly an act. She just had a military DI's attitude toward running the household. The way she saw it, after three years of looking after my daughter Emily and me, I should know the rules by now. If I'd wanted an omelet, I should have asked before the waffles were made.

As I toweled off, the man on the phone began calling out to me again. With a last swipe at the blond crew cut that passed for my hair, I put the receiver to my ear. In the background, I heard the sound of clicking keyboards and ringing phones. Office sounds. No surprise that Colonel Charles Hinkle was already at work. Since the 9-11 terrorist attacks, the OSI had been humping around the clock to plug security leaks.

"Marty? Marty? If you don't pick up, so help me—"

"Remember your blood pressure, Charlie. Now what's so damned important that I couldn't finish my shower?" Even though Charlie was my boss, I could talk to him this way because we'd known each other since our days as young captains. I wasn't all that concerned about Charlie's anxious tone, since he tended to overreact, often blowing the most mundane events out of all proportion.

Ignoring my crack, he said, "I'm only going to say this once, so listen up. You got anything scheduled, cancel it. I want you to be ready to roll ASAP—"

"Sorry, Charlie. I'm not available." I hung the towel over the shower rail, let him sputter for a moment, then went over to the bureau and began to dress.

"Why the hell not?" he demanded.

"Personal reasons."

"For instance?"

"Emily's turning thirteen tomorrow. We've got a big party planned."

Silence. There was nothing he could say. Since my wife's death from cancer three years earlier, he knew that my daughter Emily was the priority in my life.

He cleared his throat. "Look, I wouldn't ask if it wasn't important—"

"No, Charlie."

"I could order you."

A bluff. I quoted him the clause in my consulting contract, which specifically stated I could decline an investigation.

"Don't pull that legal crap on me. You've already been assigned to a task force—"

"Unassign me. Give it to Erik Olson or maybe Bob Whitcher—"

"I *can't*. The SECDEF assigned you to the task force. *Personally.*"

I was tugging on my underwear and almost toppled over. "Jesus . . ."

"Yeah. This thing is big, Marty. I just got off the horn with General Markel, the vice chairman of the Joint Chiefs. He ordered me to send a major crimes forensics team to Andrews and said that the SECDEF specifically requested that you and Major Gardner be assigned to a task force that's being put together."

I slowly donned a T-shirt as I tried to take this in. Major Amanda Gardner was another OSI investigator who happened to live next door, on a couple of acres she'd sweet-talked my dad into selling her. I asked Charlie why the secretary of defense would ask for us.

"Hell, I figured you two must have run across Secretary Churchfield on a case in the past. You didn't?"

I told him I'd never even met Churchfield and was damned certain Amanda hadn't either.

"Well, someone with a helluva lot of pull must have passed on your names. You connected, Marty?"

He meant politically. "You know better than that. Who else is assigned to the case?"

"From the OSI, just you two and the forensics techs. Doc Bowman will be the ME."

Dr. Billy Bowman was the extremely capable yet mildly irritating deputy head of the Armed Forces Institute of Pathology. I said, "So we're talking about a homicide on Andrews—"

"Not so fast, Marty. You in or not?"

As if I really had a choice now. "I'm in." Stepping into my closet, I plucked out my Sears special navy blue suit. Even for active-duty military investigators, civilian clothing was standard attire because wearing one's rank tended to hinder investigations. Enlisted members felt intimidated when grilled by someone they knew was an officer, and officers often proved less than cooperative when questioned by someone they outranked.

"The answer," Charlie grunted, "is that I don't know any specifics. According to General Markel, the task force is operating under a TS/SCI clearance."

A top-secret/special compartmentalized information clearance meant that only those with a strict need-to-know would be privy to the details of the investigation. While it was unusual that a criminal matter would be tagged with this lofty security classification, it was even more unusual that Charlie, in his capacity as OSI chief, would be kept out of the loop.

For once, Charlie wasn't crying wolf. Something big had happened.

As I finished dressing, Charlie gave me the rest of what he knew, which wasn't much. No, he didn't know who would head the investigation or which agencies would take part. Yes, he suspected the FBI would probably honcho the thing, since they were the glory boys of the investigative world. Major Amanda Gardner and I were to meet the forensic team at the Andrews AFB passenger terminal, where we would receive further instructions.

The location of the terminal suggested we might be flying to the location of the crime. When I asked, Charlie said not to bother packing a bag. The team wasn't flying anywhere.

That, of course, wasn't quite true.

While I was at the breakfast table, notifying my office that I'd be out of pocket for a few days, my call-waiting beeped. It was Charlie, telling me that the two-plus hours it would take Amanda and me to fight the rush hour traffic to Andrews was unacceptable. A helicopter would land on the grass strip in front of my house at 0730 hours, to pick us up. He asked me to pass on the change to Amanda.

When I tried, I got her machine, so I went out onto the back patio for a look.

Amanda lived in a modest ranch house a couple of hundred yards away. It was a tidy place fronted by flower beds and a lawn big enough for a game of touch football. In keeping with her rural upbringing, she'd recently added a small barn, where she kept a menagerie of animals, including a horse, a potbellied pig, and a couple of ducks. I located her in a corner of the fenced-in backyard, filling the water dish for her two dogs, a German shepherd and a golden retriever. I hollered twice before she glanced over. When I held up the phone, she nodded, tossed a ball for the dogs, and walked quickly toward the house.

Amanda had a nice walk. She's long and willowy and, at thirty-three, still moves with the easy strides of the athlete she once was. A tomboy since she could remember, she'd earned a tae kwon do black belt by the time she was sixteen and lettered in swimming at the Air Force Academy. She also has big-time smarts, graduating with degrees in engineering and physics. A tenacious investigator, she'd impressed me on the first murder case we'd worked, and I'd assumed she was one of those annoying people who did well at everything.

Then she told me about her track record with men.

I would have expected Amanda, as an attractive woman in a predominantly male profession, to get asked out constantly, but she doesn't. Since we've been neighbors, I've known her to go out on only two dates. Neither guy ever called again. The only thing I can figure is that men find her self-assurance intimidating. Her blunt assessment is that no guy wants a relationship with a bright, competent woman who can also kick his ass.

Amanda acts like it's no big deal not having much of a social life. She's often mentioned how she prefers being single and having the freedom to do as she pleases. Besides, it wasn't like she had *time* for a relationship. Not with the demands of her job and a new house to worry about.

Sometimes, I almost believed her.

I thumbed the redial as Amanda disappeared into the house, and she picked up immediately. After I dropped the dime on curbside chopper service, she said, "I've been surfing the news. Nothing. Whatever's going down, they're doing a good job keeping it under wraps."

"It's got to be a homicide. Why else would they call Doc Bowman out?"

"Since when do they classify homicides?"

The million-dollar question. Andrews Air Force Base housed the military's aircraft fleet that flew the government's elite, from the president on down. In light of the terrorist threat, I suggested that someone might have taken out a heavy hitter, which might explain all the secrecy.

"I dunno, Marty. Security on Andrews is damned tight. I don't see some Al Qaeda wanna-bes making it past the checkpoints."

I resisted the urge to say they wouldn't show up in beards, wearing "Bin Laden for President" T-shirts. Still, she had a point. Andrews was probably only a staging area for the team to meet without eyebrows being raised.

"How about the SECDEF?" she asked. "Any clue why Churchfield requested us?"

"Obviously, we were recommended."

"By who, if it wasn't Colonel Hinkle?"

"It's puzzling." By definition, the OSI was a secretive, close-knit organization. It's unlikely anyone outside the immediate chain of command would be familiar enough with our abilities to recommend us by name. Yet *someone* had.

As I was about to hang up, she said, "I'm kind of surprised you took the case. I mean, with Emily's party tomorrow—"

"Can't turn down the SECDEF."

"You okay with that?"

My silence confirmed what she knew; I wasn't. Missing your kid's party may not seem like a big deal, but it was to me. Before she died, my wife, Nicole, made me promise that I'd always place Emily at the top of my list. Over the years, I'd kept my word. Emily's soccer matches, school plays, band recitals—you name it, I was always there, sitting right up front.

"You tell Emily yet?" Amanda asked.

"She's getting ready for school. She'll be okay. Helen will be here." Helen was my stepdaughter from Nicole's first marriage. After Nicole's death, Helen had lived with Emily and me, running the crop-dusting business my father left me so I could play cop full-time. Six months ago, Helen moved out. It was a financial decision; business had been drying up because a lot of the area farms had been gobbled up by developers. Helen bought a place with a small airstrip about a hundred miles west, in tobacco country. I gave her the two planes on the condition that she retain the name Collins Aviation. When my dad retired to Florida, his dream had been for me to keep the business going. Since I hated flying crop dusters, having Helen take over was a no-brainer. Dad was happy someone in the family was still flying planes with his name on the side, and I was happy that person wasn't me.

"Emily will be disappointed," Amanda said. "So if you don't mind a suggestion . . ."

It didn't matter if I did. Over the past year, Emily and Amanda had spent a lot of time together. It was a relationship I'd encouraged; Emily needed a female role model in her life. The downside was, I had to put up with Amanda's less than subtle hints on parenting. "What?"

"Give Emily her present now."

"It's not her birthday."

"So what? You want her to be happy, right?"

"Sure, but—"

"At least bring her over and let her see it."

"I'm going to wait."

She began to argue with me. I interrupted her, saying it was because of the letter.

"Letter? What letter?"

So I explained how Nicole had written a series of letters, to be given to Emily on each birthday, until she turned twenty-one. The letters were filled with humorous anecdotes and advice on life. The kinds of things a mother tells a daughter. Over the years, I had learned to give Emily the letter a couple days before her birthday, to give her time to recover emotionally so she could enjoy her party. "Emily read it last night," I said. "She's pretty down. Even if I tell her about the pony now, it might not do much good."

Amanda was quiet. For once she seemed at a loss for words. "It must have been difficult for Nicole. To write those letters."

"It was," I said. "She wrote them shortly before she died. She could barely hold a pen. It took her almost a week."

Amanda started to say something, but her voice began breaking. Her display of emotion caught me off guard. I said, "Amanda, I didn't mean to—"

The phone clicked softly in my ear.

I returned to the breakfast table, perplexed by Amanda's reaction. She'd always been someone who prided herself on maintaining control, keeping her feelings in check. It was an image she'd carefully cultivated, to prove she was as tough as any male investigator. I'd seen her walk into the gore of a triple homicide crime scene where two of the victims were children and never bat an eye. Same thing with the funerals for victims of the 9-11 attack on the Pentagon. People getting teary-eyed all over the place, including me.

But not Amanda.

Uh-uh. Someone with her emotional discipline doesn't break down because of a touching story over the phone. That meant there had to be another reason.

As I sipped my coffee, I thought back to when I first realized something was wrong.

It had been almost two months earlier. Initially, there wasn't anything I could put my finger on. I just sensed a sadness around Amanda. A short time later, she began withdrawing into herself. She quit dropping by for dinner and frequently didn't answer her phone when I called. Last week, Emily popped over to see her and noticed her eyes were red, as if she'd been crying. What I found particularly worrisome was Amanda's recent habit of sitting on her porch in the evenings. She'd remain there for hours, sipping on wine and staring into the dark. More than once, I'd been on the verge of walking over, but for some reason, I could never bring myself to do it. If she wanted my company, she'd ask.

Emily had decided that Amanda was lonely and had been bugging me to find her a boyfriend. Maybe I'd give it a try. Deep down, I cared for Amanda more than I'd liked to admit, and to see her so unhappy—

My thoughts were interrupted by the clicking of

Emily's footsteps on the hardwood floor. I turned to the entryway and saw the dejected slope of her shoulders and the sadness in her eyes. At that moment, I hated myself for what I was about to say.

But that was the price of being a single parent.

Emily slowly made her way up the table, her curly brown hair still damp from her shower. With each passing year, she looked increasingly like her mother. Same wide-set blue eyes, lightly freckled cheeks, and dimpled chin. And she was getting tall, well over five feet. She wouldn't be a child much longer.

As she listlessly dropped her Britney Spears backpack to the floor and slipped into her chair, I said, "How are you holding up, honey?"

A little shrug. "Okay, Dad. I miss Mom."

"We all do." She sat, staring vacantly at her plate. I said, "Better eat something."

"Not hungry."

"Try."

She reluctantly fished a waffle from the serving plate. I asked, "Mind if I read the letter?" Because we always discussed them together, so I could make sure she understood everything Nicole was trying to tell her.

Emily's hand froze. She looked at me with a mixture of guilt and fear.

I frowned. "What is it, honey?"

No response. She dropped the waffle back to the plate and sat back.

"Is it the letter?" I asked gently.

She hesitated, nodded. "You . . . you can't read it, Dad."

"Oh? Mind telling me why?"

She stared at her plate, avoiding my eyes. "It's . . . personal."

"I see." But I didn't. I sat there, feeling a little hurt and confused. Nicole and I never had secrets. I couldn't believe she'd have written anything that I wasn't supposed to know about.

Mrs. Anuncio pushed through the kitchen door, took one look at Emily's downcast expression, and glared at me.

"I . . . I gotta go, Dad." Emily pushed back her chair and climbed to her feet.

"Go? You still have ten minutes until the bus."

But she'd snatched up her knapsack and was hurrying toward the door.

"Emily, wait. There's something I need to tell you."

Her pace quickened.

"Emily! I told you to get back—"

She flung open the door and was gone. Through the window, I saw her running up the gravel road toward the two-lane highway and the bus stop. She kept wiping at her eyes. From behind, I heard Mrs. Anuncio go off on me in Spanish. When I turned around, she was glaring at me, hands on her hips.

I sighed. "Mrs. Anuncio, it's not my fault. I didn't say anything."

She snorted and withdrew into the kitchen. I heard dishes banging.

For the next few minutes, I sipped coffee and tried to resist the impulse. I finally went upstairs to Amanda's room. The letter was with the others, in one of Nicole's old jewelry boxes, sitting on a corner of the dresser beside the brass-framed picture of Nicole.

I removed the envelope and stood there staring at it for what seemed a long time. My eyes went to Nicole's picture.

They're Emily's letters, Marty. Promise you won't read them unless she asks.

I promise, honey.

My hand was trembling as I returned the letter to the jewelry case. By the time I got downstairs, the phone was ringing. It was Amanda, her voice clipped, urgent.

"Better get outside, Marty," she said. "I think I hear it."

2

The helicopter cruised toward me at maybe two thousand feet. I could make out only a hazy silhouette, framed against the sun. I hurried back into the house, threw on my suit jacket, and checked that the government-issue 9mm pistol in my hip holster was loaded. After grabbing my cell phone, I found Mrs. Anuncio in the kitchen and told her not to be alarmed by the approaching helicopter. She gazed back without interest and continued stacking dishes; she was used to seeing airplanes land here.

As I returned to the living room, the sound of the beating blades had become noticeably louder. I saw Amanda already waiting on the porch, eyes fixed in the distance.

She really was a looker. Not a classic beauty, but she possessed a freshly scrubbed quality highlighted by perfectly tapered bones and tanned, seemingly flawless skin. As usual, Amanda wore little makeup, and her red hair was cut boyishly short, revealing two simple gold earrings. Her gray business suit was buttoned, hiding the gun clipped to her waist. Function over style. That was Amanda.

I studied her for a moment. Her face was a mask, suggesting that whatever had bothered her earlier was forgotten.

As I pushed through the front door, she glanced over with a puzzled expression. "Wasn't the helicopter coming from Andrews?"

"It should be. Why?"

Two steps later, I understood her confusion.

The chopper was visible below the roofline, less than a mile out. Instead of military camouflage, it was painted a metallic blue with a shiny silver roof. It crossed a power line and banked left toward the grass strip out front. At that instant, I noticed a distinctive Nike-like swoosh of red on the tail.

I recognized it at once. "What's he doing here?"

Amanda looked to me in surprise. "You *know* who's in the chopper?"

"So do you."

She frowned. "Someone from the FBI or—"

"That's a private helicopter. Probably goes for ten million easy. Take a shot on who could afford—"

"*Simon?*"

"Yeah. That's his company's logo on the tail."

"But this is a classified operation. Why would the government bring in an outsider? Hell, they wouldn't even tell Colonel Hinkle what's going on."

"We're talking about Simon," I said simply.

Amanda passed on a response. She knew if anyone was exempt from bureaucratic red tape, it would be Simon.

Lieutenant Simon Santos was the chief of the Arlington Homicide Division and over the past decade had solved a number of high-profile murder cases, most in a relatively short time. He was a brilliant, instinctual investigator with an uncanny ability to sniff out the truth. The media lapped up his successes, escalating him into something of a local law enforcement legend. Admittedly, the press's infatuation had less to do with Simon's investigative prowess than his bank account. After all, it's not like every homicide cop had a couple hundred mil burning a hole in his pocket.

Then there were his eccentricities, which also made good copy. As Simon often told me, when you're rich, you're eccentric. When you're poor, you're committed and forgotten.

By now the chopper was practically on top of us. As it chattered past, Amanda said, "If Simon's involved, that means it's a murder."

"Probably. And odds are he's the mystery man who brought us on board."

"Simon would have that kind of pull with the SECDEF?"

I shrugged. "He gives big bucks to political campaigns."

"Must be nice to be able to buy your friends," she said sarcastically.

"Hey, I thought you liked him."

"I do. It's just—" She glanced away. "Look, I know you two are tight and all. But putting up with his Simon-says bullshit gets a little old."

Simon had a controlling nature, but hey, the guy was a genius.

"Careful," I said. "I might have to mark you down for not playing well with others."

She shot me a look. "Implying what? That I'm hard to work with?"

"That was a joke."

"Don't give up your day job."

We stood there staring at each other. I smiled; she didn't.

So I said, "We'd better get going. The chopper's about to—"

She turned her back on me and went down the stairs.

Touchy, touchy.

As private helicopters go, the one we were watching was enormous. It had dual rotors and easily approximated the size of the one used by the president. After slowing to a hover, the big chopper descended to the edge of the grass strip. As Amanda and I walked toward it, we could see two pilots sitting in the cockpit. One threw up a wave and began to unstrap.

As we waited for him to open the passenger door, Amanda and I hung back, warily eyeing the spinning rotors. I removed my fingers from my ears and tested the noise. Tolerable. I gave the passenger windows a once-over and couldn't make out any faces peering out.

The cabin door opened, and stairs unfolded. A pilot hopped to the ground and beckoned to us. He was a heavy-set man with a pleasant face. As we approached, he winked at Amanda.

"Ladies first," he shouted, offering her his hand. "My name is George, and I'll—"

She blew right by George and went up the stairs.

He lowered his arm with a chagrined expression.

"Penis envy," I said into his ear.

He frowned.

I said, "Grew up with five brothers. Felt left out because they all had—"

He got it then and erupted in a big laugh. I didn't have the heart to tell him I was serious.

I clambered inside, and George followed. He thumped the door closed, and the quiet took me by surprise. From hidden speakers, we heard the sounds of classical music.

As expected, the interior was roomy and very plush. Nothing but the best for Simon. At six feet, I could almost stand without crouching, and my shoes practically disappeared into the deep-pile carpeting. I counted five rows of leather first-class seats, two to a row, an aisle in between. At that very back was a lav and a curtained area, which probably hid a small galley and a bar with good booze.

My eyes drifted over the chairs. Empty.

Amanda gave me a questioning look, which I interpreted, telling her Simon was in the lav.

"Grab any seat," George said, squeezing past us toward the cockpit door. "Flight to Andrews will take twenty minutes." He gave Amanda another wink. I sighed. Man didn't learn.

Amanda's face went cold. "Something wrong with your eye, George?" she demanded.

He looked startled.

"I asked if something was wrong with your eye."

"Well, no, but—"

"Then you're harassing me. Knock it off."

George stared at her as if he couldn't believe she was serious. He looked to me for help. I just gazed back sympathetically. George muttered an apology and dove for the safety of the cockpit. I could see the other pilot laughing.

I shook my head at Amanda. "He was interested, and

you cut him off at the knees. Not smart. Pilots are a good catch. They make good money and—"

"I'm not in the mood, Marty."

"I'm serious. You'll never meet a nice guy if you keep scaring them off."

"Drop it, or I'll hurt you."

And she could. I'd seen her bring a weight lifter to his knees with a flick of her wrist. "Violence," I said, "isn't the answer."

She ignored me and stepped over to a front-row seat. "How do you know Simon's in the lav?"

I shrugged. "He likes Bach."

On cue, we heard a click and the lav door opened.

Most people who meet Lieutenant Simon Santos for the first time are struck by the contrast between his reputation and his appearance. He looks more like a maître d' or a big-band leader than a homicide cop.

A youthful thirty-six, he is tall and dark, with a gaunt face topped by longish black hair combed straight back. As usual, he had on a pressed Armani shirt and his trademark dark blue Brooks Brothers silk suit, a red carnation pinned to his lapel. The only variation he ever made to his dress were the bow ties, which he cycled depending on the day of the week. Since this was Friday, he was wearing the red one with white polka dots. It jumped out at you with the subtlety of a face slap, which was the intent. People remembered Simon.

"It's good to see you, Amanda," Simon said warmly. "Hello, Martin."

Everyone in the world called me Marty. Not Simon. Motioning us to the seats at the back, he said, "I'm sorry about the timing, Martin. I had no choice but to request your assistance. If you miss Emily's birthday party, tell her I will make it up to her."

Which meant another expensive gift. "Uncle Simon" was always showering Emily with gifts. As Amanda and I went down the short aisle, I picked up on the conditional and said, "*If* I miss her party?"

He shrugged. "Everything is in flux. Nothing on this investigation has been decided."

"Are you in charge of the task force?" Amanda asked him.

Simon hesitated. "How much do you know?"

She deposited herself into the seat to his front, while I took the one beside him. "Not a thing," she said. "We figured it has to be a homicide. Maybe more than one."

I nodded, adjusting my seat belt. Through the open cockpit door, I could see the pilots at the controls. The engine noise became louder and the pulse rate of the rotor blades increased.

"There's only one victim," Simon said. "The initial reports suggest the death was accidental."

I clicked the belt latch and stared at him. Amanda poked her head around her seat back and did the same.

She said, "An *accident*? What the hell are we doing here?"

Simon slid a hand into his jacket. "It's a complicated situation. There are conflicting interests. So far, the two parties have only agreed that everything should be handled quietly."

"Two parties?" she said.

A vague smile. "We'll discuss the details in the air."

Amanda said, "At least tell us who the victim—"

But Simon had bent forward and closed his eyes. He

was holding a set of rosary beads in a manicured hand. His mouth began moving in silent prayer.

Amanda sighed and looked at me. She mouthed, *Fear of flying?*

I nodded.

Moments later, the big helicopter rose into the air, and Simon squeezed the rosary beads even harder.

3

At a couple thousand feet we turned east, toward the Potomac River and the Maryland border. The sky was clear and bright, the cool morning making for a smooth flight. I pressed against the window and gazed out across the northern Virginia sprawl. The helicopter made a correction to the right, and soon I could make out a blanket of fog over D.C., the top of the Washington Monument poking through. Settling back, I checked out Simon. His mouth was still moving.

Arlington County has a large number of military residents, and Simon and I have worked close to a dozen murder cases over the past ten years in which air force personnel were victims, suspects, or witnesses. Most of that time I've spent trying to figure him out—not so much his quirks, but the big stuff. Like why a religious guy with a zillion bucks wanted to be a cop.

The answer came out of the blue, from a *Washington Post* article published several years back. A murder suspect dug up dirt on Simon and tried to blackmail him into backing off. Simon wouldn't play along, so the story got leaked. For anyone else, the revelations would have ended their police career. In Simon's case, they only proved mildly embarrassing. There was no public backlash, no talking heads hollering for his badge, no editorials questioning his fitness to serve. None of that. Simon said his reputation and his close relations to the press saved him, and I agreed.

Of course, the half mil he spent hiring the big-time D.C. PR firm didn't hurt.

When I read the *Post* story, I felt as if someone had flipped on a light switch to Simon's soul. Suddenly, everything that had puzzled me about him made sense. His secretive nature, his generosity to anyone in need, his early forays into the priesthood—it was all there if you read between the lines. Specifically, the write-up was a scathing exposé on Simon's father, a Cuban exile who made a fortune in the 1960s Miami real estate boom. It turned out that between business deals, Papa Santos got his jollies strangling young girls and dumping their bodies in Biscayne Bay. Simon learned the truth when he was something like ten or eleven. Since then, it's been the defining event in his life. He'd become a homicide cop not because he wanted to; he *had* to.

And that's what the article attacked through innuendo and suspicion. Simon's motive for being a cop. A *homicide* cop. The son of a serial killer.

Why?

Frankly, I worried for Simon. Someday he was going to realize that what he was doing was ultimately pointless. No matter how hard he pushed himself or how many cases he solved, nothing would change. His father's victims would remain dead, and he would always feel the guilt. But I suppose he probably already knew—

A hand touched my arm.

When I looked over, Simon was giving me a relaxed smile. "It's cleansing for the soul, Martin."

"I'm sure it is." As he returned the rosary beads to his jacket, I said, "Ready?"

When he nodded, Amanda started unbuckling her seat belt. "The seat swivels," Simon told her.

She found the lever and swung around. I dug out my notepad.

"The victim," Simon said, "is the chairman of the Joint Chiefs of Staff, General Garber." He paused, anticipating a reaction.

Amanda and I gazed back calmly. We'd prepared for the worst, and this almost seemed like good news. To many in the military, it probably was.

Simon seemed puzzled by our indifference. But he'd never served in the military and wouldn't be privy to the rumors that swirled around General Michael J. Garber.

Since the chairman of the Joint Chiefs resided on Fort Meyers, near the Pentagon, I said, "Did General Garber die on Andrews or—"

"Andrews. A number of the Joint Chiefs attended a terrorism conference in London. Their plane landed early this morning, and Garber's body was discovered in his private compartment by his security detail."

That meant the army's Criminal Investigative Division, since they had the responsibility for protecting the chairman on international trips. I asked Simon for the name of the agent in charge.

He paused, retrieving the information from his mental file bank. He possessed what amounted to total recall. Once he heard or read something—a name, a phone number, an e-mail address, anything—he never forgot it. "Andrew Hobbs."

"Oh, *beautiful*," Amanda said.

Simon frowned at her.

"Andy," I explained, "is an old-timer and a little past his prime. You don't know him because he rarely handles homicide investigations."

"What Marty really means," Amanda said, "is no one *trusts* him to handle homicides."

"He's not that bad," I said.

"Unless he's awake. Cause of death?" She was looking at Simon, pen poised over her notepad.

"The information hasn't been verified," he said. "Secretary Churchfield had a brief conversation with the Joint Chiefs who'd been aboard the plane, and called me."

Opening my notepad, I said, "General Markel one of the chiefs on the plane?" Because this would explain his call to Colonel Hinkle, initiating the investigation.

Simon nodded. "General Johnson and General Sessler were the others."

I jotted down the names with their titles. It was a who's who of the military. General Mark Johnson was the marine commandant, and General Robert Sessler the air force chief. General David Markel, the vice chairman, would temporarily assume the chairmanship and become the military's top dog. There were twenty-four stars between the three men, if you counted both shoulders. Nothing like witnesses with horsepower to enhance credibility.

By now, Simon was recalling the events that led to the discovery of General Garber's body and I had to write fast to keep up.

Simon spoke for five minutes without stopping. My hand was cramping by the time he finished. He'd related the factual details in a rough chronology. He offered no opinion as to whether he thought the death was an accident. He didn't want to influence Amanda and me in any way. Yet.

Afterward, he sat with his chin sunk to his chest, watching as we skimmed through our notes to see if there was anything we didn't understand.

After making an initial assessment in a case, most experienced cops have an inner voice that tells them how things probably played out. At the moment, mine was whispering that we were wasting our time. That this was in all likelihood simply a case of accidental death.

According to Simon, General Garber's aide-de-camp, a Lieutenant Colonel Tina Weller, was the first to realize something might be amiss with her boss. When the C-32—the military version of a Boeing 757 airliner—landed on Andrews at 0546 hours after an eight-hour flight, Colonel Weller had gone to Garber's compartment to awaken him. Receiving no response, Weller alerted the three-man CID security team, led by Andy Hobbs. Andy had his men kick in the door, and when they entered, they found the general lying dead on the floor, still dressed in his pajamas, a deep bruise on his throat. The body's temperature had cooled significantly, indicating the general had died hours earlier. After a cursory investigation, Andy concluded that the general had tripped and fallen forward, striking his throat on a coffee table.

Two additional items supported Andy's accident theory. First, General Garber had reportedly downed the better part of a bottle of whisky earlier that evening, and second, the flight had experienced a fair amount of turbulence over the Atlantic, some occasionally severe.

The makeup of the thirty-two people aboard the aircraft also seemed to dispel any notions of foul play. Excluding the three members of the Joint Chiefs, the remainder were all either support staff or flight crew. No media types or civilians of any kind had gone on the trip.

This latter point was telling. It implied that, with everyone on the same military team, no one would have a motive for wanting General Garber dead.

A dubious assumption, but was that relevant in light of the facts? Probably not.

Before I could mention this to Simon, Amanda beat me to it, announcing, "Everyone hated General Garber."

Simon's frowned. "That's rather a harsh assessment—"

"Hated," Amanda repeated flatly. "No one in the military could stand the guy. Everyone knew the only reason he made rank was because his father happened to chair the Senate Armed Services Committee. Rumor had it that Garber was basically incompetent and a womanizing drunk. He never should have gotten one star, much less four. But Senator Garber pulled strings and made sure his kid moved up the promotion chain. You probably know General Garber's only been the chairman a couple weeks—" At Simon's nod, she went on. "Major Katie Tucker was one of my roommates at the academy. She works in Pentagon LL and gave me the scoop on how Garber got selected. It's not pretty."

"LL?" Simon said.

"Legislative liaison," I answered. "The military's lobbying arm with Capitol Hill."

"According to Katie," Amanda continued, "the SECDEF fought General Garber's appointment hard. So did practically everyone else in DoD. No one, I mean no one, wanted General Garber placed in the top billet. Garber's an air force general, and even the SECAF, his own service's secretary, tried to blackball him. Still, General Garber got the job. Know why?"

Simon said, "You're suggesting that Senator Garber—"

"*Suggesting?*" Amanda said. "Katie got this straight from her contacts on Senator Garber's staff. The senator cranked up the pressure on the president big-time. Quid pro quo with a sledgehammer. He threatened to stall the defense bill in committee unless the president appointed his kid chairman. This when we got a war going on. You believe that shit? Scumbag."

She sat back, looking flushed and morally superior. I almost said, Down, girl.

Simon still appeared skeptical. He was aware that Amanda did occasionally embellish to make a point. He glanced to me, seeking confirmation. I nodded. While I didn't know the specifics behind Garber's appointment to the military's top slot, I'd heard dozens of stories about the Air Force's Teflon general over the years—none good.

Simon adjusted his bow tie as he thought things over. To Amanda, he said, "Assuming what you're saying is true—"

"It is."

"—and even if some passengers deeply resented General Garber and had a motive—"

"They did."

"—it still might not matter without the existence of a crime."

"We don't *know* there wasn't a crime."

"Agent Hobbs has concluded—"

"Andy Hobbs should be collecting social security."

Again Simon looked to me, and again I nodded. Andy and I went back twenty years, and as much as I liked him, the bottom line was that he probably should have been put out to pasture long ago.

Returning to Amanda, Simon said, "You still must consider the facts—"

"Like what? A pickled general and a turbulent flight? That still doesn't prove— What now?" Simon was shaking his head emphatically, and I had a pretty good idea why.

"You're forgetting the door," he said to her.

At her frown, I prompted, "Andy Hobbs had to break down the door. Remember?"

"So what, Marty? I assumed he didn't have a key, and— What are you doing?"

The question was directed at Simon, who had reached behind his seat and opened the lav door. He indicated to the locking mechanism and gazed at her expectantly.

A flicker of understanding crossed Amanda's face. She asked, "That the same as the one on General Garber's compartment?"

"I was told it was similar," Simon said.

"Actually," I said, "the one on the plane is much stronger." Noting their curious looks at my sudden expertise, I explained that I'd flown as part of the SECAF's security detail some years earlier. I added, "Because the vice president often used the plane, the Secret Service added a reinforced slide latch. The Secret Service didn't like the idea that someone aboard could possibly get a hold of a key and walk in on the Veep."

Amanda said, "But you were flying on the older Boeing 707, Marty. Not the 757."

"I'll bet the door still has a latch assembly that only locks from the inside. Be silly to change it."

She was silent, considering this. His point made, Simon closed the lav door.

We sat, listening to the muffled beat of the rotors. Amanda tugged on her lower lip, her eyes shifting between Simon and me. She said, "I don't know, guys. It all seems a little too . . . coincidental. I've heard stories about how General Garber used to destroy people's careers, just to show he could. It gave him some kind of power trip. A guy like that, someone with as many enemies as General Garber, and he conveniently has a fatal accident a couple weeks after he becomes the chairman? Give me a break."

I said, "But if the door was locked—"

"I hear you, Marty. I'm just saying it doesn't *feel* right." She shrugged. "But hey, what do I care? This means we can wrap this up quick, and everyone will be happy. No muss, no fuss." She looked at me. "Looks like you'll make Emily's birthday after all."

"Possibly," Simon said. "Though we're certain to encounter resistance to a finding of accidental death."

Amanda and I looked to him in surprise. I said, "Someone *wants* this to be a murder?"

Simon hesitated. "In a manner of speaking."

"Out with it, Simon," Amanda said. "Who could possibly want this thing to be—"

Her brow furrowed at the ringing of a cell phone. I started to reach inside my jacket, then realized it was Simon's.

He stared at the caller ID box on the face but made no move to answer it. Without looking up, he said, "I was going to explain about this. Don't misunderstand."

I said, "Misunderstand?"

The phone rang again. This time Simon punched the talk button and put it to his ear. He watched Amanda and me as he spoke.

"Hello, Senator Garber," he said.

4

Simon spoke for less than two minutes. His tone was deferential and formal. He said "Yes, Senator" three times and "I'll take care of it, sir" twice. He ended with: "We'll be expecting you, sir. I see. Again, my condolences to you and your wife for your loss. If there's anything else I can do . . . Fine. Good-bye, Senator."

Not much of a conversation, but enough for Amanda and me to put two and two together and conclude that it had to be Senator Garber who wanted this to be a murder investigation.

Amanda fired eye darts at Simon. She looked at me as if to urge me to comment, but I sat quietly; there wasn't any point. Simon was being Simon. His habit of playing everything close to his chest was a reflection of his past and the years he'd spent trying to keep the secret of his father hidden. Besides, I knew Simon hadn't been feeding us a line earlier; he would have told us about his connection to Senator Garber.

Eventually.

As Simon put his phone away, Amanda cracked,

"Cozy. You and the Senator have sleepovers and everything?"

Simon appeared more amused than offended by her comment. He smiled, saying, "You're wrong about Senator Garber. He's an honorable man."

"Oh, please—"

Simon went on, "I've known the senator for years and supported his campaign. This morning he asked if I would investigate his son's death, and I agreed." He paused, eyes on Amanda. "But first I made it clear I would operate with no agenda other than to uncover the truth."

"I seem to recall," Amanda said cryptically, "that you mentioned the senator is pushing for this to be a murder."

"Because that's what he believes occurred." Simon flashed another smile. "Frankly, he voiced concerns similar to yours. He, too, feels his son's death was suspiciously . . . convenient." To me, he added, "As you've probably guessed, Secretary of Defense Churchfield has taken the opposite view and is convinced General Garber's death was nothing but a tragic accident."

I said, "The two parties you mentioned."

"Correct. Senator Garber asked Secretary Churchfield to initiate a comprehensive investigation. The secretary was reluctant, but agreed on the condition that it be handled by the military, or possibly a task force comprised of military and FBI. Senator Garber balked, insisting that he wanted someone outside the government running the investigation."

"Meaning you," Amanda said. "The senator is worried about a cover-up."

Simon nodded.

"And you requested us?"

"Through Senator Garber, yes."

"So how long until we know who else is on the task force?"

"There won't be a task force now."

"Oh?"

"That's what the senator was calling about. The secretary wouldn't agree to civilian control of the investigation. Senator Garber contacted the president to resolve the impasse. The president's overriding concern was to prevent any hint of scandal. He ordered the investigating team be kept small, to prevent press leaks. He also sided with Secretary Churchfield's position that the military retain sole jurisdiction. Since the death occurred on air force property, it was determined the OSI would take the lead with CID assisting."

Amanda said, "By CID, you mean Andy Hobbs and his boys?"

Simon nodded.

She asked, "Can we have them removed?"

"I doubt it."

"Why not?"

"It doesn't make sense to remove them. They were aboard the plane and have begun a preliminary inquiry. They're familiar with passengers and can provide us insight." He gazed at her, anticipating an argument.

For a moment, Amanda seemed tempted. Instead, she shrugged and said, "Don't say I didn't warn you."

I said to Simon, "So the FBI is definitely out?"

"Yes."

I said, "And your role?"

"A member of the team."

"That's all?"

"That's all."

Amanda had a wry smirk, which I understood. Simon was taking orders from someone else. This we had to see.

"So who is in charge, then?" I asked. "They bringing in someone with more firepower like Colonel Hinkle, or—"

"That's whom Secretary Churchfield suggested," Simon said. "Of course, Senator Garber couldn't allow it. He's convinced an active duty military officer would be too easily pressured by Churchfield."

"Imagine that," Amanda said.

Simon continued, "They reached a compromise. Someone with military connections who still retained the freedom to be objective."

As he said it, he looked at me with an odd smile. When I caught on, I felt like I'd been kicked in the stomach. Amanda followed Simon's gaze, her eyes widening. She said, "Don't tell me it's—"

"Martin," Simon said, "is the compromise. A military civilian."

They both gazed at me, waiting for my reaction. I tried to keep my cool. I told myself that I been a cop for over twenty years, solved a lot of tough cases. That this was just one more.

But of course it wasn't. This time I'd be caught in a tug-of-war between the secretary of defense and a powerful U.S. senator. And if I made one wrong move—

"Andrews, five minutes out," the copilot called out cheerfully from the cockpit.

I swore.

As the home of Air Force One and one of the most famous military installations in the world, Andrews got

more than its fair share of maintenance dollars, and it
looked like it. We approached the base from the west and
flew over wide, clean streets, perfectly manicured lawns,
and seemingly endless numbers of cream-colored build-
ings that gleamed as if freshly painted. Because it was the
morning rush hour, cars were backed up a half mile along
the access road leading from the main gate, waiting to
pass through the security police checkpoints.

Nearing the runway, the helicopter angled left, keeping clear of the traffic pattern. At the far end, I caught a
glimpse of the control tower and the newly renovated
base operations/passenger terminal building. The helicopter landing pads, which the president often used,
would be on the massive concrete ramp out front, to the
right of the grass infield with the big American flag.
Our forward speed slowed, and we began a gradual
descent.

"Martin—"

When I turned, Simon and Amanda were looking at
me. He said, "I've been assured you cannot be removed
without the consent of Senator Garber and will also be
granted the authority to do the job. Still, if you'd rather
decline, I can request—"

"Define authority," I said.

"You will have complete control in the investigation.
You can request any assistance you require, conduct any
tests you wish, and compel whomever you want to cooperate."

"Including the four-stars?"

"Yes."

"So they have to talk to me?"

"Yes."

"Cooperate in every way?"

"They've been instructed to do so, yes."

Amanda shook her head. She wasn't buying this, and neither was I. This was the military, and they were four-star generals. Regardless of my expressed authority, I wouldn't be able to compel them to do anything. I sighed. This was turning into a morning of being cornered into jobs I didn't want to take. "Relax, Simon. I'll run the investigation."

His eyes bored into mine. "You understand the generals will test you, pressure you. That's why they agreed to allow you to be in charge. They are counting on you to be deferential toward them."

I nodded.

"Remember, we are in a war. Our government cannot afford a scandal within the military hierarchy. It's imperative that the investigation be conducted quietly and efficiently. At times, that will be difficult to accomplish, but we must—"

"Simon, I'm a big boy. I can handle this."

He smiled and squeezed my shoulder, a significant gesture, since he wasn't into touching. "I'm sure you'll do fine, Martin."

Recalling his phone conversation, I asked him when Senator Garber was coming out to Andrews.

"He and Secretary Churchfield are wrapping up a meeting at the Pentagon. They're flying to Andrews by helicopter sometime within the next hour."

"Lucky us," Amanda said. "So who gets to baby-sit?"

"The senator," Simon said, "will not interfere with our investigation. He's only interested in seeing his son's body."

"And the SECDEF?" she asked.

No response.

I asked Simon where General Garber's body was now.

"In the compartment. Agent Hobbs called the senator within minutes of the landing, to notify him of his son's death. When Senator Garber told Agent Hobbs to secure the compartment, he was informed by Hobbs that he'd already done so."

I gave Amanda a little smile.

"Marty," she said, "any rookie knows you seal off a death scene."

"Cut Andy some slack, huh. He can be a good cop when he wants to be."

"Now that," she said, "is one ringing endorsement."

In response to Simon's quizzical gaze, I explained that Andy Hobbs and Amanda had worked on a series of robberies over at Fort Meyer about a year ago. "The suspect," I said, "was an air force sergeant. The case file got misplaced, and the guy walked."

Amanda almost choked. "Misplaced? Andy lost the file in a bar."

"He denies it."

She gave me a dirty look and asked Simon about the status of the passengers. His response was pretty much what I'd anticipated; the generals and key members of their staffs had returned to their Pentagon offices. Not the approved solution, but tracking them down wouldn't be difficult.

Amanda asked Simon if Senator Garber had any evidence pointing to murder. Simon replied no, saying only that the senator was aware that the other members of the Joint Chiefs were resentful of his son's appointment to the chairman's position. I told Simon my primary concern was whether the senator would believe us if we concluded his son's death was an accident.

"He'll believe me," he said. "But he must be convinced we made a thorough inquiry."

I said, "So we go through the whole drill? Conduct interviews, process the compartment, order up tests—"

"Yes."

"—even if we verify the door was locked—"

"Yes."

"—and even if Dr. Billy Bowman examines the body and determines the death wasn't homicide?"

Simon smiled. "Ultimately, it's your decision, Martin."

"Thanks a lot."

The helicopter stopped its descent, and I glanced outside. We were maybe ten feet up, following a taxiway toward the ramp. I could see a line of security policemen spaced out every hundred yards or so, to prevent access from the adjacent flight-line road. I looked for a blue-and-white Boeing 757 with "United States of America" painted across the side. It wasn't there.

Then I noticed the enormous double hangar over to the right, its entrance marked with a red-coned security perimeter. Two Humvees were sitting out front, men manning the roof-mounted machine guns. The military wasn't messing around about keeping the investigation into Garber's death quiet.

The landing pads appeared, and I could see a marshaler with his wands, waiting to park us. Thirty yards to his left, I spotted two shiny air force staff cars, a knot of air force uniforms clustered around them. Our welcoming committee. I didn't see Andy Hobbs and his CID team or the members of the OSI forensic unit, but I didn't expect to. Priority number one for the air force would be to keep them out of sight.

The helicopter turned into the ramp area, and the

marshaler motioned us forward. The group waiting by the cars spread out expectantly. I could seem them clearly now. A one-star general, two full colonels, a major with a dark blue Security Police beret, and couple of sergeants. One colonel produced a cell phone and ducked into a car, obviously to report our arrival to some Pentagon heavy hitter.

The helicopter touched down.

Showtime.

5

As we unlatched our seat belts, Simon explained that the helicopter would be returning to his mansion in Manassas—another security precaution the military had insisted upon, to lessen the chances of the two pilots guessing why we'd come here.

George came back into the cabin and opened the door. This time he was cool and distant, completely ignoring Amanda as she went down the steps. Simon followed her, and I brought up the rear.

As I emerged onto the bright concrete, George spoke into my ear and pressed his business card into my hand. I told him to forget it; Amanda wouldn't be interested. He kept insisting, and I finally agreed to try.

"What did George want?" Amanda asked, as I joined her and Simon.

"Why do you care?"

She shrugged. "Just curious."

"George likes Chinese food and wants at least two children. A boy and a girl. The boy will be named Samuel, after his grandfather—"

She'd tuned me out, and so had Simon. I followed

their eyes toward our welcoming committee. None looked happy to see us, and the general had a particularly sour expression.

"C'mon," I said. "Let's get this over with."

"Wait, Martin," Simon said, turning to me. "There's one more item that slipped my mind. The president's approval for the investigation contained a condition."

A warning bell sounded in my head. Nothing ever slipped Simon's mind unless it was intentional. I asked him what the condition was.

"Are you aware that the president will be addressing the American people tonight?"

I nodded. "Right. Eight P.M. The rumor is he's going to declare war on Iraq. So?"

"That's it. That's the condition. The president wants this issue resolved by then."

I was incredulous. "You mean *tonight?*"

He nodded.

I checked my watch. "That's twelve hours from now."

His gazed back innocently. I was furious with him. I said, "You set me up. You know there's no way in hell we can finish this in a day—"

My words were drowned out by the sudden roar of the rotor blast behind us. Simon used the diversion to wheel around toward the waiting group. Amanda strolled after him, grinning. She couldn't resist shouting out a comment that I couldn't deny.

"You've been suckered, Marty," she said.

Brigadier General Morley, the Andrews Air Force Base wing commander, was graying and angular, with a thin face and a thinner smile. He went through the introductions in an abrupt manner and made no attempt to shake hands.

Following their boss's lead, the two colonels and the security police major gave us their last names and titles and nothing else. Colonel Timmons, a wiry black man in his forties, was the support group commander, which meant he was the equivalent of a city manager for the base. Colonel Jessup, a compact guy with a barrel chest, as the operations group commander, managed all the Distinguished Visitor aircraft, including the C-32 that General Garber had died in. Major Vega, a Barney Fife clone with a surprisingly deep voice, introduced himself as the security police CO, which made him the base's top cop.

At the moment, General Morley was scrutinizing my flip-top OSI credentials as if hoping to find something out of order. He'd spent two minutes on Amanda's and was going onto his third minute with mine. He'd also given me the silent treatment when I tried to ask questions about the plane and the whereabouts of the OSI team. It was clear that he was jerking us around to reinforce the message that we weren't going to get much cooperation on his turf. I also noted that some of the armed security policeman had circled behind us in an attempt to crank up the intimidation factor.

Morley returned my credentials, then extended his hand to Simon.

Simon gave me a sideways glance and made no move to produce his badge. I said, "I'll vouch for him, General."

Morley gave me a hard look. "This is a classified operation, Mr. Collins. I need to confirm this man's identity."

"Are you satisfied with my ID, sir?"

He hesitated, then nodded.

"Then I'm vouching for him, General." Amanda nodded along, backing me up.

Morley's jaw tightened. He returned to Simon and thrust out a bony hand. Now maybe as a rigid military type, he had a natural suspicion for guys who wore wild bow ties, but I didn't think so. Simon looked to me and shook his head. He was tired of this crap, and so was I. Better to determine once and for all who was in charge.

"I'm vouching for Lieutenant Santos, General," I said for the third time.

"Now see here, Collins," Morley said. "This is a classified operation. If *I* don't verify this man's identity, he will be escorted off the base."

"What were your orders, General?" I asked politely.

"None of your damned business."

"Weren't you ordered to fully cooperate with my investigation? If not, I need to know that now." I gave him a pleasant smile accompanied by a not-so-pleasant fuck-you-sir look.

There was a long pause. Morley was struggling to keep his anger in check. He lost the battle and jabbed a finger at Simon, saying, "This is *my* base, Collins. You understand me. *Mine*. Now unless I personally see this man's ID—"

"Santos," Simon said. "My name is Detective Lieutenant Santos."

"He's often in the papers," I said helpfully.

Morley stared at me. "I don't give a damn if he's on the front page of the *Washington Post*. I want to see his ID. *Now*."

The SPs who'd circled behind us moved in closer a few steps.

Screw this. I said, "Make the call, Simon."

Simon calmly drifted back a few paces and took out his phone.

General Morley watched him, uncertainty in his eyes. So did the two colonels and the SP major. The two sergeants stood with their mouths open. In their minds it didn't compute, a civilian defying a general.

Simon carefully punched in a number and spoke louder than necessary. "Senator Garber, it's Simon. I have a problem I need relayed to Secretary Churchfield—"

Colonel Jessup stiffened. "The SECDEF? Jesus."

Colonel Timmons coughed. "Ah, General, if I might recommend . . ."

His anxious eyes locked on Morley, waiting. Colonel Jessup's blink rate kicked into high gear, and Major Vega began an anxious two-step.

The general continued to glare at me in defiance, but his twitching eyelid gave him away. He'd obviously been ordered to give us a hard time and was now wondering if he'd gone too far. Still, he couldn't bring himself to back down because—

And then Simon said Morley's name.

Loudly.

That did it. Morley stepped toward him. "Hang up," he ordered.

Simon cupped the phone and eyed him coolly.

"Hang up," Morley said again.

Simon didn't move.

I said, "General, we need to be assured of your complete cooperation."

Morley's eyes darted to me. He slowly nodded.

I said, "My men will also need office space, access to computers and phones—"

"Fine. Anything. Colonel Timmons will get you what you need. *Now hang up the fucking phone.*"

I saw a hint of panic in Morley's eyes. He knew one-star

generals who cause problems don't grow up to be two-stars. At my nod, Simon resumed talking on the phone in apologetic tones. A moment later, he returned, tucking it away.

Morley stood there, glowering at us. I expected a caustic remark, but instead he spun angrily on his heels and motioned to one of the sergeants, obviously his driver. Morley jumped into the back seat of a staff car, and they sped away.

Colonel Jessup and Colonel Timmons watched us expectantly. Major Vega had stopped dancing and was now nervously licking his lips.

I said to him, "Tell the SPs behind us to beat it, Major."

"Yes, sir." He stepped past me and barked, "Sergeant Crenshaw, get your men back to their posts."

As the SPs trudged away, I pointed to the hangar guarded by the two Humvees. "General Garber's C-32 in there?"

Jessup and Timmons nodded in unison. "Your names are on the access list, sir," Major Vega added. "You'll need these in the restricted area." He held out three bright yellow plastic badges with the words "Cleared Entry. No Escort Required."

As Simon, Amanda, and I each clipped a badge onto our lapels, Vega said, "Your team's been escorted to the hangar."

"They've already started to work?" I said, surprised.

"No, sir. After we cleared out the maintenance personnel from the hangar, Agent Hobbs figured he'd have your people set up in the vacated offices."

Andy Hobbs taking charge. Encouraging. I said to no one in particular, "I understand there are still some of the plane's passengers on base."

"In the DV lounge," Colonel Jessup said, gesturing in the direction of the passenger terminal. "There's only about a dozen or so. Mostly nonessential members of the various staffs. The rest returned to the Pentagon with the generals."

"You know which passengers are here, Colonel?" I asked.

"Agent Hobbs does. He had one of his men make a list."

"And the complete passenger manifest?"

"Hobbs has a copy."

"I'll also need all the passengers' work and home phone numbers, along with their work and home addresses."

Colonel Jessup's hesitation told me I'd finally brought up something that Andy hadn't requested. "Give me thirty minutes," he said. "Anything else?"

"The plane's crew," I said. "Pilots and flight attendants. I'd like to talk to them as soon as possible."

"That'll take longer. I've sent them home. They were pretty beat, flying all night."

I checked my watch: 0753. "Have them report at 1000 hours, in the hangar."

Jessup nodded, unclipped his cell phone from his belt, and began relaying my instructions.

"That it?" Timmons said to me.

Simon came forward. "I have a request, Colonel."

Timmons could only gaze in astonishment at the paper Simon handed him, with a name and a license number neatly written on it. Timmons said, "You want a base pass for a stretch limo?"

Simon nodded.

"*Your* stretch limo?"

"It should arrive within the hour. That's the name of the chauffeur."

Timmons slowly nodded. "Sure. Not a problem." He passed the paper to Vega, saying, "The major will clear it with his troops at the main gate. Let's go, Sergeant Rickers." As Timmons walked toward the car, he said to Vega, "A limo, huh? Must be paying cops a helluva lot more than— What was that, Major?"

Vega said something.

"*That's* the guy?" Timmons said, turning to look at Simon.

Simon leaned over and whispered a suggestion. It was worth a shot. "Colonel Timmons," I called out. "A final question—"

6

Simon, Amanda, and I stepped back with Colonel Timmons about ten paces, so we'd be out of earshot of Major Vega and Sergeant Rickers, waiting by the car. Colonel Jessup was already camped in the backseat with the door open, still talking on his cell phone. I glanced at Simon, figuring he wanted to handle this. He continued to stand quietly.

So I faced Timmons and asked, "Mind telling us who told General Morley to give us a hard time, Colonel?"

Timmons blinked, taken aback. "I don't know what you're talking about."

"No?"

"Of course not."

"It will be just between you and us, Colonel. It won't go anywhere."

"I said I don't know what you're talking about."

"General Morley was acting on his own, sir?"

Timmons hesitated, his voice turning cautious. "The general was only doing what he thought was right."

"Meaning—"

"You know. That this—your investigation—is a waste

of time and resources. For chrissakes, the man died in an accident."

"You're a doctor?" I said mildly.

Timmons's face hardened. "You know what I mean. Listen, if General Morley had orders to harass you, he sure didn't tell me about it."

"So you have no knowledge—"

"None."

I smiled. "Fine, Colonel. We'll just need you to sign a statement to that effect."

Timmons squinted. "Statement? What statement?"

"Amanda," I said, "could you take out your notepad?"

"Sure." She dug out it out.

"Write this down," I said. "'To my knowledge, General Morley was acting on his own authority when he harassed an investigation team led by Agent Martin Collins, of the Air Force Office of Special Investigations.' It will be for Colonel Timmons's signature."

Timmons was incredulous. "*I'm not signing that thing.*"

I shook my head. "Colonel . . . Colonel . . ."

"*What?*"

"Senator Garber and the secretary of defense will be arriving in the next hour. I intend to tell them we were treated rudely by General Morley. I'll inform them we think General Morley is concerned that we will uncover something unfavorable. Possibly criminal. I'll tell them that General Morley's actions were contrary to his orders to cooperate fully with—"

"Shit," Timmons said. "Fuck."

I looked at him.

Timmons ran a hand over his face. "Don't do this. General Morley's a good man—"

"I'm sure."

"—a helluva good officer. He was only acting under . . . guidance." He forced out the last word.

"So he *was* following orders, Colonel?"

Timmons paused, looking back over his shoulder at Colonel Jessup, who was still on the phone. Major Vega and Sergeant Ricker were watching us from the front seats of the car.

Returning to me, Timmons said, "You swear it won't go anywhere. If it gets out I said anything—"

"You have my word."

"It was General Markel. He said this was going to be a witch hunt because of Senator Garber's pressure. We were encouraged to be less than cooperative."

"Have a good day, Colonel," I said.

As the staff car with the four men drove away, Simon and Amanda were eyeing me with approval. He said, "Well done, Martin."

I shrugged off the compliment. After twenty years, I'd learned how to jerk the chains of senior officers.

"You know much about General Markel?" Amanda asked me.

I shook my head; he'd become the vice chairman long after I retired.

"My friend Katie," she said, "often accompanied General Markel up to the hill when he had to testify before Congress. She says he's so gung-ho about the military, it's scary. He compares serving one's country to joining a religious order. The word around the Pentagon is Markel is, well, nuts. Everyone is kinda afraid of him, including the other chiefs. Markel spent a couple tours in Vietnam as one of those lone snipers. He used to go off in the jungle by himself and come back after a few weeks with a necklace of ears. Katie figured this was just a wild rumor until she actually saw a photo in Markel's office, which showed him wearing a necklace."

Simon and I stared at her. We didn't know quite what to say.

"Anyway," she went on. "I'm telling you this because Markel's protective as hell about anything that might hurt the military. He drives Congress crazy because he won't give them a straight answer. It could be Markel told General Morley not to cooperate because he really believes we're on a witch hunt."

"That's certainly one possibility," Simon said.

None of us voiced the second: Had General Markel given the order because he was afraid of something we might uncover?

We walked toward the twin hangars to find out.

The red-coned security perimeter spanned the front of the hangar entrance in a giant semicircle. We headed for the apex, where the two Humvees were parked facing us, about twenty yards apart. The entry control point was located between them, monitored by a frizzy-haired female security cop in a green battle-dress utility uniform. Under the watchful eye of her counterparts manning the machine guns mounted on the Humvees, the female cop checked off our names against those on her clipboard, then had us sign in. Afterward, I perused the access list. Most of the OSI members I recognized; the few I didn't were new. Dr. Billy Bowman had been the last to arrive, logging in only minutes earlier.

The female cop pointed us to the rightmost of the two hangars. Since its giant doors were closed, we swung around to the small entry door around the side. A stream of maintenance troops strolled along the ramp outside the barrier, eyeing us curiously. In an adjacent alleyway, we could see about a dozen civilian cars and the two blue air force vans used by the OSI.

I stepped ahead and opened the side door. We could hear the mumble of conversation and the humming of the giant circulation fans.

Then: "Here! The SECDEF and Senator Garber are coming here! That's a load of crap, Major. I didn't sign up for this! Where the *fuck* are Collins and Gardner?"

Simon looked at me with a pained expression.

"Andy Hobbs," I said. "If it helps, his bark is worse than his bite."

He appeared less than reassured as he continued inside.

Amanda followed, muttering to me, "Man's got some mouth. You know he's a West Pointer?"

"Class of '69. Won a Silver Star in Vietnam for bravery, too."

She stopped in the doorway so suddenly that I bumped into her. "*Andy?*"

I nodded.

She slowly shook her head. "Makes you wonder, doesn't it? A guy like him, a hero."

"Andy," I said, "always makes you wonder."

An officer *and* a gentleman.

That's how the military service academy brochures described their graduates. Of course, there were always exceptions.

Thirty-five years ago, Cadet First Class Andrew Hobbs graduated from West Point as the Goat, the bottom-ranked cadet in his class. That performance foreshadowed his military career and personal life. Andy was the perennial underachiever, the guy who had the brains and talent to succeed but lacked the will to do so. Gregarious and obnoxious, Andy could be counted on to talk a good line and then promptly disappear when it was time for the work to get done. In the army, he tried an assortment of military specialties, settling on the CID because it provided an escape from the rigors of the more traditional fighting occupations. After a twenty-year career, he'd retired as a major and applied for one of the coveted full-time civil service CID billets. No one figured he had a chance of landing the job, since Andy's reputation for mediocrity had long been established, and there were a number of more qualified applicants.

But when the selections were announced, Andy's name was at the top of the list. Everyone who'd ever worked with him was stunned. The rumor mill kicked into overdrive, and the prevailing opinion was that a high-ranking sponsor must have pushed for him. When asked, Andy always denied this possibility, insisting retired majors didn't have sponsors.

He was right; they didn't. So how'd he get the job?

A screwup by the selection board? A mix-up in the personnel records? Or was Andy simply one lucky son of a bitch who'd slipped through a bureaucratic crack?

It was another mystery that surrounded Andy, right up there with his West Point appointment and why he refused to talk about the Silver Star he won in combat.

Yeah, Andy made you wonder.

7

I closed the side door. We could still hear Andy swearing. Two more security cops were standing a few paces away. They checked our yellow badges and motioned us past.

Built to house Air Force One, the hangar was cavernous and immaculate, with a gleaming gray painted floor that looked clean enough to eat off. The C-32 was parked in the center facing us, a set of portable airstairs rolled up against the forward passenger door. A Humvee sat parked at the base of the stairs, and two white-suited medical technicians were removing a wheeled gurney from its back. An inflated air hose to supply air conditioning was plugged into the plane's belly. I found this curious; it was downright chilly in the hangar.

Past the nose of the plane, we could see a gathering of OSI personnel in civilian clothes, standing in front of the big double doors leading to the maintenance offices. Pacing before them was a fat man with slicked-back gray hair, wearing a wrinkled suit, a cell phone pressed to his ear.

As we walked toward Andy Hobbs, he said, "I heard

you, Major. I'm calm. I *said* I'm calm. How the fuck should I know who's going to escort? Get one of your people. Just don't bring in a brass band. This operation's supposed to be classified, remember? Like I give a damn."

Andy Hobbs clicked off and grunted "Dipshit" to a blond man in a dark suit. A CID warrant officer whom I vaguely recognized. Carter or Carson.

By now the OSI team had spotted us, and many looked relieved. Master Sergeant Bobby Baker, the photographer, threw up an arm in acknowledgment. Others joined him. Martha Jones, the senior trace evidence specialist and team chief, said, "Thank God you're here, Marty."

Andy Hobbs spun around and squinted at us—me—accusingly. "About fucking time. Thought maybe you'd decided to take a powder, dump this thing on me."

"I've missed you, too, Andy," I said dryly.

"Yeah, yeah." He hitched his pants over his belly and came over, the blond man nipping at his heels. The collar of Andy's shirt was stained with sweat, and his florid face was redder than normal. As usual, he reeked of stale cigarette smoke. He said, "That was Major Vega on the phone. He's freaking out because he found out about Secretary Churchfield and Senator Garber flying out. Wants to know, who's going to escort?"

Before I could reply, Simon said, "Martin and I will attend to them."

Andy appraised Simon. "You're Simon Santos, huh? The pro from Dover they called in. Word I got is you're running this thing."

"Actually, I am," I said.

"Whatever," Andy said. "As long as it ain't me. I've never kissed up to the brass, and I'm damned sure too old to start now." He nodded our attention to the blond man.

"Say hi to Paul Carter. Tommy Gentry's in the plane with Doc Bowman. You know Tommy? No. Good troop. Amanda, long time no see, partner. You losing weight? You're looking kinda thin."

Amanda smiled wanly. I pointed to the air hose and asked Andy whose idea it was to hook that up.

"General Markel. It's a fucking refrigerator in the plane. And yeah, I argued with him about that. Told him that with the temp being that cold, it would screw up the doc's ability to place the time of death. But Markel didn't know how long the dick-dance between the SECDEF and Senator Garber would last. He didn't want the body to start decaying and stink up the place. The man's got four stars. What the fuck was I supposed to do?"

Markel again. I looked to Simon. His face was blank. Since Amanda had once worked aircraft maintenance, I told her to shut off the air.

As she did, Simon said, "We'd like to see the general's body now, Agent Hobbs."

"Shit, it's Andy. We're all friends here, Simon. Nice suit, by the way. Must set you back a few bucks. Me, I'm an off-the-rack man myself. Okay to call you Simon?" Without waiting for a reply, he lumbered toward the portable stairs, Paul Carter hurrying after him.

As the rest of us started to follow, I asked Amanda to escort the OSI techs into the maintenance break room located inside the double doors and brief them up on the particulars of the investigation. I told her to hit the investigation's security classification hard; no one on the team was even to hint where they were working and what they were doing. I wasn't about to earn the wrath of the SECDEF or the president because someone blabbed to their wife or significant other.

I caught up to Carter, Andy, and Simon at the foot of the stairs, where they'd stopped to don latex gloves. I dug mine out of a pocket and did the same. The two medical assistants had placed the gurney a few feet away and were now watching us from the front seats of the Humvee, a petite blond girl with braces and a chubby black guy who barely looked old enough to shave. Putting an edge in my voice, I reminded them they weren't to repeat what they were doing here to anyone. The girl gave me a frightened, saucer-eyed look and nodded. The guy barked, "Yes, sir."

Andy looked at me like I was a jerk. I ignored him.

Paul Carter led the way up the stairs, followed by Andy, Simon, and me. Andy began rattling on like a tour guide, saying, "It was one hell of a wake-up call, I can tell you. People were shitting bricks when we found the general. First thing I thought was, maybe someone decided to knock him off. I mean, it's no secret that Garber wasn't exactly Mr. Popularity. So I took me a good look. As far as I'm concerned, this thing is cut and dried. A freak accident. Hell, the guy smells like a friggin' brewery. I got to tell you it's a crying shame, us going through this bullshit just to keep some goddamn senator happy. If it was up to me, I'd have told Papa Garber to kiss my— Yo, Tom! Look alive in there! You and the doc got company." Looking back at us, he said, "Since we landed, either Paul or Tom or myself have been watching the compartment. Word I got was, anybody contaminated the scene, Uncle Andy better be looking for another job."

"Who told you that?" Simon asked.

Andy had reached the small landing at the top of the stairs. He paused, giving Simon a disgusted look. "The hell you think? The general's daddy himself. Once we got over the shock of finding the body, one of the constella-

tions—General Sessler, I think it was—tells Garber's aide
Colonel Weller that she'd better call the senator, break
the news to him about his kid. Weller was too shook up, so
I did it. I'm nice and polite, I can promise you that. I give
the senator the news real gentle-like. And he's calm at
first. Asks me how it happened, and I tell him. You know,
that the general just sorta . . . fell.

"That's when the senator loses it. The next thing I
know, he's screaming at me. Goes on about how my job
was to protect his son. Swears his kid wouldn't just fall
down. Reams me a new one, says anyone touches anything in the cabin, he'll have my ass. I tell him I know my
job and that I've already secured the cabin. He says I'd
better, and hangs up on me. Prick."

"Give the senator a break, Andy," I said. "You just told
him his son died."

"Remind me to send flowers. Fuck, I could use a
smoke."

He went through the door.

Simon watched him go, shaking his head.

I said, "Andy's an acquired taste. You'll get used to
him."

Simon gave me a look.

We continued into the plane, entering a cramped
entryway between two bulkheads. I immediately noticed
the chill in the air. It couldn't be more than sixty degrees.
Through an opening to the left, a galley was visible, and
beyond, the rows of business class seats located in the section aft of the cockpit door. Andy's bulk was disappearing
down the passageway at the end of the right bulkhead. As
we made the turn, we saw Carter and a tall, sandy-haired
man in a brown suit, whom I took to be Tom Gentry,
standing in the short passageway. Carter pointed to an

open doorway to our right. The lock was busted, and the door was pushed inward and slightly askew. From inside, we heard Andy growl, "So, Doc, whaddaya got?"

We went inside to hear Dr. Billy Bowman's answer.

Considering the compartment was on an aircraft, it was exceptionally large, almost twenty feet across and eight feet deep, with modular white walls and gray carpeting. To our front was a small faux-wood desk, two plush leather captain's chairs on either side of it, a blue terry-cloth robe draped over the back of the chair closest to us. Except for two phones—an intercom and a top-secret-secured STU III for making encrypted calls anywhere in the world—the desktop was clean, without so much as a piece of paper or a pencil visible. A passageway funneled past the desk, leading to a lav at the back. Along the left wall sat a leather couch that probably doubled as a bed, a wood-veneer-topped coffee table to its front.

And that's the area where Simon and I were focused now. Specifically on Andy and Dr. Billy Bowman, who were crouched over the body of General Michael Garber.

Garber wasn't immediately recognizable as a general. Instead of a uniform, he wore white silk pajamas and was lying prone on his stomach, his head twisted toward us. A normally handsome man with chiseled features and close-cropped graying hair, his facial muscles had relaxed in death, giving him a bloated look. Even though we were standing almost two feet away, we could smell the odor of alcohol and the hint of something flowery. Dr. Bowman was scrutinizing the back of Garber's scalp with a penlight. He turned the head and ran a gloved finger inside the dead man's mouth. As he did so, I tried to view the throat area, but Bowman was blocking my view. He peered into the dead man's nose and ears, then moved back and began studying the hands, which were lying palm-downward and close to the side, as if the general had collapsed while doing push-ups.

Andy said, "Uh, Doc, I got Marty Collins and Lieutenant Simon Santos here—"

"Six minutes," Bowman grunted.

Not five or ten. That was Billy Bowman. Mr. Precision about everything.

Andy stood and gave Simon and me a shrug. He dug a pack of cigarettes out of his jacket, looked at them longingly, put them back. Simon drifted toward the desk, contemplated it, then picked up the robe and held it up. Garber's name and rank were scrawled across the chest in big air-force-blue letters that had to be three inches high. Nothing like a little ego. Simon patted the pockets, reached into one, paused, then withdrew his hand and tossed the robe onto the chair back.

"Find something?" I asked.

"A handkerchief." He turned away and jammed his hands in his pockets, doing a slow pan around the room. He seemed to be searching for something. When he got to the couch, he said, "I assume it folds into a bed."

"Yeah," Andy said. "Should be made up. The number-one flight attendant, Sergeant Blake, told me the general called her to make it up a couple hours into the flight." Andy stepped over and pulled up a cushion. "Made up. Died before he could use it." He tossed the cushion back down.

I said, "You know who last saw the general alive?"

A shrug. "Didn't have much of chance to question the passengers. My guess is it was either his aide Colonel Weller or the flight attendant, Sergeant Blake. It sure as hell wasn't one of the other generals. They couldn't stand Garber. Avoided the guy like the plague."

My eyes sought out Simon, who moved over to the closet along the right wall. As he opened the doors, Andy said to him, "Nothing in there except his uniform and luggage. His wallet, dog tags, and security badges are on the shelf. Briefcase on the floor. Carter and Gentry already searched his bags. Nothing much. Got some classified crap in the briefcase."

I came up behind Simon and peered over his shoulder. Hanging from the rack were two bulky hang-up bags and a single neatly pressed uniform, the four stars glinting at us from a shoulder. Simon picked up the wallet from the shelf and began flipping through the inserts. I reached around him and grabbed the briefcase, which was sitting next to a couple of pillows and a folded blanket. I opened the briefcase and saw thick files. All except one had classified covers that were stamped "The Chairman's Eyes." I opened the exception and leafed through the dozen or so pages.

It was a comprehensive itinerary that listed the generals' schedules each day—the uniforms they were to wear for the various functions, who was to escort whom and to what, where they were to meet and what time. I was amazed at the detail. But the running joke in the military was that all a four-star had to do was remember to wipe his ass, since everything else was taken care of.

"Might be of use," Simon said, looking down at me.

I nodded, removed the pages, folded them, and placed them in my jacket. After returning the briefcase, I asked Andy if anyone had checked to see if any of the classified material was missing.

"I had Colonel Weller take a look," he said. "She

thought everything was there. When she leaves, she's gonna take the case back to the Pentagon and make a detailed inventory."

"She's still here on base?" I said, a little surprised.

"In the DV passenger lounge with the other pax. I had her hang around because I figured you'd want to talk to her." He patted his pockets and reached into one. "Before I forget, I got me a list of the passengers. Paul also jotted down the people still hanging around."

Andy, thinking again. "Thanks," I said, as he handed me two folded pages.

The first was actually a Xeroxed copy of the passenger manifest; the second was a neatly printed list of names with corresponding job specialities.

A total of thirteen people, including Lieutenant Colonel Tina Weller and Lieutenant Colonel Marsha Gustin, General Markel's aide. As I'd surmised, they were mostly lower-level worker bees: the enlisted and the more junior officers. Two baggage handlers, two maintenance crew chiefs, four security cops who had guarded the plane while it had been on the ground in England, a master sergeant who handled the chairman's communications equipment, a major from JCS protocol, and a lieutenant colonel who was identified as an intelligence analyst.

Glancing to the door where Carter was standing with Gentry, I said, "The intelligence analyst got a specialty?"

"Terrorism, sir," Carter said. "He briefed the generals before the conference."

I nodded, put the paper in the same pocket as the itinerary, and looked to Simon, who was staring at a picture he'd removed from the wallet. The general in uniform, standing with a striking brunette woman in her fifties, wearing a formal red dress. Neither was smiling.

"His wife," Andy said to him. "General Sessler said her name was Patricia."

Simon said, "I assume she's been notified—"

"General Sessler called her while I was talking to Senator Garber."

Simon nodded thoughtfully, returned the picture to the wallet, and placed it on the shelf. After shutting the doors, he confirmed that Doc Bowman was still inspecting the body, then made another slow three-sixty around the room. No doubt about it; he was looking for something. He said, "The general's toiletry items, Andy . . ."

Andy yawned, jerked a thumb in the direction of the john.

Simon said, "And nothing has been removed since you discovered the body?"

"Nope. Like I said, my boys and I have been outside the whole time."

"What about customs?" I asked. A customs officer would have met the plane, done a required walk-through.

The smile Andy flashed was close to a leer. "Right. Margie Benson. Good-looking divorcee, but with an attitude. About five, six months ago I was flying one of these security trips and told her she smelled nice. Man, you thought I'd tried to cop a feel, the way she acted. She went off on me, threatened to turn me in for sexual harassment. Go figure, huh?"

I said, "Andy—"

"Hey, you asked, and I'm telling you. Where was I? Right. Anyway, this morning I hustled off the plane to give Margie the customs decs and to tell her she couldn't come aboard. She asks why, and I say it's because of national security. Right away she thinks I'm bullshitting her and gives me grief. So I called Admiral Wheeler over at the SECDEF's office, explain the situation, then hand Margie the phone. She says a couple yes sirs, then hangs up. And I can see she's plenty pissed, but hey, what's she gonna do? So I give her a polite smile and ask if the plane's cleared. She says it is, and when she walks off, you know what she does? She flips me off." He grinned. "She's got an attitude. Spunky. I kinda like it. I'm thinking maybe I'll ask her out. Whaddaya think, Marty?"

I said, "You don't want to know."

Andy's grin faded when he noticed Simon's furrowed brow. "Problem?"

"You're certain no one cleaned up?" Simon asked. "Removed anything?"

Andy squinted, wary now. Dr. Bowman was also looking at Simon with interest. "I'm certain," Andy said. "Why?"

"I'm curious about the absence of glasses or—"

"Glasses? The general didn't wear glasses. At least none that I saw." Andy looked to Carter and Gentry and got two head shakes.

"Contacts," Bowman announced. "The general still has them on."

Simon started to reply, then abruptly turned for the bathroom. He appeared irritated, and I had my suspicions why. Hurrying after him, I said, "You weren't talking about eyeglasses, were you?"

"Of course not."

8

The bathroom was tiny, travel-trailer size. It contained a commode, a sink with a mirror, and a dime-sized shower. I watched from the doorway as Simon picked up the leather toiletry case, which was lying next to a tooth-brush on the edge of the sink. He unzipped the case and peered inside.

I said, "You looking for anything in particular?"

"Cologne."

The second smell I'd detected earlier. "Why?"

"An inconsistency I'm trying to understand. Here it is." He produced a small glass bottle.

"Figures," I grunted, reading the label. "For some rea-son, every air force pilot I know wears Aramis. Don't ask me why."

He gave me a funny look as he zipped up the case and set it down. He gazed into the shower. "Soap in the dish is wet." He reached to a towel hanging on a rack. "Towel, too."

I said, "And you're suddenly interested in the general's hygiene because . . ."

But Simon had bent forward to inspect the toothbrush.

He shifted his eyes to the rim of the sink, and I could see a faint green residue. A smear of toothpaste.

He turned to me with a puzzled look. "Last night, General Garber showered, brushed his teeth, and put on his pajamas. Why?"

I hesitated, knowing this was too easy. "He was going to bed."

He said, "And his use of cologne?"

"What about it?"

"If he was going to bed, why would he put on cologne?"

He had me. "He probably wouldn't."

"No." He sighed unhappily. "This is a troubling development, Martin. The general's reason for wearing cologne is—was—extremely reckless."

My eyebrows crept up. "You know why he put it on?"

A nod. He lowered his voice. "I discovered something earlier. I'm hesitant to mention it because it might not be relevant. Until I know for certain, I think it's better to wait—"

"Hey, fellas," Andy called out. "Doc says he's almost done."

I didn't move. I just stood there in the doorway, trying to understand how Simon could have found something without me noticing. That was impossible, unless . . .

I remembered.

"Shall we go, Martin?" Simon said.

He was waiting for me to step away from the door. I stayed where I was and said, "Tell me what you found."

"It's better if I wait."

"Simon, I'm running this investigation."

We argued briefly. He was determined not to tell me. I

finally said, "It was in the robe, wasn't it? You took something from it and put it in your pocket."

His eyes flickered in surprise. "Does Andy know?"

"I don't think he noticed. What was it?"

He gave me a long look. "This remains between us for
now, Martin. I don't want to tarnish General Garber's reputation unnecessarily."

"Was that something you promised his father?"

"Yes, but not for the reasons you assume. My concern
is to spare the military any needless embarrassment."

"That bad, huh?"

He shrugged.

I said, "Amanda will have to know."

Simon nodded; he knew Amanda could keep her
mouth shut.

"All right," I said. "We got a deal. Now let's hear it."

In response, Simon fished something out of his right
trouser pocket. When he opened his hand, I saw a thin
plastic packet nestled in his palm. It was no more than an
inch square, and I recognized it immediately.

A condom.

I wished I could be surprised, but I wasn't. Rumors about
General Garber's womanizing had swirled around him for
years. Like Simon, I found it mind-boggling that someone
in his position would contemplate something so reckless.

I said, "We'll have to find the woman."

Simon pocketed the condom. "If necessary."

If we had a murder on our hands, he meant.

We returned to find Dr. Billy Bowman still crouched over
the body. Andy was standing beside him, while Carter
and Gentry continued to watch from the door.

Bowman shook his head and rose. He was a small man with a mass of wiry red hair and an bony, intelligent face. Not yet forty, he was young for the full colonel's eagles he wore, and acted accordingly. Supremely confident in his own abilities, Bowman was agreeable enough to work with unless you questioned his conclusions. Then he could become petty, vindictive, and a real pain in the ass.

When he glanced our way, I went through the drill of introducing Simon. Bowman appraised him for a long moment. "So you're the wealthy cop, right? The homicide lieutenant that's in the papers?"

Simon reddened, uncomfortable either with Bowman's bluntness or his own celebrity, or a combination of both.

"Look," Bowman said quickly. "I know it's not the time, but there's a research project I'm trying to get funded. A new type of genetic marking. I was wondering if we could get together later and possibly discuss—"

"For crying out loud, Doc," Andy said. "You want to lip-lock the man, do it on your own time."

Bowman shot him an icy glare. "Andy, so help me—"

Andy threw up a hand. "Take a number and get in line, Doc. Right now we got a job to do, and my ass is dragging. So, what's the word?"

Bowman turned away stiffly and indicated to the corpse. "He died from an acute laryngeal fracture associated with massive submucosal hemorrhage and consequential asphyxiation."

"In English, Billy," I said.

Bowman flashed a superior smile.

Simon said, "A crushed windpipe asphyxiated him. If you don't mind, Doctor . . ." He was already kneeling for a closer look, and I joined him.

Simon removed a penlight from his jacket and raised the corpse's head so we had a clear view of the throat. A purple welt the size of a baseball went from an inch below the Adam's apple to the base of the neck.

I whistled softly. "That was a lot of force."

"Yeah," Bowman said. "When he tripped, he never had a chance to break his fall. His throat caught the edge of the table. Killed him."

There it was: game, set, and match. I stood and said, "So you believe it was an accident?"

"What else, Marty? There are no marks on his hands to indicate a struggle. No wounds or contusions on his head or arms. Nothing. And there sure doesn't look like there was an altercation in here. Add in the fact that the guy was drunk off his ass, and . . ." He shrugged.

"Fucking knew it," Andy muttered.

"Time of death, Billy?" I said.

"You serious? You feel the temperature in here? I got stiffs in the morgue that are warmer than this."

"Ballpark."

He sighed. "Rigor has come and gone, which makes it at least four hours. Body's cooled too rapidly to get an accurate temperature reading. Judging by the lividity, I'd say at least five hours. Could be as long as eight. That would put it somewhere between midnight and three A.M., local time. I'll check with his flight attendant, Sergeant Blake, find out when he had his meal. Get you something definitive after the autopsy. Now, if there's nothing else—"

I shook my head and looked down at Simon, knowing he'd want to bring up the missing glasses. He continued studying the edge of the coffee table. Abruptly, he stood and went over to the two CID men in the door. They stepped out into the hallway, and we could hear Simon speaking quietly.

Andy gave me a searching look. I shook my head.

To me, Bowman said, "You can get the photographers in here, Marty. When they finish shooting the body, notify the med techs. I'll be performing the autopsy at Malcolm Grow. Be quicker. The big thing is going to be keeping a lid on this thing. That's why we're using the Humvee for transport. Less conspicuous. I'll head out now and get everything set up."

Malcolm Grow was the large air force hospital located on Andrews. Bowman and I exchanged cards; he'd notify me when he completed the autopsy. Andy went to the door, saying, "I gotta grab me a smoke. I'll let the photographers know they got the green light. Unless maybe you want to hold off until show-and-tell is over, Marty?"

"No," I said. "It's better if Senator Garber sees us working. Tell everyone to come on up in five minutes."

As Andy left, Bowman said, "Senator Garber?"

After I explained that the senator and the SECDEF would be stopping by, Bowman grunted, "Better you than me." He turned to go and almost bumped into Simon, who'd reappeared without Carter or Gentry.

Simon smiled apologetically. "Before you leave, Doctor, I still have a few questions."

"Shoot."

Simon stepped over to the body. "I'm curious about why the general fell."

Bowman squinted. "I don't follow you."

"You said he fell, implying he tripped. How? There's nothing on the floor."

Bowman shrugged. "He was drunk, and it was a turbulent flight."

"So he simply tripped?"

"Sure."

"And made no attempt to break his fall? Throw an arm out?"

"Reflexes were slowed by the alcohol."

"How long would it have taken him to die?"

"A couple of minutes to pass out, depending on heart rate. Another two or three to expire."

"So he lay here the entire time?"

"It appears so. Yes."

"He would have been in pain and struggling to breath. Gasping. Unable to call out—"

"That's correct—"

"—and yet he made no move to the door. Did not try and seek help."

Bowman's face darkened at Simon's insinuation. "Lieutenant," he said, "the man was drunk. *Extremely* drunk. All I can tell you is he must have lost consciousness shortly after falling."

Simon said, "You said earlier he would have been conscious for two minutes—"

"I could be wrong," Bowman snapped.

I couldn't believe what I was hearing. Billy had to know how ridiculous his theory sounded. A troubling possibility occurred to me. From Simon's grim expression, I knew he was considering the same thing.

"Tell me, Doctor," Simon said. "Did you detect any injuries to his head? Something that might have rendered him unconscious?"

Bowman glowered sullenly, but didn't respond. His silence spoke volumes; he hadn't found anything.

Simon pressed on. "How do you know he was drunk, Doctor? You've done no blood tests or—"

"I can *smell*," Bowman said. "Can't you?"

Simon smiled easily. "But that's just it. Other than the smell, there is no evidence that the general was drinking."

Bowman blinked. "No evidence . . ."

Simon gestured around. "No glasses. No paper or plastic cups. No bottles or cans. No alcohol. *Nothing*."

A delayed reaction. Perhaps a second, and then we saw it. A flicker of comprehension in Bowman's eyes. He moved forward to look around the room. His eyes darted from one end to the other.

But there was nothing to see.

"Someone must have cleaned up," Bowman said. "Probably the flight attendant, Sergeant Blake."

"When, Doctor?"

"How the hell should I know?"

"And what about the missing bottle?"

Bowman visibly tensed. "Bottle? You mean the booze? What are you getting at?"

"I think you know, Doctor."

And then Simon turned and looked to the corpse in a suggestive way.

The effect on Billy Bowman was startling. As he followed Simon's eyes, the blood drained from his face. He stared at Simon and ran a tongue over his thin lips.

There was a long silence in the room. Twice, Bowman seemed on the verge of speaking, but didn't.

My suspicion had evolved into a certainty. A fast burner like Billy Bowman hadn't shot up the promotion food chain by not being a team player.

I said quietly, "Who got to you, Billy? Secretary Churchfield? One of the generals? What did they promise you? A star on your next promotion—"

"That's enough, Marty." His voice rising in warning.

I kept on talking. "Or maybe they promised funding for that research project. Was that it, Billy? C'mon. You can tell us if you've been bought off. We're all friends here—"

"*I said, that's enough!*"

He'd suddenly stepped toward me, literally shaking with anger. His hands curled into fists, and for an instant, I thought he might actually take a poke at me.

I said, "Now, Billy. Don't do anything stup—"

"Go to hell, you son of a bitch!"

He wheeled and stormed from the room.

We heard Billy stomp his way down the hall. Simon closed his eyes and massaged his forehead. I said dryly, "So much for the autopsy results."

He nodded absently.

"You don't seem very upset over this."

"I'm not. I anticipated this eventuality." He lowered his hand and appraised me. "The military is caught in an unwinnable situation. Public and world opinion is a fragile thing. With the prospect of war with Iraq looming, the military cannot afford to be tainted by scandal. Frankly, I find myself sympathetic with their position."

I understood what he was trying to say; I was feeling similarly conflicted. "You're questioning whether we should proceed? If finding the truth is somehow . . . unpatriotic?"

A nod. "That's also a concern shared by Senator Garber."

"It is?"

A faint smile. "Don't look so surprised, Martin. Senator Garber has no desire to embarrass the military. He's only interested in seeking the truth about the death of his son."

"He can't have it both ways," I said. "Not if this turns out to be a murder."

"I'm afraid there's no question it's a murder."

"Because of the missing bottle?"

"Among other inconsistencies. But the bottle containing the alcohol is the key. It was removed because it was evidence. Doctor Bowman knew this, that's why he reacted so . . . strongly."

"That's what I don't understand. How can you be so sure General Garber even had a bottle of booze in here? The flight attendant usually serves the drinks from the galley."

He gestured to the body. "The bruise on the throat, Martin. If you look at it closely, you'll find that it's too large to have been caused by—"

From the hallway outside, we heard a voice call out, "Lieutenant Santos, we found it. Lieutenant!"

9

===============

Paul Carter and Tom Gentry filed excitedly into the room. Carter was carrying two highball glasses, one in each gloved hand. Gentry stepped out from behind him, gingerly gripping a liter-sized bottle by the neck with two fingers. The label was facing out and read "The Glenlivet Premium Whisky." It was almost a third full.

"It was like you said, Lieutenant," Carter told Simon. "We found these in the forward galley trash bin, jammed at the bottom."

Simon's eyes went from the bottle to the glasses. "Hold them up toward the light," he directed.

Carter did. Both glasses were spotted with faint, tea-colored droplets that had long since dried. On one rim, we detected a hint of pink or red, perhaps a lipstick smear that had been hurriedly wiped away.

Simon nodded in satisfaction, and Carter lowered the glasses.

Simon asked Gentry if he'd managed to contact the flight attendant Sergeant Blake.

"Yes, sir," Gentry said. "I got her number from the

squadron. She'll be reporting here at 1000 hours, with the rest of the crew."

I checked my watch. Eight-forty-two. Simon said, "And you asked her about . . ."

"Right," Gentry said. "Sergeant Blake swears she never served the general alcohol during the flight. She admits it's possible that the general served himself, but he'd never done that before."

"Curious," Simon murmured.

"Maybe not, sir," Gentry said. "If you look at the price tag on the bottle, it appears that the general probably brought the bottle with him."

He spun the bottle a half-turn, revealing a little white sticker attached near the base. Simon and I bent forward. The price was in pounds; it had been purchased in England.

"Good work," Simon said to Gentry.

Gentry's chest puffed out, but not enough to pop his shirt buttons. "Thank you, sir."

Simon told the two men to deposit the items on the coffee table. As they did, we heard a jumble of loud voices and the sound of numerous approaching footsteps. Seconds later, Amanda poked her head into the doorway, Martha Jones peeking over her shoulder. As usual, Martha was lugging her bulky "doctor" bag full of collection equipment.

Simon smiled apologetically. "We still need a few minutes."

"A few minutes?" Amanda said. "Andy said you guys were ready for forensics."

"Tell everyone to have a seat in the front of the plane."

Groans from the hallway. Martha made a face. Amanda said, "Oh, come on, Simon. They've hauled all their equipment up here—"

"*Please*, Amanda."

She sighed and reluctantly stepped into the hallway. "Okay, you heard the man. Back on up. That's it. It'll only be a couple of minutes."

Carter and Gentry were standing before Simon, eyeing him in anticipation.

He nodded them to the door. "That's all for now. You've done well." He gave them a pleasant smile.

Their faces reflected their disappointment. They were dying to learn the significance of the bottle. But as military men, they were used to obeying orders. They left, squeezing past Amanda.

Simon said to her. "Come in and close the door."

"It's broken."

He gave her a look.

"Keep your shirt on." She entered the room and started pushing the door closed. At that moment, we heard Andy's belligerent voice: "Move aside, people. What's the holdup? Let me by, Martha. Just step into the galley for a sec, will ya? Paul, where the hell you going?" A mumbled reply, then Andy again: "Bottle? What bottle? Oh, he wouldn't, huh? Screw him."

Amanda had gotten the door closed to within an inch and was bracing it shut with a foot. Someone began pushing on it. "Open the fuck up," Andy growled.

Simon hesitated.

"Open up," Andy said again. "Or I start kicking the shit out of the door."

"He will, Simon," Amanda said lightly.

"All right."

She stepped out of the way, and Andy burst inside. He immediately looked to the table. "What's so damned important about the bottle?"

Simon said, "Please leave us for a moment, Andy."

Andy planted his feet wide. "Why the fuck should I?"

Simon gazed back, saying nothing.

"*Shit*, man," Andy said. "You're unbelievable. I thought we were all working on this thing together. But that ain't the way you see it at all. Why don't you just come out and say it? You think you're better than us. Well, I got news for you, asshole. I've been a cop since you were crapping in diapers—"

I said, "Andy, you're out of line."

"Screw you, Marty. You're supposed to be running the show. You gonna let him get away with cutting us out?"

Simon said, "It's not what you think. It's for your own good. I don't want to place you or your men in an untenable position."

"Untenable? Aw, don't tell me you think this is a murder. You heard Doc Bowman."

"Bowman," Simon said, "was mistaken."

"You got any evidence of that?" Andy's tone was flat and sarcastic.

Simon looked at me. Letting me know it would be my call.

The way I saw it, the decision to confide in Andy came down to two questions. First, whether he could be intimidated by the brass. A ludicrous proposition, considering his history. In the twenty years I'd known him, Andy had never displayed the slightest respect for authority. None. His contrary attitude coupled with his laissez-faire work ethic had cost him jobs and promotions, not that Andy cared. In a sense, this was his singular talent. A total lack of ambition. Andy had never amounted to anything because he never wanted to; he just didn't give a damn.

So that left the question of Andy's reliability. Could he

be counted on to do more than his typical half-assed job?

I looked right at him and asked if he wanted to remain on the case and why.

"Hell, yes," he snapped. "You guys are saying General Garber was murdered on my watch. That changes everything. I'm gonna be held responsible."

Amanda voted with a head shake. Andy caught it: "Dammit, this is important to me. My ass is going to be in a sling over this. I have to be in on getting the fucking killer."

In his eyes, I saw a passion that surprised me. It seemed that Andy had some pride after all.

"All right, Andy," I said.

Amanda made a derisive sucking sound to express her opinion. Andy locked her with a glare. When Amanda flipped him off, I ordered them both to cool it and told Amanda to close the door.

As she grudgingly did, Simon detailed why he thought Dr. Bowman was being pressured to rule the death an accident. Next, he brought up the condom and the cologne, which suggested that General Garber had planned on spending the evening with a woman. As evidence of this theory, he also cited the two whisky glasses found in the trash, one with an apparent lipstick stain. Finally, Simon went into his explanation of why he believed the general had been murdered. After concluding the evidence was irrefutable, he picked up the bottle and swirled the contents, pointing out that no one throws away expensive Scotch.

"Move closer so you can see. This is the crucial part." And still holding the bottle, Simon knelt down over the body.

10

Simon focused the beam of his penlight on the bruise on General Garber's neck. He shifted the beam to the edge of the coffee table and said, "The wood is less than an inch wide. From the angle he fell, General Garber's neck should have struck the upper corner of the table at no more than sixty degrees. The resulting trauma should be fairly narrow, less than an inch wide, with a sharp indentation from the table edge." The beam returned to Garber's throat again. "But as you can see, there is no indentation, and the bruising is quite extensive, covering most of the throat."

"So he couldn't have hit the table," Andy murmured.

"No. Now look closely when I hold up the bottle flush against the throat. Like this—"

Simon glanced up at us.

"Son of a bitch," Andy said.

I could only nod.

"A perfect fit," Amanda said.

Simon remained crouched as he set the bottle on the coffee table. We were all silent, picturing what must have occurred. How someone had either pressed the bottle against Garber's throat or, more likely, used it to viciously strike the general. Either way, there were still two major problems with this scenario that we had to overcome.

Amanda voiced the first one, saying, "But the general wouldn't have just lain there, waiting to die. Any bruising on his arms where he was held down, or . . . *There is?*"

Simon was nodding. "Another misstatement by Dr. Bowman." He pushed up the sleeves of General Bowman's pajamas, and we saw bruising along the triceps of each arm. The marks were roughly the size of a hand.

Simon said to Andy, "I'm surprised you didn't notice these earlier?"

Andy appeared embarrassed. "To be honest, once I saw the injury to the throat, I figured that was it. I guess I shoulda been more thorough."

"You think?" Amanda said.

I shot her a look of annoyance. She turned away, shaking her head.

Simon said, "There are also two more marks on his back. Near his shoulder blades."

He lifted the collar of the pajama top and pointed with the beam. Amanda, Andy, and I took turns, peering down. I caught a glimpse of a dark bruise near right the shoulder blade and a fainter discoloration along the left side of the upper back.

Amanda said, "So someone held him down until he died. Chose to let Garber suffocate instead of finishing him off, so the death would appear accidental. One cool killer."

Simon nodded and began readjusting the pajama sleeves.

Watching him, Amanda said, "The murderer must

have been pretty damned desperate to kill Garber here in his compartment. Jesus, talk about risky."

"Might not have been that much of a risk," Andy said. "Most everyone was asleep."

"Including you?" she said.

A grudging nod. "Our job was to baby-sit the general on the ground, not in the air. Never thought in a million years that someone would go after him in the plane. We were all racked out in the seats up front."

She said to him, "Any clue as to the identity of the woman the general might have met with?"

"You got me," he said. "If General Garber was playing slap-and-tickle with someone on the side, I never saw it. Never even heard anything from the rumor mill that he might have something going."

I asked, "How about his aide, Colonel Weller? Any possibilities there?" By definition, aides were close to their generals, and this wouldn't be the first time a sexual relationship had developed.

Andy shrugged. "All I know is she damn sure didn't kill him. Weller really became unglued when she saw the body. Crying and carrying on. For a while there, I thought we might have to get her sedated."

Simon had risen to his feet and was frowning at Andy's comment. I stepped in and told him not to read anything into Weller's emotional reaction, explaining that aides often develop an almost parental affection for their generals.

"General Garber a father figure?" Amanda snorted. "You *must* be kidding, Marty."

I shrugged. "Garber could have treated her well."

"Sure. If he was trying to cop a feel or get into her pants."

"From what I saw, he treated her okay," Andy said. "He never chewed her out like he did everyone else."

"Sloppy," Simon said.

We all looked over. He was staring pensively at the bottle and glasses on the coffee table.

"I'll bite," Amanda said. "What's sloppy?"

Simon focused on her. "The disposal of the bottle and glasses. It was clumsy, showing little forethought. Much like the use of the bottle as the murder weapon. It's as if the killer simply reacted and devised his game plan as he went along."

"You're saying the killer never intended to kill Garber?" Amanda said. "You think there was some kind of argument, and she or he just lost their head, grabbed the bottle, and lashed out?"

Simon nodded. So did Andy and I. A "crime of passion" made the most sense, since it explained away the big question: why someone would be crazy enough to knock off Garber on an airplane.

"I don't know, guys," Amanda said, after a moment. "I'm not sure we can rule out premeditation. For all we know the killer had a reason for killing Garber when he did. Could be the general was going to reveal something damning, and the person couldn't allow it. Or maybe someone had a grudge against Garber, saw an opportunity for payback, and took it."

Simon shrugged. "Anything's possible."

Amanda continued, "Of course, it'd be a good thing for us if the killer did get into an argument with Garber beforehand. Someone could have overheard them and recognized a voice— Why not, Andy?" She'd noticed his sudden scowl.

Andy waved a beefy hand around the compartment.

"For starters, the walls are completely soundproofed. You could holler your head off, and you'd lucky to hear a peep outside. Add in the plane noise, and it's damn near impossible to hear anything going on inside here."

Amanda said, "But if someone passed right by the door—"

"Doubtful," Andy said. "The door's also soundproofed, and there's an air-conditioning vent in the ceiling right outside. And it's loud. I've stood outside when the general had staff meetings. Never heard a thing. You don't believe me, give it a try."

Amanda took him up on the offer. She went out into the hallway and closed the door as best she could. I let out a yell. She reentered moments later. Even with the door open a crack, she'd barely heard me.

"Another thing bugs me," Andy said, addressing Simon. "I think it's a mistake to focus on a woman perp. Sure, she could clobber the general with the bottle. But hold him down? The general's a big guy. Take a lot of strength."

"I could do it," Amanda said.

She wasn't bragging, simply stating a fact. And if she could restrain the general, so could another athletic woman.

"Andy," Simon said quietly, "is correct to be cautious. We know a woman was in here with General Garber. We know they had at least one drink together. We know they probably didn't engage in sex, because the bed and condom weren't used—"

"Blow job," Andy said.

Simon nodded. "A valid point."

I made a mental note to have the forensic techs search for semen stains.

Simon continued, "What we *don't* know is whether the woman struck him with the bottle. Someone could have entered after she left, argued with the general, and attacked him."

More nods. Amanda said, "There might even have been more than one person involved. The woman could have had an accomplice."

Simon didn't comment. This didn't really fit his scenario of an unpremeditated act.

We all gazed down at the body, sifting through the possibilities. It came down to the woman; we had to locate her. I removed the passenger list from my pocket and scanned it. "Seven women," I said, "excluding the flight crew."

"Four female flight attendants on the crew," Andy said. "That makes eleven. Five or six are what I'd call attractive. Three are definite lookers."

"I'm sure *that's* a high standard," Amanda said.

Andy gave her a wink. "Play your cards right, I'll put you on my list."

"I'd rather be dead," she said flatly.

Andy grinned. Amanda rolled her eyes in disgust.

"Which of these women are still on base?" Simon asked Andy.

"Only Colonel Weller, Lieutenant Colonel Marsha Gustin—she's General Markel's aide—and Major Crenshaw from protocol. Oh, and Senior Airman Michelle Capello, a security cop. Capello we might want to take a look at. She's a jock. Lifts weights."

"Please," Amanda said. "I think even General Garber would draw the line at sleeping with an airman."

Andy massaged his jowls. "I dunno. Airman Marcelli's got a pretty healthy set of—"

"You're disgusting," Amanda said.

"Look," he said, "I'm just saying that's how guys are. Take Clinton and Lewinsky, or Congressman Condit and Chandra Levy. Powerful men go for good-looking girls. The younger, the better. Makes them feel more like a stud. Right, Marty?"

Amanda turned to me.

Brother. I said, "Andy's wrong. Not all men are morally bankrupt."

"So you wouldn't be tempted?" She seemed amused now.

I felt my face redden. "Of course not."

"Even a little?"

"No."

"Bullshit," Andy said.

Simon cleared his throat sharply to refocus our attention. He said, "There's another explanation we haven't considered—"

I said, "Okay."

"Drugs. The woman might have drugged General Garber. That might explain how she managed to restrain him."

I said, "So now we're talking premeditation."

Simon hesitated, then nodded.

"To prove he was drugged," I said, "we'll need the autopsy blood work results."

"Fat chance now," Amanda said.

Simon watched me, waiting for me to come up with a solution. I shook my head. "I'm firing blanks."

"I could swing by and observe the autopsy," Andy suggested. "Maybe try and sweet-talk Bowman into cooperating."

"He'll never let you in the door," I said.

Andy winked. "I'd like to see the little prick try and stop me."

"All right," I said. "But play it by the book. I don't want to give the SECDEF an excuse to toss us off the case."

He grinned. "Got it. Nothing physical."

"I'm not kidding, Andy."

"Hey, hey, relax, Marty. I'll be a fucking Boy Scout. All I'm gonna do is talk to him."

"Uh-huh."

Turning to Simon, I addressed the question that had bothered us from the beginning. How had the killer managed to lock the door from the outside?

"Logic tells us there has to be a way, Martin. We'll figure it out eventually."

Typical Simon. He'd concluded Garber had been murdered and assumed everything else would fall into place. I said, "And if we don't . . ."

He sighed and faced the door. For the next a minute he didn't move. He just concentrated on the busted lock. Finally, he surrendered with a head shake and addressed Amanda. "Were you a good engineering student?"

"Yes."

"Very good?"

"Near the top of my class."

"It should be something relatively simple. Possibly a magnet was used to slide the latch. Or perhaps there's a hidden keyhole. Something the Secret Service might have installed to gain access in event of an emergency while the vice president was flying. Whatever the secret, it would have been something that could be done quickly. Can you find the answer?"

"I can try," she said, already at the door.

11

Amanda inspected the lock with Simon's penlight. The bolt was partially bent back from the force of being pushed in. Andy said, "You're wasting your time. There's no magic keyhole. Hell, I'd know if there was. I'm the security guy, remember."

She kept on working.

Andy went on, "I'm telling you, all the doors operate exactly the same. They were one of the first things I checked. They were all locked."

I stiffened at the comment. Amanda stared at him. Simon said, "*All* the doors?"

"Sure. Technically there are five."

He went to the closet and pushed open the two doors. "Most people don't realize there's a second set of doors at the back of the closet. They were installed so the aides can iron the DV's clothes and return them without disturbing the person in the compartment. For security, they were designed like the main door, to only be locked from the inside. After I found the body, I checked the interior and exterior doors. Both sets were locked."

Simon and I came up behind him. Simon said,

"When I opened the closet earlier, it wasn't locked."

"Right. You're talking the two interior doors. I didn't lock them after I checked them out. You can tell if they're locked by the little window on the back of each door. Have a look." He twisted the latch on one door, partially opened it, and had us peer at it from the back side. We saw the window he'd described. It read "Occupied."

"Like an airline john," I said.

"Right. Same basic design. Two locks and two windows each on the interior doors and exterior doors, for a total of four. The windows tell the aides the doors are locked so they don't bother trying to open them and disturb the sleeping beauty in the compartment." Andy pushed aside the two hangup bags, revealing an identical set of doors at the back. He turned both latches to the right; they didn't move. He said, "Like I said—locked. To be honest, getting out this way would have been tougher, since you'd have to figure out how to lock two sets of doors from the outside."

He backed out of the closet, his eyes shifting between Simon and me. "It's not looking good, fellas. If someone killed him, they'd have to be fucking Casper to get out of here."

No one spoke. We all looked to Simon, not daring to voice what we were thinking: Could Simon be wrong about the mark on the throat?

"Anything, Amanda?" Simon asked quietly.

A shrug. "Your magnet suggestion could be a possibility, but the lock assembly appears to be aluminum. And if that's the case . . ."

She drifted off without bothering to point out the obvious; aluminum didn't magnetize.

Simon nodded, his face knitted in concentration.

He looked down General Garber's body and back to the door. Trying to decide if he could have made a mistake.

Abruptly his body relaxed, and the tension left his face. He smiled faintly. "Of course."

I said, "You already figured it out?"

But Simon's attention was on Andy. He asked him how long after he'd first entered the compartment had he checked the closet doors.

Andy thought. "It was pretty crazy, at first. Probably four or five minutes. Once I got the room and hallway cleared, and Colonel Weller calmed down."

"So there were people in here with you?"

Simon had expressed the question casually, but the implication hit me like a jolt. Amanda's head snapped around to me; she'd caught on, too.

Andy answered Simon, saying, "Right. Paul and Tommy were here. And Colonel Weller, of course. The three generals showed up when they heard her scream. Markel's aide, Colonel Marsha Gustin, also showed up; she's a friend of Weller's. That's pretty much it. There were a lot of people in the hall. I finally had Tommy and Paul clear everyone out so I could—"

He paused, frowning.

His eyes went from Simon to Amanda and finally to me. We were all nodding along, as if in understanding.

Andy got it then. His eyes popped wide. "Son of a *bitch*. There were people in here. That means the closet doors could have been locked *after* I came in—"

We kept nodding.

"—by someone who'd been in the room. In all the commotion, when no one was looking."

"Probably," Simon said.

"Probably, my ass. That has to be it. That's the only way it could have happened. *Fuck.*"

He gazed angrily at the closet doors. Upset with himself for not considering this possibility.

We all took a few moments to fully consider Andy's account. I removed my notepad and jotted down the names of the people who'd been in the room. It didn't take a math whiz to know we now had five prime suspects. Two women and three four-star generals.

Staring at the names, I felt a chill. If Garber had been killed by one of the women, that was one thing. Crimes of passion were understandable, possibly explainable.

But if the killer was another member of the Joint Chiefs . . .

Jesus.

"So what the hell do we do now?" Andy asked.

All eyes went to Simon, including mine. He passed the baton back to me, saying, "Martin?"

Since we were driven by the time element, I devised a plan for divvying up the workload. Andy, Paul Carter, and Tom Gentry would initially remain on the plane to monitor the forensic team and conduct a complete inspection of the passenger cabin. I wasn't holding up much hope that they'd turn up anything incriminating, since all the baggage had been removed by the passengers. Andy had entertained thoughts of getting everyone to leave them, but had been overruled by the vice chairman of the Joint Chiefs, General Markel—the same guy who'd supposedly ordered General Morley to give us a hard time.

Once the body was transferred to Malcolm Grow Hospital, Andy would tag along and try and intimidate Dr. Bowman into letting him watch. If that didn't work, he'd notify us, and we'd try to come up with something else. We needed the autopsy results to determine General Garber's level of intoxication, whether he'd been drugged, and his precise time of death.

In the meantime, Simon, Amanda, and I would set up house in the maintenance offices, where we would conduct the interviews with the eleven passengers and, later, the flight crew. After the forensic team wrapped up, Carter and Gentry would give us a hand.

"Questions?" I asked, when I finished.

Amanda prompted, "The general decs."

"Right." I asked Andy if he had the work number for the customs officer, Margie Benson. He didn't, but could get it. I told him to pass it to Amanda, so she could contact Officer Benson and find out which passenger had declared a bottle of Glenlivet on their general declaration form.

"How about I call Margie?" Andy said. "Give me an excuse to talk to her."

"Get real," Amanda said.

"What's the big deal?" he said, eyeing her with annoyance. "I can talk to her as easily as you can."

"She hates you," Amanda said. "Remember?"

"You got it all wrong. We just had a misunderstanding, is all. When I turn on my charm, Margie will realize I'm not such bad guy."

"No, Andy," I said.

"Fine," he grunted. "But you're screwing with my love life here. She could be the next Mrs. Hobbs."

Amanda said, "That make her what, number four?"

Andy gave her a slow blink. "Be nice, huh? I don't rag on you for the thing you got going."

"*My* thing?" she said, stiffening. "What thing is that?"

Andy seemed flustered by her response. His face reddened, and he looked away. "It's nothing. Forget I said anything." He poked his head out the door and hollered for Carter and Gentry.

Amanda grabbed his arm hard. "Out with it, Andy. What's that crack supposed to mean?"

He turned around, avoiding her eyes. "I said it's nothing. Really. Excuse me, huh."

As he tried to walk around her, she sidestepped and blocked his path. "C'mon, Andy. Let's have it."

He sighed, his eyes slowly crawling up to hers. He was clearly embarrassed. I tried to get his attention, but he never glanced my way. After a couple of false starts, he started to respond.

"Don't even think about it, Andy," I said.

Amanda whirled around to me. "Hey, what is this? What the hell is going on?"

"I'll tell you later," I said.

"*Now*, Marty."

"Amanda, it'd be better if we discussed this later. In private." I nodded to the door, where Carter and Gentry were watching us. Simon was also frowning, wondering what we were talking about.

Amanda gazed at me, confusion and hurt creeping into her beautiful eyes. She was imagining the worst, and I felt like a jerk. I said, "It's not that big a deal."

Of course, she knew I was lying. Andy and I wouldn't react this way if it wasn't a big deal. I braced myself, anticipating an angry response from her.

Instead, she surprised me with a resigned shrug. "Sure, Marty. Whatever you say."

I asked her to notify the SPs that we wanted someone to escort the passengers from the DV lounge. Even though she realized I was trying to get rid of her, she didn't resist. Her compliant reaction told me she'd probably suspected what Andy had been about to say. As a woman who worked in a man's world, she'd been in this situation before.

After she left, I turned on Andy. I was furious, but managed to keep my voice below a roar.

"You asshole," I said.

I went over to the coffee table to retrieve the bottle and highball glasses. Andy followed me, saying, "But I thought she knew about the rumors. How was I supposed to know she didn't? Hell, for all I knew, they were true. C'mon, you know I didn't mean anything by it. Okay, okay, I got a big mouth. I admit it. *Say something.*"

I didn't trust myself to reply. I just glared at him and walked out into the hallway, where Simon was waiting.

He said mildly, "Rumors?"

When I told him, he said, "A lesbian?" He began to laugh.

I said irritably, "You think this is funny?"

"I'm amused by the irony, Martin."

"Irony?"

"Yes. If Amanda made her feelings known, she wouldn't be in this predicament, and there certainly wouldn't be any malicious rumors. But she can't make her feelings known for a number of reasons."

He'd lost me. "What are you talking about?"

"You really don't know? Don't have any idea?"

I gave him a hard look. "Would I be asking if I did?"

"You must wonder why someone as attractive as Amanda rarely dates."

"Sure. She comes on like Lucy Lawless and scares guys off."

His face went blank.

"You know, Xena the warrior princess . . . Never mind." Simon must have a dozen TVs spread throughout his mansion, but I'd never known him to actually watch one.

"Amanda," he said, "doesn't date because she has no desire to. She turns down offers from potential suitors all the time."

"And you know this because . . ."

"Amanda occasionally confides in me."

"*Right.* She'd tell you something that she wouldn't tell me? Since when did you two become so tight?"

"We're not. That's what makes this situation so amusing, Martin. Why she feels she can talk to me, but not to you." He continued down the short hallway, chuckling to himself.

I almost told Simon that Amanda still considered him pompous, regimented, and overbearing.

But that would be petty.

12

Simon and I went to up to the front of the plane, where the forensic team had camped out. We turned over the bottle and glasses to Martha Jones, so she could analyze them for prints and conduct a color and brand comparison on the lipstick smear. I also instructed the serology people to check out the room for semen stains. Afterwards, I gave everyone a two-minute win-one-for-the-Gipper speech, explaining that General Garber's death was an apparent murder and that it was up to us to get to the truth, and fast. To hammer home the latter point, I mentioned the president's deadline of 2000 hours, which generated a lot of surprised looks and a few protests. I summed up by saying that anything incriminating they found, they were to come to Simon or Amanda or me, and no one else.

"Apparent murder," Martha Jones said. "So there's still a chance it could be an accident?"

Before I could answer, Simon said, "There's always a chance." He gave her a smile.

She sighed. "What about getting some help on running the tests? Odds are we won't make the 2000 deadline."

I looked to Simon, saw his head shake. "Do the best you can, Martha," I said.

We gazed out at the faces, waiting for more questions. There weren't any. "All right," I said. "Let's get to work."

As everyone began gathering their equipment, I handed Martha my card. "Do me a favor. Let me know if anyone from the SECDEF's office contacts you and gives you any . . . guidance."

Our eyes met. She knew what I was really asking.

She took the card, looking uncomfortable. "I can't promise anything, Marty."

At least that wasn't a no.

Before leaving the plane, Simon and I had a final house-keeping item to check out. Whenever there's a murder, you have to be able to establish both motive and opportunity. In General Garber's case, the first was a given. So that left opportunity. Specifically, how difficult would it have been for someone to enter the compartment without being observed?

Logically, we concluded that the odds of detection cor-related directly to the distance someone sat from the com-partment. The closer, the better.

The passenger manifest contained the seat numbers, so we started at the back of the plane and worked our way for-ward, noting where the five suspects were sitting. It took us less than five minutes. We passed through three separate sections, all separated by bulkheads. The largest was the rearmost one—the figurative back of the bus—where the lower-ranking officers and enlisted sat. The next section for-ward was reserved for the communications specialists and the personal staff members assigned to the four generals, including the aides, lieutenant colonels Weller and Gustin.

The third section was located directly aft of Garber's compartment. It was designed more like an intimate lounge area, with eight plush first-class chairs, four to a side, a small table between each pair of chairs. It's nice to be comfortable when planning a war.

"The generals sat in here?" Simon said.

"Yeah."

"Anyone else?"

I checked the manifest. "Nope. Each general was assigned two seats. The last pair of seats was empty. Four-stars usually don't mingle with the help."

Simon stepped forward and opened the swinging door that we'd passed through earlier. We were looking down the hallway of Garber's compartment. Members of the forensic team were still filing inside. I guessed the door was maybe five giant steps away. Four if you played in the NBA.

Simon turned to me. "No view from the front or back of the plane. It would have been easy enough for someone to wait until everyone was asleep and to slip into Garber's room without being seen."

I nodded. "And if one of the aides had paid Garber a late-night visit, he or she would have had to walk through here. One of the generals might have noticed. Or possibly someone in the second section would have seen the aide leave."

My eyes drifted over the room. It was completely empty, without so much as a coffee cup visible. But those items probably would have been collected before landing. I began opening the overhead bins. Simon crossed the room and did the same. Nothing. Andy was right; they'd cleared everything out.

"Excuse me, sir."

We turned toward the hallway. Carter was standing in the doorway of the bulkhead. I said, "Yes, Paul?"

"Andy mentioned your theory about the closet—"

"Right. Sure."

"I thought you should know that I was standing near the closet after we went inside. I didn't notice anyone open any of the doors."

"How long were you there?"

"Several minutes. I was trying to calm down Colonel Weller because she was pretty distraught. I finally asked Colonel Gustin to escort her back to her seat. By then, the generals had come in, and I was trying to keep them from interfering, so Andy and Tommy could finish checking out General Garber's body."

"Sounds like you were pretty busy," I said.

A tired smile. "You don't know the half of it, sir. But I think I'd have noticed if anyone tried to enter the closet. The only time I left was when Andy told Tommy and me to clear everyone out. There were a number of people in the hallway, and Andy wanted them to return to their seats."

"Anyone remain in the room?"

"The generals. They left pretty quickly to make phone calls. Couldn't have stayed more than a minute or two."

"I see." Simon was anxious to ask something, so I eased to the right.

"Paul," he asked, coming forward, "you said you were standing near the closet. How near?"

"A few feet. I was over by the chair at the desk. That's where I'd taken Colonel Weller to calm her."

"If she was so distraught, why didn't you remove her from the room immediately?"

"Well . . . she sort of fainted."

"Sort of?"

"She didn't lose consciousness, Lieutenant. She just sort of collapsed from the shock and all. Then she went kinda crazy when we tried to pick her up."

"And while you were attending to her, I assume your attention wasn't on the closet doors?"

"No, sir. But still think I would have noticed someone poking around. The place is pretty small."

Simon nodded at his logic. "I'm sure you're correct. Thank you, Paul."

As Carter left, I said, "He's mistaken. Someone in the room must have locked the doors. It's the only thing that makes sense."

"I agree."

But as we walked out, he still looked worried.

We emerged from the plane onto the landing at the top of the portable staircase. Below us, we could see Amanda over by the side door, talking with the two security cops. She was standing toe-to-toe with them and seemed to be dressing them down. One cop had a radio to his mouth and appeared to be trying to listen to her while he relayed something. I heard Amanda say something about passengers. The cop looked flustered. Amanda angrily snatched the radio from his hand.

I said, "Must be giving us a runaround about sending someone to escort."

Simon nodded.

"Guess my talk didn't do much good."

"They'll delay us when they can."

"If the military keeps interfering, they'll be able to run out the clock without us getting close to solving this thing."

"True."

"And that's okay with you?"

He gave me a long look. "I promised Senator Garber I would attempt to learn the truth. I never told him I would succeed."

"Come off it, Simon. Once he realizes his son was murdered, he'll never back off. He'll push this thing until he gets justice."

"That's why we mustn't commit ourselves."

"Huh?"

His eyes bored into mine. "We tell the senator that we only *suspect* his son was murdered, Martin. We make it clear we could be mistaken."

I could only shake my head. Ethics 101, according to Professor Simon. Now I understood his qualified response to Martha Jones earlier.

I said, "So we're going to keep our options open until the end?"

"Something like that."

We went down the steps.

At the bottom of the stairs, I nodded at the two med techs sitting in the Humvee. They stared back with anxious eyes. Marty the Bogeyman.

As Simon and I walked toward the maintenance offices, I said, "One thing confuses me."

He smiled. "Only one?"

"The highball glasses," I said. "They were obviously removed because they were incriminating. That tells me the killer was a woman and not some guy who came in later. He wouldn't have had a reason to take them."

"Remember," he said, "the killer was trying to make the death appear accidental. He probably removed the glasses because they could have led us to the bottle. We would have wondered what the general had been drinking."

"Why would a guy wipe away the lipstick smear?"

Silence. Like me, Simon knew the killer would only have wiped at the smear if it was personally incriminating. So unless the guy was a cross-dresser, we were back to a woman suspect.

For now.

We'd almost reached the double doors of the maintenance offices when we heard a shout. Turning, we saw Amanda frantically waving an arm at us, the radio still to her ear. Behind her, the two cops were bolting out the side door.

"They're here," Amanda hollered. "They just landed."

13

Simon, Amanda, and I waited by the Humvee with the two med techs and watched as the entourage entered the side door of the hangar. Senator Garber appeared first, followed by Secretary of Defense Churchfield and a gaunt navy admiral who I assumed was some kind of military assistant. My buddy Brigadier General Morley appeared next, followed by Major Vega and a couple of large, stern-faced men in civilian suits, wearing spy-guy earphones. No cool wraparound sunglasses, though, but maybe that was only in the movies. The two security cops brought up the rear and remained by the door.

As the group headed toward us, Senator Garber and Secretary Churchfield led the way. They walked slowly, their expressions somber. The entourage trailed them in complete silence; no one so much as whispered. It was as if we were watching a funeral procession, which in some respects, we were.

My eyes settled on Senator Garber. Like his son, he was a big man, well over six feet, with a thick chest that seemed to strain the buttons on his thousand-dollar linen suit. Now in his seventies, he had a politician's stereotypical mane of thick white hair, and his features still retained the handsome, rugged quality that had won him more than his fair share of the female votes over the years. A senator for close to thirty years, Garber had long been acknowledged as a major Washington, D.C., power broker, and not simply because of his longevity or his chairmanship of the powerful Senate Armed Services Committee.

Rather, it was Garber's legendary ability for political arm-twisting and his reputation as the consummate deal maker. Anyone who wanted legislation passed—the White House, Democrats and Republicans, corporate lobbyists and special interest groups—they all paid homage to Garber or risked having their bills incinerated in the flames of a filibuster or tabled for some innocuous rules violation known only to him. Even the *Washington Post*, a noted Garber critic, acknowledged the senator's clout in their recently published list of the country's most influential politicians. Garber had been ranked number two, right below the president and three spots above the person walking beside him now.

And that's where I shifted my eyes.

To the formidable figure in an impeccably tailored red power suit, who in three short years had risen from relative obscurity to become everybody's favorite secretary of defense and the poster child of feminists everywhere.

The Honorable Joanna Churchfield.

"The Most Admired Woman in America."

That was the title of last week's *Newsweek*, with Secretary Churchfield on the cover. It hadn't always been that way.

As one might expect, Secretary Churchfield's appointment to the nation's preeminent defense post had been sparked with controversy. Despite her impressive credentials—she'd retired from the air force as the second female three-star general in the history of the service—many in Congress and the public questioned whether a woman had the proper temperament to lead the largest military in the world. An admittedly sexist attitude, but gender stereotypes are deeply rooted and difficult to change. To the president's credit, he doggedly withstood the criticism and never wavered in his support for Churchfield. His faith was rewarded by her spectacular response to the events of September 11. She'd orchestrated a brilliantly efficient campaign in Afghanistan, winning admiration from even her harshest critics, and was continuing to methodically hunt out terrorist cells worldwide. In her press briefings, she'd further enhanced her reputation by coming across as hard-nosed, competent, and ruthlessly uncompromising. Ironically, her sex only heightened her popularity. Americans relished the notion that bin Laden and his Al Qaeda goons were getting their asses kicked by a woman.

The procession continued toward us. Churchfield's high heels clicked loudly on the concrete floor, a concession to femininity that I found surprising. But I suppose being the head of the most powerful military figure in the world doesn't make you any less a woman.

She looked much as she did on TV: a tall, sharp-featured woman in her early fifties, auburn hair cut short and feathered stylishly over her ears; a lined face that hinted of stressful decisions and years spent in the sun; large, wide-set eyes that could harden instantly when annoyed by a reporter's question.

A nudge in my ribs. Then Amanda's whispered voice: "She's staring at you, Marty."

As if I hadn't noticed.

For the last ten paces or so, Secretary Churchfield's eyes had been fixed on me. They were piercingly blue and seemed to look right through me. I tried to force myself to gaze back. Her eyes chilled, accepting the challenge. I realized getting into a stare-down with the SECDEF bordered on insanity, and looked away. As I did, I caught a tiny smile.

"A mistake," Simon murmured. "She now knows she can intimidate you."

I didn't give a damn. She was the secretary of defense. Her job was to intimidate people.

The clicking of the heels stopped. Secretary Churchfield and Senator Garber were eyeing me expectantly. So was everyone else in the entourage.

I was about to initiate the introductions, when another figure entered the side door, talking loudly on a cell phone. He ended the call and hurried over to us.

He was a short, heavy-set man with a square, flat-top haircut and an even squarer face. He moved with the rigid gait of someone marching in parade, and the arrogant set of his jaw made it clear he was someone accustomed to getting his way. Even though I'd never seen him before, his medaled army uniform and the four stars he wore immediately told me who he was.

As the vice chairman of the Joint Chiefs, General David Markel, came closer, I felt his eyes seek me out. Like Churchfield, he seemed to know exactly who I was. Unlike Churchfield, his bushy eyebrows and fierce gaze gave him a slightly unbalanced look. Watching him, I was reminded of what Amanda had said: *The word at the*

Pentagon is, Markel's a little nuts. Even the other chiefs are afraid of him.

Lucky me.

"Senator," I said, finally moving forward, "my condolences for your loss—"

Senator Garber's grip was firm, Churchfield's even firmer, and General Markel's was downright paralyzing.

He played all the textbook power games. He held my hand longer than necessary, easing forward into my personal space so I would have to step back. He rarely blinked and spoke in a menacing growl that he must have spent years practicing. The man was all about intimidation, and I had to admit it was working. He gave me the willies.

By contrast, Admiral Wheeler, Churchfield's military assistant, had a voice that sounded as if he had a mouth full of cotton, and his hand felt like a damp rag, which I thought was fitting for a navy man.

As we cycled through the introductions, General Morley and Major Vega hung back, nodding along like bobble-head dolls. No one introduced the two Mutt-and-Jeff security men, who'd drifted off to the side and pretended to be invisible—a futile exercise, considering they were both the size of my garage. Mutt had a sandy brown buzz cut and no discernible neck. His partner, Jeff, had a neck like a deflated tire, at least three chins, and tightly curled red hair that reminded me of a Berber carpet.

For a parent who'd lost a child, Senator Garber showed remarkable composure. Only by looking into his eyes could you see pain. After donning the latex gloves the med techs had given him, Garber contemplated

Simon, Amanda, and me, then said quietly, "What have you learned?"

Simon made no move to respond. I ordered the med techs to notify the forensic team that we'd be up in a minute. When they departed, I answered Garber, carefully choosing my words. "Senator, we have indications your son might have been murdered." I checked out Churchfield and Markel; she didn't even bat an eyelash at this; he did — twice. I continued, "But at this point we're not certain."

My eyes returned to Markel, who was about to speak. Churchfield touched his arm. When he glanced over, she shook her head once.

Markel's mouth obediently closed. He stood there, his face blank. Watching this exchange, I was reminded of a pit bull being restrained by his master.

Garber asked, "When will you know, Agent Collins?"

"It's difficult to say, Senator. Perhaps later this afternoon, when forensics completes some of their analysis."

Garber glanced at Simon, who backed me up with a nod.

"What you're telling us," Secretary Churchfield said, sounding puzzled, "is that you're not convinced General Garber was actually murdered?"

"It's too early to make any definitive conclusions, Madam Secretary," I said.

"So you still could decide the death was accidental?"

"Yes, ma'am."

I could almost see the gears in her head crank away as she tried to mesh this with the information Doc Bowman had almost certainly relayed to her. "I see," she said finally.

But her eyes continued to dissect me. Trying to determine whether she could believe me.

Garber said to Simon, "Now about those problems with cooperation you mentioned earlier—"

"Problems?" Churchfield said. "What problems? Why wasn't I told about this? I've instructed everyone to cooperate fully." She looked around accusingly.

"Most have been resolved, ma'am," Simon said. "We have a few minor issues remaining. One concerns the passengers on base that we still need to interview—"

He looked directly at General Markel.

Markel met his gaze with a thin smile. He said amiably, "You're a goddamn liar, Lieutenant."

Simon's face remained expressionless.

Churchfield said, "General Markel, please—"

"Madam Secretary," Markel said. "The lieutenant is implying the military isn't fully cooperating. It's not true."

Simon said, "We're still waiting for those passengers, General."

Markel smiled again. "Tell the man, Chuck."

General Morley came forward, saying easily, "A van is being arranged to transfer them here, General." He extended a folder to Simon. "The information on the passengers you requested. Office and home phone numbers, addresses—everything."

Smoothly done, I thought. Markel and Morley were trying to appear the picture of cooperation in front of Senator Garber and Secretary Churchfield.

Simon took the folder, scanned the contents, closed it. "When exactly, General?"

Morley frowned.

"The passengers," Simon said. "When will you have them here, General?"

Morley hesitated. "Twenty minutes," Markel snapped.

Simon nodded and stepped back.

Amanda whispered in my ear. I nodded; I'd already decided to get this commitment in the presence of Senator Garber.

Secretary Churchfield addressed Simon, "Well, if everything is satisfactory, Lieutenant, I think the senator and I would like to go—"

I was about to bring up the request, when Amanda cleared her throat. Churchfield frowned at the interruption. A glance at Amanda's face told me that she'd decided to handle this. I thought that unwise, since she was in the military, and tried to shake her off.

But she was already stepping past me, saying, "Madam Secretary, we still need to interview the Joint Chiefs who were aboard the plane."

Her eyes went to Markel.

No smile this time. He contemplated her with open disdain. If Amanda was unnerved, she gave no sign. She kept looking back expectantly.

"General?" Churchfield said.

"It would serve no purpose, Madam Secretary. It was an accident. We have nothing to add." He shrugged, checked his watch.

"Sir," Amanda said, "we still have questions that we need—"

"It was an accident," Markel repeated. "This is ridiculous. A complete waste of time."

A pause. Senator Garber was frowning. Secretary Churchfield quickly said to Amanda, "Something will be arranged." She nodded to the admiral, who dug out a notepad. "Admiral Wheeler will contact you with a time and date."

She looked away, signaling that Amanda was dismissed.

But Amanda didn't move. She just stood there stubbornly. While I admired her resolve, I thought she was foolish to push this now.

Yet her ploy worked, and Churchfield was forced to acknowledge her again. "Something else on your mind, Major?" Her voice was ice.

Amanda took a deep breath. "We need to talk to the generals this afternoon, ma'am."

Churchfield appeared stunned. So did General Markel and the rest of the entourage. A junior officer making demands to the SECDEF? Unthinkable.

"Major," Churchfield said, "I'm afraid that's impossible. Perhaps next Monday or Tuesday, but I cannot guarantee—"

Simon said, "Senator."

Taking the hint, Garber said to Churchfield, "Look, Joanna, the president made it clear he wants a determination by this evening—"

Churchfield angrily interrupted him. "I'm aware of that, Benton. But General Markel and the Joint Chiefs are planning the deployment for Iraq. You know the details have to be formalized by—"

"I'm not asking, Joanna."

Garber said it casually, but his words had an instantaneous effect. Churchfield froze, staring at him. She slowly nodded. "As you wish, Benton. General Markel . . ."

Markel said, "Madam Secretary, I must protest—"

Senator Garber coughed loudly.

Markel glared at him. The two men stood there, staring at each other. Markel's face darkened, and tiny veins appeared above his temples. He seemed on the verge of losing—

Abruptly his face relaxed, as if a switch had been

turned off. He turned to Amanda and said stiffly, "Twelve hundred hours. In the Tank. We can give you thirty minutes."

"Thank you, sir." She drifted back.

The Tank was the Joint Chiefs' secured briefing room, located in the Pentagon. Ideally, I would have liked to question each general individually, but I didn't want to push our luck, since I had a follow-up request.

After I asked it, Churchfield again nodded to Admiral Wheeler, who made a quick call. A plainclothes Pentagon policeman would secure Garber's office.

"Anything else?" she asked me.

"No, ma'am."

As Simon, Amanda, and I led the entourage up the stairs to view the body, we saw Markel pivot and walk rapidly toward the exit. He took out a phone and furiously began punching in a number. Simon murmured something under his breath that I was close enough to hear.

"We have a suspect," he said.

14

Andy and the entire forensics team were packed in the hallway outside the compartment. Their awed faces followed Secretary Churchfield and Senator Garber as they went inside. Even though I'd never been a fan of the senator, it was wrenching watching his reaction to the body of his son. He bent down and gently stroked a cold cheek. He kept it up until his eyes brimmed wetly. Seeing his grief reminded me of my own devastation when Nicole passed away. As painful as that was, I thought how much I loved my daughter Emily and knew nothing could compare with the loss of a child.

Glancing at Amanda and Simon, I saw they were also moved by what they were witnessing. Particularly Simon, who two years earlier had lost his chauffeur Romero, the former NYPD cop who had been his father figure, mentor, and protector.

Senator Garber rose from the body. He took out his handkerchief, wiped his eyes, and blew his nose. Simon gently placed an arm around his shoulders. They spoke quietly, and Simon removed his rosary beads.

My eyes went down the small semicircle of faces. Most were respectful, but devoid of any real empathy—an understandable reaction, considering the way they felt about General Garber.

Then I noticed the figure standing near the door.

For an instant, I thought I must be seeing things. This was the last person I would have guessed would feel any compassion for General Garber. But there was no mistaking the constant swallowing or rapid blinking. The face turned, and our eyes locked.

This time the secretary of defense was the one who looked away.

"Shall we pray?" Simon said.

When the prayer ended, Secretary Churchfield immediately ducked out the door with her security men. Everyone else slowly filed out behind them. Simon and Senator Garber left together, conversing quietly. I came up behind Amanda in the hallway and whispered in her ear. We continued up to the front of the plane as the group exited out the passenger door.

"What's up?" she said, facing me.

She was already shaking her head before I'd finished. "No way. You must have misread Churchfield's reaction, Marty."

"I didn't."

"Isn't it possible you—"

"No."

"But it doesn't make any sense. Churchfield couldn't stand General Garber."

"How do you know?"

"Everyone knew it, Marty. It was common knowledge at the Pentagon that they didn't get along."

She was talking about the Pentagon's rumor mill. I said, "That doesn't prove anything."

"Katie *told* me Churchfield despised Garber."

"She said those words exactly."

"Well, no. But she did say Churchfield considered Garber incompetent and immoral—"

She stopped. She realized what I was getting at. Just because Churchfield considered Garber professionally inept didn't mean she couldn't have had a personal relationship with him. And with Garber's history as a womanizer . . .

Amanda sighed. "You know you're reaching big-time on this."

"Maybe."

"I suppose you want me to check."

"Please."

She reluctantly took out her phone and made the call. "Katie? Amanda. Got a quick question—"

Amanda listened, then held out the phone to me. I could hear someone laughing out loud.

"Satisfied?" Amanda asked me.

As Amanda and I went down the portable staircase, we saw that the hangar was empty except for the two security cops. We headed out across the concrete toward the side door and pushed through into the bright sunlight. Simon was standing a few feet away, his back to us, his eyes on two air force staff cars that were pulling up to a military Blackhawk helicopter. The passengers, led by Churchfield and Senator Garber, emerged from the cars and began climbing aboard.

"I don't like this, Martin," Simon murmured.

"No."

The two staff cars swung around and sped out across the ramp, away from us. In the lead vehicle driven by Major Vega, we could make out two hulking shapes in the backseat, members of the SECDEF's entourage who were remaining behind. Mutt and Jeff.

Amanda eyed us grimly. "Can we stop them from interfering with the investigation?"

"I doubt it," Simon said. "They'll justify their presence by saying they only want to observe."

She gestured toward the hangar. "So we let them poke around. Intimidate the hell out of our people."

He shrugged.

The helicopter's engines roared to life. The rotors started turning, picking up speed. Moments later, the helo rose awkwardly into the air and chattered across the field toward the west.

Simon checked his watch and gazed down the flight line toward base operations. "Five minutes." He was talking about the time remaining until General Morley promised to deliver the passengers. I wasn't holding my breath.

Amanda said, "Better get here soon. We need to be on the road in an hour, to make the meeting with the generals."

"We'll question the key people first," I said. "Anyone we don't get to, Paul and Tommy can handle." As I spoke, I was watching the staff car driven by Major Vega. It had stopped at the far end of the flight line, near a group of SPs. The SPs turned to look in our direction.

"They're up to something," Amanda said, voicing the obvious.

"Screw them," I said. "I got an idea."

After I explained, Simon said I was wasting my time.

And I probably was. Still, it was better than letting them waltz in here without a fight.

When the staff car finally drove off, I walked over to the entry control point.

When the female cop passed me her access list, I saw that two pages had been added. The first contained the eleven passengers that we were expecting. The second had only two typed names: Tom Hansen and Ernie Kelley. There was no rank, and the unit affiliation read simply "Dept. of Defense."

I crumpled the page and shoved the ball in my pocket. The cop stared at me in shock.

Returning her clipboard, I smiled pleasantly and read her name tag. "Mind doing me a favor, Airman Reardon?"

She hesitated, then slowly shook her head.

"Tell Major Vega what I just did. Tell him that if anyone gets into the hangar without my okay, I will personally arrest his ass. You got that?"

She tried to speak, and coughed. Her head bobbed.

As I turned away, I heard her key her radio. Her words streamed out in a nervous falsetto. "Chief, it's Airman Reardon. You'll never believe what happened. That OSI cop Mr. Collins just ordered me to . . ."

I caught movement to my left and looked toward base operations, half expecting to see the staff car roar around the corner. Instead, a shiny blue air force passenger bus was rolling toward us.

I checked my watch. A minute to spare.

I about-faced to wait.

I glanced around as Amanda joined me near the entry point. "Where's Simon?"

"He'll meet us in the maintenance offices. He wanted to give Andy a check before he leaves."

"A *check*? Why?"

"Didn't say."

An ear-splitting screech as the bus braked to a stop. We could see the passengers in the back. As Amanda and I went over, it gradually dawned on me what Simon was up to. I shook my head, thinking I shouldn't be surprised. After all, this wouldn't be the first time he'd resorted to a bribe.

The cop started toward the bus, carrying her clipboard. I waved her off, saying, "We'll handle this, Airman Reardon."

She slowly nodded and backed away from the door.

Amanda and I entered the bus. Eleven sets of eyes were focused on us, their luggage piled on seats beside them. A female lieutenant colonel was sitting right up front, a mousy-looking blonde with stringy hair and tired eyes. I dismissed her and moved on to the remaining women. A matronly major sat to the right. Behind her, the female security cop with the killer bod whom Andy had mentioned. But I agreed with Amanda's assessment that even a oversexed hound dog like Garber wouldn't be crazy enough to screw around with an enlisted girl who might squeal to her dorm mates.

My eyes came to rest on a slender brunette sitting in the last seat. She easily passed the looks test, but seemed too young to be the aide to a four-star.

I looked to her shoulders. Her silver oak leaves glinted in the sunlight.

"Bingo," Amanda said.

Innocence.

I decided that was the quality Colonel Weller most exuded. Her rank told me she had to be in her mid-thirties, but she looked ten years younger. A fragile, petite woman with liquid blue eyes and full lips, she possessed a Kate Moss–like vulnerability that a lot of men would have found hard to resist. Then there was her voice, deep and husky and sensual as hell.

Weller hesitantly entered the big office across from the maintenance break room, where the remaining passengers were cooling their heels. I had to ask her twice before she joined Simon, Amanda, and me at the circular conference table. As she recounted the events leading to the discovery of General Muller's body, she continually clasped and unclasped a handkerchief in her hand. Occasionally her voice would quiver, as if the memory was hard on her. Everything she'd told us jived with what we'd learned from Andy.

When she finished, she looked at her perfectly manicured hands and seemed to will them to relax. Up close, I could see she wore eyeliner and a hint of rouge, but no lipstick. She focused her beautiful eyes on me, saying, "That's everything. That's what happened. Agent Hobbs suggested I wait because there would be questions. I thought that was . . . silly. I mean, it was an accident. That's what I thought, and now . . ." She trailed off with a little head shake.

I said, "We don't know he was murdered, Colonel."

"But you obviously think he was. That's what all this . . . why you're asking all these questions."

"Do you think he was murdered?"

She appeared startled. "No. Of course not."

"Isn't it true that General Garber had enemies?"

She gave me a long look. "You already know the answer."

"I'm talking about the other members of the Joint Chiefs."

"There was some . . . resentment."

"Over his appointment to the chairmanship?"

A nod.

I said, "I assume they also resented him for other reasons?"

"You mean like some kind of personal grudge?"

"Yes."

She thought, then shook her head. "Not that I'm aware of."

I frowned. "You must have overheard something. Witnessed arguments, or—"

"I didn't," she said.

"Surely, Colonel—"

"Look, I'm not saying they didn't have their disagreements. I'm only telling you I never witnessed any. The only time I was around General Garber and the other chiefs was in social settings or when we traveled. In public, their relationship was a little strained, but cordial. You might check with Garber's exec, General Bryar. He was the one who accompanied him to the meetings in the Tank. If any of the chiefs got into an argument with Garber, it would probably be there. You know. Behind closed doors."

She looked and sounded completely sincere. I said, "None of the other generals' aides ever mentioned any particular grudges their bosses had?"

"Not to me."

Amanda's head popped up from the notes she was making. Like me, she knew this couldn't be true. Generals' aides were notorious for gossiping among themselves about their bosses. Now we had to ask ourselves why Colonel Weller was reluctant to reveal what she knew.

Before I could press her, she said quietly, "You're wrong about the chiefs."

"Wrong?"

"You're thinking maybe one of them did it. Killed General Garber. They didn't."

I got it now. She was playing the loyal staff officer, unwilling to give me anything that could be construed as a motive. "You sound pretty sure about this."

She slowly interlaced her fingers and set them on the table. "I am."

"Mind telling me why?"

"I know the kind of men they are."

"That's hardly specific."

She gave a little shrug.

"You mentioned the relationship between General Garber and the chiefs was strained"—I waited for the nod—"implying they disliked him. In your opinion, who resented General Garber more? General Markel or General Johnson or—"

The head shaking began.

"—perhaps General Sessler?"

She sounded exasperated. "*None* of them. I told you they wouldn't have killed him. They *couldn't.*"

Her pretty face was locked on me in a glare. Watching her, I thought she either truly believed in the generals' innocence or was one hell of an actress.

I also detected something in her reaction that didn't quite fit. It was the same contradiction I'd noticed earlier, when she'd described finding General Garber's body. I glanced to Simon and Amanda. They were both watching her with interest.

"Loyalty," Simon said, "is an admirable trait, Colonel."

Weller blinked, as if surprised that he'd actually spoken. Since the introductions, Simon hadn't said a word. This was often his pattern during the initial phases of an interview. He liked to sit back and gauge things, coming to life only when he saw an opening.

He must have seen one now, because he continued smoothly, "You impress me as a dedicated officer, Colonel."

She appeared puzzled by his comment. "I'd like to think so."

"You took an oath to be loyal to the military and the officers above you?"

"I swore to defend the Constitution. It's not quite the same thing."

"But you swore to obey the orders of superior officers."

She flipped a few strands of hair from her eyes with a single gleaming red nail. "I see where you're going. No one ordered me to say what I did. I certainly didn't do it out of any sense of loyalty. I've been around the other chiefs enough to know they couldn't have killed General Garber. They're honorable, decent men."

"They're soldiers," Simon said. "And soldiers kill."

He said it casually, but the remark struck a nerve. Weller's face tightened, and she seemed to fight the urge to respond.

"Honorable," Simon said.

She looked at him.

"You said the chiefs were honorable men?"

"It's true."

"Including General Markel?"

"General Markel's war record speaks for itself. He's probably the most courageous man in the military. If you're insinuating anything else, you're mistaken." Her eyes were dark, angry.

Simon smiled apologetically. "I'm sure the general is very brave."

"You bet he is."

"Curious," Simon said. "I thought you said you weren't familiar with the other chiefs."

"They're heroes. They deserve my respect—and yours."

"So your defense of General Markel isn't predicated upon any personal—"

"Of course not. I'd say the same thing about General Sessler and General Johnson and any of the other chiefs."

"Including General Garber?"

A silence. She shifted in her seat and stared at her nails.

Simon said, "You must have an opinion of his character, Colonel?"

She looked up. "He's dead. What does it matter what I thought of him?"

"I take it you didn't particularly care for General Garber."

"I didn't say that."

Simon reassured her that anything she said would be kept confidential. Her brow knitted as she considered his offer. She shook her head again. "I'd rather not say."

"Colonel Weller . . ."

"No."

A trace of irritation crossed Simon's face. He leaned over the table and stared right at her. He didn't blink. It was creepy. Weller turned away, trying to ignore him. But as the seconds passed, you could see he was getting to her. She kept shooting him glances, as if expecting him to say something. *Wanting* him to say something.

But he never did. He just kept staring at her.

Frankly, I thought Simon was going to lose this test of

wills. This was a murder investigation, and Colonel Weller had to know her relationship to Garber made her a suspect. No way would she dare admit—

"Damn you." Weller glared at him. "Damn you."

"You disliked the general, then?"

She almost came out of her chair. "Disliked? I *despised* him. He was petty and mean and vindictive. He made my life a living hell. There. I said it. Satisfied?"

Simon seemed unprepared by the intensity of her response. The raw emotion. Amanda and I waited for the obvious follow-up, but he continued to sit there with a puzzled expression, as if trying to understand.

Amanda looked to me. I nodded.

"Colonel Weller," she asked, "if you despised General Garber, why were you so distraught when you found the body?"

Weller turned to her and slowly sagged back into her chair. She suddenly sounded tired. "To be honest, my reaction surprised me too. But I've been under a lot of stress from the trip. Putting up with General Garber's demands. Almost no sleep. Anyway, I think it all contributed to the shock I felt. When I walked in and saw him lying there, I . . . I sort of freaked out."

Understandable, I thought. Amanda must have thought so, too, because she changed the subject and asked Weller if she knew who purchased the bottle of Glenlivet whisky that the General Garber was drinking.

"I think General Garber bought some in London."

"You *think*?"

"I saw a bottle in his room last night. On the desk. It might have been Glenlivet. I didn't notice the label."

"What time was this?"

"A couple hours into the flight. I was returning his uniform that I'd had pressed. I stayed maybe five minutes. To discuss his schedule for the next day. Today."

"The general was alone?"

"Yes. He said he was tired and was going to bed. He told me he didn't want to be disturbed."

"Was that the last time you saw him?"

"Yes. Until this morning."

Amanda consulted her notepad. "Do you remember if his bed had been made up?"

Good question: Amanda was trying to determine if anyone saw Garber after Weller.

"It wasn't," Weller said. "When I left, I told Sergeant Blake to make it up."

Amanda made a note. "Could you tell whether General Garber was drunk?"

"He could hold a lot without showing it. But his words were a little . . . sloppy." She added, "I could also smell the alcohol on him."

"Do you wear lipstick, Colonel?"

Weller paused, thrown by the question. "Uh, sure. Sometimes."

"What color?"

"Red, mostly. Why?"

"The same color as your nails."

Weller glanced down. "Pretty close."

Amanda leaned to her left and pointed to a leather purse that was sitting on the floor beside Weller's chair. "Is your lipstick in there, Colonel?"

Weller flinched visibly, and something approaching fear appeared in her eyes. I felt a buzz of anticipation. Simon hunched forward, watching her intently.

"Why . . . why do you want it?" Weller asked Amanda.

Amanda was already on her feet and stepping over to the purse. "May I, Colonel?" She reached down.

Weller snatched up the purse and clutched it to her chest. "Why do you want it?" she demanded.

"Colonel," Amanda said, standing over her, "you're aware that anyone on a military reservation is subject to search without consent. I have the authority to physically take your purse from you."

Weller's eyes darted to Simon and me almost pleadingly. We gazed back, unsympathetic. Her small shoulders dropped as she accepted the inevitable. She held out the purse to Amanda, her hand shaking.

"Wait outside, please," Amanda ordered.

Weller rose wordlessly and walked out. The moment the door shut, Amanda dumped the contents of the purse onto the table.

15

Simon and I stood beside Amanda as she picked through the items.

The usual assortment of things you'd expect to find in a woman's purse: a leather wallet, a nail file, tweezers, gum, an opened packet of tissues, some loose change, a small cloth makeup bag with floral stitching—

Amanda unzipped the makeup bag and removed two cylinders of lipstick. Designer brands. "The lady has good taste," Amanda said. "This stuff goes for fifty dollars a tube."

She popped the caps. Both were shades of red.

Studying them, she said, "Weller must know about the lipstick smear on the glass. That's got to be why she's so frightened."

"Perhaps not," Simon said.

We glanced at him.

He was holding the wallet open, staring at something inside. He lowered it so we could see.

And there, encased in plastic next to Weller's driver's license, was a picture of a smiling man in a medaled air force uniform, standing beside an American flag. After

Weller's emotional outburst, he was the last person we expected to see.

It was General Garber.

We all stared at the picture, trying to figure it. In the photo, Garber's hair was dark brown instead of gray, and his uniform had only one star.

"It has to be at least eight to ten years old," Amanda said.

I nodded and opened the wallet. Weller's military ID was on the inside cover. I checked her birth date. She was thirty-three. She'd made lieutenant colonel at least four years earlier than her peers. Not unusual for aides to be fast burners, since they often rode the coattails of their generals up the promotion chain.

I leafed through past a few plastic inserts containing credit cards, pausing at a picture of a smiling older couple sitting in a canoe. I dug it out. An inscription on the back: "Mom and Dad at Lake Tahoe." It was dated last August. Simon tapped my arm, and I passed it over. He studied it for what seemed a long time.

I said, "Something?"

He handed it back. "Not much of a resemblance."

Unlike their thin, dark-complected daughter, the couple were both heavy-set and fair-skinned. "Probably their weight," I said. "It alters their appearance."

He nodded.

As I returned the photo to the wallet and placed it on the table, I said to Amanda, "Get Weller back in here, then take the lipstick up to Martha. Tell her we want a comparison done ASAP on whether either color matches the smear on the glass."

She was tossing the items back into the purse.

Glancing at me, she said, "Might be a good idea to search her luggage. See what else she's holding back."

"Make it fast. I don't want her to realize we're focusing on her and start screaming harassment." The passengers' luggage was still sitting on the bus, parked outside the hangar.

She handed me the purse and winked. "Goes with your shoes, Marty."

"But not my eyes," I deadpanned.

She grinned. As she headed for the door, Simon said to her, "Tell Weller we'll need a few minutes."

Which meant he wanted to talk. As we eased into our seats, I eyed him.

He tugged thoughtfully on a cheek. "It's confusing."

"Yeah." I stared at the wallet on the table. "If Weller hated Garber, it doesn't figure she'd keep his picture."

"It's more complicated than that, Martin. I'm curious about her change in attitude."

"Attitude?"

"When she described seeing General Garber's body, she tried to appear as if the process was traumatizing. But her eyes gave away her true feelings. You probably noticed."

I had. This was the inconsistency that had troubled me earlier. As she'd spoken, Weller's shoulders had dropped and her lip had quivered. She'd been the picture of worry and grief. Except for her eyes. Cold and dispassionate.

"Naturally," Simon continued, "I assumed she was trying to deflect suspicion from herself by showing remorse over Garber's death."

"And now?"

"You heard her, Martin. Why would she be so vitriolic in her hatred toward General Garber?"

"You pressured her for the truth."

"She could have simply said she disliked him, but she didn't. She specifically said she despised him."

"Your point being . . ."

He studied me. "It's almost as if she'd decided to become a suspect."

I shook my head. Simon had come up with some doozies before, but—

"I'll admit it's a little far-fetched, Martin."

"A *little*? Simon, you saw the way Weller reacted when Amanda asked for her purse. She practically laid an egg in the chair."

Simon tented his fingers, watching me. "Would you say Colonel Weller is an intelligent woman, Martin?"

I hesitated, trying to figure out his angle. "Yes."

"Very intelligent."

"Probably." As I said it, I realized where he was headed. "You're wondering why Weller kept the lipstick if it could be traced to her."

He lowered his hands and nodded. "She had plenty of time of dispose of it."

I thought. "It probably never occurred to her that we'd dig the glasses from the trash. Or better yet, she probably thought she'd wiped all the lipstick off the rim."

"And General Garber's picture . . ."

At the sound of a knock, Simon looked toward the door. "We'll see, Martin. Come in, Colonel Weller."

The change in Weller's demeanor over the last few minutes was remarkable. She now appeared calm and in control. She sat in her chair and appraised Simon and me with something approaching amusement. "You found it, I take it?"

"Found what?" Simon asked mildly.

She smiled. "The picture in the wallet. I knew you'd misunderstand."

Simon picked up the wallet from the table, opened it to General Garber's photo, and slid it to her. "Enlighten us."

"General Garber gave it to me."

"Why?"

"I suppose he wanted me to have it."

"Why?"

"He never said. I suspect it was ego. He assumed I'd want a picture of him."

"You said you hated him—"

"I did."

"Then why did you keep it in your wallet?"

Her voice hardened, matching her earlier bitterness. "You don't know him. The kind of man he was. I knew he'd check someday and see if I was carrying it. He liked playing those kinds of games. Testing people's loyalty."

Simon said, "It's an older picture—"

"The man's ego again. That was his favorite picture because he still looked young and handsome. Or thought he did. In his office, he has a big portrait of himself painted from it. It hangs over his desk, large as you please. Like he was worshiping himself. It made me sick to look at it."

"If you were unhappy working for him, why didn't you quit?" Simon asked.

A harsh laugh. "You *serious*? You know how hard I've worked to get where I am. If I tried to quit, he would have destroyed my career. You don't leave General Garber unless he wants you to go. Ask him. He knows what I'm talking about."

She was referring to me, because I was nodding. In the military, four-stars were akin to gods. Once they decided to end someone's career, whether it was justified or not, there was nothing the person could do. When I was stationed at the Pentagon, a fighter-pilot colonel with two Silver Stars for bravery committed the unpardonable sin of correcting a general's figures during a budget briefing. That the colonel was right didn't matter. The next day he was fired, his military career finished.

After I told Simon that Weller's concerns were valid, he still seemed skeptical. He was just being stubborn. Logic notwithstanding, once he got an idea in his head, he had trouble letting go.

Moving on, he asked Weller if she knew any way into the compartment, once the doors were locked. She said she didn't.

"What if the general was ill, and you had to get inside?" Simon asked.

She shrugged. "Same drill we used to enter this morning. We break the door down."

"When you discovered the body, did you notice if anyone seemed unusually interested in the closet doors?"

"No one touched them."

"How can you be sure, Colonel? You were upset and—"

"The way I was sitting. I was facing the closet. No one touched them."

Simon contemplated her, as if trying to reach a decision. This time Weller didn't seem the least bit rattled by his scrutiny. Abruptly, Simon reached down and removed the photograph from the wallet. "You mind if we keep this?"

"You can burn it, for all I care."

After pocketing the picture, he returned her wallet and purse. He looked to me: Your turn.

I said to Weller, "You have quite a career going. I assume you're min-time to light bird." Min-time meant she'd been promoted two years early to major and two years early to lieutenant colonel.

A curt nod. "I've worked hard for it."

"General Garber must have thought a lot of you, to push your promotions."

She bristled at the remark. "Implying what? That I'm ungrateful? That I *owed* him something?"

"Not at all. I was only pointing out—"

"Let me tell you something, Agent Collins. I busted my ass for those promotions. I *deserved* them."

"I'm sure you—"

But she was on a roll, angrily dressing me down. "You think being an aide is easy? For four years, I've had no life of my own. I've been on call every minute of every day. I've been a goddamn secretary, a maid, a cook, a seamstress, and any other damn thing you could think of. And now you sit here, trying to make me feel guilty because I was promoted early. Go to hell."

She sat back, her face flushed and indignant.

I didn't say anything. I just focused on her eyes and found what I expected. They were flat, devoid of any real emotion.

So this was another calculated outburst. She *wanted* us to think she was someone who got riled up easily. For the first time, Simon's theory didn't sound quite so crazy.

Bracing for another scripted eruption, I said, "I don't want you to take my next question wrong, but it has to be asked."

She sighed. "You want to know if General Garber made a pass at me."

"Yes."

"Once."

"What did you do?"

"What do you think?" she snapped. "I told him I wasn't interested and walked out."

"I'm surprised he didn't hold it against you."

"Why would he? He had other women."

"You know who they were?"

"No. He was careful. He knew even his father probably couldn't protect him from another scandal."

"How do you know he was seeing other women?"

"A few times, I answered the phone in his office. His direct line. There were women on the other end. They never left a message or their names. Just hung up when I told them the general wasn't there."

"Could they have been the same woman, or—"

"I don't know. Maybe. I didn't really notice their voices." She shrugged.

Out of the corner of my eye, I noticed Simon shift in his seat. A finger began tapping the table. He seemed impatient for me to wrap up my questions. I told him I'd be only a few more minutes.

"Take your time, Martin." But the tapping continued.

I asked Weller if General Garber's wife knew about his affairs.

She answered cautiously. "All I can tell you is, they don't live together."

"Oh?"

"Haven't for years. The separation's been kept quiet, for appearances. She still puts in face time with him at official functions." Her voice turned sarcastic. "After all, the air force can't have a general who doesn't have a spouse."

I glanced to her hand. No wedding ring. This explained her slam against the air force's informal policy of promoting only married officers to the upper ranks. I asked her where Mrs. Garber lived.

"She has a penthouse condo in the Jefferson Towers."

My eyebrows went up. That was the most exclusive apartment building in D.C. Places there started at a couple mil easy, well beyond the price range for a general officer. But then most generals didn't have a senator daddy who was worth millions.

"Do you have Mrs. Garber's number?"

She rattled it off from memory, and I jotted it in my notepad.

I was done, and I glanced at Simon to see if he had anything further. He shook his head. He seemed curiously uninterested in Weller now, displaying no signs of his earlier impatience. He did make a point of thanking Weller for her honesty and assistance. The remark seemed unnecessary, and I suspected Simon had said it to give her a false sense of security.

Which meant he still had something up his sleeve.

After I instructed Weller to wait outside and send in Lieutenant Colonel Gustin, she was incredulous. "You *still* want me to stay? Why? I've told you everything I know."

"It will only be for a few more minutes." I gave her a sympathetic smile.

She grimaced, grabbed her purse, and rose in a huff. As she went to the door, I saw Simon sit forward, his eyes fixed on her back.

Here it comes . . .

Simon had a flair for the dramatic; he waited until she was almost to the door. Then: "Did you hate General Garber enough to kill him, Colonel?"

I had to hand it to Weller. She was a cool one. She never even flinched. She brazenly continued right up to the door, as if she hadn't heard him.

He said sharply, "Colonel—"

Her hand froze on the handle. Slowly, she faced him.

The smart answer was a denial. I fully expected a denial. Instead, Weller drew in a deep breath and said, "As a matter of fact, I did."

"Did you kill him, Colonel?"

She hesitated. "Am I under any obligation to answer?"

"No."

"I'll decline, then."

"Would you be willing to submit to a lie-detector test?"

A faint smile. "I don't think that would be wise, Lieutenant."

"Probably not. Good-bye, Colonel."

"Good-bye, Lieutenant."

16

I sat there in disbelief. I said to Simon, "Okay, you called it, but I still think it's a stretch. Why would she deliberately want to appear guilty?"

"Perhaps she is, Martin."

"Then why doesn't she just confess? Why the games?"

He shook his head.

I said, "I got to tell you I'm with Andy on this. I don't see how she could have pulled off the killing. She can't weigh more than an hundred and ten pounds. Unless she drugged General Garber—"

"Don't be ridiculous. The killing was a spontaneous act."

"Right." This still made the most sense. "So we're talking about a second person in the compartment with her. Someone who helped her restrain Garber—"

"I disagree. I doubt Colonel Weller had anything to do with the crime."

Now I was completely lost. "Simon, she practically told us she was involved. Remember?"

He gave me a cryptic look. "You're jumping to conclusions. Don't. The key is the interview. Initially, she was clearly trying to convince us she couldn't be a suspect. Later, she changed her mind. Why?"

I considered this. "Go on."

"Two possibilities. First, Colonel Weller could intentionally be trying to confuse the investigation. Perhaps under orders from her superiors."

"Thin," I grunted.

"Is it? We know the military doesn't want the murder solved. It's certainly conceivable that—"

"Get real, Simon. Would the military stonewall an investigation? You bet. Would they try and intimidate us into backing off? Absolutely. But getting an officer to sacrifice herself for a possible murder rap—"

I stopped. What the hell was I saying? I sighed and shook my head. "Scratch that. You're right. Weller's not risking anything. The military will never allow us to make a case against her. They can't."

Simon nodded, squinting at the carnation on his lapel. He adjusted it, contemplated it, adjusted it again. Finally, a nod. Mr. Perfection.

I said, "You mentioned a second explanation."

"Hmm. Yes. It could be that Weller has decided on her own to protect the killer. But I think that's highly unlikely." He paused, thinking. "Not unless she had a reason. Possibly a connection to . . . but that would mean . . . I wonder if . . ."

I waited a few seconds. "If what?"

But Simon was gone, lost in his thoughts. For the next thirty seconds, he sat there like a mannequin. Right up until the moment we heard the knock on the door and Lieutenant Colonel Marsha Gustin, the aide to General David Markel, walked into the room.

•   •   •

In contrast to Colonel Weller, Colonel Gustin displayed little emotion as she related the events of the morning. She spoke slowly, in the dull monotone characteristic of military briefings. Her responses to my questions were a broken record of denials. No, she didn't know who might have wanted to kill General Garber. No, she didn't know of anyone on the plane whom he might have been sleeping with. No, she didn't know any way to enter the compartment once the door and closet were locked. No, she had no knowledge why the other generals resented General Garber. No, General Markel had never expressed any particular dislike for—

I'd had enough. My bullshit light came on bright. I asked her straight out if anyone had ordered her not to cooperate with the investigation.

She gave me a long blink, trying to mirror Weller's big-eyed innocence. She ended up looking as if she had contact lens problems.

"Colonel," I said, "are you aware that this is an official inquiry? As such, any false statements you make can be prosecuted under the UCMJ."

Her eyes popped wide, this time for real. She stammered, "I . . . I wasn't aware that—"

"Who told you to withhold information?"

She stumbled through, "No one. I swear. No one told me—"

"It was your boss, General Markel, wasn't it?"

She stared at me in shock. She shook her head.

I leaned close and spoke in a harsh whisper. "Now what if I informed General Markel that you verified he was the one who ordered you not to cooperate?"

She turned pale. "But I didn't—"

"Last chance. Did General Markel order you, Colonel?"

"No. I swear."

"Have it your way. Simon." I motioned him to pass me the folder with the passenger and crew information that General Morley had given him. I flipped to the page with the number for General Markel's office. As I removed my cell phone, Colonel Gustin watched me in growing horror.

She squeaked, "He'll . . . he'll never believe you. He'll know you're lying."

I placed the call, and a secretary who sounded about eighty answered. I said, "Ma'am, I'm Agent Collins of the OSI. I'd like speak with General Markel— If you'll take a message—"

"Don't. Please."

I cupped the phone, eyeing Gustin. "I want the truth."

She nodded dully, her face miserable.

After telling the secretary I'd call back, I tucked my phone away. To Gustin, I said, "So it was General Markel?"

"Not just him. He did the talking, but they were all there."

"General Sessler and General Johnson?"

"Yes. They called me to their section. While we were still on the plane. They said . . . they said there would be an investigation. They wanted me to stay behind, but not be too cooperative."

"They mention anything specific?"

She hesitated.

"If you lie, I'll know."

"It was . . . it concerned Colonel Weller. I was told . . . they wanted me to say that she was sitting beside me, during the whole flight."

A stunning revelation. It was all I could do keep my voice calm. I said, "So Colonel Weller left your section?"

"Yes."

"How long was she gone?"

"I'm not sure. At least a couple of hours. From around 2300 hours to a little after 0100."

She was giving me local East Coast time. The spread fit the window when Garber had probably died.

I said, "Did she say anything when she returned?"

"No. But I could tell that she was upset. Anxious. And that's not like her. Tina never gets rattled about anything. She's usually so . . . *controlled.*"

"She never told you what was bothering her?"

"No. I assumed it was General Garber. That he'd chewed her out."

This clinched it. Weller had known Garber was dead. The question was how. The most obvious conclusion was that she was either the killer or involved in the killing. When I looked to Simon, he shrugged. It was clear he still didn't consider Gustin's testimony particularly damning to Weller.

And when I thought about it, I realized he might be right.

It came down to Secretary Churchfield and the three generals. Specifically, their willingness to go along with the cover-up. Regardless of the political considerations, it seemed absurd to believe that four of the most powerful people in the military would risk their careers to protect a lieutenant colonel.

Toss in Weller's pseudo-confession, and only one conclusion made any sense. The killer had to be one of—

A phone rang, breaking in on my thoughts. Simon automatically reached into his jacket. Only this time it was mine.

I was surprised to hear Amanda's voice. She sounded furious with me. "Why the hell didn't you warn me, Marty? Son of a bitch. She walked right out and almost caught me going through her—"

I jumped from my chair and lunged past a startled Colonel Gustin toward the door. "Stop her!" I screamed into the phone. "*Stop her!*"

17

I burst into the hallway and came face-to-face with a wall of blue uniforms. All had on either pilot or aircrew wings—the plane's crew, arriving to be questioned. They recoiled at the sight of my wild face. A burly major said, "Is there some kind of a problem, or—"

I was already pushing past him. I sprinted down the hallway, trying to stuff my cell phone in my jacket. I could hear Simon right behind me. We ran into the hangar. The med techs were loading the gurney with Garber's body into the back of the Humvee. Andy was leaning against the hood, watching them. As we tore past, he called out cheerfully, "Hey, fellas, where's the fucking fire?"

I hollered out Weller's name to the two security cops. They pointed to the side door. I heard Andy say, "Aw, shit, don't tell me that—"

Simon and I reached the door. I threw it open and went out first.

We took maybe five strides before our fears were confirmed. We slowed to a walk, and I swore.

We could hear the sounds of laughter coming from the

maintenance personnel strolling across the flight line. We could see the two SPs on the Humvees, manning the machine guns. We could see the blond cop Airman Reardon still at her post by the entry control point, standing beside the driver of the bus. And a few yards to their right, we could see Amanda with her hands on her hips, staring at a maroon car that was speeding away.

Amanda faced Simon and me as we approached. She was still wearing the latex gloves she'd used in the search of Weller's luggage. She gestured at the retreating car as it disappeared around a corner. "I almost had her. Ten more seconds. Then those two walking billboards—"

"Hansen and Kelley," I said.

"Whatever. All I know is they drove up out of nowhere. I never saw them coming. They threw open the back door, and Weller jumped in." She grimaced in self-recrimination.

Airman Reardon and the bus driver were watching us. So were the two airmen mounted on the Humvees. I lowered my voice and said to Amanda, "It was my fault. I should have considered the possibility she might take off."

Amanda shook her head at me. "There's more than enough blame to go around, Marty. I should have stopped her when I first spotted her. I should have realized you guys didn't let her go." She nodded toward Airman Reardon. "We could use her radio. Call the gate and try and get them to stop the car."

"Forget it," I said. "Secretary Churchfield probably arranged this with General Morley and Major Vega."

"I know, but— *Damn!*"

She turned away, too angry to speak. No one said anything for a long moment. Maybe it was the way the wind rippled through Amanda's hair or the way the sun framed the soft curves of her perfect profile. Maybe it was her nearness to me, or the way she began chewing on her lower lip. For whatever reason, I found myself suddenly aware of her, thinking how beautiful she looked at that moment. As I watched her, the memory of my wife, Nicole, tugged at me, and I glanced down at the wedding ring I still wore. When I looked up, Simon was staring at me with an odd smile.

Amanda turned to me. "Jesus, this pisses me off. Their goddamn arrogance. They think they can waltz off with our prime suspect—"

"Colonel Weller isn't a suspect," Simon said.

Amanda's head jerked. "She *isn't?* Why the hell did she take off?"

Simon hesitated, aware of our audience. He leaned close and spoke into Amanda's ear. I couldn't hear what he said, not that it mattered.

He was telling her that one of the generals had to be the killer.

A two-ship of F-16 fighters roared overhead, the sun glinting on their wings. They pitched out into the traffic pattern and came in for a formation landing. After they touched down, we strolled back toward the hangar. Ahead, we could see Andy hanging on to the side door, gasping for air. He shouted to us and began coughing uncontrollably.

"Cigarettes will kill him," Amanda said.

I nodded. "Not that he gives a damn."

"It's unanimous. No one else does either."

I sighed. "Quit riding the guy, huh?"

"Hey," she said, "I'm just telling it like it is."

And she probably was. Andy had no close friends, and his only family was a grown son whom he hadn't seen in years. His social life consisted of drinking himself into oblivion night after night at his favorite watering hole, then staggering home to his run-down apartment, which was all he could afford after three divorces. If he died, the bartender might miss his best customer, but that would be about it.

Once we were out of earshot of Airman Reardon, Amanda said to Simon, "Tell me the rest of it."

So he did, speaking quickly. When he finished, Amanda slowly shook her head at him.

"Let me see if I understand," she said. "Colonel Weller admitted hating Garber enough to kill him—"

"Yes."

"—then she takes off, practically convincing us that she must be guilty as sin—"

"Right."

"—but you still don't believe she is, because you don't believe the secretary of defense would put her ass on the line to cover up Garber's murder simply to protect Weller. In a nutshell, that's the reason you're convinced the killer has to be one of the service chiefs."

Simon nodded.

They walked a few steps. "Sorry," Amanda said. "We're in a war. Churchfield's—the government's—only intention is to protect the military from a scandal. Any scandal. Who the killer is doesn't really matter."

"It does matter," Simon said. "If General Garber was killed by a fellow member of the Joint Chiefs, the damage to the military's reputation would be extremely egregious. Consider the propaganda value to our enemies. They could portray the American military as being led by murderers. No, no. It matters."

We were coming to the bus, parked near the front of the hangar. Andy had stopped coughing and was wheezing loudly. He gave us a feeble wave.

Amanda abruptly faced Simon. "What bugs me is that you're giving Weller a free pass. You make it sound as if she's only being used to decoy our suspicions from the real killer."

"Those men were waiting for Weller," Simon said. "That suggests Secretary Churchfield installed them as insurance, to prevent us from taking Weller into custody. If true, that proves Weller is operating under orders from Churchfield."

"Listen," Amanda said stubbornly. "All I'm saying is, there's a chance Weller was involved in the killing. A damn good chance." She gave him a meaningful look.

It took Simon a moment to catch on. "Her luggage? You found something?"

"Yeah. Had to leave it behind when I took off after Weller. If you ask me, I don't think there's much doubt what happened. Personally, I think Weller should get a medal for wasting the sick son of a bitch."

She turned and strolled quickly toward the bus.

"Yo, Marty! Hold on!"

I glanced over and saw Andy's bulk staggering toward me. I pulled up to wait for him while Simon hurried after Amanda.

Andy's face was still a splotchy red, but his breathing was down to a survivable rasp. He asked, "What the hell was that about? Why'd Weller take off?"

So I gave him a Cliffs Notes version of our suspicions concerning Weller and the three generals.

"One of the chiefs?" he said. "Guess that makes sense.

I mean, they hated the guy enough . . ." He frowned, tugging on a cheek.

I said, "You still don't sound like you're sold."

A shrug. "All I know is, Weller ain't no killer. I've flown a couple of trips with her. Got to know her pretty well. She's a good kid. I wouldn't read too much into her running off. She just got spooked. Hell, everybody thinks you guys are only looking for someone to pin this on, to keep the senator happy. Pretty clear to me that Weller had orders to get the hell out of Dodge if you guys started pressuring her too hard."

"No kidding," I said dryly. "You figure that out all by yourself?" My comment came out more sarcastic than I'd intended, and I saw at once that Andy had taken offense.

He stuck his jaw up to mine and growled, "You trying to be a wiseass, Marty?"

Christ. "No. I was only—"

"You think I'm stupid? Is that it? You think I haven't got the smarts to work a homicide? Fuck you."

"Andy—"

He poked my chest. "Let me tell you something, buddy boy. I'm only trying to stop you from wasting your time on Weller. You and Simon fuck this case up, you walk away. Go home to your cushy civilian jobs. Leave me to catch all the shit—"

He was really getting worked up. He wasn't shouting yet, but he was getting there. I said, "Andy, take it easy."

"*Screw* easy." Another poke, harder. "You know what I'm saying is true. For crying out loud, we got a dead fucking chairman of the Joint Chiefs. That's mighty tough to explain. The brass will look for someone to hang, and Andy here is going to be front and center. You blow this thing, and you might as well hand them the goddamn rope." He stepped back, glowering.

I said, "Andy, I didn't really think about—"

"Fucking right, you didn't."

"Look, I'm sorry." And I tried to sound like I meant it.

"Yeah, well . . ." He rubbed his face hard, his anger fading. When he spoke, he sounded almost apologetic. "Aw, hell. I guess I'm a little spun up. It's just that this case is important to me. You probably heard CID's been trying to force me to retire for years, prove me unfit."

I shook my head, even though I had.

"This could be their chance. Probably will be, unless you find the perp. If I get canned, I don't know what the hell I'd do. The job's all I've got. At my age . . ."

He fell silent, and a sadness crept into his eyes. I felt for him. I couldn't help it. Despite his faults, I'd always liked Andy. Why, I'm not certain. Maybe I secretly envied his lack of ambition and the freedom that gave him.

I said softly, "We'll find the killer, Andy."

"Sure you will, Marty. Sure you will."

But I knew he didn't believe it, and neither did I.

He forced a smile. "What the hell. They fire me, they fire me. Life's a bitch, and then you die. Right, Marty?"

I didn't answer him; he wasn't looking for a response. Watching him, I thought about how pathetic he suddenly seemed. Gradually, an idea occurred to me—one I tried to ignore, but couldn't. Despite my reservations, I heard myself say, "If things don't work out, you can always come work for me."

He appeared dumbfounded. "No *shit*? This is straight?"

I told him it was.

For once, Andy seemed at a loss for words. "Jeez, I . . .I really appreciate this, Marty."

"I can always use someone with your experience." I handed him my card with my office number and home numbers.

He stared at me as if he still didn't believe my offer was genuine. That someone would actually want him. He said, "Andy of fucking Mayberry."

With a crooked grin, he tucked the card away. As he did, he glanced at Simon and Amanda, who were visible at the rear of the bus. "What the hell are they looking for, anyway?"

I told him.

"Crap," he grunted. "Just like Weller's lipstick containers Amanda took up to Martha. I'll put up a month's pay nothing's going to come of it."

Again, he felt compelled to defend Weller. If I didn't know better, I'd have thought Andy had a personal interest in—

And then I realized what it probably was. Andy was always falling in love or lust. Young or old, it didn't matter. To Andy, every attractive female was a potential conquest.

"Before I forget," he said, turning to me, "I talked to that customs officer, Margie Benson."

"Andy, I specifically told you—"

"Keep your shirt on, Marty. You guys were busy, so I figured I'd call. I was cool. I didn't even come close to hitting on her. So . . . you want to know what she said about those customs decs or not?"

I sighed, already beginning to regret the job offer. "Go."

"Dead end. The Glenlivet belonged to Garber. A couple other people bought booze. Wine and Bailey's. No one else except Garber brought back hard liquor. Or if they did, they didn't declare it." He squinted, looking past me. "That didn't take long. Looks like they're finished. What's that Amanda's carrying? Can you tell?"

I turned as Simon and Amanda emerged from the bus, their heads bent in conversation. Their grim expressions told me Amanda hadn't exaggerated the importance of the evidence.

And that's where I was looking now. At the folded square of cloth in Amanda's gloved hand. The telltale baby-blue color confirmed what it probably was.

"It's a uniform shirt," Andy said.

Amanda and Simon never bothered to explain the shirt's significance; there wasn't any need. Amanda just held it up to Andy and me. I shook my head while Andy kept saying, "I still don't believe it. It can't be Weller. Dammit, it can't."

But there was no denying what we were seeing. All but one of the buttons on the front of the shirt were missing. Even more damning were the spindly tendrils of white thread hanging down.

Someone had torn off the buttons with great force.

18

A car horn blared, startling us.

We gazed down the flight line and saw a gleaming black stretch limousine rolling toward the hangar. Simon pointed to the adjacent parking area, and the limo cruised around and parked. The windows were tinted too dark for us to make out the chauffeur's face, not that I'd have recognized him. Since Romero's death, Simon had gone through dozens of drivers. Most rarely lasted more than a few weeks before he found some excuse for letting them go. Even after two years, he couldn't bring himself to replace his lifelong friend.

This was one reason Simon and I remained close, despite having little in common except our jobs. We were both coping with the loss of someone we'd loved. Not that we went around crying on each other's shoulders; we rarely did anymore. But there was a comfort in knowing that we could.

Amanda began refolding the shirt, her voice clipped, angry. "This tells us it was self-defense. That bastard Garber was drunk and jumped Weller. Tried to rape her.

She fought him off and managed to grab the bottle. End of story."

Andy said, "I know it looks that way, but . . . *Jesus.*"

"Now we know why the SECDEF is pushing to keep this quiet," Amanda said. "Think of the fallout if the word got out that the chairman of the Joint Chiefs was killed while attempting to rape his aide."

Simon had an uncomfortable expression. Like me, he wasn't completely buying this scenario. To Amanda, I said, "There's still a hole in your theory."

"Way ahead of you, Marty. It's the one thing I can't get around. How did Weller restrain Garber until he died?"

"She couldn't," Simon concluded.

"Not without help, anyway," Amanda said. "And that's the problem. Garber wouldn't have jumped her if someone else had been present in the compartment. That means they had to be alone. We also know Weller couldn't have left to get someone to help her, because if she had, Garber would have taken off. Right?"

We all nodded.

Amanda's eyes dropped to the shirt in her hand. "So what the hell are we missing? This has got to be the motive. Weller must have been the one who hit him. But how'd she hold him down without help?"

The only response was a sudden rumble from the hangar.

The hangar doors opened to a gap of maybe ten feet. We stepped clear as the Humvee containing General Garber's body drove out onto the tarmac. The giant doors immediately closed behind it.

Andy jammed two fingers in his mouth and whistled piercingly, signaling the driver to stop. To us, he said, "It seems to me you guys are forgetting something. Marty, didn't you say Weller was trying to confuse the investigation? Take the heat off the generals?"

I nodded.

"That's gotta be it, then. The shirt's a plant. Weller coulda planted it herself. I know this girl. She's smart, thinks on her feet. She knew you'd go through her bags. Take it from me, that's the way it played out. I'll let you know what I find out from the doc. Something tells me he's going to be one cooperative son of a bitch." He turned and hurried toward the Humvee.

"Plausible," Simon murmured, staring after him.

"You serious?" Amanda said. "You think Weller would go that far?"

A shrug. "Her fingernails suggest she might. Andy, hold on a moment."

He strolled after Andy, who had just opened a rear door of the Humvee. Amanda sighed and turned to me. "You agree with Simon?"

I thought back to Weller's interview. "Weller's nails are, what, close to a half inch long? If she fought with Garber, odds are she'd have broken a couple. At least scratched him."

"And if she didn't fight him?"

"Amanda, you said yourself there was a struggle."

"I said Garber attacked her. We don't know she fought back."

"Huh? Why wouldn't she—"

"Think about it, Marty. When Garber jumps her, she knows she can't possibly fend him off. He's twice her size. Screaming won't help her either, not with all the sound-proofing. So she decides to play along. When he lets down his guard, bam— She lets him have it with the bottle."

"Mind telling me who helped her restrain Garber?" I said.

"Who knows? All I'm saying is, it could have happened that way. That's what I'd have done if I'd been in her shoes. I'd go with the flow, wait my chance, then kill the son of a bitch."

Yes, I thought, she probably would.

And I decided I was okay with that.

Amanda and I watched as Andy and Simon stood by the Humvee, talking quietly. From the bits and pieces floating toward us, we knew they were discussing Weller. Amanda shook her head and turned to me. "Okay, maybe I'm mistaken."

"Can I get that in writing?"

She gave me a pained look and kept on talking. "Odds are Garber never jumped Weller. There are too many holes. She wouldn't be putting on this guilty act if she'd killed him. She's not that crazy."

"No."

She shook her head. "But for the life of me, I don't understand why she'd want to make Garber look like a rapist. It can't be simply because she wanted to confuse the investigation."

"Maybe she was trying to make a statement."

"A statement?" Her brow knitted. "Like what? You think she was trying to tell us Garber *was* a rapist? Maybe raped her?"

"Or tried to." I shrugged. "That would explain why she hated the guy so much."

She was quiet, thinking this over.

We were standing side by side, and I became aware of Amanda's nearness to me. Once again, I found myself fixating on her. I quickly looked away. What was wrong with me? Since Nicole's death, I'd never even noticed other women. Certainly not Amanda. Hell, we were just coworkers, friends. Nothing more. We couldn't be anything more. And yet . . .

I went back to the nights when I'd look out the sliding glass door and see her sitting on her porch all alone. That's when I remembered feeling the first subtle stirring of attraction. I'd find myself wanting to go over, keep her company. But I never did. I couldn't, because—

"Uh-oh," she said. "Wonder what that's about?"

Andy appeared startled at something Simon had just said. Simon kept on talking, and Andy's head bobbed. Andy patted his jacket pocket, as if responding to a question.

Amanda picked up on the gesture and said, "The check for Dr. Bowman?"

"Be my guess."

"How much, you think?"

"Enough to get Billy interested."

"So we're talking thousands?"

"Possibly more."

Amanda checked her watch. "We'd better head on back. We haven't got time to screw around, and the natives are probably getting restless."

"Simon won't be much longer."

"How about I swing by and ask Martha if any buttons turned up in the compartment? Meet you at maintenance?"

"Fine."

As Amanda turned to go, she hesitated, then asked softly, "Does Andy really think I'm a dyke?"

The statement hung in the air. "You know Andy. He shoots his mouth off before he thinks."

Her eyes crawled up to mine. "It's not just Andy. People have been spreading that stuff around about me since the academy. After all these years, you'd think it wouldn't get to me. I try not to let it, but I'm not as tough as people think. Sometimes I just get tired of putting up with all the . . ."

She bit her lip and looked away. The hurt returned to her eyes, and I found myself thinking about my comment to the helicopter pilot. My own little joke. And all the others I'd heard around the OSI office over the years. "I'm sorry," I said.

She shrugged. "Why? It's not your fault."

I didn't trust myself to reply.

Abruptly, she began speaking. Her voice had a faraway quality, as if she were talking more to herself than to me. "I've always been a jock since I was a kid. I suppose that's part of it. What makes the rumors so easy to believe. The first one started when I was a junior. There might have been some before. Probably were . . . Anyway, that was the first one I knew about. I went out with this guy for a few weeks. He was a senior. We had a fight because I wouldn't put out. He paid me back by telling his buddies I was into girls. A lez. He thought it was a joke. But it wasn't a joke. Not to me. The rumor got all over the school. People would say things to me, write things . . ." She blinked rapidly, turning to me. "It got so bad, I considered quitting. Almost did. But then, he would have won. So . . . I put up with it. When I became an officer, I thought things would change. It didn't. I suppose that's what's bothers me the most. That maybe it won't ever change. But . . . that's not true. Not entirely. It's the realization that maybe it's my fault. That there's something about me that makes guys assume—"

"Don't go there. You're not to blame. It's the way men are. We're sexist assholes."

She was silent, her face open and vulnerable.

I said, "You know you're a bright and attractive woman."

She blushed. "Marty, please . . ."

"Remember what you told me, that guys can't handle a strong, competent woman. You were right; a lot of them can't. They're too damned insecure. That's why they make up crap about you. It's a way to bring you down to their level. You have to remember that no one believes the rumors. They really don't."

"I wish I could believe that."

"*It's true.*"

"Andy believed the rumors."

I had no reply.

Neither one of us said anything for a while. Even under the bright sunlight, her skin appeared taut and smooth. Staring into her perfectly formed face, I felt something awaken inside me. I inhaled deeply, but the feeling remained.

She flashed an embarrassed smile and started to leave. "Sorry to get so heavy, huh?"

"Sure. Amanda . . ."

She looked back.

I reached for my wallet, dug out a business card, and passed it to her. "It's the helicopter pilot's card."

She frowned at it. "Why are you giving it to me?"

I tried to smile like I meant it. "Give him a call. You never know."

"Marty, I said I wasn't interested."

"Look," I said. "It's not right, what you're doing. You can't give up on relationships because of a few bad experiences—" I clammed up at a sudden coldness in her eyes.

"Relationships?" she breathed. "*You're* telling me about relationships?"

Uh-oh. "Amanda, I'm only trying to—"

"I can't believe this. I really can't. You of all people giving advice on relationships. *Please.*"

Her tone was harsh, almost mean. I had no idea why she was reacting this way. "What the hell is that supposed to mean?"

"You really don't know? Some fucking detective you are."

"Know what?"

She threw up a hand. "Forget it. It doesn't matter. Besides, you couldn't handle it."

Now I was getting angry. "What are you talking about?"

"I *said*, forget it, Marty."

"Dammit, if there's something I should—"

"I'm *tired*, Marty. I'm tired of waiting, hoping for something that will never come. But most of all, I'm sick and tired of you. Here, you like this guy so much, *you* go out with him." She flung the card at me and walked away.

Tired of me?

Amanda motored around the corner of the hangar. She was really moving, her long legs flying. I'd never seen her lose her temper like this, certainly not toward me. Whatever was behind her reaction, I was convinced it was more than my remarks. It had to be more than my remarks. Dammit, I hadn't said anything.

I turned at the sound of a car door slamming. The Humvee began driving toward the exit. Through a rear window, I could see Andy grinning at me from the back-seat, indicating he'd caught my scene with Amanda. With his big mouth, I figured I had maybe a week until every military investigator in area found out about our blow-up.

When it rains, it pours.

With a sigh, I shifted my attention to Simon, who was strolling up to me. "Want to tell me what that was about?" he asked mildly.

I fell into step beside him, and we continued toward the hangar. "Your guess is as good as mine." I explained the best I could.

Afterward, Simon shook his head patronizingly. "Martin . . . Martin . . ."

"What?"

"You. Your obliviousness. Frankly, you're a fool."

My jaw tightened. "Now just a damn minute—"

But he was talking over me, asking, "Do you really want her to go out with other men?"

"Sure. Of course. It's not healthy for her to—"

"Don't lie."

"I'm not lying. I think she should—"

"I *saw* you. I saw the way you looked at her."

My face got hot. "Simon, it's not what you think."

"It's *exactly* what I think. You have feelings for her."

I started to deny it. I wanted to deny it. But all I could think about were those nights I'd see Amanda sitting on her porch, and how much I'd wanted to talk to her. I shot back, "So what if I do?"

"Ah." His face relaxed into a smile. "Now maybe you understand why she became so angry."

I hesitated. "Actually, I'm not sure I do."

He looked at me like I was a certifiable idiot. "*She told you.*"

"But she didn't. All she said was she was tired of—"

And then I finally got it. I stared at him, unable to speak. My mouth felt like it was full of sand.

"My God," I finally managed, "it's me. She's waiting for me."

19

We came to the side door. Before opening it, I asked Simon, "How long have you known?"

"For the past six months."

"And you never said anything?"

He shrugged. "Amanda asked me not to."

"You know I can't act on this. It's too soon. I'm still not ready."

"Nicole has been gone three years."

"You're still mourning Romero."

"And I expect I always will. But I've accepted his death, and now I'm ready to move on."

"Bullshit," I said.

He gazed at me, his face softening. "She's a beautiful woman. She won't wait forever, Martin."

"I know." I swallowed. "It's Emily. It wouldn't be fair to her. She wouldn't understand. . . ."

"Have you asked her?"

I looked at him in shock. "Of course not."

"Doesn't Emily like Amanda?"

"As friends. This . . . this would be different. You don't have children. You wouldn't understand."

I saw the disappointment in his eyes. "That's the problem, Martin. I do understand."

He went inside the hangar.

As the door began to close behind him, I reached out to catch it and caught the glint of sunlight on my wedding ring. I froze, mesmerized by it.

It was a simple, gold-plated band that I'd bought for a couple hundred bucks. When Nicole and I got married, that was all I could scrape together on a second lieutenant's salary. In the twenty-three years since, I'd never removed it. And now, the thought of actually taking it off and sticking it in some box—

I felt a heaviness in my heart. Christ, how I missed her.

As I entered the hangar, Simon said, "You'll have to tell Amanda. It's kinder."

"I will."

The door closed behind us, and the two SPs moved aside to let us by. We saw Amanda going up the portable stairs. As she disappeared into the jet, I told Simon that she and I agreed with his conclusion about Weller's fingernails. "Andy's right. Weller probably didn't have a struggle with General Garber. Amanda's checking with Martha to see if any of the buttons were found in the compartment."

"I'd be surprised if they *didn't* find any, Martin."

"Oh?"

A step later it came to me. "Weller. You think she planted the buttons when she went into the compartment this morning?"

"That would explain her hysterical display."

"Display? She was putting on an act?"

"Without question. Colonel Gustin told us Weller was someone who rarely lost control of her emotions. Andy described Weller similarly. And you and I witnessed her reaction to my questions. To me, it's unlikely that someone with her composure would fall apart at the sight of the body of a man she despised."

His comment jogged my memory. In all the excitement, I'd forgotten to tell him about Churchfield. As I described her emotional reaction in the compartment, Simon began nodding.

"So you noticed her, too?" I said.

"Yes, but there's a difference. Churchfield's emotion seemed genuine. She was also clearly trying to hide her reaction from us."

"Obviously," I said, "there must be some history between her and Garber."

A nod. "It's something we should pursue, but I wouldn't put much faith that it has any bearing on the murder. Weller, on the other hand, had something to gain by her theatrics."

He glanced over, waiting to see if I could connect the dots.

"An excuse," I said. "Weller needed an excuse to stay in the compartment so she could plant the buttons."

"Yes. And if you recall where she sat . . ."

"On the chair with the robe. It would have been a cinch for her to slip the condom in the pocket. Busy girl."

An approving smile; I'd passed his little test. Still, I wasn't all that enamored of his latest theory. It bothered me that Weller, a junior aide, would be capable of orchestrating all this. Would be *willing* to do this. I mentioned my reservations to Simon.

"She had no choice. She's obviously acting under the orders of Churchfield."

I asked him why she would she want to make us think

Garber was a rapist, adding, "That seems excessive as hell. Amanda and I think maybe it's because Garber really was a rapist. Maybe he even tried to rape Colonel Weller in the past."

"That's certainly possible. I'm inclined to think the rape charge is a crucial element of the fallback plan."

"Fallback?"

"I think the military's term is contingency. You still don't see it? Think about it this way, Martin. From the beginning, Secretary Churchfield has orchestrated the cover-up like a military campaign. She had to consider that a ruling of accidental death might be unsuccessful. So, like any competent general, she developed a fallback position—"

I stopped so suddenly, he went by me a few steps. "Jesus. Blackmail."

"Yes."

"Senator Garber. She's going to blackmail him."

"If necessary, yes."

I spoke quickly, following the thread. "Hell, it all fits. If we keep pushing, get too close to the truth before the deadline expires, Churchfield will haul Colonel Weller before the senator, have her give him a song-and-dance about how she was attacked. With General Garber's reputation as a drinker and womanizer, it would be believable—"

"Yes—"

"—so the senator will be faced with a choice. The ultimate catch-22. Either he calls off the investigation, or Weller goes before the press and tells the world that his son is a rapist." I shook my head. "Churchfield had all the angles worked out. No matter what we do, she can't lose. Did I say something?" Simon was looking at me in a disapproving way.

"You're admitting defeat, Martin. Don't."

"The hell I am. I'm being realistic. This thing is over."

"If we uncover enough evidence in time, we can still prove—"

"*What* evidence? Churchfield's tainted the crime scene, thrown up bureaucratic roadblocks, pressured witnesses—"

"We have Dr. Bowman."

"Aren't you jumping the gun? He hasn't accepted your offer yet."

"He will."

I sighed as we resumed walking. "Fine. How much?"

"Initially, I told Andy to offer Dr. Bowman up to a hundred thousand."

"And now?"

"Up to a million."

I gave a low whistle. Even for Simon, this was a chunk of change. I asked, "Why the interest now? Earlier it sounded to me like you didn't care if we succeeded in solving the case."

"In some respects, I don't," he said. "But I'm committed to finding the truth."

"There's a difference?"

He shrugged.

"Fine," I said. "But I know Billy. He's gung-ho military, especially for a doc. I don't see him taking a bribe—"

Simon looked pained; he hated that term.

"—no matter how much money you toss at him. And even if he agrees to help, I doubt we'll get much we don't already know. Hell, we can pretty much guess the time of death and how much Garber had to drink. Now as to whether someone slipped Garber a Mickey, I thought we'd decided—"

I clammed up when I heard someone calling to us. It sounded like Amanda. Approaching the nose of the big jet, we turned toward the voice. She was waving to us from the top of the stairs. "Marty! Simon! Get up here now!"

Now what?

Amanda met us on the landing, looking thoroughly pissed off. A knot of somber-faced forensics team members were crowded into the entryway behind her, suggesting that I wasn't the sole source of her irritation.

"They found two shirt buttons," Amanda snapped.

I said, "So what's the problem?"

But she was already squeezing through the parting bodies. She led us into the forward section of the aircraft. Martha Jones was standing in the aisle by the cockpit door. As soon as she spotted me, Martha sprang forward and gestured to several cardboard evidence boxes on a nearby seat. "Marty, I swear I don't know how it happened. We kept the evidence in here, so it would be out of the way while we were working. I never thought to have anybody guard it. Why would I? I never even considered that anyone would . . . in all the years, nothing like this has ever . . ." She trailed off, her eyes locked on mine, searching for a sign I believed her.

By now I'd realized what had happened. I said, "Someone took the buttons?"

Martha nodded miserably.

"Not just the buttons," Amanda said. She directed me to one of the boxes; the lid was off, and we could see that it contained several glassine bags filled with blue hairs— carpet fibers that had been vacuumed. "Both the buttons and Weller's lipstick were in there. And they're gone."

"The bottle and glasses, too?" I said quietly.

"No. They're still here." She picked up a second box and raised the lid to show me.

For a moment, I was puzzled that glass with lipstick smear hadn't been taken. Then I realized it didn't matter; there was no lipstick to compare the smear with now.

There was a long silence. I could feel everyone's eyes on me, waiting to see how I was going to play this.

Martha touched my arm. "Marty, I swear to God. I had no idea that this would happen."

"No one called you from Churchfield's office. Told you to—"

"*No.*" She choked out the word.

I studied her. Martha and I went back almost fifteen years. She'd never lied to me before, and I knew she wasn't doing so now. I gave her a tiny smile. "I believe you."

She sagged with relief.

From behind me, Simon asked her, "The buttons? Where did you find them?"

"Sergeant Keele," Martha called out, looking past us. "Pete, you back there?"

We turned at a shout from the entryway. The CID men, Paul Carter and Tommy Gentry, who were standing at the front of the group, slid into nearby seats to make room for a slender, balding man who came forward.

"Wasn't it the couch, Pete?" Martha said.

Keele nodded. "One button was under it, near the right front leg. The second we found when we removed a cushion. It was lying next to one of the springs on the fold-out bed."

I said, "Did you check to see if there were any buttons on the bed?"

"Sure did, sir," Keele said. "We unfolded it. Took apart

the sheets. Nothing. Not even a hair sample. Never was slept in."

"Thanks, Pete."

Keele nodded and stepped back.

My eyes went down the tense faces, peering back at me. I knew I was wasting my time, but I had to take a shot. I repeated my question about anyone receiving calls from Churchfield's office and got negative responses all around.

I asked, "How about from the offices of General Markel, General Sessler, or General Johnson?"

Denials and head shakes.

"Did anyone of you receive a call from *anyone* in the Pentagon?"

More head shakes.

I asked if anyone had an idea who might have removed the evidence from the box. This time, the denials were even more emphatic. Then I noticed Paul Carter.

He was sitting rigidly in his seat, his eyes fixed blankly on his lap. He glanced up as if to say something, then saw me looking. His eyes dropped again.

Simon was also watching him. "Something wrong, Paul?" he asked.

Paul's head rose slowly. "No. Of course not, Lieutenant. Why?"

"You seem preoccupied."

A nervous smile. "It's my wife, Lieutenant. She's due in a few days. Our first kid and all."

Simon smiled understandingly. "We'll see if we can't wrap things up soon, Paul."

"I'd appreciate it, Lieutenant."

Afterward, another silence fell upon everyone. I knew the team members expected me to jump down their throats, read them the riot act. I didn't. In a quiet voice, I reminded them that we were acting with the support of Senator Garber. I calmly informed them that I intended to find who had removed the evidence. "When I do," I added, "the senator and I will ensure that person is prosecuted to the full extent of the law. The same goes for anyone who knows who that person is and has chosen not to come forward. Questions? No? Get back to work."

As everyone drifted away, Simon made a suggestion to Amanda. She immediately went over to Paul Carter and Tommy Gentry, telling them to stay seated.

Martha Jones said to me, "I'll personally supervise all the remaining evidence. Log everything in and out myself. This won't happen again, Marty."

I gave her hand a squeeze. "Forget it. It wasn't your fault."

She hesitated. "We've also got a problem with General Garber's classified briefcase. It's Chairman's Eyes Only. Technically, we don't have the clearance to take possession. You want me to find a safe until I get the authorization?"

"It's still in the closet?"

"Yeah."

"I'll take care of it."

"While you're there, you also might want to take a look at the lower right wall. When we bagged the pillows, we noticed some marks that are a little curious."

"Oh? What kind of marks?"

20

====

Amanda was kneeling in the aisle, talking to Paul Carter, while Tommy Gentry looked on. I slid by her, looking for Simon, but he'd disappeared.

I went to the compartment to retrieve the briefcase. It was a zoo. Nate Green and Thad Fuller were removing the door so they could analyze it in the lab. They would do the same thing with the closet doors. Inside the room, three fresh-faced latent-fingerprint specialists were in the process of dusting literally every inch of the room. The photographer Bobby Baker was standing outside the bathroom, shooting the interior. Over by the couch, I saw Simon talking with Sergeant Pete Keele. Keele removed a cushion, pointed down. Simon leaned over and stared for few moments, then nodded in satisfaction.

He came up behind me as I bent down to retrieve the briefcase from the closet. "Excuse me, Martin."

But I didn't move. I was studying the base of the right wall, the area that had been blocked by the blanket and pillows. Against the stark white siding I could see the black smudge marks that Martha had mentioned. They were roughly an inch above the closet floor. I checked the left side. Clean.

Simon said, "Martin—"

When I stood, he was slipping on latex gloves. I pointed out the marks and moved aside so he could kneel down for a look.

"Heel marks," he concluded, a moment later.

I said, "That means someone must have passed through the closet into the hallway."

Garber's uniform and hangup bags were still hanging inside. Simon slid them against the left wall, then bent forward until his face was inches from the heel marks. "I count seven—"

I said, "Martha said there were eight."

Simon nodded. "Why so many?"

I'd been wondering the same thing. One or two could be explained by someone using the closet as a passageway and catching a heel. But that many . . .

"Could be someone hid inside here," I said. "But that doesn't make much sense either. Why would the killer hang around in the closet after killing Garber?"

Simon stood. "Perhaps the marks were there previously."

"I doubt it. Left side's clean. Besides, with all the heavy hitters who use the compartment, I imagined it's cleaned thoroughly after every flight. I can check."

Simon panned over the closet interior. After a several seconds, he unzipped one of the hangup bags and started searching through the contents. I saw a short-waisted formal mess-dress blouse, another medaled jacket, a couple uniform shirts, three slacks—

"You looking for anything in particular?" I asked.

No response. He felt around the bottom of the bag,

zipped it up, then methodically went through the side pockets, removing a series of items. Shoes, socks, belts, ties, T-shirts . . .

He turned his attention to the second bag, which contained mostly civilian clothing. Finding nothing of interest, he began scrutinizing the locks on both the interior and exterior doors. He carefully locked and unlocked each one a number of times, then shook his head. "It doesn't seem possible."

He was talking about locking the doors from the outside. I said, "Try this: What if the reason for Weller's emotional display was to distract everyone so her accomplice could lock the door?"

"The interior door, perhaps. But the person would have had to open the closet, reach inside and lock the exterior door, close the closet, lock the interior door, then step away, all without being noticed."

I looked around the cramped room, picturing where everyone would have been standing. Iffy to impossible. I said, "So it has to be the main door."

Simon glanced to Nate and Thad, who had finally freed the door from the hinges. He said to me, "I assume they'll x-ray it?"

"Yeah. If they don't find a way to manipulate the locking mechanism."

"How long until they know?"

When I asked, Thad said it would be another couple of hours until they finished up in here and hauled the doors to the lab. He said he'd rush the inspection and call the moment he had something.

"Who else on the base will know whether the door can be locked from the outside?" Simon asked me.

"The flight crew and maintenance." I mentioned the

Secret Service, but Simon didn't want to go down that road; we'd have to break the code of silence and explain why we wanted to know. He clicked the closet shut, shaking his head. When he turned to me, his face was knitted with concern. Unlike earlier, he now seemed anxious to find an explanation. I asked him why.

"All along," he said, "I assumed there had to be a simple way to lock the door from the outside. That we would eventually discover it. Now I'm not so certain."

"There has to be a way, Simon. Garber sure as hell didn't kill himself."

His face spread into a tired smile. "Let's hope I'm mistaken, Martin."

As we left, I had a suspicion he was talking about more than the door.

On our way out we saw Amanda, still engrossed in conversation with Paul Carter and Tom Gentry. She signaled she was almost done, so Simon and I continued out onto the landing to wait. He sighed deeply and leaned back against the railing, eyes fixed blankly into space. For the next minute, neither of us spoke. Finally, I told him that if the crew couldn't give us the answer on the door, I'd contact maintenance. "Either way," I said, "we should have something fairly soon."

"Actually," Simon said, "I was thinking about the buttons that were found."

"What about them?"

"I'm wondering when Weller had an opportunity to plant them."

"Didn't we decide she did it after she entered the compartment and found the body?"

"How could she, Martin?"

"Easy. She just did it. In the confusion, she kicked one button under the couch and slipped the second one—"

And then I saw the problem. "Hang on. The body. It was in *front* of the couch. Andy would have kept Weller away from the body. Weller couldn't have planted the buttons then."

"You wouldn't think so."

"Later?" I said. "You think Weller planted the items later? After the body was found?"

"Andy said the room was always guarded."

"Right. So she must have done it earlier, during the flight." I paused, thinking. "Hell, anyone on the plane could have planted the buttons then. Even one of the generals."

Simon nodded, but still appeared uneasy. I asked him what else was bugging him.

"It's probably nothing."

"Try me."

A long pause. "The button under the couch. I was surprised it was found there."

"Why?"

"Various reasons." He gave a shrug and looked away.

In Simon-speak, that meant he wasn't going to confide in me. Part of his reluctance could be explained by his secretive nature. The rest could be attributed to his ego; Simon had an aversion to guessing wrong. He often played the I've-got-a-secret game until he could confirm the validity of his suspicions. An annoying trait, but after ten years of working with him, I'd gotten used to it. Sort of.

"*That* was fun."

Simon and I turned to see Amanda standing behind us. I tested her with a friendly smile. She ignored both it and me. Simon said to her, "And?"

"I think Paul Carter's just rattled because of his kid."

He said, "You *think?*"

"It's nothing I can put my foot on. But I couldn't shake the feeling he was holding back something."

Simon said, "So he *could* have taken the evidence?"

"He swore up and down that he didn't." She paused. "And frankly, I believe him."

Simon said, "Enough to let him finish questioning the passengers?"

"I don't know. Maybe."

Big help. I asked her about Tom Gentry.

She turned to me with bland indifference, trying to act as if she wasn't upset with me, which of course meant she still was. "He told me he'd searched the aft portion of the plane and never came up to the forward section."

"And you believe him, too?"

"No reason not to." She contemplated me for a moment. "You know, there's someone else we have to consider. If Tom and Paul *are* involved—"

I knew where she was going and cut her off. "Amanda, give it a rest. Just because Andy's their boss doesn't mean—"

"Get real, Marty. Andy is Andy. He's always been out for himself. If someone up the chain offered him a deal or a promotion, he'd sell out his own mother."

"That's not fair, and you know it."

"So you're saying you have no reservations about him at all? You trust him completely?"

I hesitated.

"Aha." She looked triumphantly at Simon. "I rest my case."

"Can anyone be trusted completely?" he asked her.

"Well, maybe not, but—"

"Precisely. So we must act accordingly." Addressing me, Simon said, "If it helps, Sergeant Keele is convinced someone on his team took the evidence. A number are new and inexperienced, not the usual complement who'd get assigned to an important investigation. Sergeant Keel suspects they were chosen because they wouldn't question an order to tamper with the evidence. I tend to agree."

Which almost certainly meant we were talking about more than one person. I felt a wave of frustration. "This is bullshit. How are we supposed to work this way? For all we know, half the team might have been ordered to quash the evidence."

"You expected anything less, Martin?" Simon asked.

I shot him a look of annoyance. "What? You telling me you thought they'd steal evidence from under our noses?"

"This is only the beginning," he said quietly. "We represent a threat. Someone has already killed the ranking officer in the military. Depending on who is responsible and how desperate that person becomes . . ." He fell silent, letting us draw our own conclusions.

Amanda and I stood there, weighing the enormity of what he was implying. "Jesus," she murmured.

I was going to tell Simon he was overreacting, that even if one of the generals was the murderer, he'd never dare go after us. For chrissakes, we were the cops.

Then I remembered his earlier comment to Weller, the one that put everything in perspective.

Soldiers kill.

At the bottom of the stairs, we hung a right toward the maintenance offices. I checked my watch: a little after ten A.M. Since we couldn't count on Paul Carter or Tom

Gentry or anyone else, we were now faced with the problem of questioning twenty people in thirty minutes. That meant we had to go at them in groups—all except one.

I told Simon to take the flight crew and Amanda the passengers, while I interviewed the flight attendant, Sergeant Blake. Afterward, I asked Simon about another point that had been nagging at me.

"I don't understand," I said, "why anyone would remove the buttons and the lipstick in the first place. I thought Churchfield *wanted* this to look like a rape."

Amanda's head spun around to us. "What's *this*?"

"I imagine," Simon said slowly, "it's about maintaining control."

I said, "Explain."

"Secretary Churchfield," he continued, "is leaving nothing to chance. She's established the evidence at the crime scene. She now wants the evidence in her possession. She wants to be the one to determine if and when to confront Senator Garber."

I had to admit it made sense. Churchfield certainly hadn't become the first female SECDEF by shying away from political hardball, or worse.

"You guys want to tell me what the hell you're talking about?" Amanda said.

We were almost to the double doors. I said, "Later. Right now we have to—"

I felt her squeeze my arm hard. "Someone start talking."

Simon and I found ourselves confronted by a pair of very determined green eyes.

"I'll leave you two alone," Simon said. As he continued through the door, he mouthed, *Tell her now.*

Something lurched in my stomach. I said quickly, "Simon, I think it would be better if you—"

The door shut behind him.

Amanda eyed me expectantly, releasing my arm.

I could feel my face redden. It took me a couple false starts to get up the nerve to speak. I began, "Amanda, there's something you should know, first. It's about our argument earlier . . ."

I fell silent, unable to voice the words. I tried to will them out, but they wouldn't come. It felt like my vocal cords were paralyzed.

A resigned look appeared in Amanda's eyes, as if she sensed what I was trying to say. "Just tell me, Marty."

"I . . . upset you earlier. I was out of line. I'd like to apologize."

"I see." She waited, looking a little puzzled. "Is that all?"

When I nodded, she seemed relieved. She gave me a smile. It was a nice smile.

As I laid out Simon's suspicions about Secretary Churchfield's role in the cover-up, I kept asking myself why I couldn't just tell her the truth. Was it simply that I didn't want to hurt her? Or was it that I didn't know what the hell I really wanted?

Christ.

Approaching the office, Amanda and I saw Simon leading the flight crew down the hallway. They disappeared into another room.

"I've got a few questions for Colonel Gustin about General Markel," I told Amanda. "Give me ten minutes, then send in Sergeant Blake."

"Rog." She swung left into the break room.

Moments after entering the office, I knew Colonel Gustin was through answering questions. She was seated at the table, a cell phone to her ear, staring at me with frightened eyes. She spoke loudly because she wanted me to hear.

"No, General Markel," she said. "I didn't tell them anything."

21

I took the seat across from Colonel Gustin. She ended the call moments later and returned the cell phone to her purse with a shaky hand.

I said, "Colonel Gustin . . ."

"Don't." Her head shot up. "Don't even ask."

"What weren't you supposed to tell me?"

She shook her head. "I can't say anything. He ordered me not to say anything. Please."

"Did General Markel kill General Garber?"

"No one killed him. It was an accident."

"Colonel, I need your help."

"I can't." She sprang to her feet. "Don't you understand? *I can't!*"

"At least tell me why you're so frightened of General Markel."

She was incredulous. "Haven't you seen him?"

"Yes—"

"Then you know."

I motioned to her chair. "Please sit down, Colonel."

"No. I have nothing to say."

"Tell me why Colonel Weller seems to admire General Markel so much."

"I told you, I won't answer any—"

"Tell me, and you can go." I gave her a reassuring smile.

She squinted, tempted but suspicious. "You . . . promise?"

"Yes."

A tongue flicked nervously over her lips. "Tina . . . we're not very close. I couldn't say for sure. I'd only be guessing."

"I understand."

She inhaled deeply, then nodded. "One reason Tina's attracted to General Markel is because he thinks the way she does. All that stuff they taught us in boot camp, how the military isn't a job, but a calling. Well, she believes it, and so does General Markel. They're both so dedicated it's scary. The military is their life; it's who they are." She paused, thinking. "I suppose another reason why Tina looks up to General Markel is because he won't play the political games. He's the only four-star who will stand up to Congress or the presidential staff and tell them exactly what he thinks. You remember that mission to go after the Taliban in the mountains of Afghanistan?"

"Tora Bora," I said.

"Right. All the other chiefs told Secretary Churchfield it was a good idea to get the Afghans to fight most of that battle for us, so there'd be less American casualties. General Markel argued against it, saying we couldn't trust the Afghans because a lot of them had been fighting with the Taliban only weeks earlier. Churchfield went with General Markel's recommendation, but got overruled by the president. When General Markel found out, he made an appointment with the president and told him he had no business interfering with military strategy."

"I'm surprised Markel wasn't fired," I said.

"You and everyone else." She shrugged. "But General Markel's a Special Forces legend in the army because of what he did in Vietnam. Since the Special Forces play a key role in this war, the president probably realized he couldn't fire a big hero like him without risking morale problems. He also would have risked getting into a confrontation with Secretary Churchfield; she's a big supporter of General Markel. As it turns out, the general was proved right. The Afghans we sent into the mountains did allow a lot of the Taliban to escape."

"Including bin Laden?"

A nod. "Anyway, that's pretty much why Tina admires General Markel. She sees him as this bigger-than-life warrior. A real, live John Wayne figure." She plucked the strap of her purse from the back of her chair and slipped it on. "He feels the same way about Tina. Likes her, I mean. That's what makes it so hard for me. Because she's his favorite and always will be." She sounded bitter.

I said, "Favorite?"

She shook her head at me. "Our deal was one question. You want to know anything else, talk to Tina. I've already said more than I should." She turned for the door.

I said, "I don't understand how she became Markel's favorite."

She kept walking.

I said, "At least tell me if you consider General Markel unstable, Colonel."

This was a question she couldn't resist answering. She stopped, looking back. "Do you think someone who spent two years volunteering for suicide missions is unstable?"

"Either that or extremely brave."

"Flip a coin." She opened the door and walked out.

Favorite.

I slowly circled the word in my notepad. I'd vaguely recalled seeing Weller's name, but couldn't remember where—

I dropped my pen, dug out the itinerary from my jacket, and flipped through it until I found Markel's schedule. About halfway down a page, I spotted the notation. At a dinner with the British defense minister two nights earlier, Colonel Gustin's name been lined out as General Markel's escort. And just below, someone had written: "Weller."

So it was true.

Now the question was, How did an air force officer become the favorite of an army general? I was about to jot down a few possibilities, when I heard the sound of footsteps. Through the open door, I saw a woman coming timidly across the hallway toward me. I beckoned her over.

There were two reasons I was anxious to question the flight attendant, Sergeant Blake. First, with the possible exceptions of the four-stars, she was probably in the best position to see who entered the compartment during the flight. Second, by my calculations, she was the last known person other than the killer to have seen General Garber alive.

But the problem with calculations is they're based on assumptions. In this case, my key assumption proved wrong.

Sergeant Blake wasn't the last person to see the general alive.

22

Master Sergeant Sandra Blake was a washed-out-looking peroxide blonde in her late forties. Judging by the swell of her more-than-ample bosom, she'd once been the kind of woman who could make men walk into walls. But that particular ability ended at least thirty pounds and ten years ago. I had the impression her face was still attractive, but it was hard to be sure because of the heavy makeup she wore.

Still, I liked her smile, which she targeted at me the moment she walked in. It disappeared into a tactful line at the mention of General Garber.

Unlike Colonel Gustin, Blake seemed eager to cooperate. She verified that she'd made up the bed for Garber at the request of Colonel Weller. Yes, the general had told her he intended to go to sleep and didn't want to be disturbed. No, she didn't know of anyone who entered the compartment after she left. And no, she never heard anything unusual during the flight.

"It's difficult to hear much from the hallway, sir. The compartment's soundproofed, and with the noise from the exhaust fan—"

"So I've been told. Could someone have entered the compartment without you knowing?"

She thought. "I was at my station or in the galley most of the time. Chances are I would have noticed, sir."

"Isn't your station around the corner, near the passenger door?"

"Yes, sir. But on night flights, we always darken the hallway and overhead lights. If someone had opened the general's door, I'd have seen the light from his room."

"And if his room light wasn't on?"

She hesitated, then shook her head.

I marked this on my pad and asked if she knew of a way to lock or unlock either the main or closet doors from the outside. She shook her head without hesitation.

I said, "Surely the Secret Service must have a way to get inside in case of an emergency."

"All I can tell you is that I've flown a number of vice-presidential trips. If there's a way, the Secret Service never told me."

"Would they have?"

She shrugged.

"If you knew a way, would you tell me?"

Her eyes widened. "Why, yes, sir. Of course."

Her reaction seemed sincere. I looked her in the eyes and asked if she been ordered not to tell us the truth about the door.

She met my gaze. "No, sir. No one said anything to me."

Either she was telling the truth, or she was an exceptionally practiced liar. I asked her if she'd opened the closet during the flight. She said she had, to get the bedding for the bed. She looked puzzled when I asked if she'd noticed heel marks on the right wall of the closet.

"Why would there be heel marks, sir?"

"I take it you didn't see any."

"No, sir." She hesitated.

I said, "Go on."

"I'm thinking I *should* have noticed the marks. I usu-ally watch for dirt or stains. You know, so I can notify the cleaning crews. Do you mind telling me where the marks were, sir?"

"On the right wall, just above the floor."

She looked relieved. "That explains it. I only opened the *left* door to get the bedding. I never even noticed the right wall."

Which meant the marks could have been present. I asked if she knew who was in charge of cleaning the com-partment when the plane returned from a trip.

"That would be Chief Master Sergeant Wiffel. He's in charge of passenger services cleaning crews. It's spelled e-l."

"If someone entered or left the compartment, either by the closet or the main door, would you have heard any-thing? Perhaps the sound of the doors closing?"

"Sir, no one enters through the closet."

"But they could."

"Well, yes, sir . . ."

"Assuming they did, would you have heard anything?"

"I'd have to be right up close, sir. The fan is awfully loud."

"So you wouldn't have heard anything from your sta-tion or the galley?"

"No, sir."

Great. "The other generals," I said, switching gears. "Are you responsible for serving them?"

"Yes, sir."

"Did you see any of them in the hallway outside General Garber's compartment?"

"Not once we took off, sir. While we were on the ground, the chiefs had a meeting with General Garber in his compartment."

"How long did the meeting last?"

"Five, ten minutes."

"Anyone else in the meeting besides the generals?"

"Some of the aides and execs were probably there. They often were."

"Colonel Weller and Colonel Gustin?"

"I'm not sure, sir. It was a closed-door meeting." She added, "You might ask Agent Hobbs. I think I saw him leaving the compartment around then."

I frowned. "Why would Agent Hobbs attend a closed-door meeting of the generals?"

"He normally wouldn't, sir. I assumed he was finishing his security check of the compartment. He made one before every leg."

Diligent Andy. I asked Blake if the generals remained in their section during the flight.

"As far as I know. They were always there when I saw them."

"Was anyone else with them?"

"Yes, sir. Colonel Weller."

"What time was this?"

Her forehead knitted. "I'm not sure. After 0200. Maybe 0210 hours."

"What was Colonel Weller doing?"

"She was just sitting there with General Markel. He asked me to bring her some coffee."

This seemed to validate Gustin's "favorite" comment. "They weren't talking?"

"No, sir. No one was talking. They were just sitting there."

"How did everyone appear?"

"Appear?"

"Did they seem anxious or upset?"

A head shake. "They all looked pretty normal, sir." She paused, blushing slightly. "General Markel commented he liked my perfume."

So did I. The only problem was, I could smell it the moment she'd entered the office. I asked her if she knew how long Colonel Weller had remained with the generals.

"I don't know, sir. General Markel said they didn't want to be bothered. He said they'd call if they needed anything. An hour before landing, I came by to see if they wanted breakfast. By then, Colonel Weller was gone."

"She was the only other person you saw with the generals?"

"Yes, sir."

Scanning my notes, I said, "Getting back to General Garber, when you made up his bed, did he seem drunk to you?"

No response. I glanced up.

She hesitated. "I didn't actually see him, sir."

I flipped back a page, frowning. "I thought he instructed you that he didn't want to be disturbed."

"He was in the shower when I went to make up his bed. He talked to me through the door."

"I see. Did you take him any drinks?"

"No, sir."

"You're certain? We found some glasses from the galley that we think he used."

"They didn't come from me. We took off real late from

England. The general already had dinner. Colonel Weller told me the general would ring if he needed anything. He never did. Not even to ask for a drink."

"Isn't that unusual?"

"A little. General Garber always had a martini. Sometimes several." She gave me a knowing look.

"Martinis? He wasn't a whisky drinker?"

"He might have been. I've always served him martinis. Occasionally a Manhattan."

I put a question mark by this. "I take it you flew with General Garber before he became chairman."

"A few times. When he was the vice chief of the air force."

I closed my notepad and studied her. "Did you like him?"

She considered her answer. "I guess I felt sorry for him, sir. I've been a flight attendant for fifteen years, sir. Flown a lot of important people. Presidents, senators, kings, actors, you name it. Some were nice, regular people. A lot of them were . . . difficult. Still, even if you didn't like them, you always respected them. You know, because they earned their place. I'm not sure if you understand what I'm trying to say."

"I think I do." I added, "Did you respect the general, Sergeant?"

"I thought he deserved my respect. I mean, he was the chairman of the Joint Chiefs."

"Even if he didn't really earn it."

Her eyes chilled slightly. "That's not for me to judge, is it, sir?"

A deserved rebuke; there was a lot more substance to Sergeant Blake than I'd first realized. "Yours is a minority view, Sergeant."

"I'm aware of that, sir. I don't think it's right for some- one to die and nobody cares." Her voice grew quiet. "It's true, sir. Nobody cares that he's dead. It's . . . sad."

I asked, "Do you think he was murdered?"

"I don't see how, sir. The compartment was locked."

"Forget about that."

She still seemed uncomfortable with the question. I went through the standard spiel about keeping what she said confidential.

She drew in a deep breath. "I think he *could* have been murdered, sir."

"Any guesses on suspects? Perhaps one of the other gen- erals—Yes?" She'd been shaking her head and stopped.

"I'm not sure I should say. It was more of a joke."

"Let me decide."

"About six weeks ago, I was working a trip to China. One of those military fact-finding missions. General Garber was on board. He'd been drinking quite a bit. He seemed upset. When I brought him another drink, he said something to me. You know, like he was kidding, but you could tell he wasn't. He said if anything ever hap- pened to him, I was supposed to remember a name. He even wrote it down for me. On a piece of paper. Made me take it. Kept saying it was important."

"What was the name?"

"That's just it. I can't remember."

"Where's the paper?"

"I don't know. I might have thrown it away."

"Was it a man or woman?"

"I . . . I'm not really sure. It was something foreign."

"Foreign?"

"Asian. It was Asian."

"You were flying to China."

"It could have been Chinese." She shook her head apologetically. "Maybe it will come to me later."

"Were there any Chinese people on the airplane?"

"No, sir."

"Will you look for the paper?"

Her head bobbed. "Yes, sir. As soon as I get home."

"Call if you find it." I handed her my card.

I watched curiously as she rose from the table and threw a couple glances my way. After the third one, I asked her if she had something else to tell me.

"Do you . . . do you believe General Garber was really murdered, sir?"

"Yes."

"There's no mistake?"

"No."

She grew quiet, her eyes dropping to the floor. "This isn't easy, sir. I've got a couple years to retirement. And with two kids in college . . ." She drifted off, wrestling with her decision.

I didn't say anything. I just waited for her to make up her mind.

She finally looked up at me. "What you said earlier, sir. About keeping anything I say confidential . . ."

"Your superiors won't know."

A vague nod. "I . . . I lied, sir."

"About?"

"We . . . we were instructed not to cooperate with the investigation by General Markel."

Big surprise. "He spoke to you personally?"

"He called each of us crew members at home."

"So what you were telling me about the door—"

"That part is true. I don't think it can be locked from the outside."

I contemplated her. "Why are you telling me all this now?"

A sad smile played over her lips. "Some people are saying it's a good thing General Garber is dead. That he got what he deserved. It's not right. He wasn't as bad as everyone thinks. And now that's he's been murdered . . ." Her lip trembled. "Anyway, I think it's my duty to do what I can to help."

I said gently, "You must have liked him a great deal?"

"He is . . . was . . . always good to me, sir."

Our eyes met, and an unspoken moment passed between us. I glanced to her ring finger; the wedding band was there. I smiled. "Thank you for your honesty, Sergeant."

As I watched her leave, I was torn. I liked her and was tempted to let her walk away. But I had to know.

"Wait, Sergeant."

23

After Sergeant Blake departed, I phoned the base operator for the numbers of the Andrews Support Division—the civilian maintenance contractors—and Passenger Services. I called the maintenance section first, asked for the commander, and was transferred to a Mr. Hardin.

Hardin gave me the answer I expected. No, the DV compartment's main and closet doors locked only from the inside.

"You'd swear to that, Mr. Hardin?"

"On a stack of Bibles."

"Gideon or King James?"

"I prefer Gideon. It's easier to read."

The guy was quick. "Appreciate the help."

I hung up, frowning. Hardin's familiarity with Bibles notwithstanding, I tried to convince myself he had to be lying about the doors. The operative word was *tried*. Like Simon, I was also beginning to have doubts.

When I phoned Passenger Services, Chief Wiffel was out, but I got his deputy, a Technical Sergeant Pantera. Pantera had one of those Tinkerbell voices that made her sound about twelve. After identifying myself, I asked her if the cleaning crews routinely scrubbed the closet walls after each trip.

"Always, sir."

"So if there were black smudges on the interior wall—"

"Sir," she said stiffly, "the C-32 flies the vice president, the secretary of state, members of Congress, and major heads of state. We pride ourselves on attention to detail."

"Understood, Sergeant. Thank you."

I slowly cradled the receiver. The more I thought about it, the crazier it seemed that the killer would use the closet as a passageway more than once. Each time he did, he was taking a gamble. Anyone spotting him would have wondered why he hadn't used the main door.

No. To make that many heel marks, our boy must have hidden in the closet. And if so . . .

I sat up, grabbed General Garber's classified briefcase, since I couldn't leave it unguarded, and hurried out of the office, hoping I was in time.

I poked my head into the DV compartment and relaxed. The latent print techs still hadn't gotten around to dusting the interior of the closet. After ordering them to hold off, I told Sergeant Keele to make sure no one touched the closet until he got the okay from Martha.

I found Martha in the forward section, carefully marking a glassine packet with stick-on tape. Initially, the packet appeared empty, but when she held it up for me, I saw what appeared to be a single hair.

"That's all the hairs we collected from the shower," she said.

My eyebrows went up. Usually we recovered a small nest. "You remove the drain cap?"

"How do you think we found this one? Notice the color?"

I was squinting, trying to. "Brown?"

"Closer to red. Since General Garber's got gray hair, we know it wasn't his. Could be the vice president's."

I nodded; the Veep had a full head of auburn hair.

Martha searched my face. "You're the detective. Any guesses why someone might have cleaned up the shower after General Garber used it and removed all his hair?"

I shook my head. This was another curve out of right field.

She wearily tossed the packet in an evidence box. "Some case, huh, Marty. It's days like this that make me regret not taking the early-retirement package last year. What's that you got in your hand? More lipstick? Who's the lucky girl, or should I ask?"

"The flight attendant, Sergeant Blake." I passed her the container and asked her to personally honcho the color-comparison analysis. I also told her I wanted her to supervise the fingerprinting of the closet interior, to make sure no one "accidentally" wiped away any prints.

"Marty, I'd like to help. But right now I'm a one-woman show. As it is, I'll be lucky to finish up anywhere close to the deadline."

"It's important, Martha."

She sighed, looking at me. "You're going to ride my screwup for all it's worth, aren't you?"

I winked. "What do you think?"

A wry smile. "I guess I deserve it. You win, I'll see what I can do. Might be a while until I can get around to it. Couple hours okay?"

"Thanks, Martha."

"Oh, for what it's worth—" She picked up her

notepad from a seat, flipped several pages, handed it to me.

"An informal survey," she said. "I asked my team if any of them knew who might have taken the evidence. I got denials straight down the line. That's what the n in the first column means. So I asked them whom they *suspected* might have been responsible. Big change. See the names."

I nodded, scanning the page.

"Andy," Martha said. "Nine out of twelve think it's Andy."

"They say why?"

She shrugged. "He's a jerk."

"So it doesn't mean much?"

"Probably not."

I passed her the notepad back. "You might have made a mistake on Sergeant Keele's response. You've got him down as suspecting Andy."

She looked puzzled. "Sure. That's what he told me. You heard different?"

After I related Simon's comment, she said, "Simon must have misunderstood, Marty."

"Probably."

On my way out, I swung by the compartment again and asked Keele to step into the hallway.

"Suspect the new guys, sir?" he said. "Who the hell told you that?"

It was a little after 1030 hours when I returned to the maintenance offices. I punched my mental time clock and figured we had less than ten hours to wrap this up. Simon and Amanda were both emerging from their respective rooms with their groups. From their tight-jawed expressions, I could tell their sessions hadn't gone well. Big surprise.

As I approached them, Simon gave me a questioning

look. I shook him off, avoiding his gaze and the look of disgust that came with it.

Before releasing the passengers and crew, Amanda passed out her card and instructed them to call if they remembered anything. They listened politely, but as they left, several people tossed the cards in a nearby trashcan.

"Assholes," Amanda said, as we trailed the group down the hallway.

I said, "Sergeant Blake said they were ordered by General Markel to stiff-arm us."

She and Simon looked to me in surprise. He said, "Sergeant Blake cooperated?"

"Completely. She liked Garber and wants to help us find the killer."

Simon read my face. "Define *liked*."

We pushed through the double doors into the hangar. I knew what he was really asking. "She denied that she and General Garber were having an affair."

"And your impressions . . ."

"She was telling the truth. She'd flown with General Garber a number of times, and he was always pleasant to her."

"There was no other contact?"

"Not according to her."

"Uh, Marty," Amanda said, "I hate to break the news to you, but *no one* liked Garber."

I glanced at her. "Not unless she was screwing him, you mean."

"Not even then."

"Look," I said. "Even if she was sleeping with him, I know she couldn't have anything to do with the killing. She's hasn't got it in her. Besides, she's married with a couple of kids, and—"

I gave up when Amanda's eyes glazed over. "You had to be there."

"Uh-huh."

Simon said, "Her lipstick?"

"Red. I gave it to Martha to check out."

We walked along. They kept looking at me, waiting for me to say it.

"Fine," I said, caving in. "We'll put her down as a possible suspect."

"There, now," Amanda said cheerfully. "Was that so hard?"

I ignored her and focused on Simon. "By the way, Sergeant Keele says he never told you he thought some of the new people might have taken the evidence."

"Really? How odd?"

"I thought so."

"I wouldn't worry about it. Sergeant Keele is probably confused."

"He says he isn't."

Simon shrugged. "He must be. Either that, or he lied to you."

"Why would he lie?"

He gave me a tired smile. "Possibly he doesn't want his coworkers to be irritated with him. Whatever his reason, I wouldn't worry about it."

"Maybe Keele lied to you because he's one who took the evidence."

"It's not Keele."

"How do you know?"

"Forget about Keele. It's not him."

He wouldn't discuss the subject further.

24

Most of the Arlington PD called Simon's limo the Batmobile, even though I've always thought a comparison to the Green Hornet's car might be more accurate. I'm not suggesting that Simon's limo has built-in rocket launchers, or machine guns, or any of that comic-book crime-fighter stuff. Of course it doesn't.

But it has practically everything else.

Last year, Simon blew an arrest because he didn't receive a crucial fax in time. To ensure he was never placed in that position again, he shelled out big bucks for a limo packed with every luxury item and high-tech gizmo your average multimillionaire homicide cop could possibly want. In addition to the prerequisite stocked bar and fridge of goodies, there was a plasma-screen TV, a VCR and DVD player, two independent satellite phone systems, both broadband Internet capable, a modular desk that contained a laptop and a dual-purpose printer and fax machine, and probably another half-dozen little items I still don't know about—all controlled by an overhead touch-tone screen that looked like it could launch the space shuttle.

"No hot tub?" Amanda said as we climbed in.

Simon and I took the rearmost seat while Amanda camped beside the computer desk, which swivelled on a steel arm attached to the reinforced frame. The chauffeur du jour was a bespectacled, timid-looking man in his fifties. As usual, Simon didn't bother to introduce him to us. He just rolled down the partition, instructed the guy to drive to the Pentagon, and promptly rolled the partition back up. Simon wasn't being elitist so much as determined to maintain an emotional separation from his drivers. If he didn't get close to them, it was easier to let them go.

So much for accepting Romero's death.

As the limo cruised down the flight line, Simon said, "Is there anything you haven't told us, Martin?"

"No." During the walk to the limo, I'd given him and Amanda a detailed rundown of my conversations with Sergeant Blake and Colonel Gustin, and my calls to maintenance and Pax Services. I also mentioned the fact that only a single hair had been recovered from the shower, and it apparently didn't belong to General Garber. I didn't pass on the forensics team's suspicions concerning Andy, which I considered little more than an unpopularity contest.

Simon eased against his seatback and closed his eyes. He was mentally preparing his top-ten list of items he deemed curious, interesting, suggestive, or puzzling.

Amanda and I waited, knowing better than to inter-rupt. When Simon was ready, his eyes fluttered open and settled on me. "General Markel seems to be our most likely suspect—"

"Yes."

"—and we need to pursue his relationship to Weller. Colonel Gustin's use of the term *favorite* is suggestive."

Glancing at Amanda, I said, "We'll ask around. If their relationship was more than professional, someone will know. It's hard to keep something like that secret."

He continued, "General Garber's statement that an Asian person could be responsible for his death is also puzzling. Frankly, it strikes me as ludicrous."

"Garber might have just been talking," I said. "Sergeant Blake said he was pretty drunk."

"I assume you've checked the contact information."

I fingered the papers in my jacket pocket. "No Asian names listed as either passenger or crew."

A nod. "I also find General Garber's apparent preference for martinis of interest. If true, it might indicate—"

"No dice," I said. "Andy confirmed with the customs officer that the whisky belonged to General Garber."

"I see." He looked less than pleased. "It might be worthwhile to request all the customs forms so we could check for ourselves."

I knew what he was trolling for, but considered this a dead end. Amanda obviously disagreed, saying, "It's worth a try. If someone else bought the booze and added it to Garber's customs form, the entry should be written differently. We might even find a line marked out on another form, where someone had originally declared the Glenlivet."

"I doubt it," I said. "Whoever bought the whisky would have filled out a new form. Be silly not to."

"Could get lucky," Amanda said. "The killer might have panicked. Gotten careless."

"Hasn't been careless so far."

"What about the killing?"

She won the point. This was the singular irony of the case. The contrast between a crude, hurried killing and a methodically planned cover-up.

I looked to Simon, who had flipped up the lidlike top of an armrest, revealing one of the half-dozen satellite phone receivers. It took him two calls to track down the number of the customs officer, Margie Benson. She wasn't in, so he left a message that included the limo's fax number.

"Turn on the laptop, Amanda," he said, ending the call.

She twisted around and swung the desk to her. The laptop sat in a form-fitting receptacle built into the modular top. Amanda flipped up the screen and punched the power button. As the hard drive booted up, Simon touched icons on the overhead console to route any incoming faxes to the computer. Those of interest we'd print out later.

"All set," Amanda said, pushing the desk away.

I said, "I have an explanation for the absence of hair in the drain."

Once I had their attention, I told them someone must have removed them because they were incriminating.

Amanda batted her eyes skeptically. Simon was more direct in his disagreement. "No, Martin."

I said, "So you've already considered this?"

"Among other scenarios. None are feasible."

"Marty," Amanda said. "Why would the killer take a shower? There wasn't any blood from the murder."

"I'm not necessarily talking about the killer," I said. "I'm only saying that *someone* besides Garber must have been in the shower, because—"

"Sex?" she said. You think Garber had sex in the shower?" Her tone indicated she didn't believe this at all.

"Why not? That would explain why the bed wasn't used, and why no semen traces were found."

"I understand all that, but—" She searched for a hole in my argument.

"Sex would have been awkward, Martin," Simon said. "Garber was a large man. There wasn't much room in the shower."

"They were screwing, not dancing."

A scowl of disgust. "How do you explain the unopened condom we found?"

"The obvious. He had more than one."

"We found no others in his luggage."

"What's that prove? He probably only took along a couple in case he got lucky."

"If Garber used a condom, where did he dispose of it? One wasn't found in the compartment's trash bin. Neither was the wrapping it came in."

I paused, thinking.

"Flushing is out," Amanda said. "Garber would know that's a no-no, because it could have clogged the waste disposal system."

I said, "So the woman disposed of the rubber. Or maybe Garber didn't use one. For all we know, the woman could have been on the pill."

"Wouldn't Garber have been aware of that fact beforehand?" Simon asked.

"How should I know?" I was getting tired of playing twenty questions. "Look, if you've got a better explanation—"

"I don't. Certainly nothing more plausible." He sighed. "Frankly, that's the problem, Martin. *None* of my solutions are plausible. *Nothing* fits the evidence we've uncovered. The one thing . . . the *only* thing I'm certain about is that the killer is a man. Yet everything points to a woman. It's as if . . . as if . . ."

Unable to find the word, he slumped back with a frustrated grimace. Amanda and I glanced at each other. Simon letting a case get to him?

Simon spent the next few moments staring out the window. Since it was approaching midday, the base traffic was light. As we drove past the sprawling Base Exchange complex, he said quietly, "Even here."

He was looking at the roped-off parking areas in front of the BX. Farther down, we could see more red cones in front of the commissary and the theater. This was yet another reminder of how the world had changed since 9-11. Even on a secured military installation, the home of Air Force One, even here, there was no guarantee of protection from an America-hating zealot with a car bomb.

To me, this was the damning legacy of 9-11. The realization that the world, *my* world, was no longer a safe place for me to raise my daughter.

Once again I felt unsettled. I tried to convince myself we were doing the right thing. That regardless of my personal feelings toward Garber, someone had to be held accountable for his death.

When I glanced at Simon, he was contemplating me. As if sensing my thoughts, he said, "It's not easy."

"No."

"If we pursue this, our loyalty will be questioned."

"I know—"

"People will question our motives. Our patriotism. It will be unpleasant."

"It already is."

A sympathetic smile. "We've spoken of this earlier, but before we go any further, I want—I need—a commitment of your resolve. How far you're willing to pursue the mat-

ter. *If* you're willing to pursue the matter." He looked at
Amanda.

She hesitated, then said carefully, "I'm a cop. It's who I
am and how I think. It would bother me to let a killer
walk away. I'd like to think I could put my feelings aside
and pursue an arrest."

"But you're not certain?"

"No."

He said, "Martin . . ."

"I feel the same as Amanda. I'm not sure what I'll do.
It's all too unclear."

Simon nodded and resumed gazing out the window.

Amanda said to him, "You feel the same way, don't
you?"

"Oh, yes." He gave her a smile.

But as he turned away, his smile disappeared, and I
detected something on his face that surprised me.

A look of regret.

The limo waited at the light across from the gym. Two
rights and a left would bring us to the main gate. Simon
had set the radio to a soft jazz station. For the last five
minutes, he hadn't said a word. Since he'd questioned us,
he seemed a little distant, but perhaps it was my imagination. When the light changed, he looked at me and said,
"The absence of hairs in the shower, Martin."

"What about them?"

"You're right," he said. "There is no reason for someone to have removed them unless they were incriminating. But assuming the killer was a man, why take a
shower? He wouldn't."

"That's why it had to be a woman."

"Possibly. But not because she had sex with Garber.

I'm confident we can prove General Garber didn't engage in sex before he died."

"Semen," I said, jumping on the statement. "That's what you want from Dr. Bowman, right? You want proof that General Garber didn't have sex because—"

I broke off. I thought I was onto something, but I wasn't. I couldn't see Simon forking out big bucks just to prove Garber *hadn't* been humping someone before he died.

Simon seemed amused by my confusion. "You still understand, Martin? No? Amanda?"

She was shaking her head.

"What is the common thread in this case?" he asked her. "The one constant?"

"Constant?" Her brow knitted. "I'm not sure I know . . ."

"Correct," he said.

Which only served to heighten her confusion and mine.

"The constant," Simon explained, "is the fact that we don't *know* anything. We can't *rely* upon anything we've learned." He shifted to me. "I told you earlier that Churchfield was organizing the cover-up like a military operation. No doubt with the assistance of the three generals. We can assume the scope extends beyond Colonel Weller's false statements, or the timely removal of key evidence."

He folded his arms, waiting for our response.

"What you're suggesting," Amanda said, thinking as she spoke, "is that much of the evidence has been *arranged* for us to find."

"Yes."

"Including the whisky bottle and the glasses?"

He hesitated. "It bothers me that they were hidden in the trash."

She asked, "Wouldn't we have been expected to find them there?"

"Probably."

"The military has a term for what you're describing," she said. "It's called a Deception Plan. The intent is to confuse the enemy—us—so we don't know if we're coming or going. And it's working. We don't know who the hell we can trust or what evidence we can rely on." She gave him a long look. "You could be right. They could be treating this like a war."

For a moment, no one spoke. I tried not to think about General Markel.

Turning to Simon, I said, "So the hairs in the shower might have been removed simply to deceive us. Make us think a woman could be the killer, when it was a man."

"Yes."

"Same thing with Colonel Weller's shirt, the buttons, the picture in her wallet," I said. "Everything could have been staged for us to find."

He was nodding.

"Even the heel marks in the closet."

"Yes. And don't forget the temperature on the plane. They obviously kept it cold to obscure the time of death."

That was a given. To me, this seemed a pointless exercise, since the exact time of death didn't seem to matter much. Still, this was another indication of Churchfield's resolve to alter all the facets of the case and keep us off balance.

"Dr. Bowman," Amanda said to Simon. "What you really want from him is—"

"The truth," Simon said.

"That's all?"

"That's all."

Amanda frowned, and so did I. We still didn't buy that Simon would shell out all that money unless he had something specific—

"There's the gate," Simon said, sitting up. "Amanda, take the right side. Martin, the left. Pay attention. We should know soon."

25

Three guards were manning the Andrews main gate as we drove through. A female sergeant immediately stepped into the gatehouse and picked up a phone. Her eyes stayed on us until we turned at the light.

"Be lucky if they let us back on," I said.

No response. Simon and Amanda were studying the traffic behind us. I resumed my vigil, even though I figured no one would tail us, since Churchfield knew where we were going. But Simon insisted on being certain.

Once the limo merged onto the Suitland Parkway toward D.C., we relaxed. If someone was tailing us, they were too good for us to spot them. Turning down the radio, Simon asked me to request the personnel files on our main suspects. He wanted to check out their backgrounds and assignment histories, hoping to find something that might suggest a definitive motive.

Since military personnel records were stored in giant computer databases, Simon was really seeking passwords that would allow us to access the records. Normally, obtaining the passwords was no big deal. But this situation was far from normal.

"The problem," I told him, "is I don't have the fire-power to make a password request on a four-star's records. And you can forget the SECDEF."

"Who has the authority?" he asked.

"Try the president," Amanda said. She wasn't kidding.

"Charlie Hinkle," I said, "is our best bet. He's got some clout as OSI chief."

As I reached for a satellite phone, I saw Amanda already had one out. She spoke less than thirty seconds before cupping the mouthpiece and eyeing me sourly. "This is a quote: No fucking way."

"His reason?"

"Balls the size of marbles."

I grinned, picked up a phone, and toggled the extension she was using. On the other end, I could hear Charlie engaged in his heavy, precoronary breathing. In the background, a TV was going with what sounded like the news. I said, "Charlie, we need those pass—"

And then he was all over me: "Sweet Jesus, Marty. You know what you're asking? You're talking about accessing the records of four chiefs of staff *and* the SECDEF. Everybody and their mother will want to know why. What the fuck am I supposed to tell them?"

"Nothing. You're the head of the OSI. Remember?"

"We're talking a murder, right? We gotta be talking a murder. Dammit, *I knew it.* Was the victim one of the generals? Shit, it has to be. Who was it?"

"You're not cleared, Charlie."

"Don't give me that crap. If I'm going to hang my ass on the line—"

"Charlie, I don't have time for this. I need those pass-words."

"Then you better start talking."

"*You're not cleared.*"

He made a choking sound. It was killing him, not knowing.

I decided to sweeten the pot. "Charlie, you're not thinking this through. If you get us the passwords, you could come out smelling like a rose. Senator Garber would be very grateful."

A long pause. I could almost see his fleshy face pique with interest. Like every colonel, Charlie desperately wanted to become a charter member of the constellation club.

"You better not be blowing sunshine up my ass, Marty. Because if you are, so help me—"

"I'm not."

"I thought you said you didn't have connections."

"I do now."

Another silence. Charlie was a careful guy. You didn't become the air force's top cop without being careful. He was trying to decide if I really had this much influence with Senator Garber. Finally: "Give me the names again."

I did. There were eight: the four generals, the two aides, Gustin and Weller, Sergeant Blake, and of course Secretary Churchfield, whose personnel records were in the database because of her years in the air force. I also reminded him that we'd needed a user name and password to access the Pentagon server.

Charlie still sounded reluctant. "I can't promise anything, Marty. Some general up the chain can deny the request."

"Use Senator Garber's name. Just get us the damn passwords, Charlie." I hung up before he could change his mind.

• • •

Simon was not a happy man when I told him we had maybe a fifty-fifty shot that Charlie would come through. I asked him if he knew anyone in DoD who could help, since Simon had contacts squirreled away everywhere.

He shook his head. "Not in a position to obtain the passwords."

"Try your other sources," I said. "See what they can dig up."

He was already reaching for a phone. As he made his first call, I decided to make one of my own, on the second line. On the passenger roster, I found two numbers listed for General Garber's home. The first had a Virginia prefix; the second, D.C.

I went with the D.C. number. A woman picked up. She sounded young, her tone cautious. "Mrs. Garber's residence."

"I'm Martin Collins. I'm a military investigator with the air force—"

She exploded in my ear, "I can't believe the *nerve* of you people. Haven't you harassed her enough?"

"Sorry—"

"You heard me. If you call again, I'll slap you with a restraining order so fast it will make your head spin. You got that? Now leave us the hell alone." And she banged down the phone hard enough to make me wince.

Simon and Amanda were eyeing me curiously as I ended the call. "What was all that about?" she asked.

I thumbed the redial to find out.

This time the answering machine picked up. I left a message, further identifying myself as a military criminal investigator who was looking into General Garber's death.

I said I hadn't tried to contact Mrs. Garber before and had no intention of harassing her. "Mrs. Garber," I said, "I'm convinced your husband was murdered, and it's important I talk to—"

A click. I heard breathing, but no one spoke. I said, "Mrs. Garber?"

The young woman came on, her voice still suspicious. "I was told the general's death was an accident."

"It wasn't."

A pause. "That might explain it."

"Explain what?"

She ignored me. "Why should I believe you, Agent Collins?"

"I assume you aren't Mrs. Garber, Ms.—"

"Tracy Roberts. I'm Mrs. Garber's niece. Answer the question."

"Are you an attorney, Ms. Roberts?"

"I'm in my final year at Georgetown Law."

Close enough. "Tell your aunt to call the senator. He'll vouch for—"

"Try again. My aunt and the senator don't speak. Haven't for years. Not since she moved out on his son. Besides, she's too frightened to call him or anyone else."

I said, "Frightened?"

Frowns from Simon and Amanda. On the phone, there was no reply. I had the feeling that Ms. Roberts thought she'd said too much. I said, "You can trust me, Ms. Roberts. Would I have told you the general was murdered if I wasn't on the level?"

She considered my logic. "Maybe."

"Why would I?"

"How should I know?"

I sighed. "Ms. Roberts, the government wants the murder covered up. If you don't cooperate, you're going to help them do just that. It's up to you. If you want the general's killer to go free, hang up. I won't call again."

I waited, half expecting a click. Instead she said, "You trying to lay a guilt trip on me, Agent Collins?"

"I'm telling you how it is."

A silence. Finally, in a resigned voice: "You better be on the level."

"I am."

Simon abruptly ended his call and mouthed, *speaker*. "Ms. Roberts," I said, "I'm putting you on the speaker so my colleagues can listen."

"Colleagues? What colleagues?" She was instantly suspicious again.

I quickly explained, adding, "You might have heard of Lieutenant Santos."

She seemed to relax. "Right. Sure. The homicide cop. I guess it'll be okay."

Simon touched the overhead control screen as I hung up the phone. I said, "Ms. Roberts, why is your aunt frightened?"

"That's what I'd like to know. She called me this morning, said to come over. She was crying on the phone, but wouldn't say why. When I arrived, she told me that General Garber had died in an accident. That she was supposed to keep it a secret. Later, around nine, a man came over. He said he was from the Pentagon."

"Was the man in a uniform?"

"No. A suit. And he was pretty creepy-looking. His face had a lot of scar tissue. Like he'd been badly burned."

I said, "This guy give a name?"

"Not to me. But I think my aunt knew him."

"Oh?"

"When she saw him, she didn't ask who he was. She just asked him what he was doing here, and he told her he wanted to discuss a private matter. That's when they went into the library. After he left, my aunt was close to hysterics. She was shaking so much she could barely talk. She wouldn't tell me what the man had said to her, and I could tell she was scared. All she said was, it was better if I didn't know."

"Do you think she'd tell me?"

"I know she won't. She won't talk to anybody. She's locked herself in her bedroom. I'm telling you, she's scared."

"Could you tell her General Garber was murdered, and we need her help in solving the case?"

She hesitated.

"We'll arrange protection for her," I said, receiving a nod of confirmation from Simon.

"Hang on a minute." She still sounded reluctant.

After a few moments, we heard faint knocking, followed by a muffled conversation. Then a sudden, surprised shriek and what sounded like an argument. The voices came and went as if Mrs. Garber and her niece were moving in and out of the room. Occasionally we heard clear snippets, but only for a few moments.

Mrs. Garber cried out angrily, "How could you, Tracy? *How could you?* I specifically told you—" Seconds later, in a more anguished tone, "—can't protect me. No one can. Don't you understand?"

"But they promised, Auntie. Please. If you'll just talk to them."

Mrs. Garber's response was muted, unintelligible. She sounded like she was crying. We heard Ms. Roberts ask her aunt why she thought the police couldn't protect her.

"—have to understand . . . killed Michael. They're too . . . still blaming him because . . . all these years—" Her remarks kept fading in and out. I was frustrated at my inability to decipher the words. I asked, "Anybody catch what someone's blaming General Garber for?"

Head shakes from Simon and Amanda. She said grimly, "But it's pretty clear she knows her husband was murdered."

"And why," Simon murmured.

We heard the sudden slamming of a door. Then a silence.

"I tried," Tracy Roberts said, returning to the phone. "She won't talk to you. She won't talk to anybody."

I asked her to explain Mrs. Garber's blame comment.

"Apparently people in the military blamed the general for some kind of a mistake he made years ago. She wouldn't say what the mistake was."

"Did she tell you why she's convinced we can't protect her?"

"Sort of, but I'm not sure it makes much sense. She kept saying no one can protect her from a crazy man. I asked her if she was talking about the burned guy, but she said no. That it was somebody else. You know who she could be talking about?"

Simon shook his head.

"No," I lied.

26

Since there was nothing more Tracy Roberts could tell us, I gave her my cell phone number, and requested that she keep trying to convince Mrs. Garber to talk to us. I also asked her to find out from her aunt whether the general had expressed any concerns about an Asian man.

"Concerns?" she said. "What kind of concerns?"

I related General's Garber's remark to the flight attendant, Sergeant Blake.

"I can't believe this," she said. "I really can't. It's like a bad dream. Some man from the Pentagon scares my aunt half to death. Now you're telling me General Garber might have been murdered, possibly by some Asian. The next thing you'll be telling me is that someone might actually try and harm my aunt."

I hesitated. This time Simon was nodding. I said, "It's a possibility, depending on what she knows."

"The killer. You think she knows who it is."

"Or at least suspects."

A long pause. "You mentioned something about protection—"

"Of course. Simon?"

In a reassuring voice, he outlined his plan.

"It's all arranged," Simon announced, ending his conversation with Jeff Zimmer.

Jeff was a retired homicide cop who ran a firm that specialized in protection for people rich enough or famous enough or egotistical enough to think they needed it. One of Jeff's men would remain at Mrs. Garber's until this was over.

While Simon resumed calling his contacts, I gazed out the window. Traffic was lighter than anticipated, and we were making good time. As we approached Anacostia to pick up I-395, I heard Amanda murmur, "I don't understand. . . ."

I looked over and saw her frowning at her notepad. I asked her what the problem was.

Closing her notepad, she nodded at Simon. "He said he also saw Secretary Churchfield become emotional at the sight of General Garber's body. If we assume Churchfield had some personal connection to Garber, why would she continually act like he was a dirtbag? It makes no sense."

I tossed out the obvious. "Maybe she was a woman scorned."

"Then I'd think she'd feel only contempt for him. I sure would."

She made this remark in an offhand manner. But the instant she'd uttered the words, her eyes focused on me, as if she was suddenly aware of what she'd said.

Her comment cut through me, and it was all I could do to keep my face blank. Anything less would have tipped her off that I was aware of her feelings.

After an awkward moment, she thankfully turned away. She said lightly, "I'm getting hungry. You guys want something? Marty? Simon?"

I accepted; Simon declined with a head shake.

As Amanda rummaged inside the small refrigerator, I tried to understand the emptiness that gripped me. It was an intensely hollow sensation, the kind of feeling you get when you lose something you care about.

Contempt, she'd said.

It never occurred to me that she might feel this way toward me. Possibly even hate me because—

"Turkey, pastrami, or Italian club, Marty?" she asked.

"Uh, turkey."

As Amanda passed over one of the sandwiches that were delivered daily by a deli-owner friend of Simon's, she squinted at me. "Say, Marty, you okay? You don't look too good."

"I'm fine. Never better."

And I gave her a big smile to prove it.

For the next fifteen minutes, Amanda and I ate, sipped Perrier, and watched as Simon made phone call after phone call. As far as we could tell, no one turned down his requests, but then they wouldn't.

Simon had spent years cultivating, nurturing, and protecting his army of contacts. The last aspect was by far the most important, since many were influential members of the media or held sensitive positions in the government. To ensure their anonymity, Simon never revealed their names to anyone, including me. He also never kept a written record of their identities, choosing instead to keep all their contact information in his head.

While some were paid informants, most weren't, at

least not technically. Simon was a master at making people feel obligated. Whenever he thought someone might be of future use to him, he'd begin doing them favors, usually without being asked. These favors ranged from something as small as tickets to a Redskins game or a sold-out Kennedy Center performance to arranging no-interest loans or, as he often did, simply paying off someone's mortgage or bankrolling their children's college tuition.

In my case, he'd hooked me by flying out a high-priced oncologist to consult on Nicole's cancer and hiring Mrs. Anuncio to care for Emily, so I could shuttle Nicole to her radiation and chemo treatments. After Nicole died, Mrs. Anuncio stayed on, and to this day I haven't paid her a dime in salary.

Simon's latest "favor" was the pony for Emily's birthday. He knew she'd wanted one and had called me up a few weeks earlier, saying he could get me a good deal. I told him I needed to think it over; I wasn't convinced Emily was ready for the responsibility of caring for an animal that large.

The next day, Mrs. Anuncio phoned me at work, all panicked. A man had delivered the pony. I didn't attempt to reimburse Simon; I knew it wouldn't do any good. Over the years, I'd sent him dozens of checks. None were ever cashed.

Like I said, Simon wanted people to feel obligated.

As Simon worked the phone, Amanda and I noticed he was careful not to lump all the suspects' names together. He passed on no more than three names per call. From his conversations, we figured two calls had gone to media types, three to individuals connected to a financial institution or possibly the IRS, and the rest to people in various branches of law enforcement, both federal and state. Whenever the person wasn't in, Simon hung up. He never left messages.

It was amazing, watching him work the phones. The way he would make a call, then sit for a moment and sort through the Rolodex in his head until he retrieved the number he wanted.

And it was during one of these pauses that he received a call on his cellular phone. So did I, seconds later.

Simon's tightlipped expression confirmed he'd gotten bad news.

I figured mine had to be worse.

Andy was swearing so loudly, I had to hold the phone away from my ear. Amanda eyed me quizzically, then rolled her eyes in disgust when she realized who it was.

"That goddamned cocksucker," Andy raged. "He threw me out. You believe that crap. The son of a bitch *actually threw me out.* I'm telling you it was close thing, Marty. It was all I could do not to deck the son of a—"

"Andy, calm down. Take a breath, fella."

He did, loud enough for me to hear. I heard the click of a lighter, followed by a minor coughing fit.

I said, "So Billy Bowman ordered you out—"

"Not Billy. I didn't get within twenty feet of Billy. It was that asshole SP commander, Major Vega."

"*Vega* attended the autopsy?"

This tweaked Amanda and Simon's interest, and they both looked at me. Simon turned away, resuming his phone conversation.

"Not just him," Andy said to me. "There was a squad of SPs camped outside the autopsy room. The bastards were waiting for me."

"Andy, they might have been there to ensure security—"

"Bullshit. Vega was under orders from General Morley not to let me inside. He showed me the clipboard with one fucking name. Mine. When I told Vega he could go to hell, he shoved his fucking gun in my face and ordered me to leave."

I murmured, "Jesus."

"You got that right. Someone talked. Someone tipped them off I was coming. I find out who, his ass is mine."

"Forget it. It could have been anyone in the hangar." I told him about the missing evidence and explained that a number of persons from the forensics team were probably under orders to sabotage the investigation.

"Give me an hour," he growled. "I'll find the bastards who sold us out."

That last thing I needed now was an out-of-control Andy conducting his own private witch hunt. I said, "No, Andy. We can't afford to—"

I was talking to myself.

After I gave Amanda the highlights of my conversation with Andy, we waited for Simon to finish with his call. He was listening intently, his expression tense. He said little other than the occasional "Yes" or "I understand." The limo abruptly shifted into the far right lane, and car horns blared in annoyance. Glancing outside, I saw that we were approaching the exit for the Pentagon's south entrance.

Simon said, "I'll be there in thirty minutes." He replaced the receiver and eyed me. "You first, Martin. I take it Andy wasn't able to attend the autopsy."

"No."

"It may not matter. Events are rapidly overtaking us. Everything might be out of our hands soon."

"Churchfield," Amanda said. "Don't tell me she's already contacted Senator—"

"No. That was one of my media contacts. He learned his paper is planning on releasing a story on General Garber tomorrow. An investigative piece they've been researching."

"An investigative piece?" Amanda said. "You mean the story *isn't* related to the murder?"

"He wouldn't tell me over the phone, but apparently not. The paper has been working on the story since Garber's appointment to the chairmanship."

"That's two weeks," I said. "It can't be about the murder."

"This article," Amanda said. "I imagine it's not exactly favorable."

"Damning," Simon said softly.

No one said anything. We were wondering if we'd stumbled onto the motive.

I said, "Timing fits. A damning story on Garber is scheduled to break tomorrow, so someone conveniently kills him today."

"The president and Churchfield," Amanda added. "They must have known about the story. That's why they're pushing so hard to have the case wrapped up by tonight. And if they knew about it, Senator Garber must have, too."

Her eyes went to Simon, waiting for him to acknowledge that this had to be the reason Senator Garber was so convinced his son had been murdered.

Simon turned away from her and looked out the window. For a moment, I thought he was playing that annoying game of his where he pretends not to hear something he wants to avoid discussing. When I followed his eyes to the restored facade of the Pentagon's once blackened and crumbled western wall, I realized I was mistaken. Simon was staring at it because he couldn't help himself. Frankly, neither could Amanda and I.

The limo slowed and took the exit.

As we rolled down the ramp, our eyes never left the wall. Its five-story sandstone surface looked enormous and impregnable, but of course we all knew that wasn't the case. One by one we shook our heads, reacting not so much to the memories of the attack as to the inner turmoil those memories created. Once again we were reminded that we each had to make a decision. The same one we'd been wrestling with since we'd started this case.

Do we pursue General Markel's killer and risk undermining the military, or do we let the clock run out on the investigation and walk away?

By the time we arrived at the Pentagon, I don't think any of us was any closer to an answer.

I wasn't.

27

MIDDAY

To describe the security at the Pentagon as heightened was an understatement. Armed soldiers and members of the Defense Protective Service—the Pentagon's police force—routinely patrolled the perimeter, and only big-time DoD heavy hitters were allowed to park anywhere near the building. To gain access into the Pentagon, most of the worker bees—anyone from a full colonel on down qualified—had to pass through two checkpoints. Those without an entry badge, even military members with a valid ID, were patted down and their belongings searched, then cleared inside only in the company of an escort.

As we looped past the Pentagon's cavernous South Parking, I rolled down the front partition and told the driver to pull up to the pedestrian bridge leading into the Corridor Two entrance. The limo rolled to a stop, and I checked my watch. Twenty-five minutes early. Murder suspects or not, you didn't show up late to a meeting with the Joint Chiefs.

"I disagree," Simon said, answering the question Amanda had just posed. "If Senator Garber knew about the article, he would have told me. He didn't."

"Come off it, Simon. He must have known."

"Not necessarily. The article is being kept very quiet. Do you think the paper would want the senator to know they were about to publish something damning about his son?"

She passed on a response. This was logic she couldn't refute. The driver came around and opened the door. Amanda grabbed the file containing the passenger information and started to crawl out.

"Take this," Simon said, tapping my arm.

Looking back, I saw he was holding out a card with the name of a luxury car rental agency. He explained, "I might be busy for a some time. When you're ready to leave, call, and they'll send a car."

I frowned, pocketing the card. "We'll be here for a couple hours. Your meeting with the reporter going to take that long?"

"I've made appointments with other contacts. I'll call when I'm finished."

"All right." Out of the corner of my eye, I noticed Amanda looking down on us from the sidewalk, her face puzzled. She quickly turned away and began chatting with the driver. Simon said, "Be forceful during the interview, Martin. Particularly when dealing with General Markel. Anything less, and you're wasting your time."

I nodded.

He gave me a long look. "It would help to appear angry. Can you do that?"

"I think so."

"Does he intimidate you?"

"What do you think?"

He smiled. "Good. That will keep you on your toes. Good luck."

As I turned to leave, he said, "Oh, one more thing. When will you tell her?"

It took me a second before I realized what he was asking. "I'll probably tell her in the next few days."

"Do it by tonight. When we finish the case."

"Simon, I'd rather—"

"No more delays. She has a right to know. Either you tell her, or I will."

I sighed. Simon the Godfather. "Fine. I'll tell her tonight."

As I grabbed the briefcase and emerged from the car, I guessed I had roughly eight hours to figure out how.

I'd taken a couple steps toward the pedestrian bridge when I realized Amanda wasn't with me. I turned, saw her watching Simon's limo as it drove away. As it disappeared from view, she came over to me, her face troubled. "Want to tell me about it?" I asked.

She shrugged. "The driver's a nice guy. His name is Bennie. He says he figures he'll be let go in a week. Two, tops."

"You know what I mean."

She studied me. "You probably won't believe me."

"Try me."

"Uh-uh."

But as we went up the steps of the bridge, she made a couple of false starts as if to speak. Once we alighted at the top, she said, "I don't get it."

The first checkpoint was located midway down the bridge and was manned by soldiers with M-16s slung over their shoulders. As we walked toward them, I said, "Don't get what?"

"Simon. Why he's lying to us."

My head snapped around to her.

"It's true," she said. "He told you he had appointments with other contacts. I was listening to his conversations. He made no appointments except with the reporter."

"You could have missed hearing him—"

"I didn't," she said flatly.

I shrugged. "So he probably made the appointments earlier this morning."

"Without telling us until the last minute?"

I still didn't think this was a big deal, and I told her so. Hell, we both knew Simon always kept a few cards in every hand to himself.

"But he lied to us."

"Technically, it's only a white lie."

She shot me an exasperated look. "It really doesn't bother you, huh?"

"Why should it? I trust him."

We were approaching the queue by checkpoint. Most people flashed their badges and were waved through. Two nervous-appearing young army captains were methodically being searched. Amanda and I dug out our badges, which said "NCR" in big black letters. National Capitol Region badges allowed us entry into any government facility.

Once we passed through the checkpoint, Amanda said, "I also think Simon lied about his conversation with Sergeant Keele."

I didn't react. I just kept walking.

"You hear what I said?"

"Yeah. You're mistaken."

"Am I? You've worked with Sergeant Keele. You know the guy's a straight shooter. You honestly believe he'd accuse someone on the forensics team of taking the evidence without proof? And even if he'd said that to Simon, why the hell would Keele turn around and deny making the accusation to you?"

We continued off the bridge onto a short sidewalk leading to the Corridor Two entrance. I gave her a look of annoyance. "What the hell have you got against Simon?"

"Listen, just because he's *your* hero—"

"Give it a rest, Amanda."

"It's the truth. Everyone knows that he's got you in his—" She looked away.

"Hip pocket?" I finished.

No reply.

I said, "So we're close? So what? That doesn't mean—"

She made a loud kissing sound.

I chewed on my tongue to keep from saying something I would regret. She had a knack for pushing my buttons. We passed through a set of wooden doors into a large open area where the second checkpoint, complete with an x-ray machine and metal detector, was located. A female Pentagon cop who had to weigh three hundred pounds was motioning people through with the flair of a drill sergeant.

Amanda and I stopped to dig out our OSI credentials. I said, "You're making accusations without proof. First, you thought Andy might be dirty. Now you're calling Simon a liar and implying—"

"Implying nothing. He *lied*."

"Dammit, Amanda—"

My phone rang. I ignored Amanda's glare as I fished it

from my jacket. It was Andy, calling to say he'd found out who had taken the evidence.

"Fifty bucks, he's the same bastard who sold me out. But I'll be damned if I can figure out why. Shit, I wouldn't want to be in your shoes, Marty. If it were me, I'd jack the son of a bitch up and—"

"Just tell me the name, Andy," I said irritably.

When he did, my knees almost buckled. "That's impossible."

I was in a daze as I ended the call. I tried to come up with an explanation, any explanation, but I couldn't. I made my way over to a nearby wall and leaned against it, setting the briefcase down. From somewhere I heard Amanda's voice, asking me what was wrong. Looking up, I saw the worry in her eyes.

I said, "You were right. Paul Carter saw him. That's why Paul was so nervous earlier. He didn't know who to trust."

She frowned. "Saw who? Who are you talking about?"

"Simon. Paul Carter saw Simon take the evidence."

Why?

That's what Amanda and I had to know. Why had Simon removed the evidence, and why hadn't he confided in us? Keeping his suspicions to himself was one thing. But *this* . . .

The first part, we could guess at. Simon probably suspected that someone on the team might tamper with the evidence and had simply removed the items as a preemptive measure. But if so, he should have at least told us. Hell, we were all in this together.

In the end, this is what really bothered me. That

Simon hadn't trusted us enough to let us know what he was up to.

Amanda suggested I wait, confront him in person. But I wanted to know now.

So I moved over to the far corner of the entryway and made the call. Simon picked up immediately.

"You son of a bitch," I said.

There was a long silence. When Simon responded, he sounded completely calm and unaffected. "So you know about the evidence."

It was a statement more than a question. "Damn right. Paul Carter saw you take the items. You're getting sloppy."

"Martin, I was going to tell you . . ."

"Oh, right."

"It's true. But I thought it would be easier on you and Amanda, not knowing. That way you wouldn't be faced with making a difficult decision."

"You mean on whether we should pursue the case?"

"Yes."

It dawned on me what he was driving at. "Jesus, you lied to me again."

"Martin, please—"

"Admit it. The line about how you were after the truth was a lie. You're going after the killer. You didn't confide in us because of what we said in the limo. You knew you couldn't count on us to make an arrest, so you decided to cut us out."

I was speaking in low tones, so the people filing into the building couldn't overhear what I was saying. Even so, a few glanced over curiously. Amanda ran interference and glowered at them until they looked away.

There was a long pause on the other end of the line.

Then Simon said, "You have every right to be angry—"

"No *shit*."

"—but I didn't lie to you. Not at first."

"Simon—"

"Initially, I *had* promised the senator I'd only seek the truth. I made no assurances that I would succeed. During his visit to the hangar, he asked me if I believed his son was murdered. I couldn't bring myself to lie to him. Not after seeing his grief."

I waited for him to explain the rest of it. When he didn't, I said, "So he asked you to find the killer?"

"Yes."

"And bring him to justice?"

"I'm to provide him the name, and he will take it from there."

I wanted to stay angry at him, but I couldn't keep it up. Simon didn't make promises lightly. Once he did, nothing else mattered. He'd made a commitment; it was as simple as that. I now understood his look of regret in the car. "This must have been difficult for you."

"I reacted emotionally. It was a mistake." His voice became quiet. "I need you, Martin. But in the end, this is my obligation, not yours. If you decided to quit, I would understand."

And he would. In some respects, knowing this made it harder to say no. I asked him what else he was keeping from us.

"I have a few theories, but they're rather implausible. I am concerned about Andy. I'm not sure we can rely upon him."

"Why?"

"His defense of Colonel Weller bothers me."

"Oh, that. I can explain—"

"Then there's the button. The one Sergeant Keele discovered under the couch cushion. I was surprised it had been found there, because Andy never said anything to us. Yet he must have known it was there all along."

"And you concluded that because—"

"Think back to the compartment, Martin. Do you recall Andy's response when I asked him if the couch folded into a bed?"

"Yeah. He said it did. So what?"

"Do you remember what he did next? Exactly?"

I thought. "Yeah. He reached down to check if the bed was made, and— Aw, hell."

Amanda squinted at me. She'd been listening with interest since the mention of Andy's name.

To Simon, I said, "A cushion. Andy picked up a cushion."

"The *right* cushion," Simon corrected. "The one the button was discovered under."

I shook my head, my mind drifting back to my conversation with Andy. When he'd begged me to keep him on the case. I could still hear the desperation in his voice: *Dammit, this is important to me. My ass is going to be in a sling over this. I have to be in on getting the fucking killer.*

Like Simon, I'd also given into my emotions. I'd believed Andy because I wanted to. Still . . .

"Simon," I said. "This doesn't prove anything. Andy didn't look under the cushion long. He could have missed the button. I'm sure that's what happened. He just missed it."

Amanda's head gave a little jerk. She'd finally grasped the import of what we were discussing and stepped close, placing her ear next to the phone.

"Even if he did, Martin, there is another possibility we

have to accept. Maintenance told you there was no hidden way to enter the compartment. That leaves us with only one logical explanation for how the doors were locked."

I said, "The doors?"

Amanda's eyes popped wide. I made the connection an instant later.

"My God," she said. "It could be Andy. He was guarding the compartment. He could have locked the doors at any time."

28

Amanda was silent as we stepped back in line. I kept waiting for the shoe to drop. When it didn't, I said wearily, "Get it over with, huh? Tell me I screwed up keeping Andy on board."

She shrugged. "Why? For once, I can't really fault the guy. If I'd been in his shoes, I might have done the same thing."

"I doubt it."

"Don't be too sure, Marty. That's what's so crazy about this case. I can't tell who's in the right. Us or them?"

"So the ends justify the means?"

"In this situation, maybe." She brushed a few strands of hair off her forehead. "Anyway, this just proves what we suspected from the beginning."

"What's that?"

She eyed me. "We can't afford to trust anyone."

"Next," the female cop said.

The Pentagon resembled a medieval fortress for the good reason that it had been loosely modeled after one. The most dramatic departure from tradition, other than per-

haps an absence of towers or moats, was the thematic
adherence to the number five; five sides, five stories, five
concentric rings that expanded outwardly from a central
courtyard. These rings were labeled A to E, and inter-
sected ten numbered corridors. The architects had settled
on this hub-and-spoke design for two primary reasons.
First, it was an extremely efficient layout, which allowed
someone to easily walk from one end of the building to
the other within minutes; second, it created an enormous
structural footprint that greatly enhanced the building's
survivability against a cataclysmic event, a fact chillingly
validated on 9-11.

I was familiar with the Pentagon because I'd spent a
couple years there as a major, working OSI budget issues
and avoiding generals. Back then, the hallways and offices
could best be described as depressing. The lighting was
bad, a permanent layer of grime seemed to cover the
walls, and everywhere you looked you saw the same dingy
yellows or puke greens. Now, with the billion-dollar reno-
vation project that had been under way even before the
attack, the atmosphere was considerably brighter, almost
pleasant. The walls were a spotless white, the tile floors
gleamed under bright lights, and the corridors had been
spruced up with pretty paintings.

The female cop studied our OSI credentials and our
entry badges, had us push back our jackets to verify we
were armed, then motioned us around the metal detectors. Other than casually inquiring if I was okay, she displayed little interest in Amanda and me. But as we
strolled down the hallway, I looked back and saw her
reach for a phone.

Amanda and I entered the A, or innermost, ring, followed it to Corridor Nine, and hung a left toward the

secured Joint Chiefs area. A frizzy-haired female army colonel was standing next to the Plexiglas security booth, which was occupied by a portly Pentagon cop, wearing either a furry red beret or the world's ugliest toupee.

"Agents Gardner and Collins?" the colonel said as we walked up.

Amanda and I nodded.

Her manner was brusque, professional. "I'm Colonel Tinsdale. If you'd sign in—"

We did and received a badge from the cop, marked "Escort Required."

"This won't do, Colonel," I said, passing back the badge.

She frowned.

I said, "We need visitors' badges that don't require an escort."

She shook her head emphatically. "That's not possible. You're not authorized unrestricted access."

"Then get us authorized, Colonel."

Her eyes flashed. She addressed me in a patronizing tone, as if talking to a child. "Agent Collins, my orders were to escort you to—"

"Who gave you those orders, Colonel?"

"Rear Admiral Wheeler," she snapped.

The SECDEF's sweaty-palmed military assistant. I told her to contact the admiral and relay our request.

Her jaw tightened. "I will do no such thing. The admiral is a busy man. Now either you—"

She frowned when I produced my notepad and began making a notation. "What are you doing, Collins?" she demanded.

"Hmm," I said mildly. "Writing down your name for our report."

"What report? What are you talking about?"

"'The one that will explain why we missed the meeting." I gave her a smile.

Tinsdale stared at me in disbelief. The cop in the booth was grinning, enjoying this little scene. I casually returned the notepad to my jacket and nodded to Amanda. As we turned to go, Colonel Tinsdale called out after us, "You can't do this, Collins."

We continued walking.

"You can't just leave. The generals are expecting you."

Still walking.

"Damn you, Collins. Get back here!"

We finally looked back and saw Colonel Tinsdale hurrying after us. She pulled up, saying, "There's no time. The generals are expecting you in five minutes. I simply can't—"

"You're wasting time, Colonel."

She still didn't move. She stood frozen, unwilling to yield to my power play even though she had to know she'd lose.

"You're down to four minutes, Colonel," Amanda said.

That got a reaction. She wheeled over to the booth, frantically motioning to the cop for a phone. As he handed it to her, he gave me a wink.

It took her less than a minute to get the approval.

As she held open the door for us, I said, "We know the way, Colonel."

She fixed me with a withering glare, twirled on a heel, and stalked off.

The cop was laughing as we clipped on our badges and went inside.

We went down a brightly lit corridor, past the National Military Command Center. We took a left and walked down a hallway of dark paneling and soft-blue wallpaper. Stern-faced portraits of former chairmen of the Joint Chiefs gazed down upon us from the walls. We made another left and strolled past a series of offices, including the one belonging to the vice chairman of the Joint Chiefs, General Markel. Harried-looking men and women continually streamed by us, most lugging thick files in a testament to the endless paperwork shuffle that defined the nation's military headquarters. Through open doors, we heard the constant clicking of keyboards and the hum of voices.

The chairman's office was a few doors down from the vice chairman's. We didn't see the Pentagon cop standing outside; he would have been under orders not to advertise his presence. We stopped at the double doors, and I handed Amanda the briefcase. While I played question-and-silence with the generals, she would sign it over to someone, then start searching Garber's office.

"I'd also better call Martha, tell her to keep an eye on Andy."

"All right."

"You know," she said, eyeing me, "there's one way we might be able to confirm whether Andy is part of the cover-up."

"Call Billy Bowman?" We'd discussed the possibility that Andy had fabricated the story about being denied access to the autopsy room.

"Odds are Dr. Bowman will back up Andy's story—"

I was nodding.

"—so it might be better to check Andy's personnel file, see if there's a connection to Markel or Sessler."

I realized what she was after. She was thinking that one of the army four-stars who'd been aboard the plane might be Andy's rumored sponsor. "It's a long shot. We don't even know if Andy has anyone in his pocket."

She gazed back skeptically.

I sighed. "Fine. Pull his file."

Her gaze turned sympathetic. "You sure you don't want me to come along for the interview? It could get a little rough."

I smiled to let her know I appreciated the offer, but we both knew I had to do this alone. As a civilian, I could press the generals' buttons without much fear of retribution. "I'll be okay."

Our eyes lingered on each other. She said softly, "Be careful, huh? Markel's pretty unpredictable. No telling how he'll react."

"I'm counting on that," I said, with more confidence than I felt.

She impulsively squeezed my hand, then disappeared into the office. For an instant, I felt the hollow sensation return.

I shook my head and continued down the hall. I was about to butt heads with three four-star generals, and all I could think about was what I would say to Amanda tonight.

Nuts.

At the end of the hallway, I entered a large anteroom. Faces peered up from their desks. A navy captain sitting near the door grunted, "You Collins or Gardner?"

"Collins. Gardner won't be coming."

He jabbed a thumb toward a corridor at the back. "You might want to wait a sec. The meeting's just ending."

Moments later, a line of senior officers emerged from the corridor. The chief of naval operations and air force chief of staff led the way, trailed by two three-star admirals, a one-star air force general, and a line of full colonels.

The two service chiefs eyed me as they went by, but never said a word.

As the entourage departed, the captain said, "Coast should be clear."

I nodded my thanks and headed toward the corridor. It was a dark-paneled hallway not more than twenty feet long. At the end, I could see a small wooden door. A thin man in a gray suit was standing outside.

When he spotted me, his face spread into a big, almost predatory smile. He had a raspy voice that sounded like he gargled with rocks. "Hello, Agent Collins."

Tracy Roberts had called it; he was creepy-looking as hell.

I'd seen people who had been burned before, but nothing quite like this. From his upper cheeks to his scalp, his face was a featureless mass of scar tissue. He was completely bald and had no discernible eyebrows or eyelashes. From a distance, his ears appeared normal, but as I came closer, the skin on them looked too smooth, and I realized they must be prostheses. What really got to me were his eyes. They were dark, almost black, and peered at you as if through openings cut into a flesh-colored mask. Think Darth Vader without his helmet, and you get the general idea.

I now understood Mrs. Garber's fear. If this guy had paid me a visit when I was a kid, I'd probably have had nightmares for a week.

Up close, I decided he was much older than I first thought. I could see deep wrinkles in his undamaged skin and there were the beginnings of jowls hanging from his jawline.

Looking past me, his smile faded. "Where's your partner, Collins?"

"She's won't be coming, Mr.—"

"*Colonel* Stefanski," he corrected smoothly.

Noting my surprise, he added, "Retired army. I'm General Markel's executive assistant."

That, at least, came as no surprise.

He held out his hand, which was similarly scarred and had a nub where his baby finger had once been. "If you have a cell phone or a pager, I'll take them now." The required drill whenever you entered a room classified as a SCIF, a special compartmentalized information facility. I shut off my phone and handed it over. He placed it in a metal box affixed to the wall.

We stood in silence.

Stefanski glanced at his watch. "You still have another thirty seconds."

"You sure you got a good time hack?"

Another smile, thinner. "I'm sure."

I asked, "So what do you do as General Markel's executive assistant, Colonel?"

A third smile. He seemed to enjoy smiling. Maybe he liked to show off the one part of his face that was normal. "Whatever the general requires."

"Including scaring widows?"

The mask never even blinked. "Time's up, Collins."

He reached past me and opened the door.

29

The Tank.

The first and only time I'd set foot in the Joint
Chiefs briefing room was almost ten years earlier, and it
still looked pretty much the same. It was a rather intimate,
windowless room dominated by a shiny conference table
that seated maybe ten and a floor-to-ceiling built-in projection screen. Mahogany wainscoting accented the soft
gold walls and drapes, projecting a sense of understated
elegance and power. At the very back stood the prerequisite flag display, which included the Stars and Stripes and
the colors of each service. Over to the right was a long,
narrow table where various staff members normally sat,
nervously waiting to be asked their input and often pray-
ing that they wouldn't be called.

As I followed Colonel Stefanski inside, I heard the
sounds of an angry conversation. My eyes went to the center of the conference table, to the place where the chairman of the Joint Chiefs customarily sat. General Markel
was there, talking heatedly with two four-stars seated beside
him. General Sessler, the army chief, sat to his left, and
General Johnson, the marine commandant, to his right.

"Goddammit, Dave," Sessler was saying to Markel, "I think the president is jumping the gun on this. We can't possibly deploy another hundred and fifty thousand troops in a month. We need at least two. Three would be better." Sessler had a nasal, high-pitched voice that fit his appearance. He was small and bookish, and wore thick, black-rimmed glasses that dwarfed his narrow face.

"I'm with Bob on this," General Johnson said. "A month is out. We haven't got anywhere near the airlift or sealift. We need more time." In contrast to Sessler, Johnson was a hulking man, with a square jaw and the flat, misshapen nose of a former boxer who did his share of losing. His voice boomed as if he were giving commands on a parade field, and he wore his red hair mowed to the scalp.

"The president," Markel growled, "says the timetable is non-negotiable. He's concerned the French and Germans could succeed in convincing the UN to withdraw its approval."

"I understand that, Dave," Sessler said. "But the president is assuming that the Iraqis will lose the will to fight once the bombing starts."

"They did during Desert Storm."

"But what if they don't? We could be caught without adequate forces for the ground war. We could lose a lot of boys unnecessarily."

"Thirty days," Markel said icily. "Those are your orders, General. Now if you can't handle it, I'm sure Secretary Churchfield can find someone who—"

Colonel Stefanski pointed me to the chair at very end of the table. The hot seat. As I angled toward it, I glanced up at the projection screen. A map of Iraq, with military symbols marking the estimated strength and positions of

Saddam's forces. There were literally hundreds of symbols; Saddam had been a busy boy.

I stood beside the chair as Stefanski settled behind Markel in a position of parade rest, hands clasped behind his back. The three generals continued to argue among themselves, apparently completely oblivious to us. I waited for Stefanski to say something about me to Markel, but he never did. He just stood there like a statue. A minute passed, then two. No one even looked my way.

It became clear Markel was playing another one of his intimidation games. He was telling me I was someone who could be ignored. That I didn't count.

I finally sat down and took out my notepad. No one seemed to notice. I cleared my throat sharply. Not even a glance. I said, "General Markel, if I may . . ." I might as well have been talking to myself.

What I was contemplating was completely unprofessional, not that I really gave a damn. Markel was making this easy for me. I wouldn't have to try and appear angry now; I was already there.

Reaching back, I slammed my hand flat against the table. Hard. The crack sounded like a shot, and the three generals practically jumped out of their chairs.

"What the hell."

"Jesus Christ."

"Collins," Markel snarled savagely, spinning to me, "that was insubordinate. If you ever do something like that again, I'll have you—"

I sang out, "General Garber was murdered, sir."

His mouth hung open. An instant later, all tension was gone from his face. It was creepy how he could do that. Just turn off his rage. He calmly eased back in his chair and contemplated me. "You're certain?"

"Yes, sir."

"How do you explain the compartment door being locked from the inside?"

"We're working on a theory, sir."

He looked surprised. "Which is—"

"I'd rather not say, sir."

"I see. Do you have any suspects?"

General Sessler and General Johnson rocked forward, as if anticipating my response.

"Yes, sir."

"Who are they?"

"I'd rather not say, sir."

Markel smiled thinly at my response. Gesturing to Sessler and Johnson, he said casually, "Are we suspects?"

"Sir, I'd like to ask the questions."

The smile chilled. "I'm trying to save you some time, Collins. You're obviously here because you want to know if we had a motive for killing General Garber."

"Yes, sir."

His eyes bored into mine. "You can quote me: I considered General Garber a self-serving, gutless, immoral son of a bitch. That clear enough, Collins?"

I blinked, struck by his candidness. "Yes, sir." I shifted to General Sessler. "And you, sir?"

Sessler tented his fingers, glancing at the others. "We all shared the same opinion of General Garber. Frankly, he should have been run out of the military years earlier. He certainly would have, had it not been for his father." General Johnson backed him up with a nod.

I was confused. I had no idea why they were making this so easy for me. To see how far they were willing to take this, I said to Markel, "Did you hate General Garber enough to kill him, sir?"

He seemed amused by the question. "Let's just say his death was in the best interests of the country."

"Is that a yes, sir?"

"You're a big boy, Collins. You figure it out."

I looked at Sesser; he was nodding. So was General Johnson.

I finally realized what they were up to. It was another little twist in their deception plan, to keep me off balance.

What the hell.

I bluntly asked Markel if he had killed General Garber, or knew who did. He answered as I expected, as did General Sessler and General Johnson. None of them even hesitated.

"No comment," they said.

And then Markel sat back in his chair and gave me a smug smile. He thought he had me.

But I still had a few cards to play, assuming I had the balls.

All for one and one for all.

In a nutshell, that little Three Musketeers' ditty explained their strategy. As Colonel Weller had done, they were also trying to appear guilty, knowing I couldn't possibly focus my energies on all three of them before the clock ran out. I had to admit it was a damn smart move.

But it wasn't perfect.

The weakness in this plan was that it would work only if they all stuck together. I was willing to bet they wouldn't, because of what Colonel Weller had said.

She'd called them honorable men.

For the next ten minutes, I went through my list of questions. No, they hadn't seen or heard anything suspicious. No, they had no idea how anyone could have entered the compartment without them seeing. No, Colonel Weller didn't spend more than a few minutes in their section; she'd only come up briefly to drop off a report to General Markel. Sergeant Blake was mistaken. No, they were certain no one went near the closet doors after they entered and found the body.

At that statement, General Markel said, "Is that your theory, Collins? You think someone locked the doors after we entered? Well, no one touched them. We'll swear to it."

This was my opening. I said, "You were only in the compartment for a few minutes, sir."

Markel frowned. "Are you saying someone locked it *after* we left?"

"Anything's possible, sir."

"But the compartment was under constant guard. No one could have gotten inside to lock the doors."

"General, I really can't comment."

He made a dismissive wave. "Bah. You're suggesting one of the CID men was compromised? Ridiculous."

But I could tell the seed I'd planted was starting to germinate. For the first time, I noticed a flicker of doubt in Markel's eyes. He couldn't tell if I was blowing smoke or I really had something. He exchanged glances with General Sessler and General Johnson. Colonel Stefanski smoothly came forward and whispered in Markel's ear. At a nod from Markel, he left the room. I checked the time; I had a pretty good idea what Stefanski was going to do.

Now that I had Markel guessing, I played my second card and asked him where Colonel Stefanski was going.

"None of your goddamn business."

He locked me in a flat gaze, as if daring me to respond.

It was unsettling, but I had to see this through. If I gave in to the power of his personality, I might as well tuck my tail between my legs and go home.

So I looked right at him and said calmly, "Does he usually do your dirty work for you, sir?"

Markel's reaction was instantaneous. His anger switched to the *on* position, and his face turned bright red. Sessler made a sputtering noise, and Johnson shot forward in his chair. They erupted in a chorus of indignation, led by Markel's outraged baritone:

"You son of a bitch. I'm going to have your ass. You hear me? Your *ass*."

"You're way out of line, Collins. You can't talk that way to the vice chairman."

"Jesus, who the fuck do you think you are?"

The three four-stars continued railing at me. It was a crazy scene. Confronted by their raw anger, I had to keep reminding myself that I was a civilian. That they really couldn't hurt me.

As the protests died off, I announced loudly, "So you all signed on to terrorize General Garber's widow?"

Shocked looks from Sessler and Johnson. Markel continued to fixate on me with hate. He snarled, "Don't listen to him. What he's suggesting is preposterous. He's trying to confuse the issue. He clearly doesn't know—"

Sessler was already addressing me. He demanded, "What the hell are you talking about, Collins? Who terrorized Mrs. Garber?"

I said, "You really don't know, sir?"

"Of course not."

Markel said again, "Don't listen to him. He's lying. This interview is finished, Collins."

I talked over him, saying, "Colonel Stefanski paid a

visit to Mrs. Garber this morning. Scared the hell out of her. I understand she's afraid for her life."

"My God." Sessler and Johnson both looked at Markel. Johnson said, "Dave, we *agreed*. You promised that no one would—"

"Shut up, Mark," Markel said, his voice thick.

"No. I won't stand for it. You went too far. For chrissakes, isn't it enough that her husband is—"

"*I said, shut up!*"

Johnson fell silent, his teeth clenched. Sessler sat there, looking at Markel with open disgust.

Markel spun to me, his voice trembling with barely restrained rage. "I know what you're trying to do, but it won't work. You hear me? It won't work. *Now get out of here.*"

I nodded to the other generals and pocketed my notepad. As I rose to leave, I remembered I still had a card left in my hand.

I tossed it on the table now.

30

Looking down on General Markel, I said, "Sir, we know who really killed General Garber."

He blinked, thrown either by the statement or the fact that I'd dared to speak. He recovered, saying, "You're bluffing. You don't know a damn thing."

"We have evidence that incriminates Colonel Weller, sir."

This time he showed no reaction. Neither did the other generals. I waited for them to ask me what I had against Weller, but they never did.

Which meant they already knew.

"You're pissing in the wind, Collins," Markel said. "You'll never be able to make a case against Colonel Weller, and you know it."

"Probably not, sir. I was just wondering whose idea it was for her to plant the evidence."

Again there was no response. I looked to Sessler and Johnson. They avoided my gaze. Honorable men, I thought.

"Get the fuck out of here, Collins," Markel said again.

$$\bullet \quad \bullet \quad \bullet$$

In the corridor outside, I retrieved my cell phone and made a quick call to Martha. She rarely swore, but she did so now. She was understandably furious, having learned from Andy that Simon had been the one who had taken the evidence.

"The bastard just stood there, letting me think it was my people. You know what I was going through. So help me, if I thought it'd do any good, I'd report his ass."

"You'd be wasting your time."

"I know, but— Son of a bitch."

She was seething. I gave her a few moments, then said, "Let me know when you're through."

"Don't start with me, Marty."

"Simon realizes he's screwed you over. He'll make amends."

"You bet he will." She paused. "He still handing out tickets to his sky box at FedEx Field—"

"Yeah."

"I want four. Against the Cowboys."

I had to smile. Martha was a fanatical Redskins fan. "You got it."

"The Eagles and Giants, too. *And* valet parking passes."

"Sure. Anything. Martha, I need a quick favor—"

After I told her, I could almost picture her rolling her eyes. She said grumpily, "Hang on."

She came back less than a minute later. "I got Sergeant Keele here. He says Andy got a call a few minutes ago and took off."

"Took off? Where?"

She relayed the question. To me: "All he knows is Andy left the hangar in a big hurry."

Good enough. "Thanks, Martha."

"Uh-huh. And Marty—"

"Yeah."

"Tell Simon I still think he's an asshole."

I tried Andy's cell phone, but he never answered. I hung up without leaving a message, then strolled into the outer office and looked around. I found Colonel Stefanski sitting at a desk in the far corner, talking on a phone.

I came up behind him, listened for a moment, then said, "Say hi to Andy."

He turned around, startled. I gave him a little smile.

He rose menacingly to his feet and thrust his Saran-Wrapped face close to mine. "Listen, smartass—"

By then I was already walking away.

As I headed down the hall toward General Garber's office, I checked my voice-mail messages. There were two; both from Charlie Hinkle. The first asked me to call him, and the second said he'd passed some of the passwords to Amanda.

I frowned; someone was calling out to me.

Turning, I spotted the navy captain whom I'd spoken to earlier hurrying up to me. "General Sessler would like to talk to you, Collins."

"He tell you why?"

He gave me a funny look. He was right; it was a stupid question. "Lead the way."

But instead of escorting me to the stairs that would take me up to the army chief's third-floor office, we about-faced and went down a few doors to Markel's office.

I said, "I thought I was supposed to meet with General Sessler."

We entered another anteroom with corridors on either side. More portraits hung on the walls, this time depicting recent vice chairmen of the Joint Chiefs. Markel's two executive officers, an air force colonel and an army one-star, were at their desks, tapping on keyboards. To their left sat the white-haired secretary I'd spoken to earlier. I'd been off by ten years; she was closer to seventy than eighty, and had an uncanny resemblance to Barbara Bush. The three of them glanced at the captain and me without curiosity or comment, confirming we'd been expected.

We followed the left corridor, passed a small admin room where a copy machine was buzzing away, and stepped into a spacious office dominated by an enormous portrait that covered the center of one wall. Its sheer size made you stop and look.

I found the painting's subject curious. Instead of some famous general, the face peering back at me was of a young, dark-haired soldier wearing a blue uniform with a single gold star on the collar. I asked the captain who he was.

"William Travis."

The name was vaguely familiar.

"The commander of the Alamo."

"Right." I remembered now. "The guy who drew a line in the sand and said anyone who wanted to stay should step across it. Markel a Texan? No?"

He was shaking his head. "General Markel admired Travis's balls. Markel believes soldiers should never surrender."

"Death before dishonor."

"You got it," he said. "A lot of people knock Markel for his John Wayne act, but hey, the guy puts his money where his mouth his. When he first got to 'Nam, his patrol was ambushed by the VC, and most of the survivors got the hell out of Dodge. But not Markel. Word was he single-handedly held off the VC until reinforcements arrived."

"Sounds like you're an admirer, Captain."

He shrugged. "Hell, I suppose you've got to be. Most people pay lip service to all the stuff about duty, honor, country. But man, he *lives* it. You know what he says his biggest regret is? You'll never guess in a million years—"

I shook my head.

"Not dying in combat. He says that's the only way for a warrior to go. How's that grab you? Talk about one intense son of a bitch."

"I'm not sure it'd be healthy serving under him in combat."

He laughed. "I'm no hero either. I got two kids I want to see grow up." He waved me to the sitting area. "I'd better be getting back. You're looking at the guy who's in charge of putting together Secretary Churchfield's talking paper for tonight's press conference."

"She's giving a press conference?"

"Yeah. Right after the president's speech. She's discussing the Iraq deployment. I've already sent the secretary seven drafts. *Seven*. And now I've got to crank out number eight." He shook his head gloomily. "Never should have majored in English. Two months more of this paperwork chickenshit, then it's back to the real navy."

I nodded sympathetically. While a Pentagon tour was essential for promotion to the upper echelons of the military, no self-respecting officer actually enjoyed it.

"Anyway," the captain said, "General Sessler should be along in a few minutes, but you know how it is when they get that fourth star. It's like they suddenly forget how to tell time."

As he hurried off, a female sergeant with a dimpled smile appeared, asked if I wanted anything to drink. I said no.

After she left, I took a moment to survey the room. It wasn't the size of a Fortune 500 exec's office, but it was close. In addition to the sitting area, which included a couch, a loveseat, and a couple of armchairs, there was a circular conference table and an ornately carved desk the size of a pool table. A matching hutch topped by a computer sat directly behind it, framed by a bookshelf and a steel safe. A glassed-in curio cabinet occupied one corner, and a big-screen TV another.

Not that I was paying all that much attention to the furnishings. What really tweaked my interest was a wall display that consisted of a dozen or so black-and-white photographs arrayed around a rifle enclosed in a wood-and-glass case. The rifle was obviously the one Markel had used as a sniper, and the photos all depicted haggard men in dirty fatigues, taken against a jungle background. There was something oddly reverential about the display.

I went over to the rifle. It was the military version of a Remington single-shot, bolt-action .308. I was familiar with it because I had a similar one at home, though I used mine to hunt deer, not men. A brass plaque affixed to the bottom edge of the case read simply "134." There was no further explanation, which was understandable. In the politically correct atmosphere that defined present-day America, it would be considered bad form to have a senior general highlight his prowess as a killer.

The enormity of the number was both awe-inspiring and chilling.

One hundred and thirty-four confirmed kills.

By one man.

And I'd pissed him off.

I sighed, tried to think happier thoughts, and focused on the photographs. Almost all were group shots. I scanned them, trying to pick out General Markel. It wasn't easy. Most of the photographs were small, five-by-sevens, and had been taken at a distance. There was also a sameness to the men's gaunt, unshaven faces and their vacant, world-weary expressions. These were warriors, men whose faces reflected the horrors of combat.

Below each photograph was a silver plaque engraved with a date, a unit designation—some with more than one—and a Vietnamese location, but no names of the soldiers portrayed.

I finally identified Markel in the third picture, which was larger than the rest. It showed two sergeants, standing arm in arm, each with a rifle slung over his shoulder, grinning broadly into the camera. Both were proudly holding up what appeared to be a necklace of shriveled flowers. But of course they weren't flowers.

They were ears.

A lot of ears.

My eyes went to the man on the left, a tall, lanky soldier with blond hair and ruggedly handsome features. I shifted my gaze. A shorter man, equally thin, with wavy dark hair. I studied him. There was a resemblance, but the sergeant's stripes threw me.

I looked back to the first two photos. This man was there. I also spotted him in the rest of the pictures and finally concluded he had to be General Markel.

I was about to turn away from the last photo when I froze. It was a wide-angle shot of close to twenty men. They looked like hell. Their faces were filthy, their uniforms ragged and torn. Most were sitting or kneeling, and a number had obviously been wounded, their bandages visible. In the distance behind them, I could see a blackened hillside and the prone shapes of corpses.

What held my attention was the face of a soldier at the right edge of the picture. He'd stood out because he was heavier than the rest. Much heavier.

I stared at his face, but the image was too grainy for me to be sure. Still, I had the feeling, the sense that—

And then I saw another face that seemed familiar.

I slowly shook my head at a growing realization. If two of them were there . . .

I leaned close and began studying every face.

There he was. The third man. This time his face was clearer, and I was certain of his identity.

I stood back, trying to understand. This was a coincidence I hadn't anticipated. Still, did it really mean anything? So what if they'd all fought in Vietnam together? How could that have anything to do with—

I stiffened. I was looking at the silver plaque, focusing on the name of the place where the photograph had been taken. My eyes darted to the other pictures. Most of the names were different. But two were identical to the location in the large group photo. I thought back to Sergeant Blake's words as she tried to recall the name of the person General Garber had been fearful of:

It was an Asian name.

It could have been Chinese.

I began to tremble. My God, I'd only assumed that—

Voices from the hallway outside. Then loudly: "See that we're not disturbed, Colonel."

"Yes, sir."

When General Sessler walked in, I was sitting in a chair.

31

G eneral Sessler entered the office and closed the door. As I started to rise, he gestured me to remain seated. He said sarcastically, "At least you have some respect for rank, Collins."

I didn't reply. My pulse was still racing, and I was working to appear calm.

Sessler slid his small frame into the armchair beside me and contemplated me through his Coke-bottle bottoms. "Quite a little display you put on in there. You shook up General Markel. Not an easy thing to do." He added, "Or smart."

"Did he kill General Garber, sir?"

His face darkened. "I didn't call you here to answer questions. I want to give you some advice, hoping you'll come to your senses."

Here comes the sermon. I said, "In other words, you want me to back off, sir."

"You better believe it. You have no idea what you're dealing with. If you did, there wouldn't be any question. You'd never pursue this thing. You couldn't."

"General, I'm aware of the political considerations—"

"For God's sake, man, think about what you're doing. The damage you'll cause. We're about to attack Iraq. This time it won't be as clean as the Gulf War. Saddam knows we're coming after him. He's got nothing to lose by using chemical and biological weapons. We're talking casualties, a lot of casualties. And that's only part of the problem. The second we attack, the Muslim world will be up in arms. They don't give a damn that our actions are justified or that we lost three thousand innocent Americans on 9-11. All they care about is that the great Satan is attacking one of their own. Terrorist recruiting will triple overnight. That means this fucking war—"

"General—"

"—will last for years. *Years*. Public opinion is a fickle thing. Right now, the American people are solidly behind the war. It's crucial that they continue to support us when the body bags start coming home. They need to have faith in the integrity of the military leadership—"

"General, there's been a murder. I'm a cop. It's my duty to—"

"You're an American." He jabbed a finger accusingly at my chest. "Or is that something you've forgotten?"

My jaw tightened. I was trying to keep my cool, but he was getting to me. I coldly told him he had no right to question my loyalty.

He snorted harshly. "Don't I? You know what's at stake, and yet you persist in pursuing this matter. In my book, that makes you nothing but a— *The hell you going?*"

I was out of my chair. General officer or not, I didn't have to listen to this. I turned my back on him and started toward the door.

He grabbed my arm and held it in a bony grip. "Sit down, Collins. That's an order."

I looked down at his hand. "Sir, technically, that's assault."

Our eyes met, and he slowly loosened his grip. "Sit down," he said quietly. "We need to talk."

I didn't move.

"Collins," he said, sounding tired, "I took an oath to protect this country. I've spent most of my life trying to do just that. If I came on too strong, that's too fucking bad. I've earned the right. Two Purple Hearts and four stars say I've earned the right. Now sit the fuck down. I haven't got much time."

I hesitated, then eased down.

Sessler's spoke in low tones, but with an undercurrent of emotion. "There's a lot more to this than you could possibly conceive. The political concerns are only a part of the equation. You keep pushing, people are going to get hurt. People who don't deserve it. You'll destroy reputations . . . and worse."

I caught the implication. "Sir, are you saying this wasn't an accidental killing?"

He hesitated, as if searching for a word. "It *was* an accident. Maybe not technically, but that's what it was. No one intended it to happen, it just did. If you want to hold someone responsible, there's only one person. General Garber. *He* is the one who is ultimately responsible for what happened. *He* is the one who brought this upon himself." He grimaced in disgust. "Jesus, the man really was one sick son of a bitch."

"By sick, are you suggesting—"

"I'm telling you the man had a sickness. A self-destructive streak. When he drank, he couldn't control his urges, and it killed him."

"Are you saying he tried to rape Colonel Weller?"

He gazed at me coolly. "Did I say he did?"

"No, sir." But he hadn't denied it either.

He continued contemplating me. "Think about what I said, Collins. No good can come from what you're doing. You walk away now, you'll thank me later."

"Sir, Mrs. Garber was threatened."

"That was a mistake. Colonel Stefanski got carried away. He tends to be protective where General Markel is concerned." He nodded to the photos on the wall. "That's him with Markel. They've known each other since Vietnam. After Stefanski recovered from his injuries, Markel was the one who convinced the army to reinstate him to active duty."

I knew he must be referring to the picture that showed Markel with his arm around the tall soldier with the blond hair. I said, "I noticed they were both sergeants during the war."

"Yeah. Dave—General Markel—got a battlefield promotion during his second tour. After Stefanski's burns healed, he went to school, got his degree and a commission."

I asked Sessler how Colonel Stefanski had received his burns.

A shrug. "It was war. Shit happens. Stefanski was at the wrong place at the wrong time. At least he was one of the lucky ones; he survived. A lot of young boys didn't." He shook his head somberly. "Though if you ask Stefanski, he'd probably have preferred dying. Jesus, what the poor bastard went through."

I said, "So you're convinced General Markel never asked Stefanski to speak to Mrs. Garber?"

"Of course not." He focused on me. "Let me tell you something about Dave Markel. He's the most dedicated, selfless soldier I've ever come across, bar none. All that stuff you've probably heard about him is crap. He's not crazy or psychotic or anything else. He likes to project that image to keep people off balance, so they'll do what he wants. Who in their right mind wants to go up against a guy who's supposed to be nuts? The Vietcong sure didn't. You familiar with what Markel did in 'Nam?"

"Somewhat."

"That should tell you the kind of guy General Markel is. His missions were suicide. No one expected him to survive. Dave sure as hell didn't. Yet he kept going out into the jungle because he knew it was the best way to save lives. American lives. If it cost him his own, he figured that was okay. A better-than-even trade. You know why he collected ears?"

"No, sir."

"Intimidation. Dave's a master at it. It's what he's all about. He knew playing the psycho American killer would shake up the enemy, make him more effective. And he was right. When the word got out he was working an area, the VC cleared out."

Sessler sat back in his chair, shaking his head at me. "You're barking up the wrong tree, Collins. The truth is, Dave felt sorry for Patricia Garber. We all did. It must have been humiliating as hell, being married to someone who couldn't keep his pecker zipped up. Take my word for it, Dave would never have gone along with any attempt to frighten Patricia. Why the hell would he? She couldn't know who killed her husband. She wasn't on the plane."

"Sir, she might suspect—"

"That's hardly proof."

"Sir, in the meeting, you and General Johnson reacted as if you believed—"

"We didn't know the facts. We asked Dave, and he explained Stefanski got carried away."

A bullshit answer, but I had to give Sessler his due. He was doing a helluva job singing the party line. Now the question was: Did he believe in what he was saying?

There was a knock on the door, and the navy captain poked his head inside. "General, they're waiting for you."

Sessler checked his watch, then stood, looking down on me. "Think about what I said, Collins. Let this go. It's not worth it." His glasses stayed on me, anticipating an answer.

I slowly rose, saying, "Sir, I'd like to clear something up."

"Make it fast."

"Colonel Stefanski. I'm wondering why he felt the need to visit Mrs. Garber if she didn't know anything damaging."

He looked surprised at the question. He stood there for a long moment, trying to come up with a response. Something plausible.

But we both knew there was nothing he could say.

"Leave us, Captain," he ordered.

As the captain withdrew, Sessler appraised me, disappointment in his eyes. "I guess I wasted my time. Fine, have it your way. The bottom line was, there were three people on the plane who've wanted to kill General Garber for years."

"And they are . . ."

A flat smile. "You're the detective. Why the fuck do you think I asked to meet you in here?"

"I assume you mean the photographs, sir."

But Sessler was already walking from the room.

General Sessler hadn't wasted his time. Not entirely. He'd made me stop and think. Again.

I stood in the quiet, weighing my options. In the end, it came down to the realization that the outcome was a given. Whether I participated or not, the case would be solved and the killer exposed. Perhaps not by the end of the day or the week or the month even the year. But eventually.

Because Simon had made a promise to a grieving father.

In some respects, that made everything easier. Whatever happened, I wasn't responsible. It was out of my hands.

At least, that's what I told myself.

I walked over to the wall and removed the group photo with the faces I'd recognized. After slipping it from its frame, I flipped it over. There were no names on the back. I stepped next door to the admin room and asked the dimpled sergeant for a magnifying glass. She dug through two desks before she produced one that resembled a frog.

After scrutinizing the twenty-three faces, I concluded General Sessler had lied again.

Four of the people in the pictures had been on the plane with General Garber.

Brigadier General Clay was General Markel's senior executive officer. When I handed him the receipt and informed him I was taking one of General Markel's photographs, he didn't argue or attempt to deter me in any way. I didn't expect him to.

They wanted me to have the picture.

As I strolled down the hall toward Garber's office, I made the call to Sergeant Blake. It was admittedly a long shot, but I had to try.

Her voice sounded groggy as if I'd woken her up. No, she'd hadn't found the paper with the Chinese guy's name. But she did remember that the name had reminded her of trash. Possibly because she'd been carrying one of those plastic trash bags when she'd talked to General Garber. She couldn't be sure.

Brother. "Now think. Could the name be Vietnamese? Did the general ever mention Vietnam during your conversation?"

"Not that I recall."

Glancing at the plague, I read off the location to her. No reply. I started to spell it—

She cut me off, her voice excited. "That's it. It was 'trash bin.'"

"Sorry?"

"Don't you see, sir. Trash bin. *Tranh-binh.* It's him. He's the man General Garber told me about."

"—apologize, Congressman Maloney, General Garber won't be able to make your four-o'clock meeting. Yes, sir. He's been unavoidably detained. I'm sure he'll reschedule next week. Yes, sir. I'll tell him."

As I entered General Garber's reception area, two things immediately jumped out. First, the two executive officers' desks were empty, the tops completely clean, as if they'd gone for the day. Second, there was an absence of the usual office sounds coming from the offices at the back.

My eyes settled on the secretary's desk, where the

room's lone occupant was cradling a phone. A severe-looking brunette wearing a red power suit, she made a mark in a big appointment book, then glanced up at me. "Are you Agent Collins?"

"That's the name on my ID."

She appeared more annoyed than amused by my remark. She pointed a manicured nail down a short hallway. "The general's office is the second door on the left. You'll see the officer."

I asked her where the executive officers were.

"They took ill and went home. There's a flu bug going around." She said it with a straight face.

"I see. Is Colonel Weller here?"

"She also wasn't feeling well and left for the day."

"Is *anyone* from the staff here?"

"A few of the admin personnel. Sergeant Gerard is filing papers in the back, and Sergeant Brinker went to lunch."

Two low-ranking Indians and no chiefs to man the fort. They didn't miss a trick. I read the nameplate on her desk. "Thank you, Mrs. Coughlin."

She flashed a superior smile. "I'm *Ms.* Baker. I'm only sitting in temporarily. I work for Secretary Churchfield."

Which explained the dress and the attitude.

As I entered the corridor, the plainclothes cop who was sitting outside Garber's office, a young black man with a pencil-thin mustache and a nervous flicker of a smile popped to his feet. I was curious to see that his shirt collar was dark with sweat, even though it wasn't that warm. We shook hands, and he introduced himself as Frank Gibson.

When he started giving me a play-by-play on how he secured the office, I waved him off. "You already briefed Agent Gardner?"

"Why, yes, sir."

"No one tried to enter the office since you arrived?"

"No, sir. Nobody was even in here except Ms. Baker and the admin personnel." His tone was earnest, but his nervous smile suggested otherwise.

And on it goes. "Look, Gibson, if someone ordered you not to say anything—"

"But they didn't, sir. Honest. No one tried to get in. Ask Ms. Baker. She'll tell you. Oh, Ms. Baker, could you—"

I said, "That's not necessary."

Too late. Baker appeared from behind her desk and came over to us. "Is there a problem, Officer Gibson?"

Before Gibson could reply, I said, "There's no problem. It's just a little misunderstanding. Everything's fine."

"I see."

We played the stare game for a few moments. I gave her a smile. She attempted one of her own and failed. With a final look at Gibson, she returned to her desk.

The instant she disappeared from view, I turned to Gibson. "If you're lying to me, I'll have your ass. You got that?"

He got big-eyed. "Sir, I swear I'm not—"

"Yeah, yeah." I brushed past him into the office and closed the door. After I'd taken a couple of steps, I stopped dead, my head swiveling around.

What the hell?

32

Amanda was sitting at Garber's desk, poring over the contents of an open file, a yellow highlighter in her hand. She motioned me over, but I could only stand there with my mouth open.

I'd seen senior officer "I'm-a-stud" walls that were over the top before, but this was ridiculous. You couldn't look anywhere in the room without seeing photos of General Garber's beaming face. There were pictures of him sitting in military jets, or receiving an award, or shaking hands with prominent politicians, or just posing heroically in his medaled uniform. There had to be hundreds of photographs—big, small, new or old, it didn't matter. As long as Garber was the subject, they were there someplace. What really made me gag was the large oil painting towering over the desk, which showed General Garber receiving his first star—the one painted from the photograph we'd found on Colonel Weller.

"Yeah," Amanda said dryly. "The only thing missing is baby pictures. And if you look real hard, you might even turn up those."

She was exaggerating, but not by much. The pictures were arranged chronologically and spanned Garber's entire military career, beginning with his days as an ROTC cadet. One or two even appeared to have been taken at military prep school, when Garber was in his early teens. I said, "This is . . . sick."

"But his narcissism could be a break for us."

At my frown, she said, "I searched the office. Nothing. My guess is that anything that might point us to the killer is long gone. But they made a mistake." She nodded to the lower corner of the left wall, where a half dozen or so of Garber's cadet photos were located. "Take a look at the bottom two."

So I did. In both, Garber was wearing the uniform of an ROTC cadet. The first was obviously a graduation picture and the second showed him standing with a group of classmates, holding up a banner that read "University of Virginia ROTC #1." I scanned the cluster of young men and women, but none struck me as familiar.

Amanda prompted, "I'm talking about the spacing between the pictures."

I saw it now. "It's off. These pictures are much farther apart than the rest. And the edges don't line up with the others."

"Now look down."

I was already doing so. Against the dark blue carpeting, I'd noticed white dust-like specks. More on the molding. I removed the pictures and found three evenly spaced holes where screws had been pulled from the sheetrock. When I matched up the photos with the two outer holes, the frames lined up with those on either side. The conclusion was obvious, and as I replaced the photographs, I said, "Someone rearranged these and removed a photograph that was here."

"Yeah. You know how often these offices are cleaned?"

"Nightly."

"So someone rearranged those pictures either late last night or this morning. And we know it couldn't have been General Garber." She looked at me.

I nodded thoughtfully. It seemed a stretch to believe that an old ROTC photo of Garber's could somehow incriminate a killer. Yet someone must have had a reason for removing it.

Amanda said, "Ten bucks says the pictures were changed this morning. They wouldn't have done this if Garber was still alive."

"True."

"So someone in the office must have seen the person who did it."

"Like it matters. You really think they'd tell us?"

"I was talking about the cop, Gibson. The man is not a happy camper."

"No." I told her about my confrontation with him.

"He's pretty young, Marty. Said he's been a cop less than a year. I could try and squeeze him a little, see if he'll talk."

"Watch out for Baker."

Amanda winked, rising. "The ice princess. I saw her trying to type a memo. Whatever she does for Churchfield, she's no secretary. So, how'd it go with the generals?"

"I survived." As I started to give her a recap, she said, "Tell me later. Gibson supposed to be relieved at one so he can grab lunch."

I checked my watch: 12:43.

"Here," Amanda said, thrusting out the file she'd been reading. "Colonel Hinkle gave me the passwords for Andy and Colonel Weller, and I downloaded their RIPs and some of their OPRs." RIPs were the service member's assignment histories; OPRs, their annual performance evaluations.

Reacting to the thinness of the file, I said, "I take it Charlie's still having problems getting the passwords on Churchfield and the generals?"

"They're stalling him. They keep telling him he'll get them, but so far nothing. We might have to get Senator Garber to raise a little hell."

This would be something we'd have to run by Simon. As Amanda went to the door, I headed for the sitting area.

"Uh, Marty, you mind reading that outside while I question Gibson?"

I frowned, looking back. "You want me to leave?"

"How bad do you want answers?"

I understood now. Amanda could become pretty intense during interrogations and didn't like anyone around to cramp her style. "Go easy, huh. The guy's only following orders."

"Relax, Marty. I'll be a Girl Scout. Give me ten minutes?" She smiled sweetly.

I was still worried.

As I joined her at the door, Amanda paused with her hand on the knob. "A couple quick items, Marty. I looked through the information on Andy and Weller. I came up empty on Andy; there's nothing that indicates who his sponsor is. On the other hand, Weller's file is enlightening as hell. It's clear she's been lying to us about practically everything."

"Okay."

"I also highlighted the key portions of her RIP and OPRs. It looks like my first hunch about her was wrong. She's no innocent victim, this girl. I think it's possible she might be involved in the killing. Perhaps even set him up. The most telling thing is her relationship to General Markel."

I said, "By telling, you mean—"

But Amanda had opened the door. Officer Gibson sprang from his chair and eyed us, or rather me, fearfully. Amanda disarmed his concerns with a dazzling smile and turned on the feminine charm that she rarely used. She engaged him in small talk, mostly inquiring about his job as a Pentagon cop, how long he'd worked here, what his duties were, that kind of thing. Initially Gibson seemed confused by her interest, but the longer she spoke, the more he gradually relaxed. At one point, he even puffed up a little at one of her compliments. When she finally tossed him the line about needing his assistance in making a search of the office, Gibson willingly agreed to do so. As I watched her usher him inside, I could only shake my head. The guy didn't stand a chance.

At the sound of the door closing, Ms. Baker poked her head around the corner. She frowned at me as I walked up. "What's Officer Gibson doing?"

"Why do you care?"

She said stiffly, "I don't. I just hope there's nothing wrong."

"Such as—"

She pointedly ignored me, but I could see the concern on her face. When I inquired as to the location of Weller's office, she reluctantly directed me to a room down the opposite hallway. As I left, she was again looking uneasily at General Garber's door.

No doubt about it; Gibson knew something.

I entered a room with four partitioned cubicles. I followed the nameplates to the desk in the right rear. When I tried the drawers, they were locked, as were the two file cabinets. The only items worth noting were the two framed photographs on her desk. The first was of Weller's parents—the older couple we'd seen in her wallet—and the second was of Secretary Churchfield pinning her with a medal, General Markel standing in the background, beaming like a proud father.

Markel and Weller.

The odd couple.

I got comfortable behind the desk, opened the file and began to read.

It was all there, as Amanda had promised. Weller's relationship to Markel, the lies she'd told us, everything. All I had to do was follow the yellow highlights and put the pieces together.

Weller had gone to work for Markel when she'd been a captain and he was a three-star, serving on the European Command staff. Since EuCom was considered a purple assignment—one that included members from all the services—this explained how an air force officer could become the aide to an army general.

When Markel received his fourth star and was given command of SouthCom in Florida—another purple assignment—Weller tagged along, having been promoted early to major. Two years later, Markel was made the vice chairman of the Joint Chiefs and transferred to the Pentagon, again accompanied by his trusty aide, the newly promoted Lieutenant Colonel Weller.

I stared at the date of her most recent assignment in the RIP, the one that showed when Weller had become Garber's aide.

May 12.

Less than two weeks ago.

Frankly, I didn't get it. Why would Weller leave Markel, a man she admired and who'd pushed her to two early promotions, to work for Garber, a man she loathed? It made no sense.

Unless, of course, Weller had gone to work for Garber as part of plan to set him up.

But if so, this still didn't answer the question that had bothered us from the beginning. If Weller was involved in the killing, why try and cultivate suspicion?

I shook my head and flipped past Weller's OPRs to Andy's RIP. The entry I was looking for was listed near the top. It had been his third assignment after graduation from West Point.

Twenty-sixth Infantry Battalion of the Third Infantry Division.

I glanced at Markel's photograph, which I'd placed before me on the desk. Two battalions were inscribed on the plaque, one marine and the second army.

The army battalion matched.

General Markel, General Sessler, General Johnson, *and* Andy had all fought in a place called Tranh-binh.

But, as far as we knew, not General Garber.

Yet Garber had been afraid of Tranh-binh.

Why? An air force officer wouldn't normally be found in a ground battle.

I studied the photograph, searching for answers.

Possibilities danced through my mind, but nothing jelled. I saw the blackened hillsides in the background, the shadowy outlines of bodies visible through the burned trees. I tried to count the dead, but there were too many. I felt a growing sense of horror.

What the hell happened at Tranh-binh?

33

No one. Gibson says no one tried to get into Garber's office."

I set the photo down as Amanda entered the room, her face locked in a scowl. She said loudly, "It was a goddamn waste of time, Marty. If he knows anything, he won't talk. Bastard."

She shut the door with a bang, then came over and deposited herself heavily in a chair before the desk.

She gave me a smile.

It took me a second. I said, "Baker?"

"Yeah. She was giving Gibson the evil eye when we left the office. I had to act pissed off to cover for him."

"So he talked?"

"Oh, yeah. He talked. Two people tried to get into the office after he arrived. The first was our girl Weller."

I nodded. I wasn't particularly surprised, since this might explain her sudden departure from the hangar.

"She showed about an hour ago," Amanda continued. "When Gibson told her the office was secure, Weller got upset and began to argue. Baker joined in on Weller's side, and the three of them went at it. When Gibson wouldn't back down, Weller left. Ten minutes later, a man strolls in, has a word with Baker, then walks up to Gibson and hands him a cell phone. On the other end was Gibson's boss, a Lieutenant Sanchez.

"Sanchez read Gibson the riot act and ordered him to let the guy into the office. Sanchez also told Gibson that he wasn't to mention anything about him to us. Gibson said the guy didn't stay long. Not more than a few minutes."

I asked, "Did he see him leave with a picture?"

"No, but the guy had a briefcase."

"Gibson know this man's name?"

Amanda produced her notepad and began turning pages. "Yeah. He read it off his entry badge. Gibson described him as a freak. Face was all burned. Here it is—"

"Stefanski."

She squinted at her pad, then at me. "How'd you know?"

I pushed the photo to her and began to explain.

It took me almost ten minutes to lay out everything I'd learned from my up-close-and-personal with the generals. Afterward, I gave Amanda my theories on the murder. There were three:

1. One general, probably Markel, had murdered Garber on his own, and the others were protecting him.
2. The three generals had conspired together to murder Garber.
3. Colonel Weller had killed Garber with the assistance of one of the other generals, again probably Markel.

When I finished, Amanda looked up from the notes she'd been making and immediately began tossing out questions, trying to fill in the holes. "Do you think the motive had something to do with what happened at Tranh-binh?"

"We know General Garber expressed a fear of Tranh-binh."

"But why would an air force officer have been in the battle?"

"He could have been a FAC." Air force officers often were attached to army units as forward air controllers, with the responsibility for calling in air strikes.

"I thought FACs in 'Nam usually flew, Marty."

"Most did, but a few were ground FACs. I'm all ears if you've got a better explanation."

She searched her brain, then shook her head. After scanning her notes, she brought up General Sessler's statement that Garber had urges he couldn't control. She added, "Sessler's making it sound like our initial theory was right all along, that Garber was killed trying to rape Weller."

"I know."

"You think he was telling the truth?"

I recalled my impressions. "It sounded like it, but there's no way to be sure. This could be another element in their smoke-and-mirrors campaign."

She frowned. "You're telling me Garber could have been killed because of something that happened at Tranh-binh—"

"Perhaps."

"—and not the rape?"

I sighed. "Who knows? We don't even know if a rape attempt occurred."

"So we're back to Simon's theory. The rape charge could be a fabrication, to give Churchfield ammunition to force Senator Garber into dropping the investigation."

I nodded.

"Same thing with this Tranh-binh connection; it could be pure bullshit. Another attempt by General Sessler to throw us off."

"Right."

Her eyes drifted down to General Markel's photograph. "I've got to tell you, I've got problems accepting Tranh-binh as a motive. We're supposed to believe that the other chiefs have hated Garber because of something that happened there. And that hatred is somehow linked to the killing."

"Revenge," I said, stating the obvious.

She looked up. "That's what I don't understand. The plaque says the battle took place in 1970. That's almost thirty-three years ago. If the generals wanted revenge against Garber, why didn't they do anything until now?"

I didn't even try to come up with an answer.

She shook her head. "You know what the problem with this case is, Marty? *Everybody* hated Garber. We can't really rule anybody out. Take Andy, for instance. What the hell is his role?"

"He's part of the conspiracy. If not the murder, the cover-up."

"Do you think he could have orchestrated the murder on his own?"

"No. If that were the case, I doubt the generals would cover for him. You don't buy it, huh?" I could see the skepticism on her face.

"Uh-uh. They were all war buddies. That's a bond that's hard to break. They've obviously been protecting him for years, even though he's been a fuck-up. Why would they stop now?"

I couldn't disagree.

She studied her notes. "You realize all your scenarios imply premeditation. Yet, the crime scene clearly suggests—"

"Remember, the scene was staged. I think that was Andy's role. To stage everything."

"He didn't do a very good job."

"That's probably because he didn't plan it in great detail beforehand; he had no reason to. Andy hadn't anticipated a full-blown investigation. He'd assumed he would be the investigating officer. With Billy Bowman's help as the ME, Andy figured it'd be a piece of cake to write the death off as an accident. It was only after he found out we were coming on board that he started throwing in the rest of the evidence, like the bottle and shirt buttons. He knew the accident theory wouldn't hold up, and he knew had to give us somewhere to look."

Amanda was nodding; she'd considered all this. "To focus us away from the real killers?"

"Sure."

She thoughtfully tapped a tooth. "I wish to hell we knew Weller's role. She's too involved to only be part of the cover-up."

"Not necessarily. She could just be extremely loyal to Markel."

"Why'd she leave him to work for Garber, then?"

I shook my head. Another mystery.

"By the way," Amanda added. "I forgot to mention that Weller also lied to us about the picture of Garber in her purse. I checked with Sergeant Brinker on the admin staff. He confirmed General Garber passed out photos of himself all the time. But he never insisted that anyone carry them around."

I shrugged. "Weller might have misunderstood. Or maybe she wanted to cover herself in case he did ask."

"That still doesn't explain why the photos Garber handed out were different than hers."

"They were?"

Amanda removed a wallet-sized picture from her jacket pocket and gave it to me. The smiling face of Garber peered back. He had four stars.

"There's a file full of these in the admin section," Amanda said. "Brinker told me Garber only passed out pictures showing him as a full general. Knowing the guy's ego, it fits." She paused, eyeing me. "So how did Weller get her hands on an old photo? She's only worked for him for a couple weeks."

I gave the picture a final glance and passed it back. Another loose end with no logical explanation.

We sat in a pensive silence. Amanda was hunched forward, staring at Garber's photograph. Her eyes shifted to the Tranh-binh picture, then to the one showing Churchfield pinning a medal on Weller. Without looking up, she said, "It's all about the past, isn't it, Marty? If we understood what happened, we'd understand the case."

"Probably."

"I keep thinking we're missing something. Something obvious."

I had the same feeling.

She sighed, pocketed Garber's picture, then held me in a level gaze. "You know, I'm still not sure I want to solve this thing."

"Neither am I."

Our eyes lingered on each other. Despite her reservations, I knew she was too dedicated a cop to suggest that we tank our investigation.

"So," she said finally, "what's our next move? You want to see what I can dig up on Tranh-binh?"

"Please."

Amanda took the chair behind the desk, booted up the computer, then logged in with the user name and password that Charlie Hinkle had provided. As I stood over her, I kept coming back to her earlier comment.

It's all about the past.

As I snatched up the desk phone, Amanda said, "You're thinking there could be a connection to the scandal?"

"Yeah. Simon should have finished talking to that reporter by now.

Simon never answered his cell or car phone. After leaving a messages on both voice mails, I watched over Amanda's shoulder as she began her computer search. Ten minutes later, we knew something was wrong. From the photo, it was clear Tranh-binh had been a major engagement, and Amanda should have turned up dozens of hits on old news stories with an account of what had occurred.

But there wasn't a single hit that pertained to a battle. Not in the military databases—either classified or open source—or in general search engines.

Amanda looked up from the screen. "I don't understand it. There has to be something. You think we've got the spelling wrong?"

Like I would know. I said, "Try searching Vietnam battles by date."

She did, and came up empty. She varied the spelling, dropping first one h, then the second. She brought up a map of Vietnam and tried hunting for the name. She swore.

As she continued clicking away on the mouse, I asked her for the passenger list. She pointed to the file that she'd given me. She'd stuck the list at the very back, behind Andy's OPRs.

Even though the convenient flu epidemic suggested I would come up empty, I began calling the passengers we had yet to interview.

I gave up after the first half-dozen. None were at work, and no one answered their home numbers. I tried Andy's home and his cellular. When he didn't pick up, I rang Martha Jones. She said Andy hadn't returned to the hangar, confirming he'd taken a powder for good.

I said, "Carter and Gentry there?"

"No, they went to lunch."

"When?"

"Oh, about thirty minutes ago. They should return soon."

Like hell.

Thinking back, I realized it had to be this way. They all had to be in on it.

When I asked, Martha told me she'd almost finished dusting the closet interior and hadn't found a single print.

"We won't find anything, Marty. The entire closet's been wiped. There's not even any prints on the doors."

An anticipated result. This was a detail Andy would have remembered.

After ending the call, I phoned Simon again, this time with the added purpose of having him notify Senator Garber that we were being stonewalled.

"This is Lieutenant Simon Santos. If you'll leave a number at the tone—"

I punched off after leaving another message, debated for a few seconds, then called Senator Garber directly.

His secretary gave me the usual brush-off, saying the senator was unavailable.

I said, "He'll take my call, ma'am. If you'll just let him know—"

"That's quite impossible, Mr. Collins. Are you a constituent? I can transfer you to Mrs. Ortiz. He handles the senator's—"

"This matter concerns his son."

"General Garber? Could you give me some specifics?"

Her brusque manner confirmed she hadn't been told of the murder. I backed off, explaining it was a private matter. After I gave her my number, I clicked off, thinking I was really starting to dislike secretaries.

"Marty . . ."

When I glanced over, Amanda was staring at the screen. I said, "You get a hit?"

"I'm not sure." She had a puzzled expression. "I found a Tranh-binh, but it's not a place."

As I swung around for a look, I understood her confusion. I was staring at a Web page with the words Ko Tranh-binh scrawled across the top.

And below it, the face of a man.

34

It was actually a long bio, fully two pages long, found on
a Web site that listed prominent North Vietnamese and
Vietcong generals. I skipped the part about Ko Tranh-
binh's formative years as a progressive young Communist
and focused on his military career.

> . . . a protégé of General Giap, the legendary North
> Vietnamese commander, General Ko Tranh-binh
> established his reputation as brilliant military strate-
> gist by orchestrating the bombardment against the
> French at Dien Bien Phu. . . .

I shifted down.

> . . . studied military tactics in the Soviet Union, Ko
> Tranh-binh returned to Vietnam and was a central
> figure in planning the campaign against the
> Americans. He was promoted to general in 1968
> and for two years led the North Vietnamese forces
> that operated out of the Central Highlands. . . .

Paragraphs on his exploits followed. I scanned them. Even accounting for the hyperbole, the guy had been a stud. My eyes finally settled on the last line of the bio: He'd been killed inspecting troop positions in 1970.

By an enemy sniper.

I slowly let out a breath. Another connection.

Amanda said quietly, "The year matches. Markel must have been the one who took him out."

My eyes dropped to Markel's photograph. "But why would he put Tranh-binh's name on this instead of the actual location of the engagement?"

"It could be it was some kind of morbid joke. It's not like he took out a high-ranking general every day."

I wondering if that's all it really was. Just some kind of—

"There's more, Marty."

"More?"

She opened up a new window on the screen. Another bio appeared. Only this time it had a pretty blue border and was titled "General Michael J. Garber."

Noting my blank look, she explained, "This proves General Garber couldn't have been engaged in a ground battle in 'Nam." She pointed. "Third paragraph, second line."

I saw it then. Garber had been a fighter pilot in Vietnam, not an FAC.

"I don't see a date," I said. "Was he in 'Nam in '70?"

"There's no date listed." She looked up at me. "But even if Garber was in Vietnam then, I don't think it matters. The guy was a fighter jock. Flew F-105s. He wouldn't be crawling around with the grunts."

I said, "He could have been shot down."

"And that would be the basis of a thirty-year grudge because—"

She was right; I was reaching for something that

wasn't there. I said, "I don't understand why Sessler would try and link Garber to something that occurred during the war, when it's not true. He had to know we'd check."

She shrugged. "All I can tell you is that if there was a battle, Garber wasn't there, unless maybe he was flying over. Dropping bombs or firing rockets—"

She stopped. Her eyes slowly went to the photograph.

She grabbed it and held it close. She murmured, "Could it . . ."

I said, "Could what? What do you see?"

But she was in a zone, lost in the image. She was so still she didn't appear to be breathing. I said, "Amanda . . ."

There was response. Her hand began to shake. I touched her, and she turned to me with a look somewhere between revulsion and horror. She said dully, "The hillside, Marty. It's burned. All of it."

"Yeah. So?"

"The bodies, too."

"I know. I saw—"

And then I understood. My eyes darted to the photo in her hand. What she was suggesting was unthinkable. And yet . . .

The realization sank in. It was true. It had to be true. Before I was aware of it, I heard myself speaking, saying what we both now knew. "Enemy artillery . . . it couldn't do that. Burn that much ground."

"Nothing could, Marty. Nothing except napalm."

And only America had employed napalm during the war.

Dropped by fighter pilots.

•   •   •

Somewhere in the room, a clock ticked. We heard the distant sound of a ringing phone. Amanda and I continued to stare at the photograph, imagining what must have happened. How a fighter pilot in the heat of battle had gotten confused and dropped the napalm on the wrong coordinates.

And incinerated American soldiers.

"It might not have been Garber," Amanda said. "It could have been someone else."

"Maybe," I said.

But we couldn't get around the hate.

Amanda set down the picture and looked at me. "General Sessler. He told you the truth. They all had motive."

"Including Stefanski. His burns . . . he must have been at the battle. Only, I don't recall seeing his name." I snatched up the file and checked the passenger list. "Not there, but this explains why he threatened Mrs. Garber. The last thing he'd want is for us to find Garber's killer."

"Especially if it's his buddy Markel."

I nodded, tossing the file to the desk.

Amanda's eyes searched my face. "How could this have been kept quiet, Marty? All these years? It couldn't be just because of the influence of Senator Garber. He was only a congressman back then. He wouldn't have that kind of pull."

I gave her a long look. "I think you know the answer."

She slowly nodded, a flicker of understanding in her eyes.

Even though this was before her time, Amanda knew what America was like in 1970. She knew about the riots and turmoil and the public's anger over the war. With the country on the brink of rupturing, she knew the government couldn't risk fueling the antiwar flames by revealing that dozens of young men had been killed not by the enemy, but by one of their own.

So a decision was made to keep the friendly-fire incident quiet. Tie it up in a bright red top-secret ribbon to prevent the survivors from revealing what they knew.

And for thirty-three years the cover-up had apparently succeeded.

Until now.

Suspicion was one thing, but we had to know. I picked up the desk phone and thumbed in the number. This time Simon answered.

Simon rarely sounded down, but he did so now. He said he'd meant to return my calls, but had been tied up in a meeting with Senator Garber. As he spoke, I could hear voices in the background. A man and a woman were discussing an upcoming vote. The woman said, "I'll pass on your concerns to the senator, but he hasn't decided on whether to support—"

"But he has to vote for the bill, Joan," the man said. "Senator Carson is threatening a filibuster. He thinks we're acting to hastily on this attack on Iraq. Senator Houck is relying upon—"

Simon sighed loudly. "He lied to me, Martin. He knew of the motive from the beginning, but never told me."

"Senator Garber?"

"Yes. I came here to confront him with what I'd learned. He confirmed there'd been an operation in Vietnam where— Excuse me." He turned away from the phone and spoke to someone. "She's arriving at two-thirty?" he said. "All right, tell the senator I'll attend. Is there somewhere quiet I could . . . Thank you, Margaret."

The sound of a door closing, and the background voices disappeared. Simon came back on the line. "In some respects, I blame myself. I knew there had to be a reason Senator Garber was convinced his son had been killed. I should have pressured him, but I didn't. Frankly, I don't know what he was thinking. This is a murder investigation. He should have realized his son's actions would eventually come to light." He sounded angry.

I said, "So Garber's death is linked to the story that's coming out in the paper tomorrow?"

"Of course. It goes to motive. General Garber was a fighter pilot in Vietnam. During a mission, he made a tragic error—"

"And killed American troops," I finished.

"You know?"

"Amanda put it together," I said. "We don't have any details. I assume you've read the article—"

"Yes, yes. The account is rather involved, and I'd rather not go into this twice. Is Amanda with you?"

"Yeah. Hang on." I checked the desk phone; it had a speaker. I found the button and cradled the receiver. "Go."

Moments later, Simon began detailing the tragic events that occurred three decades earlier. As Amanda and I listened, I don't think either of us expected to hear anything worse than the horror we'd imagined.

We did.

The battle of Hill 114.

A generic name derived from the map designation for a nondescript mound of earth that served no military purpose other than the fact that a regiment of NVA— North Vietnamese Army regulars—had selected it as an encampment.

On July 28, 1970, a battalion of American infantry attacked Hill 114 and were bitterly repulsed by the entrenched enemy. Over the ensuing three days, the Americans launched more futile attacks up the steep slopes, sustaining heavy casualties. In the early-morning hours of the fourth day, a battalion of marines arrived to reinforce the army troops. The plan was to make one final overwhelming assault to dislodge the NVA.

It was during the preparation for this attack, while the exhausted soldiers were sleeping or resting, that First Lieutenant Michael Garber made the mistake of his life.

"Garber was the lead aircraft of two," Simon said, "As he initiated his attack, he tried to avoid ground fire and maneuvered his aircraft too violently, tearing loose one of the napalm canisters on his wing. It fell near the base of the hill, where a number of the soldiers were gathered, including the wounded. Those men never had a chance. They were incinerated within moments. A number died later, before they could be evacuated. Apparently napalm canisters are extremely heavy and when carrying them pilots were instructed to never exceed a certain load—"

"G's," Amanda said automatically.

"Garber's maneuver," Simon continued, "far exceeded the restriction. The article alleges that the tragedy wasn't merely an error on Garber's part, but negligence. He should never have been flying. His reflexes were impaired, and that contributed to the excessive force he applied on the flight controls.

"In fairness to General Garber, he hadn't been scheduled to fly. But he was one of the more exceptional pilots, and there was pressure from his superiors. Still, Garber should have exercised better judgment. He didn't, and men died."

Simon fell silent. Amanda and I waited for him to continue. After a few seconds, I prompted, "By impaired—"

"He'd been drinking, Martin."

The speaker hissed. I looked to Amanda, and she shook her head grimly. "The dead?" she asked Simon. "How many?"

"Sixty-three."

"Lord . . ." She shut her eyes, visualizing the carnage. I felt sickened. This was a horrific number. I said, "I know the military covered this up, kept this from the public—"

"Quite effectively. The incident was immediately given the highest security classification. Anyone involved was threatened with prison if they spoke of it."

"Even so," I said, "I'm not sure I understand how General Garber continued to get promoted. There would be rumors. The pilots in Garber's squadron, his wingman during the mission, they would know—"

"Lieutenant Douglas Anderson," Simon said, "flew the second aircraft. He was shot down and killed during his attack run. Only Garber's superiors knew what had transpired, and they certainly had no desire to tell what they knew. After all, they were the ones who put Garber in the plane when they knew he wasn't fit to fly."

Amanda said, "But the survivors. At least some would certainly push for—"

"They were told that the pilot hadn't been at fault. The military concocted a story about how ground fire had struck the plane's release mechanism."

"Perfect," Amanda murmured. "Blame it on the Vietnamese."

"So who finally talked?" I asked Simon. "Leaked the story?"

"My newspaper source is trying to find out. The information in the article came from a classified report, which documented the incident. We can assume the report was leaked by one of the generals, since only someone high up in the military could have gained access to the information."

Amanda asked him if the battle had ever been called Tranh-binh.

"Why, yes," Simon said. "The survivors named it after a Vietnamese general who was killed. How did you know?"

"General Markel," Amanda said. "He shot the general."

"He told you this?" Simon said.

Amanda explained about Markel's photograph and the assumption she'd made. As she began ticking off who else had been involved in the battle, Simon interrupted her. "*Andy* was there?"

"You didn't know?"

"No. Senator Garber only mentioned the generals." Simon was clearly annoyed; he hated being the last one to know. "All right. Tell me everything you've learned."

Amanda looked to me to pass the ball, since I'd been the one who'd met with the generals. After I filled Simon in, he said, "This missing photograph of General Garber's. You're sure it's from his college years?"

"Pretty sure."

He was quiet, thinking about this. Over the speaker, we heard someone knock on a door. Then a woman's voice: "Secretary Churchfield is here, Lieutenant."

"A moment, Margaret," Simon said.

I said to him, "Churchfield's meeting with Senator Garber?"

"Yes. I'm puzzled that she's making this move so soon. Obviously, she's concerned we might succeed in uncovering the truth. Did you say something that might alarm her, Martin?"

"I never spoke to her."

"You must have said *something* to the generals."

"Only what they already knew. That they were suspects."

"Curious." Simon paused. "Not that it matters. I discussed this eventuality with Senator Garber. He's assured me he's determined to find the killer. Ironically, tomorrow's article made his decision easier. His son's reputation can't be damaged much more by the rape charge. This meeting shouldn't take long. Have you finished at the Pentagon?"

I explained that we'd been unable to interview any of the remaining passengers. He interrupted me. "They are of little concern. We have more pressing matters. Write this down—"

I fumbled for my pen, then saw Amanda already had one out. As she jotted down a Fairfax address, I asked Simon whom we were meeting there.

"Dr. Bowman. At his home. I've spoken to his wife, and she's expecting him to return around four."

I frowned. "His wife? Billy doesn't know we're coming?"

"No."

Amanda was shaking her head. I shared her sentiment and told Simon that Billy probably wouldn't cooperate no matter how much money he offered. I said, "The guy's a lock to get a star. He's not going to give that up."

"We need to know the time of death."

"Why? What's so important about—"

The woman said impatiently to Simon, "Lieutenant, please. They're waiting for you."

Simon mumbled an apology, then spoke rapidly to Amanda and me. "Don't interrupt. Do exactly as I say, and Dr. Bowman will cooperate. He will have no choice. When you call for the car, I want you to—"

He ran through his plan and hung up. As I toggled off the speaker, Amanda eyed me uneasily. "You realize what he's doing?"

"Using us for bait." I picked up the phone to call for the car.

35

Before leaving, we had one remaining item to check out. After Amanda printed out the bios on Churchfield and the generals, we perused them and came up empty. None had ever attended the University of Virginia.

"Wright College?" Amanda was scanning Churchfield's bio. "Never heard of it." She looked at me.

"Sorry."

She shoved the pages into the file. "Anything else you want to put in here?"

I checked my jacket pockets and produced General Garber's itinerary to England. As she placed it inside, she asked, "What about Stefanski? He's old enough to have been at UVA when Garber was there."

"Forget it. He got his degree after his stint in Vietnam."

"So what? A lot of guys put in a year or two of college before being drafted."

Point taken.

On our way out we stopped by Markel's office. His exec, Brigadier General Clay, seemed puzzled by our request, but he made a phone call to somebody in personnel.

"Indiana State," he said. "Graduated in 'seventy-five."

"Strike two," Amanda said as we left.

I nodded. The first strike had been the location of Wright State, Churchfield's college. Amanda had looked it up on the Net and learned it was a small liberal arts school in Idaho.

Which was also a long way from Virginia.

At precisely 3:10, we emerged from the JCS area, turned in our entry badges, and retraced our steps toward the Corridor Two entrance. We walked slowly and made a conscious effort not to turn around. The same female cop was manning the security checkpoint and as before, we saw her pick up a phone.

As we pushed through the doors into the bright sunlight, my phone rang. It was Thad Fuller, calling to say he'd x-rayed the closet and the main doors, and didn't detect anything unusual in the lock assemblies. Thad sounded a little disappointed, and I told him not to worry about it. When I hung up, Amanda pointed out the gleaming cherry-red BMW parked at the base of the pedestrian bridge. A man in a dark suit stood beside it, looking our direction. I threw up a hand, and he waved back.

"Right on time," Amanda said.

"They better be, at the prices they charge."

"You should have ordered a Rolls."

"They didn't have one in red." This had been something Simon insisted on, so we would be easier to tail.

"A Porsche would have been nice."

She had me. "Next time, you call."

We crossed the bridge and came down the steps. The man's name was Enrique. He was late thirties, pretty-boy handsome, and his silk suit probably cost more than I took home in a week. He had a firm handshake, wore a diamond in his left ear, and smelled of flowers.

As he handed me the paperwork, I gestured to Amanda. "She likes to drive."

"Of course," he said smoothly.

Once she signed the paperwork, he gave her a million-dollar smile and the keys. On cue, a green Jag pulled up, but before climbing in, Enrique whispered something into my ear. We both laughed, and I tossed him a wave as he drove away.

As we got in the car, Amanda deposited the file she'd been carrying onto the backseat, then sat back, frowning at me. "You going to tell me what's so funny?"

"Nothing. We were playing it cool. Enrique told me about a couple of guys in suits sitting in a car."

Her face went blank.

"Simon," I said, "owns the rental company. He hires a lot of former cops."

"Enrique's a cop? I thought he was gay."

"He is. He was still one helluva cop. Got tossed from the force for almost beating a child killer to death. Two rows up on the left. We should go right by them." I gave her the description of the car.

"Maroon? Enrique see the guys inside?"

"Yeah. Sounds like Mutt and Jeff."

Since it was approaching rush hour, the drive to Fairfax would take at least forty-five minutes. As we merged southbound onto I-395 to pick up the King Street exit, Amanda checked the rearview mirror, confirmed the maroon Buick was still following, then clicked on the radio and selected a hip-hop station. I gave her an exasperated look. She sighed and changed to elevator music.

I said, "You don't have to be that extreme."

"Fine," she said irritably. "You do it."

I punched *scan*. Heavy metal. I pressed again and settled for an oldies station.

It was a mistake.

Moments later, a Barry Manilow love song came on. As we listened to it, I caught Amanda looking at me. After the third glance, she said, "You know, it wouldn't hurt to take a chance on something new."

I shrugged. "What's the point? I know what I like and—"

Then I saw the disappointment in her eyes. She shook her head pityingly, and I heard the sadness in her voice.

"You're right, Marty. You'll never change, Marty. You can't."

I looked away from her, my pulse quickening. I now realized what she was really trying to say.

Even though she'd given me an opening, I couldn't take it. More than anything, I wanted to avoid a repeat of our earlier confrontation. We rode in a strained silence, neither of us willing to make the next move. When the song ended, Amanda said softly, "I know, Marty."

I felt her eyes on me. I didn't reply.

"Simon," she said. "He told you, didn't he? About the way I feel?"

I finally turned to her. Her beautiful face was a mask, eyes fixed straight ahead. I said, "How did you find out?"

"The way you've been acting. It's not like you've been exactly subtle." She wouldn't look at me. "Besides, I expected him to tell you eventually. Frankly, I didn't think it would take this long."

"You *wanted* me know?"

She hesitated. "Part of me did. I had this silly idea that

maybe if you knew, it would make things easier. Somehow."

"Amanda, I care for you a great deal. But with my situation—"

"Don't, Marty. Please. No explanations."

"No. I want you to understand that this . . . this has nothing to do with you. It's me. If things were different—"

"But they aren't. And the last time I checked, three was still a crowd." She gave me a tiny smile. "It's okay. We're still friends. Let's leave it at that, huh?"

"I don't want this to change anything between us."

She sighed, her eyes returning to the road. "It won't, Marty. We're adults. We can handle this."

But of course we were fooling ourselves. From this moment on, nothing would ever be the same between us; it couldn't. I think that's what I regretted most, the fact that our relationship was forever changed. Soon she would pull back completely; she wouldn't want to be reminded of this rejection. When that happened, I would miss her, and so would Emily.

My earlier sense of loss returned. Despite my attraction to Amanda, I knew I'd done the only thing I could. Anything else wouldn't have been fair. She deserved someone who could commit himself fully to her, who wasn't weighed down by the memories of his dead wife or a child—

"Marty, your phone's ringing."

It was my daughter Emily. Hearing her voice was the emotional boost I needed. Glancing at the clock on the dash, I saw it was three-thirty; she'd just gotten out of school.

"Dad, I don't have much time before the bus, but I had to call. I'm . . . I'm sorry about this morning."

"So am I, honey."

"If I could have shown you the letter, I would have. Mom . . . she only wanted me to read it. Please understand." Her voice quivered, and she sounded close to tears.

"Emily," I said gently, "it's okay. It's no big deal about the letter."

"But, Dad, it *is* a big deal. The letter, I mean. I'm confused. Mom told me something. I need . . . I *have* to talk to somebody."

"I'm here."

"Dad, please."

"Amanda is with me." She was listening, her face knitted with concern.

"No," Emily said with sudden feeling. "Not Amanda. It has to be . . . I was thinking . . . Uncle Simon. Do you think I could call him?"

I tried to keep my surprise in check. "I . . . well . . . I suppose. But he's kind of busy, honey."

"He's your best friend, right?"

"He's a good friend."

"It won't take long. I just want to ask him a question. Dad, I gotta go. I'll miss the bus."

"You'll need his cell phone number."

"I'll look it up in the computer. I love you, Dad."

"I love you, too."

As I tucked the phone away, Amanda said, "What was that all about?"

I sighed. "I wish I knew."

After I explained, she said, "Now you've got me wondering what's in the letter. Emily usually tells me everything. The boys she likes, what music she's into . . ."

"Boys? What boys?"

She winked. "You'd be surprised."

"She's *twelve*."

"Chill, Dad. She's thirteen tomorrow."

"Even so—"

"*Change*, Marty," she said with a sardonic smile. "Everyone changes. Moves on with their life. Get used to it."

I caught the dig. Still, I probably deserved it. "You still see our friends?"

Her eyes flickered to the rearview mirror. "Yeah. They're playing it cool. Always keeping a few cars back."

I was still thinking about the letter. I couldn't get it out of my mind. But I had a job to do, and I tried to refocus on the case by looking over my notes.

After several minutes, Amanda asked, "You looking for anything in particular?"

I shrugged. "Trying to find out what we missed. Simon must have a reason for thinking the time of death is so important."

"Maybe he's mistaken for once."

I gave her a look. "He isn't."

She reluctantly nodded. "I don't get it. How does he see stuff that we don't? He's smart, but so are we."

"He says he thinks outside the box."

"That's it?"

"That's it."

For the remainder of the drive, we discussed varying possibilities, no matter how seemingly improbable. As we turned onto a tree-lined street in a quiet Fairfax neighborhood, I threw out a final suggestion. I hadn't meant for Amanda to take it seriously, which was why her reaction caught me off guard.

She inhaled sharply, as if in surprise. She turned to

me, her face flushed with excitement. "*Shit*—that could be it, Marty. That would explain why they kept the body so cold and why he was wearing cologne. And the hairs in the shower. Why they cleaned up. We had it all wrong. It wasn't someone *else's* hairs they were worried about us finding—"

"You're not talking sense, Amanda. What about all the witnesses?"

"They're all suspects or staffers. They could all be lying. They have to be lying. We're on to something. I can feel it."

"You're forgetting Sergeant Blake. She specifically told me she saw General Garber."

"So what? She could be in on the cover-up. She could have said that so—"

She was looking at me more than the road. I sat up, pointing. "Better slow down. That's Billy's house. Simon's already here."

36

We parked behind the limo. The driver, Bennie, was behind the wheel, reading a paper. As we got out of the car, he gave us a hesitant wave. While I waited for Amanda to retrieve the file from the backseat, I checked out the maroon Buick. It had pulled against the curb a block away. I could make out faces watching us.

Amanda said, "Not exactly subtle, are they?"

"No."

"I don't like this, Marty. They're going to know why we're here."

"It can't be helped. Besides, their orders are probably only to keep tabs on us."

She said uneasily. "And if it's more than that?"

I knew what was bothering her. She was reacting to Churchfield's apparent concern that we might uncover the truth before the clock ran out. "Relax," I said. "They're not going to jump a couple of cops in broad daylight."

"Thanks," she said sarcastically. "I feel a whole lot better now."

The Bowmans lived in a cookie-cutter colonial two-story fronted by colorful flower beds and a neatly trimmed lawn. As we headed up the walkway toward the front door, Amanda said, "Call Sergeant Blake."

"Amanda, it's not possible—"

"It was your suggestion."

"I was joking."

"You said we should consider the improbable, think out of the box."

"Not that far out."

She slapped the file to my chest. "Call, or I will."

I sighed and opened the file for the number. This time Sergeant Blake sounded wide awake.

"Well, now that you mention it, sir—"

Amanda was ringing the doorbell when I ended the call. She read my stunned expression and said, "My God, Marty, I honestly didn't think—"

The door opened.

A small, doughy woman with an annoyingly bubbly personality, Deloris Bowman could probably dethrone Martha Stewart for the title of America's Homemaker if she tried. Bridge parties, wives' teas, charity dinners, you name it, Deloris always volunteered to play hostess. While she enjoyed being the center of the military social scene, her main purpose was to ingratiate herself to the generals' wives, so she could whisper Billy's accomplishments in their ears. So far, her efforts had paid off spectacularly; her hubby was a boy colonel on the fast track to a star. Even though it had been a few years since we'd last met, I knew Deloris would remember me, or at least pretend to.

"Marty, it's been ages." We went through the drill of hugging like long-lost friends. After I introduced Amanda,

Deloris brought up Nicole's passing, saying how sorry she was that it happened. I just nodded, hoping she'd read my silence as a message that I didn't want to go there.

"How about a brownie?" she asked, taking the hint. "They're still warm. I just took them out of the oven. Something to drink?"

When Amanda and I declined the offer, she looked genuinely disappointed. "Billy's with your friend in the study. If you change your minds—"

"Thanks, Deloris. It's tempting."

Amanda and I continued down the hallway past an immaculate formal living room filled with freshly cut flowers, stopping at a set of double doors. At my knock, we heard a grunted reply and entered a typically masculine study of dark paneling, heavy wooden furnishings, and shelves brimming with medical books.

Simon nodded to us from one of the armchairs near the desk. Billy was standing by the wet bar in the corner, fixing a drink. Since he rarely drank during the day, I took this as an encouraging sign.

Dr. Billy Bowman, it seemed, was a worried man.

He carefully swirled a glass of what appeared to be Scotch, ignoring Amanda and me. The cold-shoulder treatment meant he was still stewing over my comments in the plane.

Returning to the desk, Billy sat down heavily, fortified himself with a swallow, then said to Simon, "Your offer is generous, Lieutenant. Hell, a million would go a long way toward funding my research."

"I could deliver the check tomorrow."

"I wish you would, Lord knows. But that won't change what I'm telling you. General Garber died between one and two A.M. The autopsy proves it."

"Does it?" Simon said mildly.

Garber studied him. "You questioning my conclusions?"

Simon smiled pleasantly. "I think you're lying, Doctor."

Billy's face reddened, matching his hair. Normally his temper would kick in and he'd tell Simon to go fuck himself. But apparently Billy wasn't quite ready to give up on the money yet.

So he calmed himself with another sip. Afterward, he said coolly, "My time of death stands, Lieutenant."

"Like your determination of accidental death."

Billy's face turned to stone. "Maybe you'd better leave, Lieutenant."

"Come now, Doctor. I'd hoped we could reach some kind of agreement."

"You're asking me to fabricate evidence. I won't do it."

"I'm only asking for the truth."

"I'm telling you the truth."

Simon shook his head regretfully. "Then it seems we're at an impasse. I must apologize. I wanted to avoid unpleasantries, but you leave me no option."

Billy squinted at the implication. "Unpleasantries? Is that some kind of threat? You trying to threaten me? Because if you are, you can go straight to—"

But Simon wasn't listening to him. Instead, he turned to Amanda and me and asked, "Were you followed?"

We nodded; she identified the men.

"*Churchfield's* men?" Billy said, sitting up. "What are they doing here? What the hell is this?"

His eyes darted to each of us, demanding a response. No one said anything.

He glowered at Simon. "You want to play hardball, fine. Discussion's over. I want you all to leave. *Now.*"

Simon remained seated and addressed him calmly. "I'll ask you once more: When was General Garber murdered?"

"I told you. Now get out of here."

Simon shrugged and looked to me. "Advise those men outside that we've spoken to Dr. Bowman. Tell them that he's informed us of General Garber's time of death. Speak in generalities. Just say we know it was"—Simon's eyes returned to Billy; he wanted to see his reaction—"significantly earlier than previously assumed."

He sat back and gave Billy a knowing smile.

There was a long silence. We all watched Billy.

At first, nothing. Billy was working hard to keep his face blank. But if you looked close, you could see the cracks start to appear. First came a slight tightening along the jawline, then a nervous shifting in his chair. When Billy spoke, he tried to sound casual but couldn't quite pull it off. "You're bluffing. You can't possibly know anything."

"We do," Simon said.

"How?"

"It doesn't matter," Simon said. "We know the truth."

"We all figured it out," Amanda said.

Simon looked to her in surprise. She smiled faintly. One for the B-team.

Billy shook his head, insisting, "That's impossible. You're guessing. You can't—"

Simon interrupted him. "We can place the general's death within a few hours. If you don't cooperate, we will reveal to those men outside that you provided us this information. They will believe us. They know that's why we came here. Things will go badly for you. Your safety could be jeopardized. There have been threats against

Mrs. Garber, to prevent her from revealing what she knows."

Billy stared at Simon in astonishment. His mouth moved, but there was no sound.

Simon went for the kill, talking fast. "Frankly, I'd rather avoid that step, Doctor. At the very least, the consequences to your career would be severe. Your wife seems a very pleasant woman, and I'd rather not take such a drastic measure. I have no desire to destroy you professionally or ruin your lives. But make no mistake, I will. *I want to know the exact time of death.*"

Billy's eye twitched under Simon's relentless gaze. He drained his Scotch and coughed. For the first time, we detected defeat in his eyes. He looked at Simon and said bleakly, "It seems I don't have any options."

"One."

Billy slowly set down the glass on the desk. "Hell, I'm screwed either way. If I tell you, they'll know I talked."

"Not from us."

"C'mon, Lieutenant. They'll figure it eventually."

"They might suspect," Simon said. "But we'll deny it. We'll insist we learned the truth from the evidence."

It wasn't much of an out, but it was all Billy could hope for. He nodded his acceptance.

By now, Amanda and I had our notepads out. She took the chair beside Simon, and I sat on the sofa against the wall.

In a resigned voice, Billy began describing his analysis of the stomach contents, which was the key to establishing when Garber had died. He said the contents were only partially digested, which indicated that the general had died less than two hours after consuming his last meal, give or take thirty minutes. Since Garber didn't eat during the flight, that left one irrefutable conclusion. The one I'd considered impossible only minutes earlier.

General Garber had been dead before he'd ever been placed on the plane.

37

B illy wrapped up his summary of the autopsy results by explaining that he was still awaiting the toxicology reports that would confirm whether or not Garber had been drugged.

"But he was definitely drunk," he said. "General Garber's blood tested at .022. Over twice the legal limit. The guy was bombed off his ass."

Simon said, "Did you note his inebriation level on the autopsy?"

"Yeah. It supported the accidental death theory. That he'd fallen because he was drunk."

Simon asked him if he'd been told when Garber had eaten his last meal.

"No," Billy said, "and I wasn't about to ask. I figured the less I knew, the better."

I looked up from my writing. "Hang on a sec."

As everyone watched me, I removed Garber's itinerary from the file. I found what I was looking for on the last page. "Here it is. All the generals attended a dinner party the evening before they left. At the officers' mess on Brize Norton Air Base, near London. Cocktails at 1900, dinner at 2000. If we subtract five hours to get local time, that means Garber ate around 1600."

"So time of death would be around 1800," Amanda said.

Simon and Billy nodded. Simon said, "And the plane departed England at—"

I looked. "At 0200. That makes it 2200 our time. They took off from Brize Norton"—I checked at the first page—"which is also where they were quartered."

"Convenient," Simon murmured.

"Yeah," I said. "That probably explains how they were able to get his body on board without anybody noticing. They were on a military field. They could have driven right up to the plane without being stopped."

Everyone was quiet for a moment.

Amanda said, "Timing works out. We can assume Garber was killed somewhere around 2130 to 2200, British time. That means they could have easily gotten his body aboard the plane before the other passengers arrived."

I nodded, my eyes on Billy, "Who ordered you to fabricate the autopsy?"

"Secretary Churchfield and General Markel. Churchfield contacted me first. She called last night. It must have been around 2130. She said she wanted—"

"Back up," I said, doing the math. "She called you *before* the plane took off from England."

"Apparently."

Simon turned to me, "You're wondering how Churchfield knew about Garber's death so quickly?"

"Yeah. Churchfield phoned Billy within an hour after Garber was killed. Assuming she needed time to figure out how to deal with the situation, that means the killer must have contacted Churchfield within minutes of Garber's death."

"Implying what?" Amanda said. "You think Churchfield *arranged* the killing?"

I massaged my scalp, trying to think this through. "Hell, I don't know. I just find it hard to accept that someone murders Garber and immediately calls the SECDEF. If I'd been the killer, I'd get as far away from the scene of the crime as I could and work on setting up an alibi. I sure as hell wouldn't phone the secretary of defense and tell her I'd killed the chairman of the Joint Chiefs. How would he know how she'd react? How would he know she'd go along with the cover-up?"

Another silence. Simon closed his eyes and shook his head. This didn't make sense to him either. I said to Billy, "Getting back to Churchfield's call—"

"Right. Sure. At first, I didn't really believe it was her. The SECDEF calling me at home? I mean, I'd met her before. After the attack on the Pentagon, I was in charge of processing the bodies. Anyway, she told me there'd been a tragic accident involving General Garber, and she needed my help. That's why I went along. What was I supposed to do? How the hell do you turn down the Secretary of Defense?"

His eyes searched my face, seeking a response. I nodded, tried to appear sympathetic.

Simon said to him, "Secretary Churchfield's demeanor—how would you describe it?"

Good question. He was trying to determine whether her emotional reaction to Garber's corpse had been genuine.

"She was understandably uptight," Billy said. "Kept asking me over and over if I knew what I was supposed to do."

"Did she express any regret over General Garber's death?" Simon asked.

"Not to me. All she was concerned about was how I was going to handle my end of it. Whether I'd do what she wanted and keep my mouth shut."

So much for the confirmation we wanted. Simon said, "You mentioned you also spoke with General Markel—"

"Churchfield told me I'd autopsy General Garber's body at Walter Reed. General Markel called me this morning to say that the plan had changed, and I was now supposed to go to Andrews."

"Who else was involved in the cover-up?" Amanda asked him.

Billy shrugged. "As far as I knew, only Andy. He's the only other person I talked to about it."

She said, "What about his men?"

"I'm sure they were in on it. I mean, they'd have to be, right? But I never actually discussed any details with them or anyone else."

"Why were they trying to make it look like a rape?"

Billy looked puzzled. "Rape? What rape?"

"You didn't know?"

"Listen," he said, "my job was to call it an accident and adjust the time of death. That's all."

"How about Colonel Weller?" she asked. "Did anyone mention her role in the cover-up?"

"She General Garber's aide?"

"Yes."

"All I know was that Andy wasn't happy with her. He said something about her acting stupid and screwing things up."

This comment generated raised eyebrows all around. Amanda asked, "You know why Andy said that?"

Billy started to shake his head, then stopped.

She said, "Yes?"

He was still thinking. "When we were riding over to the hospital, I remember Andy mentioning something about buttons." He looked at Simon. "It was right after he talked to you. Andy was pretty angry; he said the buttons weren't supposed to be in the compartment. Right after that is when he said Colonel Weller had screwed things up."

My eyes went to Simon. He caught me looking and nodded fractionally. We now knew Andy *had* missed seeing the button when he'd lifted the couch cushion.

Amanda said to Billy, "Andy never specifically stated Weller left the buttons in the compartment?"

"No."

"But that was the distinct impression you had? That she was responsible?"

"Yeah."

Amanda and Simon were frowning again; they were troubled by the same thing I was. While Billy's account supported the staged rape theory, we wondered why Andy hadn't been aware of it.

Checking his watch, Simon said to Billy, "So you don't know if any of the other generals were involved in the cover-up—"

Billy shook his head.

"—and no one ever told you *how* Garber had died—"

More head shaking.

"—or who was responsible?"

"No. No one told me a damn thing other than to make the death look like an accident."

Simon abruptly stood. "Thank you for your cooperation, Doctor."

•   •   •

As I followed Simon and Amanda out the door, Billy said, "Uh, Marty, can I talk to you for a minute?"

I glanced back. "Sure."

"Close the door, huh? I don't want Deloris to hear this."

I did as he asked and waited expectantly.

Billy's eyes locked on mine. "What Santos said, about keeping me out of it—"

"He'll try, Billy. We all will."

"But no guarantees?"

"I wish I could." I shook my head.

"I guess it doesn't matter. If you guys make an arrest, it'll all come out anyway. Including the fact that I falsified the goddamn autopsy."

There was nothing for me to say, so I didn't even try.

Billy sat very still for a few moments, lost in his private thoughts. I watched him, wondering if I should leave.

He sighed deeply and began speaking in a quiet, regretful tone. "You know this is going to kill Deloris. It really will. Not a lot of docs make general. She always wanted that—worked so hard—volunteering for every goddamn thing that came along. Always pushing for me to get that star. And now, when we're so close . . ."

His eyes flickered up to me. "Guess that's life, huh. Make one fucking mistake, and it's over."

"I'm sorry, Billy."

"I thought I was doing the right thing. I really did."

I nodded.

He attempted a smile. "No hard feelings if I hope you guys don't make it."

"None."

As I walked out, I saw Billy pouring another drink and recalled General Sessler's words: *People are going to get hurt. People who don't deserve it.*

I gently closed the door behind me.

Simon and Amanda were slowly moving down the walkway, heads bent in conversation. I caught up to them and glanced at the Buick; it hadn't moved. As we approached the limo, Bennie started to get out of the driver's seat. Simon motioned him to stay seated.

Even though I knew what Simon's response would be, I had to give it a shot. I tapped him on the shoulder, and when he looked back, I asked him if Emily had called him.

"Yes." He was smiling.

"Mind telling me what she wanted?"

"I can't."

"Dammit. She's my daughter. I have a right to know."

"And you will, very soon."

I blinked. "Oh? When?"

"Patience, Martin." He gave my arm a reassuring squeeze and opened the rear door. "We'll all ride together. Leave the keys in the car. I've arranged for someone to pick it up."

Amanda said, "Already?"

He nodded. "You won't be needing it. Things are progressing rapidly. Unless I'm mistaken, we should resolve the case within the next few hours."

She and I stared at him. Amanda said, "Resolve it? How can we possibly—"

But Simon had ducked into the limo. Amanda turned toward the BMW, shaking her head. She couldn't bring herself to believe him, and neither could I.

I crawled into the back seat beside Simon. "All right. Let's have it. Are you saying you know who the killer is?"

No reply. He was staring down the street. I said, "Simon—"

"Wait for Amanda, Martin."

I sighed. The frustrations of working with Simon. As I followed his gaze, I'd assumed he was looking at the Buick, but soon realized he was focused on a second car parked farther down the street. When it dawned on me who was in it, I could only shake my head. I should have considered this eventuality. Simon was someone who considered all the angles; he never left anything to chance.

Abruptly, he faced me with an approving smile. "Amanda explained how you concluded General Garber had been killed before he was placed on the plane. Well done."

I shrugged. "We got lucky. When did you figure it out?"

He settled back and adjusted his bow tie. "I initially considered the possibility when you mentioned your confusion over the hairs in the shower. Why they'd been removed. I never accepted your theory that the hairs were incriminating to someone. Who else would have taken a shower except General Garber?

"So it occurred to me that perhaps the hairs had been removed because they would prove Garber *hadn't* taken a shower. But if that were true, why make it appear as if he did? For the longest time, that puzzled me. Then I realized the scene had been necessary to convince the flight attendant, Sergeant Blake, that Garber was alive. It must have been common knowledge they were friendly, so they couldn't simply ban her from the compartment. Yet they had to devise a plausible reason for the general to avoid her during the flight. The shower scene offered the perfect solution; someone pretending to be Garber could simply tell her he did not want to be disturbed."

"Frankly, that's what threw me," I said. "When Sergeant Blake told me she'd spoken to Garber, I never considered that the person wasn't him. But when I called her, she admitted she'd never actually seen the general during the trip."

By now Amanda had returned and was sitting in the seat beside the computer. As I shut the door, I said to Simon, "We've got a quorum. Who killed Garber?"

"I don't know."

"Huh?"

Amanda said, "Simon, you just told us—"

"What I *told* you was that I expect to resolve the case in the next few hours. That's true."

"Mind telling us how?" she asked dryly. "In case you haven't noticed, General Garber was killed in England. That means it's now possible someone who *wasn't* on the plane could have—"

"Correct," he said. "The location of the killing changes everything. Our task has just gotten easier. One person knows the identity of the killer. It was his job to know." He punctuated the comment with a knowing look.

The light finally came on. Amanda and I knew Simon was referring to the head of Garber's security team. The man who was responsible for protecting the general wherever he went in England.

Andy.

"You know," I said, following the thread, "this could be one reason why they put Garber's body on the plane. To give Andy an out. Once Garber was safely aboard, Andy wasn't responsible for guarding him."

Nods from Simon and Amanda; they realized this.

She cautioned, "We might be jumping the gun, guys. Andy still might not talk. Odds are he probably won't."

"He'll talk," I said. "He has no choice now. At the very least, we'll get him for accessory to murder after the fact. We know he had to be in on moving the body." I added, "We can also squeeze Paul Carter or Tom Gentry, see if they'll give us some leverage to use against Andy."

"Perhaps they already have," Simon said.

Picking up a car phone extension, he touched the message icon on the overhead console. He listened, shook his head, then hung up. He explained he'd left messages on Carter's and Gentry's answering machines, informing them we knew General Garber had been killed in England and that it was in their best interest to cooperate. "Frankly, I expected a response by now."

"You know where they live?" Amanda asked.

A nod. "First things first. If it doesn't work out with Andy, we'll pay them a visit."

We heard the partition whir down. Bennie glanced back and asked Simon where he wanted to go. Simon immediately looked to me.

"Andy wouldn't go home," Amanda said. "And he damn sure wouldn't go to the office."

I said, "No . . ."

But there was one place. If I could only recall—

I was startled when Simon suddenly sat forward with a surprised expression. He shouted for Bennie to start the car. Bennie said, "I'm trying, I'm trying . . ." An instant later I heard Amanda say, "They're crazy. What the hell are they doing?"

Even before I looked out the window, I knew what must have happened.

Mutt and Jeff were making their move.

38

The Buick fishtailed wildly as it roared down the street toward us. It would be upon us within seconds. Amanda and I fumbled for our guns, the only thing we could think to do. From the front seat, we heard Bennie saying, "My God. Oh, my God . . ." He managed to get the limo started, but by then it was too late. At that moment the Buick swerved and squealed to a stop, boxing us in against the curb. The front doors popped open, and the two huge security men hopped out. They came over and rapped on the window nearest Simon.

He confirmed that Amanda and I had our weapons drawn before partially lowering the window.

The crew-cut one with no discernible neck did the talking. "Everyone out of the car. We've got a few questions."

Simon said politely, "I can hear fine from here."

"I'm not asking, Lieutenant. You know who we are and why we're here. And we're telling you to get out of the car."

His red-haired partner casually slid a hand inside his jacket. Simon said, "Martin."

I stuck my barrel out the window. "I wouldn't."

Bennie made a whimpering sound and ducked below the seat.

Red Hair froze, glowering at me. He slowly lowered his hand.

"Hey, easy, fella," Crew Cut said to me. "You got us all wrong. We just want to have a friendly talk."

"Suppose you start?" Simon said. "Were you sent by Secretary Churchfield?"

"We ask the questions," Red Hair growled.

Simon gave him a hard look. "Then we have nothing to discuss. Good day, gentlemen."

"Up to you," Crew Cut said. "But we're not moving until you get out of the car."

Simon nodded. "I understand."

The window whirred shut.

"This is just what they want," Amanda said. "Keep us sitting here until the clock runs out. So—how do you want to handle it?" She was addressing Simon.

He was silent, looking down the street.

Amanda waited a few seconds, then said, "You just going to sit there?" She made it sound like an accusation.

"That's appears to be the most sensible option."

Amanda turned to me. "Well? How about it?"

I could see the excitement in her eyes. She wanted to kick ass and take names. But even as good as she was in the martial arts, she couldn't handle two guys that size. I knew I couldn't. I said, "Relax. It's not necessary for us to confront them."

"Oh, no? What are you going to do? Talk them into leaving?"

"Amanda, you don't understand—"

"Damn right, I don't." She opened the door. I immediately reached around her and closed it.

She spun to me. "Someone's got to do something. If you guys are going to sit around and—"

She shut up when I pointed.

Her eyes widened. "Say, isn't that—"

"Enrique. Now stay in the car and don't get in his way."

The green Jag slowly cruised up the street and parked against the opposite curb. It sat there with the motor running. We could see Enrique in the passenger seat, another man I didn't recognize behind the wheel. Simon's cell phone rang. He listened, then said coldly, "Whatever is necessary."

This tweaked my interest. He was giving Enrique the green light. As Simon ended the call, I said, "You sure about that?"

"I don't want them harassing Dr. Bowman."

"So it's not because you're pissed and want to teach them a lesson?"

He shrugged.

Another of Simon's little inconsistencies. Despite his religious convictions, he had a capacity for ruthlessness that I always found surprising.

We all watched the Jag as Enrique emerged. He carefully removed his suit jacket, hung it on the back of the passenger seat, then slowly approached the two men.

"How long has he been here?" Amanda asked Simon.

"Since you arrived. He was following those men."

"Shouldn't we at least give him a hand?" she asked.

"He won't need it," Simon said.

"C'mon, Simon. Those guys are twice his size."

"Enrique was in the military," Simon said, as if that explained it all.

Amanda snorted. "So what? That doesn't mean he can—"

"He was a SEAL," I said.

I could still see the doubt in her eyes. A gay cop was one thing. But a gay SEAL team member? I said, "Just watch."

Simon lowered the window again, this time all the way.

Enrique was smiling at the men, saying, "Move along, fellas. Lieutenant Santos would like to leave, and you're blocking his way."

"Beat it, buddy," Crew Cut said, putting on his tough look. "This is official business."

"Hey, Ernie," Red Hair said. "This guy's got a real pretty earring." He laughed meanly.

Ernie grinned at Enrique. "Beat it, fella, and you won't get hurt."

Enrique's smile remained fixed on his face. When he spoke, his voice was quiet, but with a hard edge. "I'm asking you to move your car. Please."

"Look, friend," Ernie said. "You're starting to piss me off. I'll tell you one more time. Leave, and nobody gets hurt."

"That's good advice," Enrique said, the smile gone now. "You and your friend should take it. It's healthier."

"Okay, asshole," Ernie said, moving forward. "You had your chance. Now I'm going to—"

Then it happened.

Ernie reached out as if to shove Enrique. We never saw Enrique move, because Ernie's bulk blocked our view. The next thing we knew, Ernie was rolling on the ground, screaming, clutching his knee. His partner said, "Why, you fucking son of a—"

Enrique's hand snapped out, and we heard a crunching sound. Blood spurted from Red Hair's nose. Enrique brought up a knee viciously, and Red Hair dropped with a howl of pain.

"Now," Simon said to Amanda and me. "Get their weapons, then order them to leave."

By the time we walked over to Enrique, he'd already disarmed the men. As he handed me the weapons, he grinned. "Nice to see I haven't lost my touch."

Ernie sat up, glowering at him with hate. "My knee. You broke my fucking knee, you son of a bitch."

"I'm getting all teary-eyed. Get your friend and beat it."

Ernie started to respond, but thought better of it. He grimaced and struggled to his feet.

"What about our guns? We can't leave without our guns."

Enrique looked to me. I removed the clips, pocketed them, then cleared the chambers and held the guns out to Ernie. He took them, muttering, "Shithead." He hobbled over to his partner, who was still moaning, and helped him over to the car. As he got behind the wheel, Ernie said, "You haven't heard the last of this."

As the car peeled away, we became aware of several people watching us from their front yards. One woman hurried back inside her house.

That was our cue to get going. But before we could, we had one other minor problem to overcome.

"Bennie just quit," Simon called out.

As Amanda and I got into the limo, Simon was handing Bennie a wad of bills through the window and telling him he was sorry things didn't work out. A visibly shaken Bennie nodded dumbly, then made his way over to the Jag.

"Simon," Enrique said, looking back from the driver's seat, "you understand this is only temporary. I told you before, I'm not the chauffeur type."

"I understand."

"I'd also like to wear my own clothes. No uniform." He plucked a piece of lint from his suit jacket, which he'd retrieved moments earlier.

"I'm amenable to that."

"Now, about the pay—"

"Double your previous salary."

Enrique grinned. "Well, okay. Where to?"

"I'll know it when I see it," I said.

Puzzled looks from Simon and Amanda.

I explained.

All I knew about the bar Andy frequented was that it was within walking distance of his apartment in northwest Alexandria. For someone of Andy's girth and limited lung capacity, I guesstimated he could handle around three blocks, tops. Our best shot was to go to Andy's place and drive around the neighborhood, check out the bars within the prescribed perimeter. One of them had to be it.

Would Andy be there?

I put the odds at better than even. For a borderline alcoholic like Andy, it was the logical place for him to hang out until the 2000 deadline passed. More importantly, as far as I knew, he'd never told anyone the name of the bar. In fact, he went out of his way to keep the location secret.

When I'd once asked him where it was, he bluntly told me he'd rather I didn't come there.

"It's nothing personal, Marty," he'd said. "But I go there to forget about work, hang with my own kind."

"What kind is that, Andy?"

He never answered me.

Alexandria was a straight shot down Route 7 from Fairfax. Since we were going against traffic, the flow was moving. We spent the ride scanning through the various faxes and e-mails Simon printed out from his computer — the information he'd requested from his sources.

As usual, Simon had gone overboard. There were hundreds of pages pertaining to our key suspects, everything from credit histories to newspaper stories to school transcripts. You name it, if the information was a matter of public record, and sometimes if it wasn't, we had it there someplace.

Amanda wearily tossed down a handful of customs declarations she'd been perusing and announced, "Andy told the truth. Only General Garber bought a bottle of whisky."

Simon glanced up from the computer screen. "Could you tell if his form was tampered with?"

"Looks okay to me, but I'm no expert." She plucked a page free and held it out to him.

"Give it to Enrique."

She hesitated.

"Pass it up," Enrique sang out. "I worked forgery for a year."

As she crawled forward and handed him the page, she gave me a knowing look. I nodded, suppressing a smile. After three long years, it seemed like Simon had finally found a chauffeur to replace Romero.

Simon was clicking furiously on the keyboard. He thrust out another stack of pages he'd just printed. Taking them, I said, "You know we'll never get through all this in time."

"We might learn something important, Martin." He smiled. "If it helps, you can ignore the data on the generals. We understand their motive. Concentrate on Weller and Secretary Churchfield."

Churchfield I understood, but . . . "Anything in particular you're looking for on Weller?"

"There are a number of questions about her that are troubling." He shrugged. "The most pressing one is why she was so intent on implicating herself in the murder."

This again. Amanda stepped on my comeback line, saying, "I thought she was acting on orders to confuse the investigation."

"So did I," he said. "But apparently we were in error."

I knew what was bugging him. "Listen, just because Andy wasn't aware that she'd planted the shirt buttons doesn't mean— Go ahead." He was about to interrupt me anyway.

"Secretary Churchfield," he said, "didn't know about the buttons either, Martin. Or the condom we found."

My eyebrows went up.

Amanda said, "How do you know?"

"Churchfield's meeting with Senator Garber," he said. "I fully expected her to try and blackmail him with the fabricated rape charge. She never did. She only asked him if he would drop the investigation for the good of the military and the country. She also added that it would be better for the senator if he never learned the truth."

"A threat?" Amanda said. "Was she threatening him?"

"It didn't come across that way. Her tone was straight-forward, as if stating a fact."

I said, "And this ties in to Weller how?"

"I confronted Churchfield with the evidence implicating Weller. I asked her why she thought it necessary to have one of her officers incriminate herself. Her initial reaction was one of shock. Later, she became very angry with me. Incensed, really. She insisted Weller had nothing to do with the crime and ordered me to leave her alone."

I said, "Churchfield could have been lying."

"She wasn't. Her surprise—and anger—were genuine."

"Simon, the generals were aware of what we had on Weller. They would have told Churchfield."

"Obviously, they didn't."

Amanda asked him what reason the generals would have had for keeping this information from Weller.

"I don't know. It's suggestive that both Churchfield and Andy weren't aware of Weller's actions. From that, I think it's clear Weller acted on her own."

"Aren't you forgetting Markel?" Amanda said. "He could have ordered her."

"I disagree. I suspect Markel was similarly unaware of Weller's intentions. If he'd known, he would have told Andy. There would be no reason not to. Then there's Weller's emotional display in the compartment to consider. The only people in the room were the generals and Andy and his men. Why would she stage the scene if they were aware of her intentions?"

I felt like we were going in circles. "Simon, when I spoke with Markel, I told you he *knew* about Weller planting the—"

And then I recalled the timing, and the hole in his argument disappeared. I sighed. "Never mind. Andy found out about Weller the same time we did. He could have called Markel before I met with him."

Amanda said to Simon, "So you're telling us that Weller was the only one who wanted the murder to look like it had been motivated by a rape attempt? That Garber really did try to rape her?"

"I think it's likely, yes."

We listened to the hum of the tires as we digested this new wrinkle. I glanced to Enrique and saw him watching us in the rearview mirror. He was trying to follow along, but looked as confused as I felt.

Amanda said grudgingly, "If, and I still think it's a big if, *if* Weller acted on her own, she did it to protect someone. That's the only reason she would have for framing herself."

"Markel," I said, jumping on the obvious. "She's covering for him without his consent."

"Maybe," Simon said. "And maybe not. All we know is that Colonel Weller has her own agenda. Any assumptions as to her motive are unwise."

Amanda looked at me. I nodded. Simon was thinking out of the box again.

As Amanda and I began searching through the pages for information on Weller, the car phone rang. Simon picked up an extension, then turned to me and pointed at the console. I thought he wanted me to flip on the speaker, but as I reached up, he mouthed a different word. It took me a few seconds to locate the icon. I nodded when I had it.

"Okay, Carter," Simon said. "Start at the beginning and leave nothing out."

39

Andy lived in a tired-looking eight-plex in the Latin section off Beauregarde Road, about five miles northwest and a world away from the upscale glitz of Old Town Alexandria. We looked out front for Andy's car, but didn't see it. As we circled the block, we spotted the first bar. Julio's Hacienda. "Not a chance," Amanda said.

But I checked it out anyway. No Andy.

Fifteen minutes later, we had hit four more bars and still came up blank. It was well after five; we had less than three hours until we turned into pumpkins. Simon shook his head in frustration. Even though he wouldn't say it, I knew what he was thinking.

I'd guessed wrong.

Enrique said cheerfully, "Looks like people like to drink around here."

No one smiled.

We turned a corner and spotted another bar. The last one within the three blocks. As we drove up, I knew at once we'd finally found it.

Sunlight streamed through the enormous plate-glass window out front. Squinting against the glare, we could see several patrons sitting in inside. A heavy-set man at the end of the bar might have been Andy, but he wasn't wearing a jacket, and his back was to us. If it was him, we now had the problem of him spotting us as we came in.

Simon barked instructions to Enrique. After parking the limo, he took off down the sidewalk while Amanda, Simon, and I strolled up to the front door. Before we entered, I recalled what Andy had told me.

I go there to forget about work . . . hang out with my own kind.

That prophetic comment and the big sign mounted over the tattered awning confirmed this was the bar Andy often frequented. Club 114, it read.

The same number as the hill in Vietnam.

The bar was small, no bigger than the fast-food restaurant it probably once was. I counted seven Formica-topped tables on the scarred wooden floor, a long bar running along the back wall. The air was thick with smoke, and a battered jukebox in the corner was playing a scratchy version of Lynyrd Skynyrd's "Sweet Home Alabama." On the wall adjacent to the door, I saw dozens of photographs of young men in military fatigues. Above them hung a wooden sign that read "Duty, Honor, Country." Below, in smaller letters: "The Good Die Young." There were only four patrons inside, all males in their mid- to late fifties. Three were at a table, one leaning against the bar.

All were staring at us, and none was Andy.

The song on the jukebox ended.

The bartender, a heavy woman with a gaudy Hawaiian shirt and teased red hair, said, "Can I help you?"

Simon walked over and showed her his badge. "We're looking for Andy Hobbs."

Her face went blank. "Never heard of him."

Simon looked at the men at the table. They shook their heads. The man at the bar said, "Nobody by that name comes here."

"I see."

Amanda and I went over to the end of the bar, where the man we'd seen earlier was seated. A freshly lit cigarette burned in an ashtray.

Amanda said, "Andy's brand."

I looked around. "Whose cigarette is this?"

"Mine," the man at the bar said. He sauntered over, picked up the cigarette, took a drag, and casually retreated.

At a nod from Simon, Amanda and I sat on a couple stools. Simon took the seat beside me and smiled at the bartender. "Nice place you have here. Quite . . . rustic."

"We like it." She kept staring at him. "I told you we never heard of this guy Hobbs."

Simon shrugged. "I'll have a Coke, no ice." He looked at Amanda and me, saw our heads shake.

The bartender brought him the Coke. Simon sipped it. No one spoke. The bartender watched him, and we could see she was getting increasingly nervous. So were the patrons. The men at the table got up and walked out. The man at the bar killed his beer and followed.

Finally, from somewhere at the back, we heard, "Quit pushing. Oww. Dammit, I'm going, *I'm going!*"

The bartender got a stricken look.

Amanda got up and locked the front doors, turning over the Closed sign.

Simon and I watched the swinging doors located behind the bar. Moments later, Andy appeared, followed by Enrique, who was holding Andy's gun. Andy's jacket was torn, and there was a slight reddening below his left cheek. He stood there, glaring at us.

Enrique wedged the pistol in his pants, then produced a cell phone from his trouser pocket and passed it to Simon. "He was talking to someone when I spotted him."

Simon frowned at the phone. The flip-top hinge was bent, and there was a large scratch along the side.

"He fell on it when I took him down," Enrique said apologetically.

Simon tried to key the phone; it was dead. He asked, "Who were you calling, Andy?"

"None of your damned business," he snapped.

Simon smiled, laying the phone on the bar. "Can I buy you a beer?"

"Fuck you. I'm not saying shit."

"A beer, please." Simon handed the bartender a twenty. "Whatever he normally drinks. Keep the change."

She poured out a large draft and placed it before Andy.

Simon said, "You're in a lot of trouble, Andy."

"For what? I didn't do anything."

I said, "We know about Hill 114 and what General Garber did to the men in your unit."

"What's that prove? Nothing."

"It proves you had a motive."

Instead of a denial, he gave a harsh laugh. "See those?" He pointed to the photos by the door. "Sixty-three men— boys—dead because of that son of a bitch. Oh, yeah, I had a motive, all right. *But I didn't kill him.*" He was fixated on me with an intensity that made his jowls shake. He abruptly snatched up the beer, spilling some on his coat. He didn't even notice. We watched as he stalked around the bar, sat down, took a long drink. He lit a cigarette and glanced at the bartender. "Tell them, Doris. Tell him what happened to Jerry."

She said, "Andy, I really don't . . ."

"Tell them," he said again.

She took a deep breath and looked to us. "Jerry was my husband. He . . . he was burned horribly. They amputated his legs, one of his hands. He lived . . . he existed . . . for years. But he couldn't take it anymore. One day, while I was at work, Jerry decided . . . I found him . . ." Her eyes misted. She wiped at them and smeared her mascara.

We were silent, watching her.

Simon gently said to Enrique, "Could you take her in the back?"

"Sure."

As he led her through the swinging doors, Amanda said to Andy, "So what happened? Did Jerry kill himself?"

Andy nodded, his eyes on his beer. "Blew his brains out." He looked at her dully. "He was my best friend in 'Nam. Left Doris with two kids. The boy, Jake, is my godson. I helped Doris set this place up. Give her a way to make a living."

I said, "I'm sorry, Andy."

"Don't be. Jerry should have done it earlier. That way he wouldn't have had to suffer." He took another drink.

Amanda watched him with a compassion that mirrored mine. We now understood his fuck-the-world attitude and why he never gave a damn about anything. If we were in his shoes, maybe we wouldn't either. I said, "We understand the survivors of the battle were never told Garber was responsible."

"No."

"When did you find out?"

He shrugged, knocking an ash off his cigarette. "About a year ago."

I said, "When General Markel became vice chairman and pulled the file?"

Andy blew out a cloud, scratched an ear.

I said, "You really had us going. We couldn't figure out how the compartment doors were locked from the inside. We now know you must have locked the main door, then left by the closet. Later you locked the closet doors after you broke in."

He yawned and reached for the beer.

I decided to hit him with the kicker. I said, "We know Garber was killed in England, and you moved the body."

I had to admire Andy's self-possession. His only reaction was a slight pause as he raised the glass to his lips.

He set the beer down, crushed out the cigarette. "I'm leaving. I've got nothing else to say." He went toward the door.

Simon called after him, "There's something you should listen to, first."

Andy threw back his hand and kept going.

"Andy!"

He whirled around. "Listen, either you arrest me, or you can kiss my—"

He broke off, frowning at what Simon was holding in his hand. It was one of those small recorders, the kind used for dictation.

"I'm truly sorry, Andy," Simon said.

He pressed *play*.

●　　　●　　　●

A soft hiss.

Abruptly, Paul Carter's anguished voice came on, talking about his new baby and how he didn't want to go to jail.

Then Simon, telling him to start at the beginning and leave nothing out.

I was watching Andy. Almost immediately, his facade of denial started to crumble, then fell away completely. His shoulders sagged, and his head dropped. He suddenly looked tired and old and vulnerable. He stared down at the floor and shook his head as he accepted the inevitable.

It was over.

Amanda went over and led Andy back to the bar. He didn't resist. By the time he sat down, Paul was telling us what happened.

"Fuck," Andy said.

Paul spoke slowly and deliberately, as if aware of the consequences of what he was saying. "Tommy and I got a call from Andy in our room. It was late, around 2330 hours, after the dinner with the Brits at the officers' mess. The generals were in their quarters, getting ready for the trip home. Andy was watching General Garber, and he told us to get over to Garber's room ASAP. That something had happened. When we got there, we found Garber slumped on the couch. He was dead. The other generals were already there. Markel, Sessler, and Garber. And Andy. No one else.

"General Markel did all the talking. He told us there'd been an accident. He said General Garber was drunk and had stumbled, crushed his throat against the edge of the coffee table. You know, like the way we tried to make it look on the plane. I remember no one seemed panicked. Everyone was real cool, like they knew exactly what they were going to do. Markel gave this little speech about how humiliating it would be for America to have its top soldier die because he'd gotten drunk. So he told us—ordered us—to put Garber's body in his compartment on the plane. He said it would be better, you know, politically.

"Hell, I knew the way he was saying General Garber had died couldn't be true. I've been a cop long enough to know a guy doesn't suffocate that quick. Not before he could get help. Plus Andy was with him. The other generals' rooms were right down the hall. They would have heard Garber if he—"

At this point Carter's voice rose slightly. "What could I do, Lieutenant? Shit, I'm a warrant officer, and here's a four-star general—*three* four-star generals—ordering me to move the body. So I fucking moved the body. Tommy, Andy, and me. It turned out it wasn't any big deal, getting Garber out of there. His suite was on the ground floor and had a private entrance through this little garden. Andy made sure the coast was clear, and Tommy and I each stuck our head under Garber's arms and carried him to the car like he'd passed out. Anyone one who saw us would have believed that. Garber had hit the booze hard at the dinner. Like he always did.

"We put General Garber into the staff car, drove out to the plane. It was close to midnight by then, and there weren't many people around. Our main concern were the security cops guarding the plane, but Andy took care of them. He kept them back so they wouldn't get a good look and gave them the story about the general being drunk. They bought it. They knew his reputation. They'd seen him drunk on the plane. We hid Garber in the closet of the compartment. Wedged him in—"

At this, Simon shot me a look. This explained the black heel marks we'd found in the compartment.

Carter continued, "Andy said he didn't need Tommy and me anymore, so we went to our seats up front. Later, the generals showed up, and everyone had a meeting in the compartment. What went on, Tommy and I couldn't tell you. All I know is that Andy came by later and told us they'd arranged Garber's death to look the same as back in his room. He said it would be more believable that way. You know, because that's what really happened. Andy also told us what we were going to do when we landed. How we were supposed to find the body and go through the motions of conducting an accidental death inquiry.

"That's what we were doing when General Markel came in and told us that General Garber's father was pushing for a murder investigation. It got really tense for a while. I mean, *tense*. Andy and the generals had this big discussion on what the hell they were going to do now. They knew a finding of accidental death would never stand up, but they also decided they couldn't, wouldn't frame anybody. I guess that was when Tommy and I finally realized the truth. If Garber had died accidentally, the generals would have said so, right? I mean, why hide that fact now? Why even talk about framing somebody?

"Anyway, the generals figured they'd be logical suspects because of the bad blood between them and General Garber. They didn't think that was necessarily a bad thing. I mean, you couldn't go after them all, right? General Sessler also suggested they should give you someplace else to look. Confuse you. That's why we hid the booze bottle and the glasses in the trash. Make you think a woman might have killed him when she really couldn't. I mean, a woman would never be strong enough to kill General Garber. Not like that.

"That's pretty much all I know, Lieutenant. You were there for the rest of it. I only did it because I was ordered to. Same with Tommy. Probably Andy, too. I like Andy. He's not the jerk a lot of people think." Carter's voice grew quiet, apologetic. "When you see him, tell him I'm sorry. But I've got my wife and kid to think about. Tell him I hope he understands. Tell him for me. Christ, I'm sorry."

He fell silent. The taped hissed.

We looked at Andy. He was smoking a cigarette, his face the picture of dejection.

On the tape, Simon asked, "Who planted the condom and the shirt buttons, Paul?"

"Andy said that Weller must have done it. He told us you'd found the buttons, which came from a shirt that you'd found in her bag. None of us knew why she'd do something so crazy. But she did. Go figure."

"So that had never been part of the cover-up?"

"Hell, no. I told you the plan wasn't to frame anyone."

"Whose lipstick was used to mark the glass?"

"I don't know. Andy handled that. Got it from someone on the plane. He threw the container away later."

"Do you know or suspect who killed General Garber?"

"No."

"So you never heard or saw anything that might suggest who the killer was?"

There was no reply.

"Paul?"

"I was in the compartment. The generals were talking. It was right after they were told you were coming on the case. They were worried because of your reputation."

"What did you hear, Paul?"

"General Markel. He was talking to General Sessler and General Garber. Look, maybe I shouldn't say anything. I couldn't swear they were discussing the killing. They could have been talking about anything."

"What did Markel say?" Simon pressed.

A long silence. Then, almost in a whisper: "'Me.' Markel said, 'Remember, tell them it was me.'"

"That's a goddamn lie."

This came from Andy, who'd sprang from his stool and was staring at us with wild eyes. He shouted, "Paul Carter is lying. General Markel never killed—"

Andy never finished his statement, because he was interrupted by a soft tinkling sound. Like the sound of glass breaking.

Then his forehead exploded in a mist of red.

40

Something wet hit my face. I watched in horror as Andy's body slid down the front of the bar. "Down!" Amanda screamed. "Get down!"

I was already dropping to the floor. She fell on top of me, and I could feel her breath hot against my face. We heard another brittle crackling sound, and something thumped hard against the bar. Simon lay prone to us, shouting, "Can you see him? Can you see him?"

Amanda rolled off me, fumbling for her gun. As I jerked mine free, I frantically looked out the window. "There's a car—"

Wood splintered inches above our heads. We couldn't hear the gunshots. The silence heightened the terror. We had no warning when the bullets would—

More splintering wood. Amanda swore savagely. I raised my weapon, tried to aim. We heard a squeal of tires.

I sagged back, panting like I'd run a race. I looked at Andy. He was sitting like a rag doll, his back propped up against the bar, his head slumped forward. Portions of his scalp were gone, and I could see pulverized bone and brain matter. I turned away, sickened.

From behind, we heard Enrique call out, "What happened? What's going on?"

Simon ordered, "Stay there. Don't come out until we're sure."

"Sure of what?"

Amanda was crawling forward, keeping behind the door to shield herself. I went after her, kissing the floor. We stood together and peered around the edge of the window.

Cars. A lot of cars.

But the one I had seen was gone.

To be certain, we watched for a full minute. People casually strolled up the sidewalk. A woman pushing a baby carriage window-shopped across the street. No one appeared alarmed in any way, since the shooter had used a silenced gun.

"He's gone," I said finally.

Amanda went over to Simon and helped him to his feet. Enrique came out through the swinging doors, the bartender Doris behind him. I said, "Enrique, don't let her see—"

But it was too late. Doris was already past him, walking around the bar. She took one look at Andy and let out a piercing scream. Amanda took her hand and tried to comfort her, but Doris just stood there screaming. Enrique finally led her away as she sobbed.

Amanda handed me a bar napkin and pointed to my face. I wiped it and inspected the napkin. Tiny red streaks; Andy's blood. My stomach lurched, and I hurried over to the washbasin behind the bar.

When I returned, Amanda and Simon were standing over Andy. Simon removed his rosary beads and said a prayer. Afterward, I was surprised to see Amanda's eyes moist. She turned to me and I heard the emotion in her voice. "All those things I said about him. If I'd known what he was really like. I mean what he did for Doris . . . helping her . . ." She bit her lip.

It was an impulse. She was feeling guilty, and I wanted to reassure her. I placed my hand gently on her shoulder—

She immediately tensed at my touch. Our eyes met. She said quietly, "I'm fine, Marty."

I got the message. In light of our understanding, she considered the gesture inappropriate. As I lowered my hand, I realized it had already begun. She was pulling back from me.

An awkward silence followed. I looked at Simon. He shook his head.

Amanda's eyes again drifted down to Andy. "He was trying to cover for them, and they killed him. It's not right." She glanced up, her eyes turning cold. "Until now, I wasn't sure. But this changes everything. I want the bastard who did this."

I nodded; I felt the same way. This was personal now.

As we stepped away from the body, Simon asked me if I could identify the shooter, and I had to tell him no—I'd only caught a glimpse. There appeared to be one person in the car. I had the impression that he was a white male. His vehicle I was more certain about. I described it as a blue Lincoln or a possibly a Caddy. A mid-nineties model, with a boxy frame.

Amanda pointed to the starred holes in the window. "Fairly large-caliber rounds. Be hard to drive and fire a rifle, so he probably used a silenced handgun. Figure he was forty to fifty feet away, shooting into dim light. Not an easy shot." She gave me a knowing look. "I'd say that nails it down to one of two guys."

I was already taking out my cell phone to find out which one.

I tried the most likely first.

The Pentagon operator gave me Stefanski's office number. When I called it, a navy commander told me Stefanski wasn't in. No, he didn't know when he'd return. And no, he didn't expect him back today.

I immediately phoned General Markel's office.

"He's unavailable, Agent Collins," his executive officer, Brigadier General Clay, said.

"Make him available, General."

"Now see here—"

Maybe it was my frustration over the case or the anger I felt over Andy's death. Maybe it was the fact that after going toe-to-toe with three four-stars, a one-star didn't intimidate me. Whatever the reason, I lit into Clay, snarling, "General, you tell General Markel that his boy Stefanski just blew away a military investigator. You tell Markel that I'm holding him personally responsible for the murder. You tell Markel I'm coming after him."

"*My God.* Are you certain that—"

"Damn fucking right, General."

A pause. When he spoke, Clay was clearly rattled. "General Markel. I . . . he's meeting with Secretary Churchfield. I'll put you through."

Elevator music. I grimaced at Simon and Amanda. Simon's cellular rang. He answered it, and judging by his reaction, Amanda and I could tell bad-news floodgates were still wide open. He tensed. "When did it happen?" Then later: "Where is she now? All right."

Simon disconnected with a grim head shake.

"What is it?" Amanda asked. "What happened?"

In my ear, I heard Markel's furious voice demand, "What the hell is this, Collins? What kind of crap are you trying to—"

Simon came over to me. "Let me talk to Markel."

I cupped the mouthpiece. "No. I want to do this. Andy was my friend. I want this bastard to know—"

"That was Jeff Zimmer, Martin. Someone tried to kill Mrs. Garber."

Amanda inhaled sharply. "Jesus."

Simon held out his hand to me.

I passed him the phone.

I knew Simon had to be as angry as I was, but he never raised his voice while speaking to General Markel. In a businesslike manner, Simon first described Andy's shooting, then shifted to the attempt on Mrs. Garber. The details on the latter were sketchy.

Roughly an hour earlier, someone had fired a shot through Mrs. Garber's bedroom window from a building across the street. Mrs. Garber wasn't struck, but she understandably went into hysterics. Simon said to Markel, "Mrs. Garber was taken to the hospital and is being treated for shock. No one saw who fired the shot, but I think we both know it had to be Colonel Stefanski. Do you know what kind of car he drives?" He nodded at the response. "That matches the description of the vehicle we saw. Now, do you know where he is? I understand, General—" Simon paused, listening. "All right. Call him. Yes, that's amenable to me. I'll hold."

When Simon covered the phone, I said, "An hour? The attempt on Mrs. Garber took place over an hour ago, and Jeff Zimmer only told you about it now?"

"Jeff has been testifying in a trial. He learned of the

attempt when he checked his messages." He flashed a hard smile. "General Markel is insisting he had nothing to do with either attack. That Stefanski was acting completely on his own."

"Like hell," I grunted.

"What I don't get," Amanda said, her brow furrowing, "is how Stefanski managed to pull off *both* shootings."

I said, "An hour is plenty of time to drive here from Mrs. Garber's apartment in D.C."

"I know that," she said. "But if we assume Stefanski was the person Andy called—"

"Right," I said, seeing the problem now. "You're wondering how he got here so fast."

"Yeah. I figure Andy called him no more than twenty minutes ago. Unless Stefanski was in the area already, he couldn't make it here that quickly. Not in rush hour."

We all thought for a moment. One obvious explanation came to mind.

After voicing it, Amanda hurried off to ask the bartender Doris if Andy had planned on meeting Stefanski here.

Simon resumed his conversation with General Markel. From what I overheard, it sounded as if the general had arranged a meeting with Stefanski. When Simon hung up, he said, "Markel appears to be cooperating. He confirmed Stefanski owns a blue Lincoln Town Car. General Markel also told Stefanski to come to his office at seven this evening."

It took me a moment. "He's going to gift-wrap him for us?"

"Apparently."

I recovered from my surprise and eyed Simon skeptically. "You do realize Markel's probably stalling us. He can't afford to have Stefanski talk. He's trying to give Stefanski a chance to get away."

Simon nodded. I wasn't telling him anything he hadn't considered.

Amanda reappeared from behind the bar and came over. "It was Stefanski. He was a bar regular. Get this. Doris said Andy and that bastard were friends."

I felt a tightening in my chest. I knew it was hate.

Simon began punching in a number. I assumed he was going to report the murder and issue an APB on Stefanski's car. Instead, he called Senator Garber and informed him of what had happened and what we were about to do. The plan Simon laid out was fairly comprehensive. Even though he didn't believe Stefanski was going to show for the meeting with Markel, he couldn't discount the possibility. Simon said, "Senator, we'll need you to ensure that the Pentagon police cooperate. Yes, sir. Mr. Stefanski works directly for General Markel. Yes, I agree it appears as if General Markel was responsible for your son's death. No. Don't say anything to the president yet. I'm still working on building a case. I understand, sir. We have only two hours. Have you spoken with the president about extending the time? I see. I'll do what I can, Senator. Good-bye."

Amanda and I were frowning at him as he ended the call. She said, "It *appears* Markel is responsible?"

Simon deflected her implication with a shrug. "We needed Andy. Without him, we still have no proof Markel killed General Garber."

There was a delayed reaction by Amanda and me. I said, "No proof? What about—"

And then Amanda went off on Simon. She stepped so close to him that she was practically spitting in his face.

"Are you serious? We *know* Markel organized the cover-up. We *know* he told the CID team to move the body. We *know* he was behind the attempt on Mrs. Garber—"

Simon said, "Amanda, please. If you'll just—"

But she was talking a mile a minute. She turned and gestured angrily toward the bar. "What about Andy? We *know* he had Stefanski kill Andy."

"Amanda, we need evidence. All we have is innuendo and—"

"We've got evidence. We've got the tape. It proves Markel *ordered* the cover-up."

"Amanda, calm down."

"I am calm." She placed her hands on her hips, glaring at him.

Simon hesitated, anticipating another tirade. Finally, he said, "The tape proves nothing. It's Carter's word against Markel's."

"Gentry will talk," she said stubbornly. "That will make it two against one."

"Three against two," Simon corrected. "General Johnson and General Sessler will support General Markel."

"What about Dr. Bowman? He'll testify that Garber was already dead before he ever left England."

"I'm talking about *proving* murder. We need evidence pointing to the killer. Definitive evidence. Something to convince the president that Markel is responsible. Without it, the investigation is finished."

I said to Simon, "You'll stay on the case. You won't quit. You gave your word."

He sighed. "But it will be difficult, Martin. You know what will happen. Anything pointing to Markel's culpability will conveniently disappear. I will have no access to the evidence or the witnesses. The reality is no one wants this case solved. Not the president or the military. So in the end, it won't be."

I said, "But Senator Garber—"

"Is a politician," Simon said firmly. "He understands the reality of the situation he's facing. The article tomorrow will destroy his son's reputation. The outraged families of the men Garber killed will be all over the media, demanding to know why they were never told the truth. The senator will be vilified because of the strings he pulled to ensure that the incident in Vietnam remained classified. If he continues to insist his son was murdered—without evidence supporting the charge—he will be regarded as a vengeful and bitter man. Will that stop him from pursuing his son's killer? Of course not; he's a father. But it will greatly curtail his influence."

No one said anything for a while. Twice Amanda attempted a response. She desperately wanted to counter Simon's logic, but she couldn't. The anger in her eyes was replaced by a frustrated acceptance—the realization that we were facing a wall that we couldn't get over.

She threw up her hands. "So we let the son of a bitch go?" She meant Markel.

"For General Garber's murder, the likely answer is yes. Our only hope now is Stefanski. If we locate him, and he cooperates, we might implicate Markel in Andy's killing."

"Fat chance," I said. "He's extremely loyal to General Markel. Hell, he just killed for him."

"What about Mrs. Garber?" Amanda asked. "She knows something. Stefanski wouldn't have tried to kill her unless she had something on Markel."

"Actually," Simon said, "General Markel told me Stefanski wasn't trying to harm Mrs. Garber. He insisted

Stefanski only intended to frighten her, prevent her from talking to us." He shook his head. "I've no doubt he achieved his objective."

"You got the name of the hospital she's at?"

"Yes, but it won't do any good to talk to her now. If she wouldn't confide in us before, I doubt she'll—"

"Simon," she growled, "just give me the name of the fucking hospital."

He blinked, taken aback. "Of course. It's Walter Reed."

I watched through the window as Amanda got in the cab and drove away. Simon was beside me, talking to the Alexandria police about Andy's murder. After he relayed a description of Stefanski's car, he ended the call and eyed me accusingly. "You told Amanda how you felt."

He'd obviously figured it out from the awkward scene between me and Amanda. "Yeah, I told her."

He shook his head. "Martin . . . Martin . . ."

"What?" I said, with a trace of annoyance.

"You were premature. You should have waited."

I stared at him. *"But you told me to tell her."*

"You said you would tell her tonight. You should have waited until tonight."

"Why?" I said. "Nothing was going to change the way I felt. What the hell difference would it have made?"

"More than you know."

"What's that supposed to mean?"

He grimaced unhappily. "Never mind. It's not important any longer. Get Enrique. Tell him to take Doris over to the flower shop across the street and have her wait there until the police arrive." He turned for the door.

I said, "We're leaving? Shouldn't we at least wait to give our statements?"

"There's no time. We need to ensure that everything is in place if Stefanski arrives." He opened the door, looking back at me. "I wish you would have waited, Martin."

This time I wasn't going to give him the satisfaction of asking why. Not that it mattered.

Simon had already walked out.

41

During the ride to the Pentagon, Simon spent much of the time on the phone, coordinating Stefanski's possible apprehension with Captain James Roche of the Pentagon's Defense Protective Service. Simon decided it was safer to arrest Stefanski after he passed through the metal detector, since we could be certain he wouldn't be armed. As far as I could tell, the only tricky part of the operation was trying to determine which entrance Stefanski would use. The closest one to Markel's office was the river entrance, which was usually reserved for the Pentagon's heavy hitters, so Roche had to check whether Stefanski, in his capacity as an executive assistant to the vice chairman of the Joint Chiefs, was on the access list. He was.

While Roche's men would cover all the entrances, Simon and I would stake out the river entrance. We wanted to be there if and when Stefanski was taken into custody. Afterward, we'd obtain a warrant to search his car and home, and pray like hell he hadn't ditched the guns he'd used to kill Andy and take the potshot at Mrs. Garber. Without the weapons and a subsequent positive ballistics match of the bullets, we'd have to let the son of a bitch go. That was the law.

Sometimes, I thought, the law sucked.

Simon was still on the car phone, working out the details with Roche, when he received a call on his cellular. He removed it from his jacket and promptly passed it to me.

The familiar gruff voice on the other end caught me by complete surprise—but not as much as the statement that followed.

I sat there, my mind racing, trying to think. It was a trick. It had to be a trick. He couldn't possibly—

"You heard what I said, Collins?"

"Yes, sir."

"Lieutenant Santos there?"

"Yes, sir."

"Put him on."

"I'm in charge of the investigation, sir."

"I *said*, put Santos on."

I got the message; I didn't count. I pocketed my ego and tapped Simon on the shoulder.

"It's General Markel," I said. "He wants to work out a deal."

Simon held the phone out so I could listen in. He said, "What kind of deal, General?"

"I'll confess to killing General Garber."

As easy as that. My heart thumped against my chest. When I looked at Simon, his face was completely composed.

"In exchange for what, General?" he said.

"I understand you're in the process of surrounding the Pentagon. Is that true?"

"Yes."

"Stupid move. I thought we had an understanding."

Simon's smooth face hardened. "Colonel Stefanski killed Agent Hobbs."

"If we do it your way, he'll kill a lot more. In 'Nam he didn't miss. Ever. That's why I know he never intended to kill Mrs. Garber. If he had, she'd be dead. Now think: Why the hell do you think I asked him to come to my office? Because I can control him."

"General, I can't risk—"

"Let me finish. What I'm trying to tell you is that Stefanski is a hunter. He hunts men. I taught him everything he knows. I can tell you that he'll smell the trap you're setting from the moment he drives up. When he does, it's over. You might get him, but it will cost you. You want that?"

Simon hesitated. "You want me to pull back the Pentagon police?"

"You better pull them back."

"If I do, you'll hand over Stefanski, give me a signed confession—"

"Yes."

"—and detail how and why you killed General Garber?"

"Yes. Everything."

Enrique kept glancing back at Simon and me. I mouthed, *Confession*. The cop in him reacted with a disbelieving head shake.

Simon said to Markel, "Mind telling me why you're doing this?"

"The price of command. Stefanski exceeded my

orders. He wasn't supposed to hurt anyone. Now that he
has, I have to accept responsibility for his actions."

"So you're doing this out of a sense of honor?" Simon
said.

"You could call it that." He paused, then added with
feeling, "That was the difference between General Garber
and me. I have honor."

"You really expect me to believe you, General?"

Markel sounded angry. "I'm a professional soldier. I
live by a code. I don't kill men I've served with, and I sure
as hell don't shoot at women—"

Simon interrupted him. "What did Mrs. Garber know,
General? What was it you were trying to prevent her from
telling us?"

A pause. "She heard me."

"Heard you?"

"On the phone. When I entered General Garber's
suite, he was on the phone with her. I'd leaked the story to
the press that he was responsible for a friendly-fire incident—"

"I've read the article, General."

"Oh? It's not supposed to be published until—"

"Tomorrow morning. Please continue."

He sighed audibly. "The article. That's the reason I'd
gone to Garber's room. I wanted the son of a bitch to
know that what he did in Vietnam was finally going to
come out. I wanted to see him sweat, knowing his career
was over and he was finished. Anyway, after I told him, we
got into an argument. He was drunk. One thing led to
another. He threw a punch, and I just reacted. I picked up
the bottle, and that was it."

"Mrs. Garber heard you kill him?"

"No. General Markel had hung up by then. But she

could put me in his room that night. Look, there's no time to get into this now. If you don't call off the police—"

"I'll require more than your word, General. I need your confession now, on tape. I also need to read you your rights."

"Dammit, there's no time."

"Call me back, sir."

"What the hell for? Jesus, man, don't you understand I'm trying to confess?"

"Yes, sir. That's why I need you to call me back." Simon gave him the number of the car phone and disconnected.

Once Simon read Markel his rights, the actual confession, including Simon's questions, took less than five minutes. It was short and sweet, and included only the essential elements. The details we'd get from Markel's formal statement. I was struck by the chilling calmness in Markel's voice as he described Garber's killing. How he held him down as he gasped for air. Markel said, "It took almost three minutes before he passed out. Another minute to stop breathing. I could have finished him off quick, but I knew my only chance was to make it look like an accident."

He fell silent, signaling he was finished. Simon asked, "Where was Andy?"

"He's the one who'd answered the door. I'd sent him out, told him to get a cup of coffee."

"So he didn't know what you intended?"

"Don't play it cute, Lieutenant. I said I didn't go to Garber's suite to kill him."

"Tell me who was involved in the cover-up."

The phone hissed.

"General—"

Markel answered mechanically, overpronouncing the words so there would be no misunderstanding. "I alone gave the orders for the cover-up. I am completely and solely responsible. No one else."

Simon didn't argue this point; he had no desire to go after Churchfield or the other generals, and neither did I.

Still, Simon couldn't resist tying up a few questions that troubled us. He started with: "What about Colonel Weller? Why did she stage the scene to appear as if General Garber had tried to rape her?"

"Leave her out of this. She had nothing to do with any of it."

"General, we know she—"

"I said, leave her alone."

"At least tell me why she left you to work for General Garber."

"I guess I'm not getting through to you, Lieutenant. I'm not saying a damn thing about Colonel Weller or anyone else. You have any other questions about the killing, save them for later. We had a deal, and I expect you to call off the cops. And if you've got an APB out on Stefanski, cancel it. Either that, or you better make damned sure the morgue's got a fresh supply of body bags. My office. 1900 hours. Stefanski will be here." He hung up.

Simon turned off the speaker, frowning. "This doesn't make any sense. There is no reason for him to do this. He knows we don't have the evidence for an arrest. He knows the investigation will be terminated within hours. Yet he willingly confesses. Why?"

He was looking at me for a response. I came up with

the only one I could think of: Markel might have been telling us the truth. Perhaps he did feel responsible for what happened to Andy and Mrs. Garber, and was confessing to make amends.

"So you believe he's an honorable man?"

"I think he *believes* he is."

"Try this," Enrique tossed out. "What if the general confessed because it was the only way to get something he wanted?"

His handsome face was watching us in the rearview mirror. I said. "Like what?"

He shrugged. "He sure seemed anxious for you to pull off the cops around the Pentagon."

I caught the implication and countered with the obvious: Why would Markel confess and then try and make a run for it?

"Yeah, you're probably right," Enrique said with a reluctant shrug. "I guess it's a crazy idea."

But when I glanced at Simon, I saw his eyes were riveted on the back of Enrique's head. I knew at once what that expression meant.

Unlike me, he thought Enrique was on to something.

I hated rush hour.

Two miles from the Pentagon exit, I-395 suddenly turned into a parking lot. Enrique tuned in to the traffic report, and we learned there was a three-car pileup just ahead. A Care-Flight helicopter came in and removed the injured. A Channel Five news helicopter flew over, reporting on the scene. After twenty minutes, traffic began moving again. I checked my watch. We'd still make the meeting with a few minutes to spare.

To describe Simon's second conversation with Captain Roche of the Pentagon police as unpleasant would have been charitable. Roche was understandably furious. I could hear him yelling at Simon over the phone. Roche had called in men on their days off; he'd mobilized SWAT. Next time, Lieutenant Santos better have his shit together before he cried fucking wolf.

As Simon cradled the receiver, I said to him, "Aren't you carrying things a little far?"

His face went blank. "Sorry?"

"Don't give me that. I heard you tell Roche that Stefanski was no longer a suspect. *And* you canceled the APB."

Simon nodded. "I think it's better that way. I don't want Stefanski stopped prior to reaching Markel's office."

"I hope to hell you know what you're doing. If he escapes, it's going to be hard to explain."

He shrugged. "At this point, I think we should let the situation play out. Do this the way General Markel wants."

"At least call Roche back. Have a few men available in case—"

"No. I think I'm right about this." He yawned, reclined against the headrest, and closed his eyes. I wasn't fooled. He was trying to avoid discussing this.

I pressed, "Right about what? Trusting Markel?"

Simon didn't reply. His eyes remained closed.

"Simon—"

The only response was the hum of tires over the road.

I sighed in annoyance. Enrique asked, "He's not really asleep, is he?"

I leaned close and spoke into Simon's ear. "Not a chance."

Simon never flinched. Moments later, we heard faint snoring.

"I'll be damned," Enrique said.

I still didn't believe it.

42

I said, "We're here, Simon."

He blinked sleepily and saw that we were rolling to a stop near the Corridor Two pedestrian bridge. He checked his watch, realized we had almost ten minutes, then popped the tape of Markel's confession from the limo's recorder and pocketed it. He rummaged around a side compartment, dug out a fresh tape, and inserted it into his handheld recorder. Flipping down a mirror over the door, he scowled disapprovingly at his appearance, then began combing his hair. I reminded him that he wasn't authorized to take his gun into the building. He nodded and reached down to remove it.

I got out and waited for him on the curb. The early evening air was cool, thickening clouds hinting at rain. Before joining me, Simon spoke to Enrique in Spanish. I caught the name Christopher. As the limo drove off, I said to him, "Who's Christopher?"

"The man who drove the Jaguar. I had him retrieve a package and hold it in the rental office." He smiled. "A gift from a woman."

This was news, since Simon had only one serious girlfriend in his life, a reporter who'd been shot during one of our earlier cases. It seemed like a new chauffeur wasn't the only change Simon was making in his life.

Walking up steps of the bridge, Simon produced his phone, saying he was going to have Amanda verify whether Mrs. Garber had overheard an argument between her husband and General Markel. When I told him I'd already passed the word to Amanda, he appeared surprised. I guess he really had been asleep after all.

As we started across the bridge, we could see people emerging from the building, but few were going in. I didn't notice anyone who remotely resembled Stefanski, but I didn't expect to. Chances were, he was already here; if not, he'd be using the river entrance.

My eyes drifted over the parking area. Because of the hour, the majority of vehicles were gone. Of those that remained, a number were press vans and satellite trucks, which had arrived to cover Churchfield's news conference. I didn't spot any Pentagon cops or men in SWAT team Ninja suits. Captain Roche hadn't wasted any time in recalling his men. Once again, I found myself hoping Simon wasn't making a mistake.

After searching Simon, the soldiers cleared him past on my entry badge, since I was authorized to escort. Three minutes later, we were through the metal detectors and heading down the A-ring toward the JCS area. This time there was no welcoming committee, but the guard was the same man I'd met earlier, who had been told to expect us. As he handed us our badges, he mentioned my earlier confrontation with the female colonel. We both had a chuckle.

It was a little before seven when Simon and I entered Markel's anteroom. A crowd of close to a dozen, a mixture of military and civilians, was wedged into the small sitting area. Most were seated; the rest stood. All were leafing through identical blue folders marked with a gold DoD seal. General Clay, Markel's exec, addressed the group, saying, "The secretary's press conference will begin immediately after the president's televised remarks. If you'll turn to the schedule, you will see the secretary will answer questions for thirty minutes. That's all. Please note, she's only going to discuss the deployment—the size, scope, and a rough timetable. She doesn't want to get into justifying the war against Iraq. The president already has made a strong case for— Yes, Maria?"

A pretty brunette seated on the couch pointed a nail at something in her folder. "It says here that General Markel will accompany the secretary on the podium—"

"Correct. He'll also make a few remarks and entertain follow-up questions, once the secretary departs."

"Where's General Garber, sir? Shouldn't he be the one—"

"General Garber is indisposed."

She frowned at him.

"That's all I know," Clay said.

"And that's what we tell the press?"

"Yes."

She persisted, "So General Garber is ill?"

"Indisposed," Clay repeated.

Maria still seemed confused as Clay resumed his briefing. Simon and I hung by the door, waiting for someone to notice us. A lieutenant colonel and a captain darted past, disappearing into the hallways to the right. Against the windows at the back, two sergeants were standing at a long table, collating foot-high stacks of pages into more blue folders, which were obviously press kits. Markel's white-haired secretary was hunched over the keyboard, typing away.

Simon and I went over to her. She smelled of lilacs. I said, "Excuse me, ma'am."

Without glancing up, she said, "Collins and Santos. The 1900 meeting. Right?"

"That's us."

My smile was wasted, since she was already picking up a phone to inform Markel we'd arrived. Hanging up, she said, "He'll be with you shortly. If you'll please have a seat."

I looked around. None were available. Simon asked her, "Is Mr. Stefanski with the general?"

"No. He called and said he was running late."

"Thank you."

We drifted toward an open space near the table where the two sergeants were working. We gazed out the window, which overlooked the river entrance parking area, the gray-black waters of the Potomac beyond. The two sergeants chatted away as they mindlessly stuffed the folders. The topic was sports, specifically Redskins football and Coach Spurrier's fun-and-gun offense. After a while, they shifted to basketball and argued whether Michael Jordan would play a third season.

"Doesn't really matter," one sergeant said gloomily. "Either way, the Wizards will suck. Always have and always will."

A conclusion I unfortunately shared. Fingering my watch, I said to Simon, "It's been five minutes. Could be Markel's stalling."

Simon ignored my comment and the intimation it contained. He continued to gaze out the window, following each car as it pulled into the parking area. He was looking for Stefanski's blue Lincoln.

More minutes went by. I began an impatient two-step. The sergeants had covered all the local sports teams and were now discussing hunting. One mentioned that Markel hunted deer every year in North Carolina. "The general's been hunting since he was a kid," the man said. "That's the reason he was one helluva sniper in 'Nam. Shooting, to him, was like breathing. He'd been doing it since he could walk." He went on talking about Markel's marksmanship as if he were a modern-day Daniel Boone.

I became aware of the silence behind me. Glancing back, I saw that General Clay had returned to his desk. The crowd in the sitting area was filing out the door. I made another time check. Seven-twelve.

Screw this. Stefanski wasn't going to show. I was about to urge Simon that we should make our move now. Throw cuffs on Markel and pressure him into—

I stiffened at a comment by one of the sergeants. Turning, I saw Simon staring at the two men. He'd heard the remark, too.

I tried to keep my voice casual. "What was that you said, Sergeant?"

They both glanced at me in surprise. I was addressing the shorter of the two, the beefy guy with dark hair. I said, "Just now. You were discussing General Markel."

The sergeant still seemed puzzled. "You mean that he likes to hunt, sir?"

"After that. You said something about a bolt—"

"Oh, right. I was telling Joey here that I just returned from General Markel's house, over on Fort Myer. The general sent me there to pick up the original bolt and a box of shells for his rifle. He's thinking about using it for deer hunting next month and wants to shoot a few rounds at the range over at—"

But I wasn't listening to him any longer. I stood there, trying to convince myself that Markel really *was* making the gun serviceable only to hunt. But the little voice in my head kept talking about another possibility.

Shit—

As I pivoted toward Markel's office, someone grabbed my arm. It was Simon. He spoke in soft tones, telling me that it was better this way. That we should let things play out.

There was something in the way he said it, the calm acceptance in his voice. I stared at him. *"You knew this would happen?"*

He gave me a sad smile. "The general is a proud man. I realized it would be humiliating for him to—"

And then we heard it. The loud, cracking sound of a gunshot. The secretary gave a gasp and dropped the phone she was holding. General Clay grunted, "What the hell—" He was out of his chair, sprinting down the hallway. Simon and I ran after him, the two sergeants following. From up ahead, a woman shouted, "It came from General Markel's office!" We got to his door. The cute admin sergeant I'd met earlier was standing outside, frantically trying the knob. It was locked. Clay pushed her out of the way and called out Markel's name. He tried the knob again, swore, fumbled a hand into his pocket.

He removed a key chain, selected a key, and inserted it into the lock. I ordered him to step back. He turned as if to argue, then saw I had my gun out. I went in first, Simon right behind me. The smell of cordite was heavy in the room. Markel wasn't at his desk, and when we looked toward the window, we finally saw him.

My voice was wrong.

43

In an instant, my surprise gave way to confusion and then to fear. Markel stood with his back to the window, his rifle trained on Simon and me. Markel's eyes were flat, dead. When he saw the pistol in my hand, he shifted the barrel fractionally to my chest. We stood there with our weapons pointed at each other, like a scene out of *High Noon*. Any second, I expected to feel the impact of a bullet.

Even though the room was chilly, I began to sweat.

Simon said, "Please put the rifle down, General."

Markel said, "I had to do it. I had no other choice."

Simon nodded as if he understood, but I had no idea what Markel was talking about. Behind us came the sound of Clay's voice: "General, please. Do as they say."

"Close the door, Jim," Markel ordered.

"Sir, I don't think—"

"*Close the fucking door.*"

A murmur of anxious voices. There were shouts to call for the police. Someone said, "Jesus, he really is crazy." Then we heard the door close. It was quiet. From outside the window, there was more shouting, but the words were too faint to make out.

Simon said again, "General, please put down the rifle. This isn't necessary."

Markel didn't answer him. He'd turned to look at the portrait of William Travis hanging on the wall. His attention was completely off me. This was my chance. All I had to do was pull the trigger, and—

Abruptly, Markel began to speak. His voice was somber, almost reverential. As I listened, I grew increasingly mesmerized by his words. He was talking passionately about things like courage and honor and duty. Slowly he drifted toward the portrait, as if drawn by an invisible force. That's when I noticed the hole cut into the window behind him. His body had blocked me from seeing it. But Simon had a different angle, which explained how he'd known what had occurred.

Since the Pentagon's windows didn't open, the hole had been necessary. A small glass-cutter on the desk confirmed that Markel had planned this. I shook my head, still having difficulty accepting what had just transpired.

Markel was talking about loyalty now, the kind of loyalty forged only in the heat of battle. He kept mentioning someone named Denny. I soon realized he was referring to Colonel Dennis Stefanski. He said, "That night on Hill 114 was pure hell. So many men, dying or dead. I found Denny barely alive. Everyone told me to leave him, that he wouldn't make it. But we'd been through so much. Two tours. I carried him to the chopper. His skin came off in my hands.

"But he made it. He lived. God knows how. Ever since then, he felt he owed me. His loyalty to me drove him to do what he did. He was only trying to protect me. It was my fault. I placed him in the position. I told him that I'd killed General Garber. I told him about the phone call and that Garber's wife had heard me. It was Denny's idea to talk to her, scare her into keeping quiet. I went along with it because I was desperate. What other option was there? But I never foresaw the lengths he would go to. And Andy. Why the hell did he have to shoot Andy? Dammit, we all fought together. We were brothers . . . He should have realized that Andy would never . . ."

He trailed off with a pitying head shake. Simon and I watched him. We knew better than to say anything. After several seconds, Markel gathered himself with a ragged breath and nodded to a thin sheaf of pages on his desk. "It's all there. I wrote out a complete confession."

Simon came forward and picked up the pages, which were handwritten. As he scanned them, Markel said, "Read it later."

"General, I need to ensure—"

He broke off when Markel pointed the rifle at him. My finger tightened on the pistol trigger. "Don't, General."

No reaction. Markel was focused on Simon. His eyes had that unbalanced look, the one I recalled from the hangar. He said, "You have your confession, Lieutenant. The case is closed. I want you to leave."

Simon gazed back coolly, completely unafraid. For a moment, I was worried he might try and argue. Thankfully, he pocketed the pages without comment.

"General," I said. "Put down the rifle. It doesn't have to end like this."

"You think I'm crazy, Collins?" He still had the unbalanced look.

I hesitated, thrown by the question. "No, sir," I lied.

"*Are* you crazy, General?" Simon asked bluntly.

Jesus— I held my breath, expecting Markel to react with anger.

But he appeared amused by the question. He even gave Simon a little smile.

"In some respects," he said, "I suppose I am. A lot of people say they have values they would die for, but they don't mean it." His voice hardened. "I do."

"Including honor?" Simon said.

"*Especially* honor."

"Suicide has no honor, General."

Markel laughed harshly. "You're wrong, Lieutenant. The crucial element is the motive behind the act. Mine is noble. I am repaying a debt the only way I can."

"A debt?" Simon said.

There was a long pause. Markel seemed reluctant to respond. He finally did, peering right at Simon, as if to be certain he understood.

"I owed Andy," he said with feeling. "He saved my life in Vietnam."

Simon passed on making a comment. There was nothing he could say.

Markel motioned impatiently with the rifle, signaling he was through talking and it was time for us to go. Simon asked him if he was a religious man. Markel shook his head, no.

Producing his rosary beads, Simon said, "Do you mind if I say a prayer, General? It won't take long."

Markel stared at him in disbelief. "Look, either you get out of here or—"

But Simon had already begun to pray, reciting the Twenty-third Psalm from memory. It was an eerie feeling, hearing the haunting finality of the words and being with someone who was about to take his own life. I suspect the reason Simon had chosen this prayer was to give Markel a final chance to reflect. Perhaps reconsider.

When he finished, Simon gazed at Markel as if waiting for a comment. Markel's only response was to motion once more with the rifle. This time Simon complied, and we left. Within seconds of the door closing behind us, we heard an audible click. Then came the sound of the gunshot.

44

Chaos.

That's the only way to describe the scene that greeted us in the hallway. The moment we emerged from Markel's office, uniformed Pentagon cops swarmed upon us and shoved guns in our faces. One wrenched the pistol from my hand. A short, balding cop confronted Simon and me and demanded to know what the hell was going on. He wore captain's bars, and his name tag said Roche, confirming he was the guy whom Simon had pissed off earlier. As Simon was about to answer him, we heard the rifle shot. A few cops flinched, but none ducked or flattened against the wall—a notable display of self-control, considering they were dealing with a crazed general who'd killed over a hundred men.

Captain Roche angrily repeated the question. Simon calmly replied that General Markel had just killed himself.

Roche ordered us to remain in the reception area. "Don't move. Don't even fucking blink. I'm going to want some goddamn answers." He grabbed the mike clipped to his collar and radioed for the SWAT team.

"That's really not necessary, Captain." I grabbed the doorknob. Locked.

Roche tore my hand away. "Richie, get them out of my hair!"

A big cop came forward and puffed up his muscles to make sure we noticed. He followed Simon and me down the hall. More cops were in the anteroom, the staff having been cleared out. Richie went over to the door, which was open, and stood by it, eyeing us. From the outer hallway, we could hear shouts—cops ordering people to clear the offices.

Two civilian women walked past but didn't seem unusually alarmed. A major followed, talking on a cell phone. Two colonels calmly strolled by moments later.

Simon remarked on everyone's composure. I mentioned this could be a lesson gained from 9-11. In the Pentagon, people had learned that there was nothing to be gained by panic.

"I disagree, Martin. They should be frightened. It's human nature to be frightened."

I shrugged. I wasn't about to get into an argument over this.

At the sound of a siren, we walked over to the window. It was almost dusk, and we could see two Humvees blocking the entrance to the nearly empty parking lot, uniformed cops taking cover behind the vehicles, their rifles aimed at Markel's office. Looking right, we spotted the blue Lincoln Town Car parked in the front row. The body of a man lay face-up a few steps from the driver's door. In the dim light, we couldn't make out his facial features, but we could see the shininess of the blood on the asphalt.

Another Humvee roared up, squealing to a stop near

the first two. This time soldiers piled out, their weapons trained on the building. "I don't understand this," Simon murmured.

My brow furrowed. "What? That Markel blew Stefanski away?"

"Yes. It's inconsistent. From the beginning, General Markel has sought to protect the military from negative publicity. Yet he does this in full view? Kills Stefanski in such a dramatic fashion?" He looked uneasy. "No. I don't understand it."

Brother. Simon always had to dot all the i's and cross the t's. I said, "Markel told us why. He was repaying a debt. Andy saved his life, so he feels honor-bound to avenge him. Besides, Markel's got a few loose screws. Who the hell really knows what motivates a guy like him . . ."

I trailed off. Simon wasn't listening to me. He was shaking his head, murmuring to himself. Something about a door . . .

He became still, as if a thought had just struck him. Abruptly, he walked over to the table, dug out a blue folder from a box, flipped it open, and began to read.

A radio squawked loudly behind us. A scratchy voice estimated twenty minutes until SWAT arrived. Moments later, we heard another radio call: "This is an exercise. All units treat this as an exercise. Repeat, all units—"

"Turn that damn thing off!"

I turned, saw the big cop, Richie, click off his radio. Another cop with lieutenant's bars was glaring at him. Richie's face reddened.

"That explains it," Simon said softly.

I nodded. In an effort to keep the press in the dark, the military was officially referring to the shooting as an exercise. We now understood why no one had appeared panicked.

Simon shut the blue folder he was holding. He no longer seemed troubled. Apparently, the radio call had also tempered his concerns about Markel killing Stefanski in such a public fashion, though I had no idea why.

Simon produced Markel's confession and began to read. He handed me the pages as he finished. There were only three. I deciphered Markel's scrawl and realized he hadn't told us anything new.

That meant we were still left with unanswered questions. This bothered Simon. He still wanted to know why Markel had called Secretary Churchfield so soon after killing Garber, and why Colonel Weller had tried to make Garber look like a rapist. In Simon's way, he was telling me he wasn't finished with investigation.

Even with the confession.

Even with the killer dead.

Even though we generally knew what had happened and why.

Even though there was nothing to be gained except to embarrass the military even more.

He still wanted to continue.

It was too much.

It had been a long, trying day, and I was spent, both physically and emotionally. I didn't want to think about the case anymore. I didn't want to think about Andy, who was lying on a slab in a morgue. I didn't want to think about Markel, who in the end proved to be more of a man than I could ever envision being. I didn't want to think about my roles in their deaths and how they'd probably be alive if I'd simply walked away. I didn't want to think about Amanda, and how she was going to withdraw from my life.

I just didn't want to think.

All I wanted to do was go home and spend a few hours with my daughter, Emily. Hold her close and see her excitement when I told her she was going to have a birthday party she'd never forget.

So I asked—I *begged* Simon to let everything go. What did it really matter about Weller or Churchfield? We'd done what had seemed impossible. We'd found the killer and solved the case in a day. Simon had kept his promise to Senator Garber. *Let the damn thing go.*

Simon was genuinely surprised by the passion of my response. It never occurred to him that I would have no desire to continue.

But then, I had a life.

"All right, Martin," he said reluctantly. "But there's something you need to know." He passed me the blue folder. "Look at the schedule."

"Simon, I'm really not interested—"

"*Look.*"

I sighed, opened the folder.

"The third page."

I turned to it. There wasn't much there. Seven little bullets, indicating the sequence of the press conference. The Pentagon Press secretary would play emcee. At the conclusion of the president's address, he would introduce Secretary Churchfield and General Markel. Churchfield would make her remarks, answer questions, then leave. Markel would remain to make additional remarks and also field questions.

An hour after the press conference began, it would be over.

I glanced at Simon. "So?"

He gave me a little smile. "You don't think it's odd?"

"What's odd?"

"Agent Collins!"

Simon and I turned away from the window and saw General Sessler standing by the door, grimly motioning to us. No mystery what he wanted to discuss.

I returned the folder to Simon. "Let me do the talking."

"Martin, I think it's best if—"

"You said I was in charge. You said this was my case."

He sighed. "I don't think—"

"You promised me."

It was my trump card. I'd reminded him he'd given his word. He surrendered with a nod, but clearly wasn't happy about it.

As we walked over to Sessler, I told the big cop, Richie, to retrieve my pistol. He hesitated.

"Get it, officer," Sessler ordered.

So Richie hurried over to Captain Roche, who was still standing with a knot of his men outside Markel's door. The two men conversed briefly, looking back at us. Roche's grimace made it clear he wasn't enthused about the prospect of his two key witnesses leaving, even for a little while. Still, he knew better than to argue with a four-star general, and I saw him turn to a second police officer, the one who had disarmed me.

After Richie returned with my pistol, Sessler led Simon and me out into the hallway.

"We'll talk in my office," he growled. "It's on the third floor."

I nodded; I knew where the army chief's office was.

As we headed for the staircase, Simon asked if there

was a rest room nearby. Sessler shot him a look of irritation, but directed him to a door behind us. When Simon rejoined us five minutes later, Sessler glared at him. Like me, Sessler suspected that whatever Simon had been doing in the john, he hadn't only been taking a piss.

Sessler strode into his office and pointed Simon and me to armchairs before his desk. As he sat down, he muted the television, which was tuned to CNN. On the monitor, a former secretary of defense continued to talk soundlessly. A scrolling banner below him read: "President Addresses Nation on Iraq War, 8 P.M. EST."

Tossing the remote aside, Sessler eyed Simon and me. "Tell me what happened."

Simon handed him Markel's confession, then sat back with his arms folded, letting me know this would be my show. Once Sessler looked over the confession, I filled him on what we'd uncovered. The only item I withheld was Billy Bowman's role in confirming Garber's time of death. I danced around this topic by saying we'd deduced Garber had been killed in England, and left it at that. As I went through my spiel, General Sessler's expression never changed. I had the feeling he knew beforehand what I was going to say.

As I thought about it, I realized I shouldn't be surprised. Markel certainly would have told him about Andy's death and that Stefanski was responsible. Markel may have even mentioned his intention to confess.

But as to Markel telling him he'd planned to kill Stefanski and commit suicide? No way.

"Any additional issues that I need to be concerned about?" Sessler asked.

I told him that civilian police could pose problems,

since they were pursuing Andy's killing and the shooting at Mrs. Garber's.

"We'll attend to them," he said.

I wasn't about to ask him how. I said, "Captain Roche also wants us to give a statement."

"Forget about Roche."

Another anticipated response.

"Anything else?" Sessler asked.

I shook my head, struck by his matter-of-fact tone. Like we were completing a business transaction. I'd continually been on edge, waiting for him to lash out that our pursuit of the investigation was somehow responsible for Markel's death. After all, this was the man who earlier had laid the guilt trip on me, saying I was going to hurt innocent people.

But he never once played the blame card. Even more curious, he didn't appear all that upset over Markel's death.

I began to wonder if my initial hunch was mistaken. Perhaps Markel *had* told Sessler about his intentions to—

Sessler held up the confession. "Is there any reason you need this, Collins?"

I glanced at Simon. His eyes were fixed straight ahead. He intended to hold me to my statement that I'd do all the talking. I said to Sessler, "I don't think so, sir."

"I understand there's a tape."

Confirmation that he had spoken with Markel. Again, I looked to Simon.

He sighed, his hand reaching into his jacket. He produced the tape and placed it on the desk.

"Play it," Sessler said.

Simon hesitated, dug out his tape player. He popped in the tape and hit *play*. Markel's voice: "I'm responsible for the death of—"

"That's enough," Sessler said.

Simon removed the tape and passed it to him.

"Any copies?"

Simon shook his head.

"Now," Sessler said, sitting back, "Secretary Church-field has one more request. She'd like to be assured the matter is fully resolved. The president speaks in a few minutes." He looked to the TV screen in a particularly suggestive way.

I understood what he was asking. I waited to see how Simon would respond. This was the test. If he really believed there was anything in the case worth pursuing, he would never make the call.

But moments later, he took out his cell phone.

"Senator Garber? Simon. You can inform the president that your son was murdered by General Markel."

As Simon and I left, the president's voice blared out from the TV. The witching hour had arrived and I still had a call to make. I phoned Martha Jones and told her to tell the forensics team to go on home.

45

Petulant.

That's the only way to describe Simon's demeanor during our seven-minute walk to the Corridor Two exit. He never said a word the entire time. He wouldn't even look at me. He reminded me of the proverbial spoiled kid who was pouting because he didn't get his way.

Did I care that he was ticked off with me?

Not particularly. We'd been through these disagreements before. After a few days, he'd get over it, and all would be forgiven.

But he'd never admit he was wrong to want to pursue this case further. He'd never admit that every investigation had questions that were impossible to resolve and that it was crazy to even try.

Frankly, this fanaticism for answers is what set him apart, made him such a good cop. Usually, I was willing to play along. But not tonight.

Not tonight.

We stepped out onto the bridge. It was noticeably colder, the night air filled with a light mist. At first I didn't see the limo, but once we started down the steps on the other side, Enrique drove up. He'd obviously been parked where he could watch for us.

As Simon and I got in back, Enrique handed him a yellow manila envelope—the package Simon had wanted. Across the top someone had written "Hold for Lt. Santos." Rather than open it, Simon placed it in a side compartment and stared out the window.

After grabbing a beer from the fridge, I returned to my seat beside him. I sipped, watching him. Finally, I said, "You want to talk about it?"

Nothing. I shrugged; I'd given it a shot.

Enrique called out, "Where to now?"

Simon remained silent.

I told Enrique to head for Walter Reed so I could catch a ride home with Amanda. Before she'd left the bar, Simon had arranged for a car to be delivered to her.

Enrique cranked the engine, began pulling out. He asked, "So how'd it go? You arrest General Markel?"

I started to explain what had happened.

"Stop the car," Simon ordered. "We're not leaving."

Enrique hit the brakes so suddenly, I lurched forward, spilling my beer. I swore, turning to Simon. "Dammit, I knew it. You couldn't let this go. You always have to—"

He cut me off with a sharp: "The truth, Martin. Do you want to know the truth?"

"*We know the fucking truth.*"

"You're certain? You have no doubts?"

"Markel's dead. It's over. None of it matters. Churchfield, Weller—"

"But it *does* matter, Martin. Markel played us for fools. It was an illusion. We were deceived. I will not allow him to— Where are you going?"

I'd jammed my beer into a cup holder and had clicked

open the door latch. Without looking back, I climbed out and shut the door hard. The Pentagon had a Metro stop, and I swung back toward the bridge. After a few steps, I heard the window whir down behind me.

Simon called out, "Markel was lying. He didn't kill Garber."

I picked up the pace. I was his ticket into the Pentagon. He'd say anything to get me to return.

"I can prove it, Martin. I can prove he set us up."

I slowed.

"Senator Garber believes Markel was innocent."

I came to a stop. I stood there, shaking my head. Aw, hell—

When I turned around, I saw Simon looking up at me, his face dimly visible from glow of nearby streetlights. "Simon, if you're bullshitting me—"

"Senator Garber received confirmation that neither Markel nor the other generals could have killed his son."

I frowned. "When did you— The bathroom?"

"Yes. Senator Garber phoned me after speaking with the president. That's when he told me about the sworn statements the president had received from Secretary Churchfield. The ones Churchfield had requested from the British."

"What sworn statements?"

The interior lights came on. Simon opened the door and gave me a sardonic smile. "Come on back, Martin. Our job isn't completed. We still have work to do."

After a deep breath and a final head shake, I returned to the limo.

Simon hadn't misstated or exaggerated; Markel's confession was a complete fabrication.

From Simon's conversation with Senator Garber, he learned that seventy-three British officers and dignitaries had attended the dinner with the four American generals. At the behest of Churchfield, all the attendees had faxed signed statements, stipulating that during the course of the evening, only one American general had left the dais prior to 2300 hours.

Garber.

If their statements were true, Markel's innocence seemed irrefutable.

I said, "The Brits could be lying."

"All of them? Including the civilians?"

I tried again. "Did Churchfield tell them *why* she wanted the statements? Because if she did, and the attendees were pressured to—"

"Unlikely. She wouldn't risk the story of Garber's death being leaked."

We were parked at the end of a mostly empty row, about a hundred yards from the bridge. Enrique and Simon were both watching me. I gathered my thoughts with a swig of beer. "What about Billy Bowman? What if his estimate of the 2130 time of death was wrong?"

"You're familiar with Dr. Bowman's proficiency. Could he be mistaken by two hours?"

He was allowing for the time it would take Garber to travel from the dinner to his room and get into the confrontation with Markel. "No," I admitted. "Billy's too good an ME to be off by that much. So unless he lied to us about the time of death—"

Simon shook his head.

"Then Markel's out. He couldn't have done it. Neither could Sessler and Johnson. Not if they also were at the dinner until 2300."

"So," Simon said quietly, "it seems Andy was telling us the truth after all."

He was referring to Andy's defense of Markel, moments before he was killed by Stefanski.

"Let me get this straight," Enrique said. "You guys are telling me this guy Markel confessed to a murder he didn't commit and then killed himself. Why?"

Simon didn't reply; he was frowning at his watch. He turned and began rummaging in the side compartment, the one where he'd placed the manila envelope earlier.

Tell them it was me.

Those were the words that Paul Carter had overheard Markel say to Sessler and Garber. In light of that statement, there seemed to be only one response to Enrique's question. I told him General Markel was obviously covering for the real killer.

"He'd shoot himself to do that?"

"Possibly. If he thought it was the only way to protect someone he cared about. The one candidate who fits the bill is his former aide, Colonel Weller." I grimaced as my train of thought derailed. "But the problem is, Markel had no reason to protect Weller. None. We weren't anywhere close to making a case against her."

"So there has to be someone else," Enrique said. "I mean, a guy just doesn't kill himself—"

"*Now,*" Simon said. "Now we'll know if I'm right."

In a sudden, dramatic gesture, he thrust a remote toward the television, which was affixed to the roof in a manner similar to those on aircraft. Under the soft glow of the interior lights, we could see the hard set of his jaw and the tension in his eyes. Enrique cocked an eyebrow at me. *What's with him?* I shook my head.

The screen flared, and an instant later, we saw the

president sitting at his desk in the Oval Office. His voice was low, barely audible. Enrique said, "You mind, Simon? I'd like to see this."

A nod. Simon tapped on the remote, increasing the volume.

Enrique hopped out from behind the wheel, jogged around, and took the seat to my right.

I said to Simon, "Mind telling us what you're looking for?"

"Patience, Martin."

So I nursed my beer and listened to the president. His demeanor was somber, almost regretful, belying the emotional undercurrent of his words. He reminded us of the three thousand innocent lives that had been lost and promised that this war with Iraq was necessary to prevent an even greater catastrophe in the future. He listed a wide array of chemical and biological weapons in Saddam Hussein's arsenal and chillingly detailed their lethality. Staring directly into the camera, he asked whether America could afford to wait until these weapons fell into the hands of Islamic extremists.

"In two short years," the president continued, "we estimate that Iraq will possess two to three nuclear weapons. If the terrorists on 9-11 had been in possession of one, America would still be grieving over the deaths of untold thousands and possibly even millions. Much of New York City would be uninhabitable for generations. Our country, this beacon of freedom, would cease to exist as we know it. No, my fellow Americans, there is no other alternative. The terrorists started this war, and America will finish it. We will not be victimized by such horror again. Saddam Hussein's weapons threaten not only America but the world. If the world is unwilling to join us in this

fight for peace, America and her allies will wage this battle alone."

He paused. The camera closed in tight, and the president's face filled the screen. "The threat is real. Let's roll,
America."

The camera slowly faded back as the president continued to sit at his desk.

"Wish I was still a SEAL," Enrique murmured.

I nodded. With his three final words, the president had
simultaneously reminded us of the courage of the passengers on Flight 93 and awakened a surge of patriotism.
Suddenly, it didn't seem to matter who killed General
Garber or why Markel had confessed. I said, "Simon—"

"Wait. We'll soon know."

He was sitting at the edge of his seat, eyes riveted on
the television. I returned to the monitor, where a solemn-
faced Harvey Jenkins was sitting at the CBS anchor desk.
"As of eight P.M. Eastern Standard Time, America is again
at war with Iraq. Now to the Pentagon for Secretary
Churchfield's press conference . . ."

The familiar blue-draped Pentagon press room
appeared. Ron Hammond, the silver-maned Pentagon
press secretary, was standing at the podium. Ron leaned
toward the microphone and said, "Ladies and gentlemen,
the secretary of defense."

Simon sprang forward, thrusting out a finger. "Look.
You see him? *Look.*"

I almost dropped my beer.

I stared at the screen in disbelief. I couldn't accept the
reality of the image I was seeing. It was impossible. It had
to be impossible.

And yet . . .

My mind went back. Slowly, event by event, I shifted through the inconsistencies, the little things that seemed to not quite fit:

Markel locking his office door after Simon and I left.

The controlled reaction of the Pentagon police, at the instant Markel fired the second shot.

Captain Roche's grabbing my hand to prevent me from reentering the office.

The radio call, saying it was an exercise.

General Sessler's seeming lack of concern over Markel's death.

Simon's comments: Why would Markel do this? Why would he kill Stefanski in such a public fashion?

And, of course, the schedule in the press kit. The one that still showed Markel accompanying Churchfield on the podium.

Taken singly, none of these items meant anything. But together . . .

I felt angry with myself. I should have noticed. I should have paid attention. But I didn't because . . .

Because I'd been in turmoil over this case from the beginning. Deep down, I never wanted it solved. I never wanted to know the truth. So I'd let myself be fooled. Let myself see only what they wanted—

Someone was tapping my arm.

Enrique's voice: "Look at *who*? All I see is Secretary Churchfield, on the stage with a four-star general."

"That's him," I said. "That's the guy Simon's talking about."

"Doesn't look familiar," Enrique said. "Have I heard of him?"

"Yes," Simon said. "He's General Markel."

46

On the screen, we watched Secretary Churchfield approach the podium, while General Markel remained a few respectful paces behind her. The camera moved in, framing Churchfield. Her sharp features were set in a taut, confident line, matching her gaze. She looked out over the audience as cameras flashed continually. It occurred to me that she was posing. This was the image she wanted plastered on the front pages of the world's newspapers tomorrow, that of a tough, supremely competent military leader.

Gradually, the flashes tapered off, and she began to speak, but not about the war. Rather, she opened by announcing a tragedy, the death of a great American soldier.

General Michael Garber.

She didn't discuss the details of his death, other than to say he'd fallen in the compartment of his plane and suffered a fatal hemorrhage. She briefly mentioned that an investigation of the accident had been completed, and a summary of the report would be available after the briefing. She went on for a several minutes, eulogizing General

Garber. She recounted his career, described him as her right arm, and magnanimously credited him with orchestrating the campaign to be employed against Iraq.

"Our success in the upcoming war," she said, "can directly be attributed to General Garber. America will miss him in this crucial time. I will miss him. Our prayers and thoughts go out to his family and to his parents, Senator and Mrs. Garber."

She paused, as if looking down at the podium for her notes.

"Did you hear it?" Simon murmured.

"Yes," I said.

"Hear what?" Enrique asked.

"The catch in her voice," I said. "When she said she'd miss General Garber."

Enrique still appeared lost. I explained our suspicion that Churchfield had some emotional attachment to Garber.

As Churchfield began discussing the troop deployment, Simon muted the volume. No one said anything for a few moments.

Enrique gave a little cough. "Look, I'm still confused—"

I said, "You should be."

"This guy General Markel," he continued, tugging on his earring, "confessed because it was the only way to get you to pull off the cops. Give his buddy Stefanski a chance to get away?"

I nodded. Out of the corner of my eye, I watched Simon, wondering if he'd admit he never should have canceled the APB on Stefanski. But he continued to sit quietly; his ego didn't allow him to own up to mistakes.

Enrique asked, "What about the rest of it? Why'd

General Markel stage Stefanski's shooting and his own suicide?"

Simon's eyes sought out mine, to see if I had a response. I did. I said part of the reason he'd staged the stunt was his arrogance. By making us look foolish, Markel was sending us the message that he was smarter than we were. I added, "But the main reason was that Markel needed a way to get us to turn over his confessions. Once we thought he was dead, we had no reason to keep them."

"But his confessions were bogus," Enrique said. "Markel could prove he wasn't the killer—" He broke off with a head shake. "Jeez, I must be tired. The press. They couldn't take the chance that the confessions might fall into the hands of the press. If that happened, Markel would have to explain why he confessed to a killing he didn't commit."

"You got it," I said. "And that's the reason General Sessler appeared so soon after we left Markel's office. Sessler's job was to get us to hand over—"

I sighed. Simon was giving me his unsettled look, which meant he disagreed. "Am I missing something?"

A nod. "You're partially correct; they wanted to retrieve Markel's confessions. But only *after* I called Senator Garber and told him Markel was the killer. This was a crucial element. They were trying to destroy Senator Garber's credibility with the president. Make it appear as if the senator really was on a witch hunt."

"Okay . . ." But I only had a vague idea where he was going.

"You see, Martin," he went on, "that was the purpose of those sworn statements. The ones proving Markel's innocence— Ah, you understand now?"

My head was bobbing. "I think so. Once Garber informed the president that Markel was the killer, the president would confront him with those sworn statements. Without Markel's confessions to back him up, Senator Garber couldn't prove he wasn't accusing Markel without cause. Gotta give them credit. They're damn good. They had all the bases covered."

"Except they made a mistake," Simon said, "It never occurred to them that the president would call Senator Garber *before* Garber made the accusation, and reveal to him the existence those sworn statements."

True, not that it really made much difference in the long run. They'd jerked us around so much that we still had no idea who really killed Garber or why.

Enrique said, "And General Markel staged the shooting of Stefanski because—"

I couldn't even venture a guess, and I didn't see how Simon could either. But he did, without hesitation.

"A message," he said. "Markel was telling us he would take care of Stefanski." He punctuated the comment with a knowing look.

My eyebrows widened at the implication. Before I could respond, Enrique said, "Are you suggesting—"

"I'm not suggesting anything; I *know*. Markel not only demonstrated his intention, he told us." Simon turned to me. "Do you recall his exact words when we entered the office? He said he had no choice, that he had to do it. This was a direct reference to killing Stefanski. Later, Markel spoke of honor, said he was repaying a debt, told us he owed Andy. At the time, the general seemed to be explaining his suicide, but now we know the truth." He shook his head emphatically. "I don't think there's any question. In Markel's eyes, Stefanski's crime was unforgivable; he'd killed one of their own. If he isn't dead already, he soon will be."

Enrique squinted dubiously. In his mind, it didn't compute that Markel would kill a friend. Frankly, this bothered me, too. But we were talking about a man who defined himself by his own rigid moral code and a sense of honor few could understand. And if his code required him to kill a man whose life he'd once saved, I had no doubt he would do so.

Like I said, the man was nuts.

"So what now?" I asked Simon.

A shrug. "Nothing. We wait for Amanda's call. I'm hopeful she'll learn something useful from Mrs. Garber." He pushed past me, sat down by the computer, and lifted up a seatback to reveal a row of shelves. After removing a thick file—the one containing the background information on the suspects that he'd downloaded earlier—he clicked closed the seatback and began scanning the file's contents.

"Mrs. Garber, the murdered general's wife?" Enrique said.

"Yeah." I frowned at Simon. "Hopeful? Earlier, you said Mrs. Garber would be too frightened to—"

I stopped. He was smiling at me. I'd missed something obvious.

"Amanda," I said, catching on. "She's the real reason you went to the rest room. You called her, had her tell Mrs. Garber that Stefanski and Markel were both dead."

"Yes. Here." He handed me a thick sheaf of pages, then passed a similar stack to Enrique.

"Anything in particular I'm looking for?" Enrique asked.

Simon's explanation was cut short by the ringing of a

car phone. His hand snaked out to a receiver. At the mention of Amanda's name, I punched the speaker icon on the overhead console. When I heard her excited voice, I immediately grasped the significance.

Simon's call had worked, and Mrs. Garber had finally decided to talk.

Amanda spoke at a frenetic pace, the words pouring from her in a series of disjointed phrases—"told me everything. Mrs. Garber said she received *two* phone calls from her husband. That's how I know she was in Garber's room. She was supposed to meet him. *Son of a bitch*. This changes everything. Our rape theory could be right. That would explain why—"

Simon said, "Amanda, slow down. You're not making any sense."

"I'm trying to tell you, General Markel *lied*. He wasn't the one who argued with General Garber. He tried to make it appear as if he did, but his call—the one Weller made—came too late. Hours after Garber was already dead—"

Simon, clearly annoyed: "Amanda, will you please—"

"*Just listen*. I'm telling you, she was there. She was the one who came to Markel's room. She was the one Mrs. Garber heard—"

"Weller?" Simon said. "Are you talking about Weller?"

A pause. When Amanda answered, she spoke in a hushed tone, as if afraid someone would hear.

"Churchfield," she said. "Churchfield was with Garber in England."

47

Five minutes later, I punched off the speaker. Afterward, we all sat around with stunned expressions. None of us felt like talking; we couldn't. We were still reeling from what Amanda had revealed.

Mrs. Garber had indeed told her everything. Most of the loose ends were wrapped up. What we didn't know for certain, we could now make educated guesses at.

Simon should have been pleased at the dramatic turn of events, but he wasn't. He was staring gloomily out the window. I asked him what was wrong.

He sighed. "The past. I knew the truth had to be connected to the past. The missing photographs, Churchfield's connection to Garber, Weller's behavior—the signs were all there. I should have realized. But I let myself become rushed by the time constraint. I lost my focus."

I said, "They put up too many roadblocks. No one could have known."

He shook his head. "I should have known, Martin."

The disappointment in his voice told me he really believed it.

A car slowly drove past. We watched in silence until it disappeared around the corner.

"Evidence," Enrique said. "You guys still don't have any evidence supporting Mrs. Garber's statement."

Which wasn't quite true. We had the evidence. At least some of it.

Now all we had to do was find it.

So we each took our stacks and began going through them. Since we knew what we were looking for, it took only about fifteen minutes. Afterward, Simon phoned Mrs. Garber's home number. I turned on the speaker, so we could listen in. When her answering machine picked up, Simon punched in the code that Amanda had given him.

General Garber's call was the sixth one, after a message from a dry cleaner. A metallic voice gave yesterday's date followed by the time: 1848 hours local.

Over two hours after Garber's death.

Instead of the dead general's voice, we heard a woman say tentatively, "Mrs. Garber, this is Colonel Weller. General Garber wanted me to call and say he would be returning home tomorrow—"

Weller broke off, as if surprised by something. In the background we heard male voices arguing. One man's words were garbled; the second we understood clearly. It was General Markel. He sounded enraged. "You gutless son of a bitch. You killed all those men and never had the balls to admit—"

Colonel Weller, rattled: "Mrs. Garber, I . . . I . . . Good-bye."

The phone went dead.

Simon slowly cradled the receiver, looking at Enrique and me.

"Smart," Enrique grunted. "General Markel was doing his damnedest to look like the killer. Cover up for the earlier call General Garber made to his wife."

Simon and I nodded. According to Amanda, General Garber had phoned his wife at around 1735 local time, within minutes of his death. While they were speaking, Mrs. Garber heard a woman enter General Garber's suite and ask to talk to him. Even though the woman never said her name, Mrs. Garber knew it was Churchfield because her husband had told her he'd returned from the dinner early, to meet with the secretary of defense.

More significantly, General Garber had also mentioned to his wife *what* Churchfield wanted to discuss. It was this topic, a similarly shocking revelation, that had been our focus as we sifted through the pages of background information.

The key document had been in Enrique's stack. After I pocketed it, I assumed Simon would want to immediately return to the Pentagon. Instead, he slumped back in his seat and closed his eyes. A minute passed, then two. He never moved. This time I knew he wasn't sleeping.

Simon's pride was bruised. He'd been made to appear foolish. To ensure it didn't happen again, he was taking his time, analyzing every facet of the case.

He finally opened his eyes, sat up, and adjusted his bow tie; he was ready.

I said to him, "You realize the investigation is officially closed. They don't have to talk to us. Odds are, they won't. They could even have us forcibly removed from the Pentagon."

Simon pressed his lips into a tight line. "So we make them a offer they can't refuse."

I nodded.

But rather than contact Churchfield directly, he phoned Senator Garber. Three minutes later, the senator called back. As we anticipated, Churchfield had reluctantly agreed to meet.

"Looks like the press conference is over," Enrique said.

Simon and I glanced at the TV, which was still on, the sound turned down. The camera was trained on Markel, who'd stepped back from the podium and was talking to Ron Hammond, the press secretary. While the two men conversed, Markel handed a folder to a female officer who'd approached the stage. She pivoted and slipped out a rear door.

"Weller, " I grunted. "It seems she's not wasting any time, reclaiming her old job."

"Looks young," Enrique said.

"Good genes."

He smiled, picking up on the irony of my statement.

As I opened the car door, I heard a sudden hiss of disapproval. Turning, I saw Simon staring fixedly at the television. He began shaking his head.

I sighed. "Now what's the matter?"

But his attention was still on the screen. He looked increasingly disgusted. "I'm a fool. *I'm a fool.*" He spun to me and demanded, "Who is responsible for packing a general's luggage?"

I blinked. "Uh, usually the aide—"

"Colonel Weller's number? Do you have it?"

I gestured vaguely to the cabinet he'd opened earlier. "I think Amanda put it—"

He popped up the seatback and located the file, which contained the contact information for the passengers. He opened it, pawed through the pages. He stopped, reading quickly. Enrique and I watched him with a puzzled expression. I said, "Simon . . ."

He shut the file and looked up at the monitor. Markel was still talking to Ron Hammond. Simon gave a grunt of satisfaction, picked up a phone, and made a call. To me, he said, "There is a second possibility, Martin."

"There is?"

"Yes. We have to be certain which one—" Into the phone: "Colonel Weller? Lieutenant Santos. I'm advising you that you are a suspect— *Do not hang up.* I know you packed General Garber's luggage the night he died. That places you in his room at the time of his murder." He paused; she'd interrupted him. Whatever she told him, it was the wrong thing to say. He snorted angrily. "I know you were there. I know why you tried to incriminate yourself. If you do not cooperate, I will arrest Secretary Churchfield. *Do you understand?*"

The arrest statement was a flat-out lie; we had no real evidence against Churchfield. Still, the threat apparently generated the response Simon was seeking.

His face relaxed. "Good. We understand each other. Listen closely. I want you to do exactly as I say . . ."

When Simon cradled the phone, Enrique still looked bewildered, but I wasn't. I now grasped what Simon was trying to do and why.

After he explained his plan, Enrique said, "Hey, I get it. They screwed with you, so now it's your turn. Play one against the other. Not bad. It might even work."

"It will," Simon said. To me: "You understand about the phone call?"

"Yes."

"You have the number?"

I patted my coat.

He eyed me. "It's better if you don't draw attention to yourself."

I nodded. "I'll keep my mouth shut. Churchfield won't even know I'm there."

"Good."

As we got out of the limo, I said to him, "If this works, I will have a request for General Markel."

He frowned. "What kind of request?"

He was shaking his head even before I finished. "The general will never agree, Martin. He would risk incriminating himself."

I gave him a hard look to show him I wasn't going to back down. "I don't care. I have to be certain. I owe it to Andy."

He seemed to smile. "All right, Martin."

We walked through the mist toward the Pentagon.

48

Twenty minutes later, Simon and I were cooling our heels in Churchfield's waiting room. For obvious reasons, it was a scene of frenzied activity. High-ranking DoD civilians and officers constantly came and went, anxious aides scurrying after them. Two prominent talking heads stopped by and requested interviews with Churchfield. They were rebuffed by a squat navy captain who seemed to double as the office bouncer. The civilian secretary answered call after call, a number of which were from members of Congress. In each instance, she deflected their requests by saying Churchfield was in a meeting. Finally, we heard a lone exception. "One moment, Mr. Vice President." She put his call through.

Simon yawned, drained his coffee, and went to refill his cup from the pot in the corner. He stopped to chat briefly with the secretary. He laughed at something she said. To look at him, he appeared completely relaxed; you'd never know he was about to confront the secretary of defense.

I shook my head and tossed aside the copy of the *Air Force Times* I'd been reading. Unlike Simon, I felt tense. I didn't share his view that our success was guaranteed. Churchfield was arguably the second most powerful person in the country. We had no idea how she'd react when cornered. She could put up a wall, decide to play hardball. And if that happened—

From somewhere a clock chimed. Ten o'clock. I sighed. So much for spending time with my daughter before she went to bed.

I fished out my cell phone and punched in my home number. After a half dozen rings, Emily picked up. She told me she was on the other line with her latest best friend, Trisha. Hint: She was too busy to talk to me. I told the birthday girl not to stay up too late, and I'd see her in the morning.

"Don't go, Dad. I'll be right back."

Ditching her Trisha for me. This was a first.

A moment later, she said, "Did you talk to Uncle Simon? Did you?"

I frowned at her excited tone. "He mentioned you'd called."

"Cut it out, Dad. What else did he say? *Tell me.*"

I could almost picture her squirming in her chair. I glanced at Simon. He was now conversing with the navy captain. I said, "That was it. He just said he'd spoken with you."

"Huh? He didn't say *anything* about Mom's letter?" She sound absolutely crushed.

"Honey, we've been busy. There really hasn't been time—"

"*He promised.*"

She was on the verge of tears. I didn't get it. What the hell was in the letter that would make her so upset?

When Simon looked my way, I motioned to him. As

he came over, I said to Emily, "Uncle Simon's here. You can ask him yourself."

"Emily," I said, shoving the phone into his hand. "You're in trouble."

Simon placed it to his ear and looked at me. "Uh, Martin, if you don't mind . . ."

"I do."

He shrugged, handed me his coffee cup, and strolled out the door.

Simon returned a few minutes later and handed me back the phone.

I said, "Well?"

"Emily understands. I told her I needed to complete the arrangements."

"What arrangements?"

"Martin. This really isn't the time."

"Make time. You're supposed to tell me about the let-ter— What?" He was pointing past me.

I turned, saw the navy captain striding over to us. He announced, "This way, gentlemen."

Instead of leading us down the hallway toward Churchfield's office, he swung out the door into the E-ring.

Simon shot me a look of concern. This was something we hadn't counted on. I quickly sidled up to the captain and asked, "Where are we going?"

He gave me a room number. Noting my blank expression, he added, "It's a conference room."

"Is it a SCIF?" If we were being taken to a secured com-partmentalized information facility similar to the Joint Chiefs meeting room, we'd have to turn in our cell phones.

The captain shook his head.

I drifted back, reassured Simon with a nod. He came forward to shield me in case the captain turned around. As we walked along, I thumbed the speed-dial on my cell phone. She answered on the first ring. Moments later, we arrived at a set of double doors. The captain knocked once, opened the door, and ushered us inside. By then, I had my phone safely tucked into my shirt pocket.

The sight that greeted us wasn't what we'd been led to expect. Instead, they were *all* waiting for us in the briefing room.

As Simon and I entered, no one said a word. They just stared at us with open resentment. Churchfield was seated at the head of the gleaming conference table. To her left were Markel, Sessler, and Johnson. Ernie and his red-haired partner stood along the back wall and were doing their best to appear menacing. No easy feat for Red Hair, who looked like a clown reject with his swollen and purple nose.

Before withdrawing, the captain directed Simon and me to the seats on Churchfield's right. As we walked over, twelve pairs of eyes followed. I risked a glance at Markel. He met my gaze with an arrogant grin. At least he'd left his rifle in his office.

As we slipped into our seats, Churchfield said, "You have five minutes."

Simon focused on her. "Did Senator Garber mention why I requested this meeting, Madam Secretary?"

She hesitated. "He said you know who killed General Garber."

"Crap," Markel grunted. "They're bluffing."

Simon gave him a cool smile. "Then why are you here, General?"

Markel's face reddened. "Listen, you son of a—"

"Be quiet, Dave," Churchfield said wearily.

"No. I've had it with—"

"*Dave.*"

Markel folded his arms, glowering.

To Churchfield, Simon said, "We requested to speak with you privately, Madam Secretary."

She said smoothly, "I have no secrets from my staff."

Simon said, "I suggest you reconsider—"

"You now have three minutes, Lieutenant."

Simon nodded agreeably. "Martin, your notepad—"

I fished it out and passed it over. He opened to a clean page and began to write.

"Aw, Christ," Markel said. "What the hell is this?"

Simon tore the page free, folded it in half, and slid it across the table to Churchfield.

She gazed down at it, making no move to pick it up. "I don't play games, Lieutenant."

Sarcastic grins from the generals. Johnson, the marine, openly laughed.

Simon said, "Please."

Churchfield reluctantly picked up the paper and unfolded it. The instant her eyes fell on the words, her head gave a little jerk. She stared at Simon.

He nodded once.

Seconds passed. She kept looking at Simon as if trying to make a decision. The generals shifted uncomfortably in their seats. They knew something was wrong. Markel tested the waters, saying, "Well, what is it? What did he write?"

When Churchfield ignored him, he bent forward and tried to read the paper in her hand. She twisted toward him, a hard look. He slowly sat back.

Churchfield's eyes scanned the generals' faces. "I want you to leave us."

Their eyes widened in surprise. They exchanged glances, but no one moved.

"Leave us, gentlemen," Churchfield repeated more firmly.

Markel coughed. "Uh, Madam Secretary, I don't think—"

"I gave you an order." Her voice was like ice.

Markel's mouth cycled open and closed a few times. He seemed uncertain as to what to do next.

"For the last time, *get out of here*."

Churchfield was glaring at Markel, her nostrils flared. He blinked, too stunned to react. Finally, he rose to his feet, and the other generals followed.

"Take security with you," Churchfield said.

Markel motioned to Mutt and Jeff. As he trailed them out the door, he looked back at Simon and me with a fierce, almost psychotic look. At that instant, seeing his face, I knew Simon was right. This was someone who could kill a friend who'd wronged him.

Returning my attention to Churchfield, I saw she'd placed the paper on the table. Even though it was upside down, I could easily read the two sentences Simon had written.

General Garber is Colonel Weller's father.

And below: *You are her mother.*

The door closed. In the ensuing quiet, we heard the soft rush of air blowing through a vent. For several seconds, Churchfield didn't say anything. She just kept looking at the paper on the table. As she did, we could see that the emotion of the moment was getting to her. An eyelid twitched, and we noticed a tremble in her upper lip. From his jacket, Simon produced a copy of Weller's birth certificate and slid it before her. To remove any lingering doubt she still might have.

Churchfield glanced at it, then slowly looked up at Simon. "Have you told Senator Garber?"

"Not yet."

"How much do you know?"

"We've interviewed Mrs. Garber."

"She told you I was . . . there?"

She was referring to England. Simon nodded.

She swallowed hard and turned away. "I didn't think we would get away with it. But Dave—General Markel— said we had to try. That it was our duty to try. When I heard his plan, I thought . . . I thought maybe he was right. Maybe it would all work out. Somehow . . ."

Her eyes returned to Simon. "I didn't do this for myself. I did it for the country—and for women. I . . . I was the first female defense secretary. If it came out that . . . the scandal . . . it would have taken years . . . decades . . . until another woman got the opportunity. I had a responsibility, an obligation beyond myself. Do you understand?"

Simon and I nodded sympathetically.

Another silence followed. Churchfield again stared down at the paper with Weller's name. She closed her eyes briefly, and began to speak haltingly. "I never wanted Mike to know about Tina. I didn't think he had the right—not after what happened. But Tina kept insisting. She wanted to know who her father was. She said she had a right to know. So I finally told her last month. That's when she decided to work for him. She wanted to get to know him, understand what he was like. Natural, I suppose. Of course, I knew what would happen next. And it did. She gave me an ultimatum. If I didn't tell Mike that he was her father, she would. So I had no choice. That's why I was going to meet him last night. I'd been flying around Europe, trying to shore up support for the war—"

Simon said. "There was no mention in the news that you'd left the country."

"That was the idea. Our allies insisted the meetings be kept secret. They were concerned my presence would inflame the antiwar movements and the radical left in their countries. My last stop was England. I'd met with the prime minister earlier that day. After the meeting, I received a call from Tina. She told me that she'd already broken the news to Mike. So when I met with him, he already knew. I regretted that; I should have been the one to . . ."

She trailed off, lost in her thoughts.

Simon said gently, "We need to know everything, from the beginning."

She gave him a slow blink. Nodded.

"Tell me when you first met General Garber."

She inhaled deeply and began.

49

Churchfield continued to speak in soft, hesitant tones, pausing occasionally to rein in her emotions. As the story unfolded, we understood why the process of remembering was so difficult.

"We first met in ROTC . . . at the University of Virginia. Mike was handsome . . . almost beautiful. I fell for him from the moment I saw him. Love at first sight, you could call it. I was seventeen, impressionable. He was two years older, popular. I never thought he'd notice me. But one day—it was in September—he invited me to spend the Labor Day weekend at his family's summer house in Virginia Beach. A group from the school were going, so it wasn't like we were going to be alone. Still, I almost turned him down. I knew why he was asking me. I knew about his reputation, all his girlfriends . . . But Jesus, he was so damned good-looking.

"So I accepted. For the first couple of days, Mike was a perfect gentlemen. We talked, got to know each other. It was sweet. Nice. Then the night before we left, we had a big party. Mike drank heavily. Around midnight, he asked me to take a walk along the beach. I could tell he was drunk. I knew I shouldn't go. But everybody was watching us . . . watching *me*. And I was worried what they would think. You know, that I was some kind of . . . prude. So I went. Mike took me to a secluded place, near some rocks. He knew right where to go. He'd been there before. As soon as we stopped, I told him that . . . that I'd never been with someone. A man. I told him I didn't think I could go through with it. When I said it, he got this strange look. And then he went crazy. He was like . . . like an animal. I tried to fight him, but . . ."

She blinked rapidly. "Jesus, this is difficult."

Simon gave her a moment, then said, "You never pressed charges?"

She shook her head. "The next day he apologized. He said it was the booze. He didn't know what he was doing. He was so damned sorry that . . . I don't know. It sounds crazy, but . . . but I didn't hate him. I never could hate him. I suppose that's why . . . that's why I kept his picture. The one he gave me when he made general. Part of me wanted to throw it away. But somehow I couldn't."

Simon said gently, "You gave the photograph to your daughter?"

A vague nod. "Tina saw it. She asked to have it." Her eyes locked on Simon. "What you don't understand is that Mike was so different when he was sober. It was the alcohol that changed him, brought out his demons. I often thought that if he could have only controlled himself, his urges . . . But he couldn't seem to . . . such a shame . . ." She trailed off, shaking her head sadly.

At that moment, it occurred to me how much she must have loved him.

Once.

Simon said, "And when you told him you were pregnant?"

"His family . . . his father . . . he was a congressman back then. He called me. He offered to pay for an abortion. I initially agreed. But when the time came, I couldn't go through with it. So I left school and went home to have the baby. My parents helped me put it up for adoption."

"Did you keep in contact with your daughter?"

A nod. "The Wellers were family friends. I transferred to a college close to where they lived, so I could see Tina, watch her grow up. For years, she thought I was her aunt. I . . . I told her the truth when she turned twenty-one. That's why she joined the air force. Because I was already serving." She smiled to herself at the thought.

"Did General Markel know Colonel Weller was your daughter?"

"No. No one knew."

"You asked him to hire her as his aide?"

"Yes. General Markel and I have been close for years. I knew he'd look after her."

Simon edged forward, tenting his fingers. He lowered his voice, sounding apologetic. "I need to know about last night, Madam Secretary."

She shut her eyes, as if trying to will the question away. When she opened them, she said, "I could still deny it. All you can prove is that I was there. You have no evidence that I killed anyone."

Simon's jaw hardened. "You assured me you would cooperate."

"I have. I've told you—"

"Did you kill General Garber?"

She hesitated. "No. When I left he was alive, and—"

As she answered, I was watching Simon. His face darkened, his lip curling in disgust. He was making a show of
being upset with her. He knew he had to appear convincing. *Now*, I thought. *Now he will make his move.*

An instant later, he did and in a stunning fashion.
Springing from his chair, he replayed my scene with the
generals by slapping his hand on the table with an ear-
splitting crack. Churchfield recoiled in shock.

Before she could recover, Simon leaned over her,
speaking harshly. "Do not test my patience, Madam
Secretary. You have many enemies. People who don't
think a woman should be in the position you hold. Once
I reveal that I believe you are a murderer, you will be finished. The innuendo and suspicion will damn you.
Within a month, you will be forced to resign. General
Markel, General Johnson, and General Sessler will
almost certainly suffer the same fate. To protect yourself,
you will destroy their reputations as well as cause great
harm to the military. Don't do it. Choose the honorable
path and tell me the truth. *Did you kill General Garber?*"

Churchfield's face turned bright red under his verbal
onslaught. She appeared both angry and frightened. She
struggled to form a response, but couldn't get the words
out. I watched her, thinking Simon had overplayed his
hand. He'd wanted to lay it on thick, but—

She finally lashed back at him, furiously spitting out
the words. "*You son of a bitch.* You have no right. You
weren't *there.* You don't know what happened."

"Tell me."

"*Go to hell.*"

Simon didn't respond to her rage; there wasn't any
need. He given her two options, both bad. Now she had to
decide whether to resist or—

"Oh, Christ—" Churchfield turned away. Her lip was quivering uncontrollably. She bit at it.

Simon slid into his seat. He repeated softly, "Tell me."

She was silent, fixated on the wall. I thought she wasn't going to answer him. Finally, in a strained whisper: "He was drunk. He attacked me."

"So it was self-defense?"

She turned to him. Her eyes were dark with anger. She said, "He was furious over Tina. Because I hadn't told him. We argued . . . said some things. I slapped him. He . . . he went wild. Attacked me."

"Did he try and rape you?"

"He . . . he had that look. He said he was going to teach me a lesson. Like before. He mentioned the beach. I tried to fight him, but he was too strong. I don't remember grabbing the bottle. I . . . I only remember that it was in my hand. And I swung and hit him."

"Was anyone there? Were there any witnesses, or—"

"No. No one else was present."

"Where were your security men?"

"Outside. In the car. I made them wait in the car. I didn't want them there."

"And Colonel Weller?"

"I said no one was—"

She stopped, looking around the table with a puzzled expression. She settled on me, her eyes widening in disbelief. I gave her an apologetic smile and removed the cell phone from my shirt pocket. In the quiet of the room, we could hear the woman's tinny voice clearly. She was shouting the same thing, over and over.

"It wasn't her, I killed him. It wasn't her, I killed him . . ."

Churchfield gave a strangled cry and lunged toward me.

•   •   •

Her move took me by surprise. I yanked away the phone before she could grab it from my hand. Churchfield kept swinging an arm at me, tears of frustration in her eyes. Simon was instantly on his feet and by her side. As he pulled her back into her chair, she looked up at him pleadingly. "She doesn't know what she's saying. She wasn't there. She's only doing this because—"

"It's the truth," Simon said.

"But it isn't. I'd sent her away. I wanted to talk to Mike in private."

"It *has* to be the truth," Simon said again. "Because it's the only way to end this."

Churchfield stared at him in confusion. She started to say something, then noticed he was smiling. He said softly, "Your daughter knew this was the only solution. That's why she incriminated herself."

She stared at him. "My God. Are you saying you're willing to—"

"Yes." He was still smiling.

"But what you said earlier. About accusing me publicly. All the rest of it."

"It was harsh, but necessary. I needed a confession. Something I could use."

"Use? For the senator?"

"Yes."

Her voice tentative now: "Are you sure he will . . . agree?"

He nodded, looking to me. My cue.

I said, "There is a condition for our help, Madam Secretary. I'd need a favor."

She turned to me, her tone wary. "What kind of favor?"

"It's a message for General Markel. Tell him he has a week."

She frowned. "A week for what?"

"The general will know." I slid a card across the table toward her. "Tell him to contact me when it's finished."

She glanced at the card, then looked at me. "I'm afraid I'll need to know what this is all about."

"Agent Hobbs was my friend . . ." I left the statement hanging.

I saw it then, a flicker of comprehension in her eyes. She said quietly, "We never had this conversation, Collins."

"What conversation, ma'am?"

She picked up the card.

Simon spent the next five minutes talking to Colonel Weller on my cell phone, getting her account of what happened the night General Garber was killed. Once that conversation ended, he immediately called Senator Garber. In a regretful tone, Simon detailed the events of his son's death to the senator. Much of Simon's version mirrored what Churchfield had described. The only difference was that when General Garber had tried to rape Churchfield, it was Weller who came to her rescue, picked up the bottle, and struck Barlow with the fatal blow.

Simon said, "Yes, Colonel Weller is quite traumatized, Senator. No, I don't think medical care is necessary. I'll tell them. I'm truly sorry it turned out like this. No, don't blame yourself. Good night, sir."

As he passed me the phone, he looked at Churchfield. "He would like to meet Colonel Weller someday. Apologize to her."

Churchfield nodded.

"The senator would also like to apologize to you."

She swallowed hard. "This is very difficult for me to accept. Maybe it's better to go with the truth. Perhaps the senator will understand it was self-defense."

"It's a risk," Simon. "He might think you were lying."

"I'm aware of that. But I don't want him to spend the rest of his life believing that his granddaughter killed her own—"

"It's over, Madam Secretary," Simon said.

50

It was almost eleven by the time we made the return trek to the limo and drove from the Pentagon. Simon and I sat in the back, sitting in the dark and nursing drinks. He had a glass of wine, and I had a designer beer.

At the moment, Simon was relating the details of the case to Enrique. He enjoyed discussing investigations once they were finished; it was how he wound down, decompressed. When Nicole was alive, I used to engage in a similar routine. Anytime I'd make a big arrest or bust, we'd sit out on the porch with a couple of drinks, and I'd tell her what a big hero I was. I knew my stories probably bored her to tears, but she always acted completely fascinated by what I was saying. That was Nicole. During our entire marriage, she always made me feel like I was the most important thing in her life. Since she passed away, I still went out on the porch to unwind. Sometimes I'd even close my eyes and talk through a case, pretending she was still there sitting beside me.

But when I opened my eyes, I saw only an empty chair.

I waited for the familiar ache in my chest to appear. The one I'd lived with every day for the last three years.

When it came, I took a deep breath and stared at the flickering streetlights until it went away.

We turned north on the GW Parkway. Simon was still talking. As I listened, I found it hard to believe that we'd started the investigation only this morning. It seemed such a long time ago. It was even more difficult to accept that we'd actually succeeded.

I sipped my beer.

Of course, the truth was that we *hadn't* succeeded. Not if our purpose had been to identify the killer of General Garber to his father.

Walking from the Pentagon, I'd asked Simon if this bothered him. Not only hadn't he fulfilled his promise to Senator Garber, but he'd also lied to him.

"I didn't lie, Martin."

"C'mon. We both know Colonel Weller didn't kill General Garber."

He shrugged. "She confessed."

"Because you manipulated her."

"Not at all. She provided her account freely. I didn't advise her on what to say." He gave me a smile.

I let it go. The bottom line was, he'd made the only decision he could. Still, I found it amusing the way Simon modified his ethics to fit the situation. As long as he hadn't personally coerced Weller's confession, he felt justified in citing it to Senator Garber as fact.

I said, "There's one other aspect about the killing you haven't mentioned."

We walked along. He gave me a sideways glance. "Andy?"

I nodded.

He shrugged. "We could never prove his role."

"No."

But we both realized that Churchfield could never have immobilized General Garber for the time it took him to die. That meant someone—a male—had helped her. Since the generals and Churchfield's security team weren't present, that left only Andy. Now I had to ask myself, would Andy have willingly helped murder General Garber?

He wouldn't have been able to resist. After thirty long years, Andy had an opportunity to avenge the deaths of his friend Jerry and the rest of the men Garber had maimed and killed. In Andy's mind, he probably saw it as a noble, almost heroic act.

Simon began telling Enrique how he believed General Garber's killing occurred. I got comfortable and closed my eyes, visualizing his words. One by one, the images shuttered across my tired mind like snapshots on a conveyor belt. I saw Garber's crazed and drunken face as he lunged at Churchfield, tore at her clothes. I saw her fighting him off as she cried out for help. I saw her flailing hand grab the bottle from the coffee table and swing a vicious blow. I saw Garber clutch his throat and crumple in agony to the floor. I saw Andy rush into the room, responding to Churchfield's cries. I saw Churchfield turn to him, trying to explain what has just happened.

At that point, the image freezes.

Andy is standing over General Garber, watching him as he gasps, frantically trying to breathe. Churchfield tells Andy to do something, get help. Andy makes no move to go. Instead, he leans close to Churchfield and makes a suggestion. Her eyes widen in shock. She shakes her head, no. Andy points to the bottle she is still holding and tells her what a scandal would mean. That perhaps it was better this way. This time Churchfield hesitates. For a moment, she is torn; she knows what he's telling her is true.

She again shakes her head, no. She can't bring herself to do it.

Get help, Agent Hobbs.

But Andy has seen her uncertainty and bends over Garber. He grips the general's hands and lies on top of him, using his weight to pin him down. Garber thrashes wildly, trying to throw Andy off. But the general's reflexes are slowed by the alcohol, and Andy is too heavy.

Garber soon weakens, his screaming lungs starved for air.

His struggles fade into stillness. Churchfield watches in horror, but does nothing.

The image fades to black; Simon has stopped talking.

Maybe his assumptions were off, and this wasn't the way everything played out. Maybe it was Andy rather than Churchfield who actually struck Garber with the bottle. In my mind, who actually administered the blow wasn't as critical as understanding Churchfield's response afterward. Why hadn't she tried to prevent Andy from killing Garber? Did she let him die because she was afraid of what a scandal would mean to her reputation and career, or was she simply paralyzed with fear?

Or was there a deeper, more calculated reason?

While we could never know the answer, I believed it was the latter. Specifically, the fine line between love and hate. Even though she'd once been in love with General Garber, she'd also grown to hate him for what he'd done to her. In the end, when it counted, the hate won out.

The limo slowed, and I heard the soft click of a blinker. Then Enrique's voice: "We're almost there."

I opened my eyes.

• • •

We were cruising through downtown Rosslyn, not far from the Key Bridge. Here the mist had thickened, turning into a fog. Enrique made a left and pulled in front of gray office building. Ahead, we could see a single car parked along the curb. It was a shiny red BMW, the same car Amanda and I had driven earlier.

I said to Simon, "Why did you ask Amanda to meet us here, anyway? I could have waited for her at the Pentagon."

He shrugged. "We didn't know how long we would be. I thought she'd be more comfortable in Crysto's."

Crysto's was the ritzy penthouse restaurant that Simon owned. As we got out of the car, I told Simon he didn't have to hang around; Amanda and I were going to drive right home.

"I want to tell her she did a good job, Martin."

We took the elevator to the twelfth floor. The restaurant had a Closed sign on the door. Within seconds of Simon's knock, a maître d' with slicked-back silver hair appeared and peeked at us through the frosted glass. Seeing Simon, his face lit up, and he unlocked the door with a flourish.

We entered a grottolike foyer, complete with ivy-covered stone walls and a bubbling fishpond. Simon said, "Wait here, Martin."

So I stayed by the pond while he took the maître d' by the arm and led him to the reservation desk. Simon said something, and the maître d' made a quick phone call. Afterward, they conversed in hushed tones for several minutes. The maître d' kept looking my way, grinning broadly. After the third time, I checked my zipper. That wasn't the problem.

A second man in a tuxedo appeared from a door at the back. He was carrying a bottle of wine, which he immediately took over to Simon. Simon inspected the label, gave a nod of satisfaction, then handed the guy a wad of bills. The man smiled appreciatively and continued down the short hallway toward the dining room. Moments later, the maître d' winked at Simon, flashed me another grin, then also departed for the dining room.

I strolled over to Simon, my curiosity meter pegged. I asked him what the hell was going on.

He smiled, reaching into his jacket. "I'm fulfilling my obligation to your daughter."

"Emily? What does she have—"

Then I saw the manila folder he was holding out to me. Across the front were written the words "Hold for Lt. Santos." It was the same one that Enrique had picked up for him earlier. I shook my head when the realization sank in. "Jesus. Emily was the woman?"

"Yes. Take it, Martin."

As I did, I knew what it would contain. I slowly peeled back the flap. Inside was a white envelope addressed to Emily, the one I'd found on her dresser this morning.

Simon said, "Emily was quite confused. You're her father. She didn't feel comfortable broaching this subject with you. She said whatever you decide is fine with her. Her only concern is your happiness. She also wanted me to tell you that she cares for Amanda very much."

I blinked. "Amanda?"

Simon smiled again. "We'll talk at Emily's party. You can tell me how the evening turns out."

"'The evening turns out'? What are you talking about?"

But he was already striding out the door.

I stared down at the envelope, my heart pounding.
I removed the letter inside.

My dearest daughter,

You're thirteen now. You must be so beautiful. I wish I could be with you on this day, share your joy, and tell you how much I love you. I'm so proud of the woman you're becoming. You may not realize it, but I am always there with you, watching you from afar. I know when you are happy and when you are sad. I know when you're thinking of me, and I hope you can tell when I'm thinking of you. If you have any doubts, feel your heart. Whenever you feel the beat, that's me, telling you that I love you.

My eyes began to mist. I could barely read. I looked around. I was alone in the entryway. I swallowed hard and kept going.

The next few paragraphs were easier. Nicole wrote about things like maturity and responsibility and temptation, often citing examples from her own teenage years to highlight what she meant. My name finally appeared at the top of the third page.

Emily, this is hard for me to say, so I'm just going to say it. I loved your father with all my heart. But by the time you read this, I'll have been gone three years. My absence isn't fair to you and it isn't fair to your father. You need a mother, and he needs a companion. God didn't make us to live our lives alone. If he hasn't found someone by now—and knowing your father, he hasn't—I want you to tell him it's okay. We had twenty glorious years. Nothing will

*ever change that. But the reality is, life is for the
living.*

*Will you do that for me, Emily? Will you tell him
it's okay to find someone?*

Please.

Lord—

I lowered the pages, wiping at my eyes with my jacket
sleeve. The maître d' appeared from behind me, his face
soft and sympathetic. "Is everything all right, sir?"

"Is . . . is there a rest room?"

He pointed down a corridor by the coat closet.

It took me a few minutes to clean up and rein in my
emotions. The maître d' was waiting where I'd left him. I
said, "I'm ready."

He smiled and led me toward the dining room. It was
empty except for a woman sitting at a table by the fire-
place. Her back was to me, and she was sipping wine.

As I walked toward Amanda, I still had no idea what I
was going to say.

Epilogue

I received the package five days later.

It was early Wednesday morning, and I was just leaving the house for work when I saw it sitting on the welcome mat by the front door. It was a small package, not more than three inches square, wrapped in butcher paper and heavily taped. I knelt down and studied it. No postage markings that I could see. When I picked it up, it was curiously light, only a few ounces. I slowly turned it over and saw a single word, written in block letters.

HONOR.

I now realized who had sent it, but I'd been expecting a phone call or an anonymous letter, not a package.

Returning to the house, I continued downstairs to my basement office. Using my pocket knife, I cut the tape and removed the butcher paper, revealing a small white cardboard box. I lifted the lid.

Lord—

I stared, overcome with revulsion.

Ears. Two of them. Sitting on a bed of cotton.

I placed the box on the desk and sagged into a chair. It took almost a minute before I could get up the nerve to look in the box again. My impulse was to throw it in the trash, but I had to be sure.

Taking a deep breath, I forced myself to touch one of the ears. The moment I felt the rubberized skin, I jerked my hand away. I had my confirmation.

Of course I had to call Simon and Amanda and let them know. But first I had something important to do. A final commitment I had made to a friend.

So I went upstairs to my portable bar in the living room and poured out a shot of whisky.

What I was about to do wasn't appropriate, not that I cared. While General Garber hadn't deserved to die for a mistake he'd made during the heat of battle, he was still a sick son of a bitch and a rapist.

I raised the glass in a silent toast. *Andy, you finally gave a damn.*

I took a drink.

Visit
❖ **Pocket Books** ❖
online at

....

www.SimonSays.com

....

Keep up on the latest new
releases from your favorite
authors, as well as author
appearances, news, chats,
special offers and more.